Behind a Mask

Louisa May Alcott

Behind a Mask

The Unknown Thrillers of Louisa May Alcott

Edited and with an Introduction and

Afterword by Madeleine Stern

HARPER ● PERENNIAL

NEW YORK ● LONDON ● TORONTO ● SYDNEY

HarperCollins books may be purchased for educational, business, or sales promotional use. For information please write: Special Markets Department, HarperCollins Publishers Inc., 10 East 53rd Street, New York, NY 10022.

First Quill edition published 1997.

Reprinted in Perennial 2004.

Book Design by Helen Roberts

Library of Congress Cataloging-in-Publication Data

Alcott, Louisa May, 1832–1888.
Behind a mask.

Contains an introd. by M. B. Stern and four stories by L. M. Alcott: Behind a mask; or, A woman's power. The abbot's ghost; or Maurice Treherne's temptation, Pauline's passion and punishment, and The mysterious key and what it opened. The first two of these were published under the pseud. of A. M. Barnard.
Includes bibliographical references.
I. Stern, Madeleine Bettina. II. Title.
PZ3.A355Be [PS1017] 813'.4 74-31046
ISBN 0-688-15132-9

12 13 14 15 QG 20 19 18 17 16 15 14

❧ *Contents* ❧

❧ *Introduction* ❧

BY MADELEINE STERN

I intend to illuminate the Ledger with a blood & thunder tale as they are easy to "compoze" & are better paid than moral & elaborate works of Shakespeare so dont be shocked if I send you a paper containing a picture of Indians, pirates, wolves, bears & distressed damsels in a grand tableau over a title like this "The Maniac Bride" or The Bath of Blood A Thrilling Tale of Passion.

The quotation is not by a writer associated with the gore of Gothic romance but by the future author of a domestic novel known to all the world as *Little Women*. On June 22, 1862, Louisa May Alcott wrote those lines to a young man named Alf Whitman, whose charms she would one day incorporate into the fictional character of Laurie.[1]

The statement itself evinces her powers, for within the briefest compass it touches upon her facility in composition, her ostensible motive, and the type of periodical or audience at which she aimed. The fact that Louisa May Alcott—"The Children's Friend"—let down her literary hair and wrote blood-and-thunder thrillers in secret is in itself a disconcerting if titillating shock to readers in search of consistency. Like Dr. Johnson's dog that stood upon its hind legs, it is *per se* remarkable. Equally remarkable is the story of their discovery, an intriguing byway in literary detection. Most remarkable of all perhaps is the fact that those gory, gruesome novelettes—written anonymously or pseudonymously, for the most part—were and still are extremely good: well paced, suspenseful, skillfully executed, and peopled with characters of flesh and blood.

Now, for the first time, after more than a century, they are reprinted—a belated though well-deserved tribute to a multifaceted genius who hailed from Concord, Massachusetts. They merit not only the avid attention of the general reader, whose appetite will grow with what it feeds on, but closer study by the astonished yet delighted critic, who may wonder precisely why and when, how and for whom these colorful forays into an exotic world were written. The analysis will disclose not only the nature of the creation but the nature of the creator, for Louisa May Alcott brought to this genre of escapist literature both an economic and a psychological need.

There is no doubt the economic need was there. The four "little women" whose name was not March but Alcott—Anna, Louisa, Abby, and Elizabeth—grew up not only in the climate of love but in the colder climate of poverty. Their father, Amos Bronson Alcott, the Concord seer, who was sometimes regarded as a seer-sucker, had many gifts but none for making money. As Louisa put it in a letter to a publisher: "I too am sure that 'he who giveth to the poor lendeth to the Lord' & on that principle devote time & earnings to the care of my father & mother, for one possesses no gift for money making & the other is now too old to work any longer for those who are happy & able to work for her." [2]

The cost of coal, the price of shoes, discussions of ways and means, all the essentials of living formed an obbligato to Louisa's early years, a background as basic to her life as romps with the neighboring Emerson children, berrying excursions with Henry David Thoreau, glimpses of a mysterious Hawthorne hovering in the Old Manse, and echoes of her father's lofty discourses on universal love and Pythagorean diet. Returned from a lecture tour in the West, Bronson Alcott was asked, "Well, did people pay you?" He opened his pocketbook, flourished a single dollar bill, and replied, "Only that! My overcoat was stolen, and I had to buy a shawl. Many promises were not kept, and travelling is costly; but I have opened the way, and another year shall do better." [3] He was the recipient of gifts from his wife's distinguished relatives, the Mays or Sewalls, or from his friend and neighbor the illustrious Ralph Waldo Emerson, who would place a bill under a book or behind a candlestick "when he thinks Father wants a little money, and no one will help him earn." [4]

To solve the mundane question of ways and means, to pay the family debts and end the necessity for a charitable Alcott Sinking Fund, Louisa May Alcott was prepared to do any kind of work that offered, menial or mental. "Though an *Alcott*"—and Louisa underlined not the condition but the name—she would prove she could support herself. "I will make a battering-ram of my head," she wrote in her journal, "and make a way through this rough-and-tumble world." [5]

She tried what was available, and what was not she tried to make available: teaching, working as a seamstress or as second girl, doing the wash at two dollars a week. At midcentury the family poverty had never been more extreme. At this juncture Louisa went out to service and garnered from her experience no money but a villain for her tales and a consuming inner fury to explode.

The full story of what might be entitled "The Humiliation at Dedham" has never been told, although Louisa herself years later wrote a bowdlerized account of it in "How I Went Out to Service." Since it was grist for the mill of a writer of thrillers, it merits recounting. [6] At the difficult midcentury the Alcotts lived for a time in Boston, for it was better to be earning a living in a city than to be starving in a country paradise. Mrs. Alcott, the Marmee of the as yet unwritten *Little Women*, worked as a city missionary and opened an intelligence office. When an ancient gentleman from Dedham applied for a companion for his sister, Louisa decided to take the position herself. The gentleman—now for the first time identified as the Honorable James Richardson, Dedham lawyer, president of a local fire-insurance company, author of several orations, and devotee of the Muses—seemed to her tall, ministerial, refined. Waving black-gloved hands about, he assured her that his home was graced by books and pictures, flowers, a piano, the best of society. She would be one of the family, required to help only in the lighter work.

Fortified by those assurances, Louisa in 1851, age nineteen, went out to service. The Richardson home was not precisely as it had been represented. The light housework included not only bed making but the kindling of fires and the destruction of cobwebs. What was more, Louisa was expected to play audience to Hon. James Richardson, who invited her into his study for oral readings or metaphysical discussions. The aged Richardson's attentions soon became maudlin. He plied her with poems while she washed the dishes and he left reproachful little notes under her door. Stranded on an island of water in a sea of soapsuds, Louisa finally delivered an ultimatum: she had come to serve as companion to Hon..James Richardson's sister, not to him. As a result of her display of independence, all the household work was assigned to her: digging paths through the snow, fetching water from the well, splitting the kindling, and sifting the ashes. The final degradation was the command to polish the master's muddy boots with the blacking hose, at which the young domestic balked. After seven weeks of drudgery she announced her intention of leaving. Richardson shut himself up in sulky retirement while his sister tucked a sixpenny pocketbook into Louisa's chilblained hands. The pocketbook contained four dollars, which the outraged Alcotts returned to Dedham. Although Louisa subsequently made light of this experience in "How I Went Out to Service," there can be no doubt that from her humiliation an anger was born that would express itself both obliquely and directly when she sat down to write her blood-and-thunder tales.

Another devastating experience a few years later could also be caught in a net of words, provided the author remained anonymous. Frustrated in her attempts to find work—teaching Alice Lovering, sewing for Mrs. Reed or Mrs. Sargent—Louisa found that her courage had all but failed. As she looked at the waters of the Mill Dam she was tempted to find the solution of her problems in their oblivion. Though her immediate problem was resolved, surely that "Temptation at the Mill Dam," however fleeting, became, along with the "Humiliation at Dedham," part of the psychological equipment of a young woman who would shortly take her pen as her bridegroom.[7]

There was much else in Louisa's life in Concord or Boston that formed part of that equipment. There were characters not merely in books but in life—like Hawthorne, whose dark figure had glided through the entry of a somber Manse, a fitting shadow to inhabit a house of shadows. There were fugitive slaves who passed through the village, a stop on the Underground Railway. There were the ghost stories with which Louisa thrilled the boys of Frank Sanborn's school as apples and ginger cakes rounded out an Alcott Monday Evening. Surely the report of Professor Webster's hanging for the murder of George Parkman at Harvard provided her with a store of bloodcurdling detail. Louisa's short but indelible service as a nurse in the Civil War brought her a harvest of characters along with a shattering illness in which delirium alternated with unconsciousness, aspects of disease most adaptable to the blood-and-thunder variety of fiction. As companion to a sickly young woman, Louisa went abroad in 1865. Europe yielded her dramatis personae ranging from a Russian baron to an English colonel, from a mysterious lady resembling Marie Antoinette to a charming Polish boy. There too she saw Mazzini, pallid, diaphanous, wearing deep mourning for his country, the perfect hero for a dramatic destiny in a sensational story. For a Louisa Alcott who never stopped taking notes, Europe provided also a panorama of backgrounds—exotic, colorful, romantic. As her father wrote to her: "Your visit to Chillon and description of . . . the Prison, is as good for the romancer as for the poet, and this with the legend the best matereal [*sic*] for a story by the former." [8]

Bronson Alcott called his scribbling daughter "an arsenal of powers." [9] In that arsenal was stored still another personal source for stories. All her life the redoubtable Louisa May Alcott had gone barnstorming and all her life she had dreamed of the ten dramatic passions. [10] The "Louy Alcott troupe," of which Louisa May, age ten, was author-director, gave way to family tableaux and dramatic performances in the Hillside barn. At fifteen Louisa dipped her pen into gaudy ink as, with her sister Anna, she wrote the scripts of a succession of melodramas whose titles and subtitles foreshadow those of the thrillers that were to come: "Norna; or, The Witch's Curse"; "The Captive of Castile; or, The Moorish Maiden's Vow." The props and appurtenances, the backgrounds and characters of these early plays staged for the Concord neighbors are familiar to readers of blood-and-thunder tales: ghosts and stolen scrolls, duels and magic potions, dungeon cells and gloomy woods, murder and suicide.

Throughout her life Louisa carried the theater with her wherever she went. She took the roles of director, author, and actress in drawing-room charades or plays in the Boston kitchen. With lightning changes of costume she ranged from a prince in silver armor to a murderer in chains, until she confided to her journal that she would be a Siddons if she could. From her later work in the Amateur Dramatic Company of Walpole and the Concord Dramatic Union, Louisa gained a certain professionalism in her attitude toward the theater. In 1860 her farce, *Nat Bachelor's Pleasure Trip,* was actually staged at the Howard Athenaeum, Boston, and the playwright received a bouquet as she viewed the performance from a private parlor box. Louisa received more than a bouquet from her experience in theatricals and her romance with greasepaint. She developed a skill in lively dialogue, in suspenseful plotting, and in broad-stroke character delineation, skills she would one day apply to her blood-and-thunder tales. "I fancy 'lurid' things," she wrote in her 1850 journal, "if true and strong also" [11]—a fancy she would gratify a decade later. Like many of the episodes of her life, Louisa's addiction to the theater provided both a source and a training ground for what would follow.

So too did her reading. Dickens she devoured, reading aloud with her sister Anna the dialogue of Sairey Gamp and Betsey Prig, thrilling to the tale of Reuben Haredale's murder, reinaugurating the Pickwick Club in Concord. Books from Emerson's study could be borrowed: Dante and Shakespeare, Carlyle and Goethe. "R.W.E. gave me 'Wilhelm Meister,'" she noted, "and from that day Goethe has been my chief idol." [12] (Her chief idol, it needs no reminding, had delved into matters alchemical and antiquarian, and his Faust had made a world-famous pact with the devil.) *The Heir of Redclyffe* was a favorite of Louisa's and so too was Hawthorne's *Scarlet Letter*. Indeed, she was so enthralled by novels that in one lofty moment she "made a resolution to read fewer novels, and those only of the best." [13]

There can be no doubt at all that the fiction addict Louisa Alcott dipped from time to time into the gore of the Gothic novel. In America that type of romance was so enthusiastically received that as early as 1797 both "dairymaid and hired hand" amused themselves "into an agreeable terror with the haunted houses and hobgoblins of Mrs. Radcliffe." [14] By the time she had become an omnivorous reader a host of Gothic novels was available to her in English or in English translation. In their pages Louisa could envision settings, mouth language, and cogitate themes. She could wander from ruined abbey to frowning castle, from haunted gallery and feudal hall to pathless forest and chilly catacomb. She could savor romantic words—*repasts, casements, chambers*. She could revel in unholy themes—deals with the devil and the raising of the dead, secret sects and supernatural agencies. Horace Walpole's marvelous machinery, Mrs. Ann Radcliffe's ghosts, Monk Lewis's horrors, William Beckford's Oriental terror, Ludwig Tieck's vampires were all available to her. So too, of course, were the strange stories of Washington Irving, the haunting stories of Nathaniel Hawthorne, the subtle tales of Poe the master, whose horrors were the unknown horrors of the mind. [15]

Probably Louisa Alcott had been moved to write as soon as she had learned to read. The compulsion was hers early to combine threads of her own experience with the threads of the books she had read and interweave them into a fabric of her own creating.[16] Her first published work was a poem, entitled "Sunlight," that appeared in the September, 1851, issue of *Peterson's Magazine.* Interestingly, it was pseudonymous, for it was signed "Flora Fairfield." The poem was followed in May, 1852, by Louisa's first published prose narrative, "The Rival Painters: A Tale of Rome," for which the author received five dollars along with the delight of seeing her initials in print.

Despite a devastating rebuke from the publisher James T. Fields, who advised her, "Stick to your teaching, Miss Alcott. You can't write," Louisa persisted. In 1854 "Flora Fairfield" adorned the *Saturday Evening Gazette* with "The Rival Prima Donnas," a tale of vengeance in which one singer crushed her competitor to death by means of an iron ring placed upon her head. In the garret with her papers around her and a pile of apples nearby, the twenty-two-year-old spinner of tales evolved plots about strong-minded women and poor lost creatures until she became the mainstay of the *Gazette.*

At the same time, in 1855, her full name appeared as the author of her first published book, *Flower Fables,* "legends of faery land" she had devised for Emerson's daughter Ellen. The book netted her thirty-two dollars. In the sky parlor of a Boston boardinghouse Louisa continued to write when she was not teaching or sewing. "Love and Self-Love," the story of an attempted suicide woven from her own temptation at the Mill Dam, was accepted by James Russell Lowell, editor of *The Atlantic Monthly.* "M. L.," a story of slavery and abolition, was rejected. The author went on consuming piles of paper. She had caught the writing fever and boasted to Alf Whitman, "My 'works of art' are in such demand that I shall be one great blot soon." [17] She worked on two novels: *Moods,* a medley of death, sleepwalking, and shipwreck; and *Success* (later changed to *Work*), an autobiographical romance in which she would one day insert a chapter on insanity, suicide, and thwarted love. After her brief service as a Civil War nurse, Louisa converted her experience into a realistic narrative, *Hospital Sketches,* first serialized in *The Commonwealth* and subsequently published in book form.

Seated at her desk, an old green-and-red party wrap draped around her as a "glory cloak," Louisa pondered in groves of manuscripts. In 1855 her earnings included fifty dollars from teaching, fifty dollars from sewing, and twenty dollars from stories.[18] Yet she not only

preferred pen and ink to birch and book—or needle—she was committed. Her pen was never and would never be idle. She lived in her
inkstand. Some years later, when she supplied *The New York Ledger*
with an article on "Happy Women," [19] she would include a sketch of
herself as the scribbling spinster.

The scribbling spinster had already had a variety of writing experience. From flower fables to realistic hospital sketches, from tales of
virtue rewarded to tales of violence, she had tried her ink-stained hand.
Now, in her early thirties, she would attempt still another experiment.
The letter to Alf Whitman revealed the plan: "I intend to illuminate
the Ledger with a blood & thunder tale as they are easy to 'compoze'
& are better paid than moral . . . works." For Louisa May Alcott they
were indeed easy to compose. She could stir in her witch's caldron a
brew concocted from her own experience, her observations and needs,
as well as from the books she had read, for, like Washington Irving,
she had "read somewhat, heard and seen more, and dreamt more than
all." Louisa's blood-and-thunder tales would be not only "necessity
stories" produced for money—from fifty to seventy-five dollars each—
but a psychological catharsis. What is more, although their author
never publicly acknowledged them, these experiments would stand the
test of time. The future author of *Little Women* added much of her
own to the genre. Indeed, had she persisted in the writing of thrillers,
the name of Louisa May Alcott may well have conjured up the rites
of a Walpurgis Night instead of the wholesome domesticities of a
loving family.

In 1862, in the midst of the Civil War, *Frank Leslie's Illustrated
Newspaper,* a popular New York weekly devoted to alluring pictures,
gossip, and murder trials, offered a one-hundred-dollar prize for a story.
To pay the family debts and at the same time to give vent to the
pent-up emotions of her thirty years, Louisa Alcott wrote the first of
her blood-and-thunder tales. Though it would be published anonymously, "Pauline's Passion and Punishment" [20] bore the stamp of its
author, who immediately developed her own technique and outlined
a theme to which she would often return. While her plots were violent
enough and her backdrops remote enough to merit classification in the
Gothic genre, Louisa was principally concerned with character. Of
all the characters she adumbrated in these narratives the one who
came most completely to life and who obviously was as intriguing to
her author as to readers was the passionate, richly sexual *femme fatale*

who had a mysterious past, an electrifying present, and a revengeful future. In such a heroine—so different from the submissive heroine of the Gothic formula—Louisa May Alcott could distill her passion for dramatics and her feminist anger at a world of James Richardsons. At the same time she could win a sorely needed hundred dollars.

In "Pauline's Passion and Punishment," as in all the Alcott thrillers, the reader is immediately introduced to problems of character rather than of plot. The suspense lies less in what the heroine will *do* than in what the heroine *is*, although both considerations become entwined as the character develops and the plot advances. In a fascinating opening, the anonymous author places onstage her Pauline, a proud and passionate woman who has lost all—fortune and, as a result of one man's perfidy, love. She is left with her fury and her desire for revenge, emotions which become the motivating forces in an ironic plot.

Against the background of an exotic paradise, a green wilderness where the tamarind vies with the almond tree, the spotlight falls upon Pauline Valary, pacing "to and fro, like a wild creature in its cage," a "handsome woman, with bent head, locked hands, and restless steps." She is a woman scorned by her lover, Gilbert Redmond, who has abandoned her for a moneyed bride. In swift course she arouses the devotion of the sensitive, young, southern romantic Manuel, who, attracted by her implicit sexuality, becomes not only her husband but her accomplice in the intended destruction of Gilbert Redmond. She does not plan Gilbert's murder but some more subtle revenge. "There are fates more terrible than death, weapons more keen than poniards, more noiseless than pistols. . . . Leave Gilbert to remorse—and me." And so, on page 1 of her thriller, the already skillful author has sketched in her characters, spotlighted her heroine, set her scene, and suggested a suspenseful plot.

The suspense mounts in the search for Gilbert and the dramatic encounter with him and his bride. The character is embroidered as Pauline's "woman's tongue" avenges her and "with feminine skill" she "mutely conveys the rebuke she would not trust herself to utter, by stripping the glove from the hand he had touched, and dropping it disdainfully." The meeting of Gilbert and Pauline is the meeting of man and woman, a meeting in which Pauline silently accepts Gilbert's challenge to the "tournament so often held between man and woman —a tournament where the keen tongue is the lance, pride the shield, passion the fiery steed, and the hardest heart the winner of the prize, which seldom fails to prove a barren honor, ending in remorse." And so faint alarms and excursions subtly suggest without overtly revealing the denouement.

Pauline's inexorable anger intensifies until she is possessed by a devil—not one with a cloven hoof but a subtle psychological force for evil. Her little stage performance and "drama of deceit"—all Louisa's heroines are actresses on the stage or off—her machinations to bankrupt Gilbert "in love, honor, liberty, and hope" fail utterly in the end.

The winner of Frank Leslie's one-hundred-dollar prize adopted the pseudonym of A. M. Barnard for a tale she submitted to another flamboyant weekly, *The Flag of Our Union.* Despite her preoccupation with passionate and angry heroines, Louisa was already too skillful a writer to repeat herself without variation. "The Abbot's Ghost: or, Maurice Treherne's Temptation" [21] is set in no exotic Cuban paradise but a haunted English abbey replete with screaming peacocks, thick-walled gallery and arched stone roof, armored figures and an abbot's ghost. A Dickensian flavor attaches to these Gothic appurtenances as, sitting round the hall fire, the dramatis personae tell tales of ghosts and coffins, skeletons and haunted houses. The star of that dramatis personae is less the hero of the title than the magnificent Edith Snowden, a strong-willed woman burdened by a heavy cross, a mysterious past, and jealousies that conflict with "contending emotions of . . . remorse and despair." "The Abbot's Ghost" is filled with psychological insights that illuminate the subtle relationships of the characters. The plot, revolving principally about the sudden cure of the crippled Maurice Treherne and ending with a triple wedding in the abbey, is basically a love story narrated against a strongly Gothic background. It comes to life through the brilliant depiction of a woman of passion and power whose furies are banked by her innate nobility.

Unlike the anonymous "Pauline's Passion" and the pseudonymous "Abbot's Ghost," *The Mysterious Key* [22] has a male hero, a charming young Italianate Englishman, and unlike either of those narratives, *The Mysterious Key* was published over the name of Louisa May Alcott. The possibility suggests itself that Louisa insisted upon secrecy less for her blood-and-thunder stories in general than for her passionate and angry heroines in particular.

The hero of *The Mysterious Key* combines a touch of that Polish boy who, with Alf Whitman, was to become the Laurie of *Little*

Women, and a strong hint of the pale and ardent Italian patriot Mazzini. Paul's appearance at the Trevlyn home in Warwickshire—an estate adequately equipped with haunted room and state chamber—touches off an elaborate plot. Well paced, it depends for its unfoldment upon a prophetic rhyme and a mysterious black-bearded visitor, a sealed letter and an ancient family volume, pretended sleepwalking, a touch of bigamy and a blind ward, Helen. The silver key that opens the Trevlyn tomb and discloses a mildewed paper proving Helen's identity is less mysterious and less intriguing than the hero Paul who, as Paolo, had been—like Mazzini—a hero in the Italian Revolution. All loose ends—and there are many—are neatly tied as the silver key slips into the door of a grisly tomb unlocking "a tragedy of life and death."

Between "Pauline's Passion," written in 1862, and *The Mysterious Key,* which appeared in 1867, Louisa wrote other gaudy, gruesome, and psychologically perceptive thrillers. Sitting incognito behind her pen, she produced "V. V.: or, Plots and Counterplots," an involved tale about a danseuse, Virginie Varens, whose flesh bore the tattooed letters *V. V.* above a lover's knot. A mysterious iron ring, drugged coffee, four violent deaths, and a viscount parading as a deaf-and-dumb Indian servant were the ingredients of this heady witch's broth. Poison vied with pistols or daggers for "the short road to . . . revenge," garments were dyed with blood, the heroine concluded her dark bargain, and the author doubtless recalled with nostalgia the comic tragedies of her childhood. This flight into the all-but-impossible not only emblazoned the pages of a sensational newspaper but was reprinted as a ten-cent novelette.[23]

Like "V. V.," "A Marble Woman: or, The Mysterious Model"[24] was filled with a variety of plots and counterplots as well as a colorful cast of characters that included a sculptor, Bazil Yorke, and an opium-eating heroine. The plight of Mme. Mathilde Arnheim was pursued by the indefatigable writer in *The Skeleton in the Closet,*[25] the narrative of a woman married to an idiot husband and bound to him by a tie which death alone could sever.

Of all the blood-and-thunder tales conceived by Louisa May Alcott when her hair was down and her dander up, the most extraordinary—in this critic's opinion at least—is the one that gives this book its title. "Behind a Mask: or, A Woman's Power"[26] is not only *per se* a suspenseful story recounted in a masterly manner; it fuses in its crucible many of the elements that had gone into the life of its author.

It engrosses the reader while it makes use of and reflects the experiences and emotions of its creator. "Behind a Mask" is therefore a Gothic *roman à clef*, a fast-moving narrative whose episodes unlock the past not only of the heroine Jean Muir but of the writer Louisa Alcott. Behind this mask, perhaps, the future author of *Little Women* sits for a dark but revealing portrait.

Jean Muir is many things: a woman bent, like Pauline Valary, upon revenge; a woman who, to achieve her ends, resorts to all sorts of coquetries and subterfuges including the feigning of an attempted suicide; a woman filled with anger directed principally against the male lords of creation. But she is primarily an actress.

The arrival of a new governess at the ancestral Coventry estate in England—a role played by Jean Muir—sets the plot in motion. She appears, pale-faced, small, and thin, not more than nineteen years old, and the first scene she enacts is an effective, sympathy-arousing faint. "Scene first, very well done," murmurs the astute Gerald, to which she replies, "The last scene shall be still better."

The mystery is suggested, the suspense begun, the plot laid down when, in the privacy of her room, Miss Muir proceeds to open a flask and drink "some ardent cordial," remove the braids from her head, wipe the pink from her face, take out "several pearly teeth" and emerge "a haggard, worn, and moody woman of thirty. . . . The metamorphosis was wonderful. . . . her mobile features settled into their natural expression, weary, hard, bitter. . . . brooding over some wrong, or loss, or disappointment which had darkened all her life."

Very gradually Miss Muir's transformation is made intelligible until she develops into one of Miss Alcott's most fascinating heroines. Like Pauline Valary she is, of course, a *femme fatale* with whom every male member of the Coventry household, including the fifty-five-year-old Sir John Coventry, falls madly in love. Her background is mysterious. She has lived in Paris, traveled in Russia, can sing brilliant Italian airs and read character. Her powers are fatal. She confesses to one of her lovers, "I *am* a witch, and one day my disguise will drop away and you will see me as I am, old, ugly, bad and lost."

Jean Muir is indeed a psychological if not a Gothic witch. Proud and passionate, mysterious and mocking, she wields a subtle spell. Motivated like Pauline by thwarted love, she carries out her intention of ruining the Coventry family with deliberation, using all the dramatic skills known to the theater. She lies or cries at will, feigns timidity or imperiousness to suit her needs. In a remarkable episode, when impromptu tableaux are performed in the great saloon of Coventry Hall, Miss Muir darkens her skin, paints her brows, and writes hatred on her face. Success crowns all her efforts for she captures her prize —the middle-aged head of the House of Coventry and with him a title and an estate. Meanwhile her secret is out. And what a feminist secret it is!

The temptation at the Mill Dam, the humiliation at Dedham, the theatrical barnstorming, the readings in Gothic romances were all stirred in the caldron of "Behind a Mask." So too were Louisa's conflicting emotions, her hates and her loves, her challenge to fortune. Weaving from these varied threads a tale of evil and passion, of fury and revenge, A. M. Barnard had used her sources well.

Just why Louisa May Alcott selected that pseudonym remains conjectural. "A.M." were her mother's initials—Abigail May; "Barnard" might have been suggested by the distinguished Connecticut educator Henry Barnard, who was a family friend. For the most part, the thrillers, whether pseudonymous, anonymous, or upon one or two occasions in her own name, were issued by two publishing firms. One of them boasted an editor who was as much of a *femme fatale* as L. M. Alcott could conjure up. The other included a partner whose life strongly suggested the episodes of a sensational novel. In her editorial and publishing negotiations therefore, A. M. Barnard—whether she was aware of it or not—was among kindred spirits.

"Wrote two tales for L.," Louisa noted in her 1862 journal. "I enjoy romancing to suit myself; and though my tales are silly, they are not bad; and my sinners always have a good spot somewhere. I hope it is good drill for fancy and language, for I can do it fast; and Mr. L. says my tales are so 'dramatic, vivid, and full of plot,' they are just what he wants." And a few months later: "Rewrote the last story, and sent it to L., who wants more than I can send him." [27]

1862 was the year of Antietam and Fredericksburg. It was not for the home circle alone that so-called family newspapers and cheap paperbacks were printed, but for soldiers in camp who could while away tedious hours between battles by escaping to an ancestral estate in Britain or a tropical paradise in Cuba. As the war gathered momentum, the market for such literature widened and with it the need for new authors and new stories.

The "L." of Louisa's journal, to whom she offered "Pauline's Passion" in competition for the announced hundred-dollar prize, was well aware of this need. Frank Leslie,[28] publisher of *Frank Leslie's Illustrated Newspaper,* had his hand on the public pulse. He had begun life as Henry Carter, wood engraver in England, adopted the pseudonym of Frank Leslie, and migrated to America. Ruddy, black-bearded, aggressive, dynamic, he had in 1855 launched his *Illustrated Newspaper,* a project that was to make him a power on New York's Publishers' Row. With its graphic cuts of murders and assassinations, prizefights and fires, the weekly was to dominate the field of illustrated journalism for nearly three-quarters of a century. It sported just enough text to float the pictures instead of just enough pictures to float the text. Thanks to a clever and ingenious device, Leslie was able to produce his pictures—sometimes mammoth double-page engravings —with unprecedented speed. Thanks to his editorial staff, he was able to select text that titillated an ever-expanding readership whether it gathered at hearth or campfire.

It was E. G. Squier who wrote to Louisa May Alcott in December, 1862, when she herself was nursing at the Union Hotel Hospital: "Your tale 'Pauline' this morning was awarded the $100 prize for the best short tale for Mr. Leslie's newspaper, and you will hear from him in due course in reference to what you may regard as an essential part of the matter. I presume that it will be on hand for those little Christmas purchases. Allow me to congratulate you on your success and to recommend you to submit whatever you may hereafter have of the same sort for Mr. Leslie's acceptance." [29]

E. G. Squier, scholar-archaeologist serving temporarily as a Leslie editor, was married to another Leslie protégée who could have served as prototype for every one of Louisa's *femmes fatales.* Miriam Florence Squier [30] had been born in New Orleans in 1836, and throughout a stormy, flamboyant, and successful life in the North she remained a southern belle. Much of that life would have fascinated A. M. Barnard. Between Miriam's first two marriages she had gone barnstorming with Lola Montez under the stage name of Minnie Montez. As knowledgeable editor of the House of Leslie she sported a blue stocking on one leg, but her other leg was encased in a stocking as scarlet as any worn by Pauline Valary or Jean Muir. Eventually Mrs. Squier would marry not only Frank Leslie but his publishing domain, becoming a *grande dame* and a forcible power as head of the House of Leslie before going on to other conquests marital and extramarital.

In A. M. Barnard's heyday, during the early 1860's, this was the colorful trio who managed the Leslie publications. With the new year of 1863 *Frank Leslie's Illustrated Newspaper* announced that, after deliberating over the moral tendency and artistic merit of over two hundred manuscripts, the editor had decided to award the first prize to "a lady of Massachusetts" for "Pauline's Passion and Punishment." [31] In the next number, the first half of a story of "exceeding power, brilliant description, thrilling incident and unexceptionable moral" was anonymously published, with appropriate illustrations of "Manuel reading Gilbert's Letter" and "Gilbert's Despair at Pauline's Final Rejection." "Received $100 from F.L.," Louisa commented in her journal, "for a tale which won the prize last January; paid debts, and was glad that my winter bore visible fruit." [32]

Other seasons also bore visible fruit that ripened in the Leslie periodicals. "A Whisper in the Dark," [33] a tale too mild for A. M. Barnard but too lurid for L. M. Alcott, and "Enigmas," [34] a mystery about Italian refugees, a spy and a woman disguised as a man, made their bows in the *Illustrated Newspaper*. In 1866 Miriam Squier reminded Louisa May Alcott that Frank Leslie would be glad to receive a sensational story from her every month at fifty dollars each. [35]

By that time the tireless author was receiving between two and three dollars a column for thrillers produced for a Boston publishing firm headed by yet another remarkable trio. In the ears of those three gentlemen the call of the wild still echoed, for one had edited tales that embodied it, a second had yielded to it by sailing to New Granada aboard the *Crescent City*, and a third had been the hero of a sensational novel which, if written, would have included chapters on the conquest of California, gold digging, a jaunt to the Sandwich and Fiji islands, China, and Australia. If A. M. Barnard was ever at a loss for a plot she needed merely to hearken to the lives of Messrs. Elliott, Thomes, and Talbot of Boston. [36] William Henry Thomes, who had succumbed to gold fever, had also encountered Indians, coyotes, and grizzlies, had sailed aboard an opium smuggler that plied between China and California, and was himself a mine of suggestions for authors whose thrilling romances he would publish. As publisher of the *True Flag*, James R. Elliott had edited the type of story William

Thomes had lived. The two formed a publishing partnership in 1861, a year after the New York firm of Beadle had introduced their dime-novel series to an avid American reading public. Joined by Newton Talbot, who had listed to the call of the wild by sailing to New Granada, the trio set out their shingle on Boston's Washington Street and, like the House of Leslie in New York, proceeded to issue a chain of periodicals and novelettes that would bring adventure and romance to a nation at war.

The mainstay of their business was *The Flag of Our Union*,[37] a miscellaneous weekly designed for the home circle. Though, according to its publishers, it contained "not one vulgar word or line," it did seem to specialize in violent narratives peopled with convicts and opium addicts. It was for that periodical that Louisa May Alcott under the pseudonym of A. M. Barnard produced her bloodiest and most thunderous thrillers.

A series of five letters from James R. Elliott to Louisa M. Alcott written between 1865 and 1866 reveals her relations with the Boston trio, their terms, and their reactions to her effusions:

> *Jan. 5. 1865.*
>
> *I forward you this evening the 3 first copies of the "Flag" in its new form.*
>
> *I think it is now a literary paper that none need to blush for, and a credit to contribute to its columns, rather than otherwise.*
>
> *Now I have a proposition to make you. I want to publish your story "V.V." in it, in place of publishing it as a Novelette in cheap style, as I had intended, and will give you $25. more for the story provided I can publish it under your own name.*
>
> *Please look the "Flag" over & let me know as early as Saturday. . . .*[38]

Louisa resisted the additional twenty-five dollars and "V.V.: or, Plots and Counterplots," its authorship unacknowledged, appeared as a four-part serial in *The Flag of Our Union* in February, 1865. It was later reprinted as No. 80 in the firm's series of *Ten Cent Novelettes of Standard American Authors*—this standard author bearing the name of A. M. Barnard. Elliott's subsequent letters reflect his own growing addiction for the productions of that standard author and his repeated desire to use the name of Louisa May Alcott, known now for her *Hospital Sketches*, in place of A. M. Barnard:

Jan. 7. 1865.

> *I should be pleased to have you write me some stories for the Flag, of about 25 to 40 pages of such Ms. as "V.V." I want them over your own name of course, & will give you $2.00 a column (short columns you will notice) for them. That rate will be fully equal to $16.00 for a first page story in the "American Union" . . . I have entered your name on our gratis list, & you will receive the "Flag" regularly. . . .*
>
> *P.S. I will purchase another Novelette of you at any time you may wish to dispose of one. . . .*

On January 21, 1865, Elliott followed this with the brief but revealing note that was to provide the clue to the Alcott pseudonym:

> *You may send me anything in either the sketch or Novelette line that you do not wish to "father", or that you wish A. M. Barnard, or "any other man" to be responsible for, & if they suit me I will purchase them.*
> *. . . I will give you $3,00 per column (run in inside length) for sketches under your own name.*
> *Let me hear from you.*

Between January and June of 1865, when the next extant letter is dated, Elliott did indeed hear from Miss Alcott, for her "Marble Woman" was run in May and June. The insatiable publisher demanded more, writing on June 15:

> *Have you written anything in the novel line you would like to have me publish "by A M. Barnard, author of "V.V." "The Marble Woman" &c. &c.? If not can you furnish me with a sensation story of about 145 to 150 pages such Mss. as your last "The Marble Woman" so that I can have it by the middle of July? I don't care about even any particular name, if you prefer any other nome [sic] de plume for this one story, use it, as it is for one of my cheap Novelettes.*
> *I will give you $50. for such a story, & don't want it to exceed 150 pages of Mss. the size of "The Marble Woman," 140 pages will answer, or 145 will be better.*
> *By the way my friends think the "Marble Woman" is just splendid; & I think no author of novels need be ashamed to own it for a bantling. I am sorry you should have had any feeling in regard to the nome [sic] de plume. I am sure that I have not given*

currency to the idea that "A. M. Barnard" & yourself were identical.

Please let me hear from you by return mail, if possible; in regard to the short novel.

In August, 1866, the last extant letter in this extraordinary correspondence was written:

The story entitled "Behind A Mask" is accepted. I think it a story of peculiar power, and have no doubt but my readers will be quite as much fascinated with it as I was myself while reading the Ms. I will give you $65. for it. . . .
I should like another by the 20th of September.
Can I have one? . . .

The source of supply seemed as limitless as the demand. "The Abbot's Ghost" followed "Behind a Mask," and in 1867 both *The Skeleton in the Closet* and *The Mysterious Key* appeared in paperback—the former in the *Ten Cent Novelettes* series as No. 49 along with Perley Parker's *The Foundling* and the latter as No. 50.

There is little doubt that Louisa enjoyed not only the monetary rewards for her surreptitious labors but the use of a pseudonym, the secret correspondence with her publishers—the whole clandestine procedure involved in producing thrillers from "behind a mask." There is little doubt too that she would have enjoyed the story of the discovery of her pseudonym and of her anonymous and pseudonymous narratives. If the ghost of A. M. Barnard still haunts an earthly realm it will surely hover close at hand as that mystery is unraveled.

The unmasking of Louisa May Alcott took place while the country was engaged in another conflict, the Second World War. I was at work on a biography of Louisa May Alcott. With my lifelong friend and future business partner—Dr. Leona Rostenberg, printing historian and founder of our firm, Leona Rostenberg—Rare Books—I visited a distinguished Alcott collector. Carroll Atwood Wilson was a handsome and urbane gentleman, an attorney and a bibliophile who showed his bookish treasures with an enthusiasm equaled only by our intense interest.[39] He knew his Alcott well, and his Alcott characters, especially Jo March of *Little Women,* who, it will be recalled, offered sensational stories to the publishers of the *Weekly Volcano* and *Blarneystone Banner.* Mr. Wilson showed us many volumes by Louisa May Alcott, among them the copy of *The Mysterious Key* that was

used in the preparation of the present collection. And as he dusted off
the books, handing them to us one by one, he remarked, "Miss Stern,
you must get yourself a Guggenheim Fellowship and complete your
biography of Louisa May Alcott." Then, mindful of Leona Rostenberg's preoccupation with bibliographical problems and printing history, he turned to her. "Miss Rostenberg, we know that Louisa Alcott
wrote blood-and-thunder stories just as Jo March did. And we know
she had some sort of pseudonym. We don't know what the pseudonym
was and we don't know anything about the stories. You identify the
pseudonym and locate the stories."

Both Miss Stern and Miss Rostenberg proceeded to carry out
Mr. Wilson's injunctions. At Houghton Library, Harvard University,
where we delved through piles of manuscript and mountains of family
letters, Leona came upon the five letters from James R. Elliott of
Elliott, Thomes & Talbot to Louisa May Alcott that revealed the
pseudonym, the titles of three of the thrillers and the name of the
periodical that issued them. For the Sherlock Holmes of Houghton
Library the rest was elementary—or would have been elementary had
the exigencies of war not intervened.

The Flag of Our Union, it appeared, was and is, in the language
of booksellers, an uncommon periodical. The Library of Congress
boasts one of the more complete runs. To wartime Washington, therefore, Sherlock Rostenberg repaired, having paved the way with the
necessary correspondence. Armed with her deerstalker and her magni-
fying glass, not to mention the all but intolerable anticipatory palpita-
tions of the scholar bent on discovery, she awaited the arrival of the
Civil War run of *The Flag of Our Union,* only to be informed that
the periodical had been placed in safekeeping "for the duration."
Despite this frustration, Leona Rostenberg was able to announce her
extraordinary discovery in an article entitled "Some Anonymous and
Pseudonymous Thrillers of Louisa M. Alcott," published in the
Papers of the Bibliographical Society of America in 1943.[40] In the
thirty years that have followed that announcement the discovery has
been referred to in bibliographies, biographies, and publishing his-
tories. But it is not until now that the stories themselves have been un-
earthed and reprinted.

The author herself, whose secret was so well hidden, viewed her
clandestine productions with some ambivalence. Like her illustrious
mentor Ralph Waldo Emerson, many critics objected strongly to the

"yellow-covered literature of the Sylvanus Cobb, Jr. stamp," and Louisa was sometimes inclined to agree with this denunciation. When she converted *The Flag of Our Union* into the *Blarneystone Banner* and *Frank Leslie's Illustrated Newspaper* into the *Weekly Volcano* as media for Jo March's "necessity stories," she might have had her tongue in cheek but she was also looking down her nose. Later, reprinting "The Baron's Gloves" in a collection of *Proverb Stories,* she explained her motive: "As many girls have asked to see what sort of tales Jo March wrote at the beginning of her career, I have added 'The Baron's Gloves,' as a sample of the romantic rubbish which paid so well once upon a time. If it shows them what *not* to write it will not have been rescued from oblivion in vain." [41]

Yet there was another side to the complex Louisa May Alcott. Her thrillers were "necessity stories" of course, but the necessity was not merely monetary. In a revealing conversation she once doffed her mask and confessed her addiction to blood-and-thunder:

> I think my natural ambition is for the lurid style. I indulge in gorgeous fancies and wish that I dared inscribe them upon my pages and set them before the public. . . . How should I dare to interfere with the proper grayness of old Concord? The dear old town has never known a startling hue since the redcoats were there. Far be it from me to inject an inharmonious color into the neutral tint. And my favorite characters! Suppose they went to cavorting at their own sweet will, to the infinite horror of dear Mr. Emerson, who never imagined a Concord person as walking off a plumb line stretched between two pearly clouds in the empyrean. To have had Mr. Emerson for an intellectual god all one's life is to be invested with a chain armor of propriety. . . . And what would my own good father think of me . . . if I set folks to doing the things that I have a longing to see my people do? No, my dear, I shall always be a wretched victim to the respectable traditions of Concord. [42]

Actually, Louisa May Alcott was a victim less to "the respectable traditions of Concord" than to her own success. In September of 1867 she noted in her journal, "Niles, partner of Roberts, asked me to write a girls' book. Said I'd try." [43] The result was *Little Women,* the first part of which appeared in 1868, the second in 1869. The families of New England, the merchants of Boston, in time the American public itself laughed and cried over a story destined to become a perennial best seller. The girl who had gone out to service and hemmed pillow-cases to fill the gaps in the Alcott Sinking Fund had made her fortune. At the same time, the author who had dispatched thrillers to Frank Leslie and James R. Elliott had presumably found her style. The niche she had walked into with *Little Women* was too comfortable to abandon. Henceforth Louisa May Alcott would have neither the necessity nor the time to play A. M. Barnard.

Only when her publishers, Roberts Brothers of Boston, projected a "No Name Series" would the author of *Little Women* revert to the literary subterfuge of the author of "Behind a Mask." In *A Modern Mephistopheles,* published anonymously in that series in 1877, Louisa Alcott fused the influences of Hawthorne and Goethe and added to her cast of "lurid" characters the pagan figure of Felix Canaris, who sold liberty and love for fame; the sybarite Jasper Helwyze, her "modern Mephistopheles," who sought out the evil in mankind; and Olivia the mellow beauty. "It has been simmering," the author wrote in her journal, "ever since I read Faust last year. Enjoyed doing it, being tired of providing moral pap for the young." [44] Surely The Children's Friend must have found nostalgic pleasure in returning to the ingredients of earlier caldrons: hashish enclosed in a tortoiseshell bon-bonnière; mesmerism; "skins mooned and barred with black upon the tawny velvet"; a heroine who walked, as Pauline Valary had done, with the "restless grace of a leopardess pacing its cage."

Yet No. 6 in the "No Name Series" could not restore the past to the author of No. 50 in the *Ten Cent Novelettes* series. The past was buried between the fading blue wrappers of those *Ten Cent Novelettes* or in the dusty pages of the once gaudy weeklies *The Flag of Our Union, Frank Leslie's Illustrated Newspaper.* It is time to brush the dust away, for the stories are better than their author realized and their reprinting is long overdue.

Although they are rare and all but impossible to find today, rarity alone would not entitle them to the wide readership which should be accorded this collection. Like all the authors of sensational literature, Louisa Alcott was equipped with a riotous imagination, a dramatic instinct, and an indefatigable right hand. If she borrowed from other Gothic romancers the trappings of a rich aristocracy in which she could forget her own penury, if her language upon occasion was high-style pompous and her themes ghostly-gruesome, she nonetheless added much of her own to the genre she had adopted. Her plotting

was tight and well paced and she used the serial form to heighten the mounting suspense of her narratives. Her characterizations were natural and subtle and her gallery of *femmes fatales* forms a suite of flesh-and-blood portraits. Her own anger at an unjust world she transformed into the anger of her heroines, who made of it a powerful weapon with which to challenge fate. The psychological insights of A. M. Barnard disclose the darker side of the character of Louisa May Alcott, and so her stories must appeal enormously to all who have been enthralled by the life and work of the author of *Little Women*. Since those same psychological insights reveal her as intensely modern, intensely if obliquely feminist, her stories must command an immediate response today. They are rich with interest for those in search of current themes and preoccupations as well as for those in search of Louisa May Alcott. And for those who seek merely the thrills of the cliffhanger, they bring the delights of the suspenseful tale well told.

The four narratives selected for *Behind a Mask: The Unknown Thrillers of Louisa May Alcott* are, it is hoped, an earnest, a foretaste of others that will follow. For Louisa Alcott was indeed a natural—an almost limitless—"source of stories." Here her "gorgeous fancies" and her flamboyant characters do "cavort at their own sweet will." And here, in an extraordinary union, the excitements of escape are coupled with the excitements of self-discovery. She writes in a vortex behind her mask and she proves, if proof is needed, that "the writers of sensation novels are wiser in their generation than the children of sweetness and light." [45]

NOTES

[1] Louisa May Alcott to Alf Whitman, Concord, June 22 [1862] (Houghton Library, Harvard University).

[2] Louisa May Alcott to James Redpath, n.p., n.d. (New York Historical Society).

[3] Ednah D. Cheney, ed., *Louisa May Alcott: Her Life, Letters, and Journals* (Boston, 1889) p. 70 [hereinafter Cheney]. For biographical details about Louisa May Alcott, see also Madeleine B. Stern, *Louisa May Alcott* (Norman, Okla., 1971).

[4] Cheney, pp. 124–125.

[5] *Ibid.*, p. 89.

[6] Louisa May Alcott, "How I Went Out to Service," *The Independent*, XXVI:1331 (June 4, 1874); Stern, *Louisa May Alcott*, pp. 64–66. The Dedham family was identified with the help of the late Mr. Frank W. Kimball and Dr. Arthur M. Worthington, both of Dedham, Mass. In *An Address . . . before . . . the Massachusetts Charitable Fire Society* (Boston, 1810), James Richardson announced, "Benevolence is both a sentiment and a duty." See also Alvan Lamson, *A Discourse on The Life and Character of Hon. James Richardson* (Boston, 1858).

According to "Gossip," *Frank Leslie's Lady's Journal*, XIX:476 (December 25, 1880), p. 115, Louisa May Alcott had worked as a servant in a former Senator's household. A young theological student who boarded with the family asked her to black his boots shortly after her term as a servant had expired. Her reply was that while studying divinity he should have learned humanity. Despite inaccuracies, this is an interesting record, especially since it appeared in a Leslie periodical.

[7] Stern, *Louisa May Alcott,* pp. 89–91.

[8] A. Bronson Alcott to Louisa, Concord, December 17, 1865, in Richard L. Herrnstadt, ed., *The Letters of A. Bronson Alcott* (Ames, Iowa [1969]), p. 379.

[9] A. Bronson Alcott to Mrs. A. Bronson Alcott, St. Louis, November 30, 1866, *ibid.,* p. 397.

[10] *Comic Tragedies Written by "Jo" and "Meg" and Acted by the "Little Women"* (Boston, 1893); Stern, *Louisa May Alcott, passim;* Madeleine B. Stern, "Louisa Alcott, Trouper," *The New England Quarterly,* XVI:2 (June, 1943); Madeleine B. Stern, "The Witch's Cauldron to the Family Hearth: Louisa M. Alcott's Literary Development, 1848–1868," *More Books, The Bulletin of the Boston Public Library* (October, 1943), p. 363.

[11] Cheney, p. 63.

[12] *Ibid.,* p. 45.

[13] *Ibid.,* p. 68.

[14] Edith Birkhead, *The Tale of Terror: A Study of the Gothic Romance* (New York [1920]), p. 197.

[15] For a fine anthology of Gothic novels with extremely informative introductions, see Peter Haining, ed., *Gothic Tales of Terror,* I and II (Baltimore, 1973).

[16] For Louisa May Alcott's writings, see the Bibliography appended to Stern, *Louisa May Alcott,* pp. 342–360; Madeleine B. Stern, *Louisa's Wonder Book: A Newly Discovered Alcott Juvenile* (Mount Pleasant, Mich., 1975); Jacob Blanck, *Bibliography of American Literature* (New Haven, 1955), I, 27–45.

[17] Louisa May Alcott to Alf Whitman, April 5 [1860] (Houghton Library), quoted in Stern, *Louisa May Alcott,* p. 97.

[18] Cheney, p. 80.

[19] Louisa May Alcott, "Happy Women," *The New York Ledger,* XXIV:7 (April 11, 1868).

[20] "Pauline's Passion and Punishment," *Frank Leslie's Illustrated Newspaper,* XV:379 and 380 (January 3 and 10, 1863). Published anonymously. Now reprinted from issues at the New York Public Library and the New York Historical Society Library.

[21] "The Abbot's Ghost: or, Maurice Treherne's Temptation," *The Flag of Our Union*, XXII:1, 2, 3, and 4 (January 5, 12, 19, 26, 1867). Published under the pseudonym of A. M. Barnard. Now reprinted through the courtesy of Mr. William Matheson, Chief, Rare Book Division, Library of Congress.

[22] L. M. Alcott, *The Mysterious Key, and What It Opened* (Boston: Elliott, Thomes & Talbot, [1867]). Issued as No. 50 in the *Ten Cent Novelettes* of *Standard American Authors* series. Reprinted as No. 382 in *The Leisure Hour Library* by F. M. Lupton of New York, ca. 1900. For bibliographical details, see Blanck, *op. cit.*, No. 152 and No. 231. Now reprinted through the courtesy of Dr. Julius P. Barclay, Curator of Rare Books, and Miss Joan Crane, Alderman Library, University of Virginia. The copy at the University of Virginia had belonged to Carroll Atwood Wilson.

[23] "V. V.: or, Plots and Counterplots," *The Flag of Our Union*, XX:5, 6, 7, 8 (February 4, 11, 18, 25, 1865). Reprinted as No. 80 in the *Ten Cent Novelettes* of *Standard American Authors* series under the pseudonym of A. M. Barnard. For bibliographical details, see Blanck, *op. cit.*, No. 165.

[24] "A Marble Woman: or, The Mysterious Model," *The Flag of Our Union*, XX: 20, 21, 22, 23 (May 20, 27, June 3, 10, 1865). Published under the pseudonym of A. M. Barnard.

[25] L. M. Alcott, *The Skeleton in the Closet*. Published with Perley Parker, *The Foundling* (Boston: Elliott, Thomes & Talbot [1867]), as No. 49 in the *Ten Cent Novelettes* of *Standard American Authors* series. For bibliographical details, see Blanck, *op cit.*, No. 151.

[26] "Behind a Mask: or, A Woman's Power," *The Flag of Our Union*, XXI:41, 42, 43, 44 (October 13, 20, 27, November 3, 1866). Published under the pseudonym of A. M. Barnard. Now reprinted through the courtesy of Dr. Marc A. McCorison, American Antiquarian Society, Worcester, Mass.

[27] Cheney, p. 131.

[28] For details of Frank Leslie and his *Illustrated Newspaper*, see Frank Luther Mott, *A History of American Magazines 1850–1865* (Cambridge, Mass., 1957) II, 452–465; Madeleine B. Stern, *Imprints on History: Book Publishers and American Frontiers* (Bloomington, Ind., 1956), pp. 221–232; Madeleine B. Stern, *Purple Passage: The Life of Mrs. Frank Leslie* (Norman, Okla., 1970), *passim*; John

Tebbel, *A History of Book Publishing in the United States* (New York and London, 1972) I, 357–358.

[29] E. G. Squier to Louisa May Alcott, ca. December 18, 1862 (Orchard House, Concord, Mass.). Quoted in Leona Rostenberg, "Some Anonymous and Pseudonymous Thrillers of Louisa M. Alcott," *Papers* of the Bibliographical Society of America, XXXVII:2 (1943). See also Stern, *Louisa May Alcott*, p. 123.

[30] For Miriam Squier's tumultuous life and career, see Stern, *Purple Passage, passim.*

[31] Stern, *Louisa May Alcott*, p. 128.

[32] Cheney, p. 151.

[33] "A Whisper in the Dark," *Frank Leslie's Illustrated Newspaper*, XVI:401 and 402 (June 6 and 13, 1863). Reprinted in *A Modern Mephistopheles and A Whisper in the Dark* (Boston, 1889).

[34] "Enigmas," *Frank Leslie's Illustrated Newspaper*, XVIII:450 and 451 (May 14 and 21, 1864).

[35] Miriam F. Squier to Louisa May Alcott, New Rochelle, September 17, 1866 (Houghton Library, Harvard University). See also Stern, *Purple Passage*, p. 220.

[36] For Elliott, Thomes & Talbot, see Rostenberg, "Some Anonymous and Pseudonymous Thrillers of Louisa M. Alcott," *passim*; Stern, *Imprints on History*, pp. 206–220; Tebbel, *A History of Book Publishing in the United States* I, 438–440.

[37] The periodical ran from 1846 to 1870. See Mott, *A History of American Magazines* II, 35.

[38] The letters, which were found in the Louisa M. Alcott MSS., Box II (Houghton Library, Harvard University), were first printed in Rostenberg, *op. cit.* Quotations have been made from their text, and two of the letters have been reproduced by permission of the Harvard College Library.

[39] See Carroll A. Wilson, *Thirteen Author Collections of the Nineteenth Century and Five Centuries of Familiar Quotations.* Edited by Jean C. S. Wilson and David A. Randall (New York, 1950).

[40] Rostenberg, *op. cit.*

[41] Louisa May Alcott, Preface, *Proverb Stories* (Boston, 1882). See Madeleine B. Stern, "Louisa M. Alcott's Self-Criticism," *More Books, The Bulletin of the Boston Public Library*, XX:8 (October, 1945), p. 341.

[42] From a conversation with Louisa May Alcott. See L. C. Pickett, *Across My Path: Memories of People I Have Known* (New York, 1916), pp. 107–108. See also Stern, "Louisa M. Alcott's Self-Criticism," *loc. cit.*, p. 341.

[43] Cheney, p. 186.

[44] *Ibid.*, p. 296. See also Stern, *Louisa May Alcott*, pp. 264–265; Madeleine B. Stern, "Louisa M. Alcott: An Appraisal," *The New England Quarterly*, XXII:4 (December, 1949), pp. 494–496.

[45] Dorothy L. Sayers and Robert Eustace, *The Documents in the Case* (New York, [1972]), p. 81.

AMERICAN UNION,
Three Dollars a year.
FLAG OF OUR UNION,
Four Dollars a year.
MONTHLY NOVELETTE,
Two Dollars a year.
DOLLAR MONTHLY,
$1.50 a year.

OFFICE OF **Elliott, Thomes & Talbot's Publications,**

63 CONGRESS STREET,

Boston, Aug. 11 1866,

Dear Miss Alcott

The story entitled
"Behind A Mask" is accepted. I
think is a story of peculiar
power, and have no doubt
but my readers will be quite
as much fascinated with
it as I was myself while
reading the Ms. I will
give you $65. for it. That
amt awaits your order.
I should like another
by the 20th of September.
Can I have one? I sh'd
be happy to pay you $5.
each for two or three
poems by Miss Alcott.

Very Truly Yours
J. R. Elliott.

Boston Jan. 27, 1865.

Dear Miss Alcott

You may send
me anything in either the
sketch or Novelette line
that you do not wish
to "Father", or that you
wish A. M. Barnard, or
"any other man" to be responsible for, & if they suit me
I will purchase them.
I will pay for poems
under your own name.
Also I will give you
$3.00 per Column (Union inside
length) for sketches under
your own name,
Let me hear from
you. Very truly Yours

J. R. Elliott

Behind a Mask

~ or ~

A WOMAN'S POWER

BY A. M. BARNARD

⋟ chapter I ⋞

JEAN MUIR

"HAS she come?"
"No, Mamma, not yet."
"I wish it were well over. The thought of it worries and excites me. A cushion for my back, Bella."

And poor, peevish Mrs. Coventry sank into an easy chair with a nervous sigh and the air of a martyr, while her pretty daughter hovered about her with affectionate solicitude.

"Who are they talking of, Lucia?" asked the languid young man lounging on a couch near his cousin, who bent over her tapestry work with a happy smile on her usually haughty face.

"The new governess, Miss Muir. Shall I tell you about her?"

"No, thank you. I have an inveterate aversion to the whole tribe. I've often thanked heaven that I had but one sister, and she a spoiled child, so that I have escaped the infliction of a governess so long."

"How will you bear it now?" asked Lucia.

"Leave the house while she is in it."

"No, you won't. You're too lazy, Gerald," called out a younger and more energetic man, from the recess where he stood teasing his dogs.

"I'll give her a three days' trial; if she proves endurable I shall not disturb myself; if, as I am sure, she is a bore, I'm off anywhere, anywhere out of her way."

"I beg you won't talk in that depressing manner, boys. I dread the coming of a stranger more than you possibly can, but Bella *must* not be neglected; so I have nerved myself to endure this woman, and Lucia is good enough to say she will attend to her after tonight."

"Don't be troubled, Mamma. She is a nice person, I dare say, and when once we are used to her, I've no doubt we shall be glad to have her, it's so dull here just now. Lady Sydney said she was a quiet, accomplished, amiable girl, who needed a home, and would be a help to poor stupid me, so try to like her for my sake."

"I will, dear, but isn't it getting late? I do hope nothing has happened. Did you tell them to send a carriage to the station for her, Gerald?"

"I forgot it. But it's not far, it won't hurt her to walk" was the languid reply.

"It was indolence, not forgetfulness, I know. I'm very sorry; she will think it so rude to leave her to find her way so late. Do go and see to it, Ned."

"Too late, Bella, the train was in some time ago. Give your orders to me next time. Mother and I'll see that they are obeyed," said Edward.

"Ned is just at an age to make a fool of himself for any girl who comes in his way. Have a care of the governess, Lucia, or she will bewitch him."

Gerald spoke in a satirical whisper, but his brother heard him and answered with a good-humored laugh.

"I wish there was any hope of your making a fool of yourself in that way, old fellow. Set me a good example, and I promise to follow it. As for the governess, she is a woman, and should be treated with common civility. I should say a little extra kindness wouldn't be amiss, either, because she is poor, and a stranger."

"That is my dear, good-hearted Ned! We'll stand by poor little Muir, won't we?" And running to her brother, Bella stood on tiptoe to offer him a kiss which he could not refuse, for the rosy lips were pursed up invitingly, and the bright eyes full of sisterly affection.

"I do hope she has come, for, when I make an effort to see anyone, I hate to make it in vain. Punctuality is *such* a virtue, and I know this woman hasn't got it, for she promised to be here at seven, and now it is long after," began Mrs. Coventry, in an injured tone.

Before she could get breath for another complaint, the clock struck seven and the doorbell rang.

"There she is!" cried Bella, and turned toward the door as if to go and meet the newcomer.

But Lucia arrested her, saying authoritatively, "Stay here, child. It is her place to come to you, not yours to go to her."

"Miss Muir," announced a servant, and a little black-robed figure stood in the doorway. For an instant no one stirred, and the governess had time to see and be seen before a word was uttered. All looked at her, and she cast on the household group a keen glance that impressed them curiously; then her eyes fell, and bowing slightly she walked in. Edward came forward and received her with the frank cordiality which nothing could daunt or chill.

"Mother, this is the lady whom you expected. Miss Muir, allow me to apologize for our apparent neglect in not sending for you. There was a mistake about the carriage, or, rather, the lazy fellow to whom the order was given forgot it. Bella, come here."

"Thank you, no apology is needed. I did not expect to be sent for." And the governess meekly sat down without lifting her eyes.

"I am glad to see you. Let me take your things," said Bella, rather shyly, for Gerald, still lounging, watched the fireside group with languid interest, and Lucia never stirred. Mrs. Coventry took a second survey and began:

"You were punctual, Miss Muir, which pleases me. I'm a sad invalid, as Lady Sydney told you, I hope; so that Miss Coventry's lessons will be directed by my niece, and you will go to her for directions, as she knows what I wish. You will excuse me if I ask you a few questions, for Lady Sydney's note was very brief, and I left everything to her judgment."

"Ask anything you like, madam," answered the soft, sad voice.

"You are Scotch, I believe."

"Yes, madam."

"Are your parents living?"

"I have not a relation in the world."

"Dear me, how sad! Do you mind telling me your age?"

"Nineteen." And a smile passed over Miss Muir's lips, as she folded her hands with an air of resignation, for the catechism was evidently to be a long one.

"So young! Lady Sydney mentioned five-and-twenty, I think, didn't she, Bella?"

"No, Mamma, she only said she thought so. Don't ask such questions. It's not pleasant before us all," whispered Bella.

A quick, grateful glance shone on her from the suddenly lifted eyes of Miss Muir, as she said quietly, "I wish I was thirty, but, as I am not, I do my best to look and seem old."

Of course, every one looked at her then, and all felt a touch of pity at the sight of the pale-faced girl in her plain black dress, with no ornament but a little silver cross at her throat. Small, thin, and colorless she was, with yellow hair, gray eyes, and sharply cut, irregular, but very expressive features. Poverty seemed to have set its bond stamp upon her, and life to have had for her more frost than sunshine. But something in the lines of the mouth betrayed strength, and the clear, low voice had a curious mixture of command and entreaty in its varying tones. Not an attractive woman, yet not an ordinary one; and, as she sat there with her delicate hands lying in her lap, her head bent, and a bitter look on her thin face, she was more interesting than many a blithe and blooming girl. Bella's heart warmed to her at once, and she drew her seat nearer, while Edward went back to his dogs that his presence might not embarrass her.

"You have been ill, I think," continued Mrs. Coventry, who considered this fact the most interesting of all she had heard concerning the governess.

"Yes, madam, I left the hospital only a week ago."

"Are you quite sure it is safe to begin teaching so soon?"

"I have no time to lose, and shall soon gain strength here in the country, if you care to keep me."

"And you are fitted to teach music, French, and drawing?"

"I shall endeavor to prove that I am."

"Be kind enough to go and play an air or two. I can judge by your touch; I used to play finely when a girl."

Miss Muir rose, looked about her for the instrument, and seeing it at the other end of the room went toward it, passing Gerald and Lucia as if she did not see them. Bella followed, and in a moment forgot everything in admiration. Miss Muir played like one who loved music and was perfect mistress of her art. She charmed them all by the magic of this spell; even indolent Gerald sat up to listen, and Lucia put down her needle, while Ned watched the slender white fingers as they flew, and wondered at the strength and skill which they possessed.

"Please sing," pleaded Bella, as a brilliant overture ended.

With the same meek obedience Miss Muir complied, and began a little Scotch melody, so sweet, so sad, that the girl's eyes filled, and Mrs. Coventry looked for one of her many pocket-handkerchiefs. But suddenly the music ceased, for, with a vain attempt to support herself, the singer slid from her seat and lay before the startled listeners, as white and rigid as if struck with death. Edward caught her up, and, ordering his brother off the couch, laid her there, while Bella chafed her hands, and her mother rang for her maid. Lucia bathed the poor girl's temples, and Gerald, with unwonted energy, brought a glass of wine. Soon Miss Muir's lips trembled, she sighed, then murmured, tenderly, with a pretty Scotch accent, as if wandering in the past, "Bide wi' me, Mither, I'm sae sick an sad here all alone."

"Take a sip of this, and it will do you good, my dear," said Mrs. Coventry, quite touched by the plaintive words.

The strange voice seemed to recall her. She sat up, looked about her, a little wildly, for a moment, then collected herself and said, with a pathetic look and tone, "Pardon me. I have been on my feet all day, and, in my eagerness to keep my appointment, I forgot to eat since morning. I'm better now; shall I finish the song?"

"By no means. Come and have some tea," said Bella, full of pity and remorse.

"Scene first, very well done," whispered Gerald to his cousin.

Miss Muir was just before them, apparently listening to Mrs. Coventry's remarks upon fainting fits; but she heard, and looked over her shoulders with a gesture like Rachel. Her eyes were gray, but at that instant they seemed black with some strong emotion of anger, pride, or defiance. A curious smile passed over her face as she bowed, and said in her penetrating voice, "Thanks. The last scene shall be still better."

Young Coventry was a cool, indolent man, seldom conscious of any emotion, any passion, pleasurable or otherwise; but at the look, the tone of the governess, he experienced a new sensation, indefinable, yet strong. He colored and, for the first time in his life, looked abashed. Lucia saw it, and hated Miss Muir with a sudden hatred; for, in all the years she had passed with her cousin, no look or word of hers had possessed such power. Coventry was himself again in an instant, with no trace of that passing change, but a look of interest in his usually dreamy eyes, and a touch of anger in his sarcastic voice.

"What a melodramatic young lady! I shall go tomorrow."

Lucia laughed, and was well pleased when he sauntered away to bring her a cup of tea from the table where a little scene was just taking place. Mrs. Coventry had sunk into her chair again, exhausted by the flurry of the fainting fit. Bella was busied about her; and Edward, eager to feed the pale governess, was awkwardly trying to make the tea, after a beseeching glance at his cousin which she did not choose to answer. As he upset the caddy and uttered a despairing exclamation, Miss Muir quietly took her place behind the urn, saying with a smile, and a shy glance at the young man, "Allow me to assume my duty at once, and serve you all. I understand the art of making people comfortable in this way. The scoop, please. I can gather this up quite well alone, if you will tell me how your mother likes her tea."

Edward pulled a chair to the table and made merry over his mishaps, while Miss Muir performed her little task with a skill and grace that made it pleasant to watch her. Coventry lingered a moment after she had given him a steaming cup, to observe her more nearly, while he asked a question or two of his brother. She took no more notice of him than if he had been a statue, and in the middle of the one remark he addressed to her, she rose to take the sugar basin to Mrs. Coventry, who was quite won by the modest, domestic graces of the new governess.

"Really, my dear, you are a treasure; I haven't tasted such tea since my poor maid Ellis died. Bella never makes it good, and Miss Lucia always forgets the cream. Whatever you do you seem to do well, and that is *such* a comfort."

"Let me always do this for you, then. It will be a pleasure, madam." And Miss Muir came back to her seat with a faint color in her cheek which improved her much.

"My brother asked if young Sydney was at home when you left," said Edward, for Gerald would not take the trouble to repeat the question.

Miss Muir fixed her eyes on Coventry, and answered with a slight tremor of the lips, "No, he left home some weeks ago."

The young man went back to his cousin, saying, as he threw himself down beside her, "I shall not go tomorrow, but wait till the three days are out."

"Why?" demanded Lucia.

Lowering his voice he said, with a significant nod toward the governess, "Because I have a fancy that she is at the bottom of Sydney's mystery. He's not been himself lately, and now he is gone without a word. I rather like romances in real life, if they are not too long, or difficult to read."

"Do you think her pretty?"

"Far from it, a most uncanny little specimen."

"Then why fancy Sydney loves her?"

"He is an oddity, and likes sensations and things of that sort."

"What do you mean, Gerald?"

"Get the Muir to look at you, as she did at me, and you will understand. Will you have another cup, Juno?"

"Yes, please." She liked to have him wait upon her, for he did it to no other woman except his mother.

Before he could slowly rise, Miss Muir glided to them with another cup on the salver; and, as Lucia took it with a cold nod, the girl said under her breath, "I think it honest to tell you that I possess a quick ear, and cannot help hearing what is said anywhere in the room. What you say of me is of no consequence, but you may speak of things which you prefer I should not hear; therefore, allow me to warn you." And she was gone again as noiselessly as she came.

"How do you like that?" whispered Coventry, as his cousin sat looking after the girl, with a disturbed expression.

"What an uncomfortable creature to have in the house! I am very sorry I urged her coming, for your mother has taken a fancy to her, and it will be hard to get rid of her," said Lucia, half angry, half amused.

"Hush, she hears every word you say. I know it by the expression of her face, for Ned is talking about horses, and she looks as haughty as ever you did, and that is saying much. Faith, this is getting interesting."

"Hark, she is speaking; I want to hear," and Lucia laid her hand on her cousin's lips. He kissed it, and then idly amused himself with turning the rings to and fro on the slender fingers.

"I have been in France several years, madam, but my friend died and I came back to be with Lady Sydney, till—" Muir paused an instant, then added, slowly, "till I fell ill. It was a contagious fever, so I went of my own accord to the hospital, not wishing to endanger her."

"Very right, but are you sure there is no danger of infection now?" asked Mrs. Coventry anxiously.

"None, I assure you. I have been well for some time, but did not leave because I preferred to stay there, than to return to Lady Sydney."

"No quarrel, I hope? No trouble of any kind?"

"No quarrel, but—well, why not? You have a right to know, and I will not make a foolish mystery out of a very simple thing. As your family, only, is present, I may tell the truth. I did not go back on the young gentleman's account. Please ask no more."

"Ah, I see. Quite prudent and proper, Miss Muir. I shall never allude to it again. Thank you for your frankness. Bella, you will be careful not to mention this to your young friends; girls gossip sadly, and it would annoy Lady Sydney beyond everything to have this talked of."

"Very neighborly of Lady S. to send the dangerous young lady here, where there are *two* young gentlemen to be captivated. I wonder why she didn't keep Sydney after she had caught him," murmured Coventry to his cousin.

"Because she had the utmost contempt for a titled fool." Miss Muir dropped the words almost into his ear, as she bent to take her shawl from the sofa corner.

"How the deuce did she get there?" ejaculated Coventry, looking as if he had received another sensation. "She has spirit, though, and upon my word I pity Sydney, if he did try to dazzle her, for he must have got a splendid dismissal."

"Come and play billiards. You promised, and I hold you to your word," said Lucia, rising with decision, for Gerald was showing too much interest in another to suit Miss Beaufort.

"I am, as ever, your most devoted. My mother is a charming woman, but I find our evening parties slightly dull, when only my own family are present. Good night, Mamma." He shook hands with his mother, whose pride and idol he was, and, with a comprehensive nod to the others, strolled after his cousin.

"Now they are gone we can be quite cozy, and talk over things, for I don't mind Ned any more than I do his dogs," said Bella, settling herself on her mother's footstool.

"I merely wish to say, Miss Muir, that my daughter has never had a governess and is sadly backward for a girl of sixteen. I want you to pass the mornings with her, and get her on as rapidly as possible. In the afternoon you will walk or drive with her, and in the evening sit with us here, if you like, or amuse yourself as you please. While in the country we are very quiet, for I cannot bear much company, and when my sons want gaiety, they go away for it. Miss Beaufort oversees the servants, and takes my place as far as possible. I am very delicate and keep my room till evening, except for an airing at noon. We will try each other for a month, and I hope we shall get on quite comfortably together."

"I shall do my best, madam."

One would not have believed that the meek, spiritless voice which uttered these words was the same that had startled Coventry a few minutes before, nor that the pale, patient face could ever have kindled with such sudden fire as that which looked over Miss Muir's shoulder when she answered her young host's speech.

Edward thought within himself, Poor little woman! She has had a hard life. We will try and make it easier while she is here; and began his charitable work by suggesting that she might be tired. She acknowledged she was, and Bella led her away to a bright, cozy room, where with a pretty little speech and a good-night kiss she left her.

When alone Miss Muir's conduct was decidedly peculiar. Her first act was to clench her hands and mutter between her teeth, with passionate force, "I'll not fail again if there is power in a woman's wit and will!" She stood a moment motionless, with an expression of almost fierce disdain on her face, then shook her clenched hand as if menacing some unseen enemy. Next she laughed, and shrugged her shoulders with a true French shrug, saying low to herself, "Yes, the last scene *shall* be better than the first. *Mon dieu,* how tired and hungry I am!"

Kneeling before the one small trunk which held her worldly possessions, she opened it, drew out a flask, and mixed a glass of some ardent cordial, which she seemed to enjoy extremely as she sat on the carpet, musing, while her quick eyes examined every corner of the room.

"Not bad! It will be a good field for me to work in, and the harder the task the better I shall like it. *Merci,* old friend. You put heart and courage into me when nothing else will. Come, the curtain is down, so I may be myself for a few hours, if actresses ever are themselves."

Still sitting on the floor she unbound and removed the long

abundant braids from her head, wiped the pink from her face, took out several pearly teeth, and slipping off her dress appeared herself indeed, a haggard, worn, and moody woman of thirty at least. The metamorphosis was wonderful, but the disguise was more in the expression she assumed than in any art of costume or false adornment. Now she was alone, and her mobile features settled into their natural expression, weary, hard, bitter. She had been lovely once, happy, innocent, and tender; but nothing of all this remained to the gloomy woman who leaned there brooding over some wrong, or loss, or disappointment which had darkened all her life. For an hour she sat so, sometimes playing absently with the scanty locks that hung about her face, sometimes lifting the glass to her lips as if the fiery draught warmed her cold blood; and once she half uncovered her breast to eye with a terrible glance the scar of a newly healed wound. At last she rose and crept to bed, like one worn out with weariness and mental pain.

✥ *chapter II* ✥

A GOOD BEGINNING

ONLY the housemaids were astir when Miss Muir left her room next morning and quietly found her way into the garden. As she walked, apparently intent upon the flowers, her quick eye scrutinized the fine old house and its picturesque surroundings.

"Not bad," she said to herself, adding, as she passed into the adjoining park, "but the other may be better, and I will have the best."

Walking rapidly, she came out at length upon the wide green lawn which lay before the ancient hall where Sir John Coventry lived in solitary splendor. A stately old place, rich in oaks, well-kept shrubberies, gay gardens, sunny terraces, carved gables, spacious rooms, liveried servants, and every luxury befitting the ancestral home of a rich and honorable race. Miss Muir's eyes brightened as she looked, her step grew firmer, her carriage prouder, and a smile broke over her face; the smile of one well pleased at the prospect of the success of some cherished hope. Suddenly her whole air changed, she pushed back her hat, clasped her hands loosely before her, and seemed absorbed in girlish admiration of the fair scene that could not fail to charm any beauty-loving eye. The cause of this rapid change soon appeared. A hale, handsome man, between fifty and sixty, came through the little gate leading to the park, and, seeing the young stranger, paused to examine her. He had only time for a glance, however; she seemed conscious of his presence in a moment, turned

with a startled look, uttered an exclamation of surprise, and looked as
if hesitating whether to speak or run away. Gallant Sir John took off
his hat and said, with the old-fashioned courtesy which became him
well, "I beg your pardon for disturbing you, young lady. Allow me to
atone for it by inviting you to walk where you will, and gather what
flowers you like. I see you love them, so pray make free with those
about you."

With a charming air of maidenly timidity and artlessness, Miss
Muir replied, "Oh, thank you, sir! But it is I who should ask pardon
for trespassing. I never should have dared if I had not known that Sir
John was absent. I always wanted to see this fine old place, and ran
over the first thing, to satisfy myself."

"And *are* you satisfied?" he asked, with a smile.

"More than satisfied—I'm charmed; for it is the most beautiful
spot I ever saw, and I've seen many famous seats, both at home and
abroad," she answered enthusiastically.

"The Hall is much flattered, and so would its master be if he
heard you," began the gentleman, with an odd expression.

"I should not praise it to him—at least, not as freely as I have to
you, sir," said the girl, with eyes still turned away.

"Why not?" asked her companion, looking much amused.

"I should be afraid. Not that I dread Sir John; but I've heard
so many beautiful and noble things about him, and respect him so
highly, that I should not dare to say much, lest he should see how I
admire and—"

"And what, young lady? Finish, if you please."

"I was going to say, love him. I will say it, for he is an old man,
and one cannot help loving virtue and bravery."

Miss Muir looked very earnest and pretty as she spoke, standing
there with the sunshine glinting on her yellow hair, delicate face, and
downcast eyes. Sir John was not a vain man, but he found it pleasant
to hear himself commended by this unknown girl, and felt redoubled
curiosity to learn who she was. Too well-bred to ask, or to abash her
by avowing what she seemed unconscious of, he left both discoveries
to chance; and when she turned, as if to retrace her steps, he offered
her the handful of hothouse flowers which he held, saying, with a
gallant bow, "In Sir John's name let me give you my little nosegay,
with thanks for your good opinion, which, I assure you, is not entirely
deserved, for I know him well."

Miss Muir looked up quickly, eyed him an instant, then dropped her eyes, and, coloring deeply, stammered out, "I did not know—I beg your pardon—you are too kind, Sir John."

He laughed like a boy, asking, mischievously, "Why call me Sir John? How do you know that I am not the gardener or the butler?"

"I did not see your face before, and no one but yourself would say that any praise was undeserved," murmured Miss Muir, still overcome with girlish confusion.

"Well, well, we will let that pass, and the next time you come we will be properly introduced. Bella always brings her friends to the Hall, for I am fond of young people."

"I am not a friend. I am only Miss Coventry's governess." And Miss Muir dropped a meek curtsy. A slight change passed over Sir John's manner. Few would have perceived it, but Miss Muir felt it at once, and bit her lips with an angry feeling at her heart. With a curious air of pride, mingled with respect, she accepted the still offered bouquet, returned Sir John's parting bow, and tripped away, leaving the old gentleman to wonder where Mrs. Coventry found such a piquant little governess.

"That is done, and very well for a beginning," she said to herself as she approached the house.

In a green paddock close by fed a fine horse, who lifted up his head and eyed her inquiringly, like one who expected a greeting. Following a sudden impulse, she entered the paddock and, pulling a handful of clover, invited the creature to come and eat. This was evidently a new proceeding on the part of a lady, and the horse careered about as if bent on frightening the newcomer away.

"I see," she said aloud, laughing to herself. "I am not your master, and you rebel. Nevertheless, I'll conquer you, my fine brute."

Seating herself in the grass, she began to pull daisies, singing idly the while, as if unconscious of the spirited prancings of the horse. Presently he drew nearer, sniffing curiously and eyeing her with surprise. She took no notice, but plaited the daisies and sang on as if he was not there. This seemed to pique the petted creature, for, slowly approaching, he came at length so close that he could smell her little foot and nibble at her dress. Then she offered the clover, uttering caressing words and making soothing sounds, till by degrees and with much coquetting, the horse permitted her to stroke his glossy neck and smooth his mane.

It was a pretty sight—the slender figure in the grass, the high-spirited horse bending his proud head to her hand. Edward Coventry, who had watched the scene, found it impossible to restrain himself any longer and, leaping the wall, came to join the group, saying, with mingled admiration and wonder in countenance and voice, "Good morning, Miss Muir. If I had not seen your skill and courage proved before my eyes, I should be alarmed for your safety. Hector is a wild, wayward beast, and has damaged more than one groom who tried to conquer him."

"Good morning, Mr. Coventry. Don't tell tales of this noble creature, who has not deceived my faith in him. Your grooms did not know how to win his heart, and so subdue his spirit without breaking it."

Miss Muir rose as she spoke, and stood with her hand on Hector's neck while he ate the grass which she had gathered in the skirt of her dress.

"You have the secret, and Hector is your subject now, though heretofore he has rejected all friends but his master. Will you give him his morning feast? I always bring him bread and play with him before breakfast."

"Then you are not jealous?" And she looked up at him with eyes so bright and beautiful in expression that the young man wondered he had not observed them before.

"Not I. Pet him as much as you will; it will do him good. He is a solitary fellow, for he scorns his own kind and lives alone, like his master," he added, half to himself.

"Alone, with such a happy home, Mr. Coventry?" And a softly compassionate glance stole from the bright eyes.

"That was an ungrateful speech, and I retract it for Bella's sake. Younger sons have no position but such as they can make for themselves, you know, and I've had no chance yet."

"Younger sons! I thought—I beg pardon." And Miss Muir paused, as if remembering that she had no right to question.

Edward smiled and answered frankly, "Nay, don't mind me. You thought I was the heir, perhaps. Whom did you take my brother for last night?"

"For some guest who admired Miss Beaufort. I did not hear his name, nor observe him enough to discover who he was. I saw only your kind mother, your charming little sister, and—"

She stopped there, with a half-shy, half-grateful look at the young man which finished the sentence better than any words. He was still a boy, in spite of his one-and-twenty years, and a little color came into his brown cheek as the eloquent eyes met his and fell before them.

"Yes, Bella is a capital girl, and one can't help loving her. I know you'll get her on, for, really, she is the most delightful little dunce. My mother's ill health and Bella's devotion to her have prevented our attending to her education before. Next winter, when we go to town, she is to come out, and must be prepared for that great event, you know," he said, choosing a safe subject.

"I shall do my best. And that reminds me that I should report myself to her, instead of enjoying myself here. When one has been ill and shut up a long time, the country is so lovely one is apt to forget duty for pleasure. Please remind me if I am negligent, Mr. Coventry."

"That name belongs to Gerald. I'm only Mr. Ned here," he said as they walked toward the house, while Hector followed to the wall and sent a sonorous farewell after them.

Bella came running to meet them, and greeted Miss Muir as if she had made up her mind to like her heartily. "What a lovely bouquet you have got! I never can arrange flowers prettily, which vexes me, for Mamma is so fond of them and cannot go out herself. You have charming taste," she said, examining the graceful posy which Miss Muir had much improved by adding feathery grasses, delicate ferns, and fragrant wild flowers to Sir John's exotics.

Putting them into Bella's hand, she said, in a winning way, "Take them to your mother, then, and ask her if I may have the pleasure of making her a daily nosegay; for I should find real delight in doing it, if it would please her."

"How kind you are! Of course it would please her. I'll take them to her while the dew is still on them." And away flew Bella, eager to give both the flowers and the pretty message to the poor invalid.

Edward stopped to speak to the gardener, and Miss Muir went up the steps alone. The long hall was lined with portraits, and pacing slowly down it she examined them with interest. One caught her eye, and, pausing before it, she scrutinized it carefully. A young, beautiful, but very haughty female face. Miss Muir suspected at once who it was, and gave a decided nod, as if she saw and caught at some unexpected chance. A soft rustle behind her made her look around, and, seeing Lucia, she bowed, half turned, as if for another glance at the picture, and said, as if involuntarily, "How beautiful it is! May I ask if it is an ancestor, Miss Beaufort?"

"It is the likeness of my mother" was the reply, given with a softened voice and eyes that looked up tenderly.

"Ah, I might have known, from the resemblance, but I scarcely saw you last night. Excuse my freedom, but Lady Sydney treated me as a friend, and I forget my position. Allow me."

As she spoke, Miss Muir stooped to return the handkerchief which had fallen from Lucia's hand, and did so with a humble mien which touched the other's heart; for, though a proud, it was also a very generous one.

"Thank you. Are you better, this morning?" she said, graciously. And having received an affirmative reply, she added, as she walked on, "I will show you to the breakfast room, as Bella is not here. It is a very informal meal with us, for my aunt is never down and my cousins are very irregular in their hours. You can always have yours when you like, without waiting for us if you are an early riser."

Bella and Edward appeared before the others were seated, and Miss Muir quietly ate her breakfast, feeling well satisfied with her hour's work. Ned recounted her exploit with Hector, Bella delivered her mother's thanks for the flowers, and Lucia more than once recalled, with pardonable vanity, that the governess had compared her to her lovely mother, expressing by a look as much admiration for the living likeness as for the painted one. All kindly did their best to make the pale girl feel at home, and their cordial manner seemed to warm and draw her out; for soon she put off her sad, meek air and entertained them with gay anecdotes of her life in Paris, her travels in Russia when governess in Prince Jermadoff's family, and all manner of witty stories that kept them interested and merry long after the meal was over. In the middle of an absorbing adventure, Coventry came in, nodded lazily, lifted his brows, as if surprised at seeing the governess there, and began his breakfast as if the ennui of another day had already taken possession of him. Miss Muir stopped short, and no entreaties could induce her to go on.

"Another time I will finish it, if you like. Now Miss Bella and I should be at our books." And she left the room, followed by her pupil, taking no notice of the young master of the house, beyond a graceful bow in answer to his careless nod.

"Merciful creature! she goes when I come, and does not make life unendurable by moping about before my eyes. Does she belong to the moral, the melancholy, the romantic, or the dashing class, Ned?" said Gerald, lounging over his coffee as he did over everything he attempted.

"To none of them; she is a capital little woman. I wish you had seen her tame Hector this morning." And Edward repeated his story.

"Not a bad move on her part," said Coventry in reply. "She must be an observing as well as an energetic young person, to discover your chief weakness and attack it so soon. First tame the horse, and then the master. It will be amusing to watch the game, only I shall be under the painful necessity of checkmating you both, if it gets serious."

"You needn't exert yourself, old fellow, on my account. If I was not above thinking ill of an inoffensive girl, I should say you were the prize best worth winning, and advise you to take care of your own heart, if you've got one, which I rather doubt."

"I often doubt it, myself; but I fancy the little Scotchwoman will not be able to satisfy either of us upon that point. How does your highness like her?" asked Coventry of his cousin, who sat near him.

"Better than I thought I should. She is well-bred, unassuming, and very entertaining when she likes. She has told us some of the wittiest stories I've heard for a long time. Didn't our laughter wake you?" replied Lucia.

"Yes. Now atone for it by amusing me with a repetition of these witty tales."

"That is impossible; her accent and manner are half the charm," said Ned. "I wish you had kept away ten minutes longer, for your appearance spoilt the best story of all."

"Why didn't she go on?" asked Coventry, with a ray of curiosity.

"You forget that she overheard us last night, and must feel that you consider her a bore. She has pride, and no woman forgets speeches like those you made," answered Lucia.

"Or forgives them, either, I believe. Well, I must be resigned to languish under her displeasure then. On Sydney's account I take a slight interest in her; not that I expect to learn anything from her, for a woman with a mouth like that never confides or confesses anything. But I have a fancy to see what captivated him; for captivated he was, beyond a doubt, and by no lady whom he met in society. Did you ever hear anything of it, Ned?" asked Gerald.

"I'm not fond of scandal or gossip, and never listen to either." With which remark Edward left the room.

Lucia was called out by the housekeeper a moment after, and

Coventry left to the society most wearisome to him, namely his own. As he entered, he had caught a part of the story which Miss Muir had been telling, and it had excited his curiosity so much that he found himself wondering what the end could be and wishing that he might hear it.

What the deuce did she run away for, when I came in? he thought. If she *is* amusing, she must make herself useful; for it's intensely dull, I own, here, in spite of Lucia. Hey, what's that?

It was a rich, sweet voice, singing a brilliant Italian air, and singing it with an expression that made the music doubly delicious. Stepping out of the French window, Coventry strolled along the sunny terrace, enjoying the song with the relish of a connoisseur. Others followed, and still he walked and listened, forgetful of weariness or time. As one exquisite air ended, he involuntarily applauded. Miss Muir's face appeared for an instant, then vanished, and no more music followed, though Coventry lingered, hoping to hear the voice again. For music was the one thing of which he never wearied, and neither Lucia nor Bella possessed skill enough to charm him. For an hour he loitered on the terrace or the lawn, basking in the sunshine, too indolent to seek occupation or society. At length Bella came out, hat in hand, and nearly stumbled over her brother, who lay on the grass.

"You lazy man, have you been dawdling here all this time?" she said, looking down at him.

"No, I've been very busy. Come and tell me how you've got on with the little dragon."

"Can't stop. She bade me take a run after my French, so that I might be ready for my drawing, and so I must."

"It's too warm to run. Sit down and amuse your deserted brother, who has had no society but bees and lizards for an hour."

He drew her down as he spoke, and Bella obeyed; for, in spite of his indolence, he was one to whom all submitted without dreaming of refusal.

"What have you been doing? Muddling your poor little brains with all manner of elegant rubbish?"

"No, I've been enjoying myself immensely. Jean is *so* interesting, so kind and clever. She didn't bore me with stupid grammar, but just talked to me in such pretty French that I got on capitally, and like it as I never expected to, after Lucia's dull way of teaching it."

"What did you talk about?"

"Oh, all manner of things. She asked questions, and I answered, and she corrected me."

"Questions about our affairs, I suppose?"

"Not one. She don't care two sous for us or our affairs. I thought she might like to know what sort of people we were, so I told her about Papa's sudden death, Uncle John, and you, and Ned; but in the midst of it she said, in her quiet way, 'You are getting too confidential, my dear. It is not best to talk too freely of one's affairs to strangers. Let us speak of something else.'"

"What were you talking of when she said that, Bell?"

"You."

"Ah, then no wonder she was bored."

"She was tired of my chatter, and didn't hear half I said; for she was busy sketching something for me to copy, and thinking of something more interesting than the Coventrys."

"How do you know?"

"By the expression of her face. Did you like her music, Gerald?"

"Yes. Was she angry when I clapped?"

"She looked surprised, then rather proud, and shut the piano at once, though I begged her to go on. Isn't Jean a pretty name?"

"Not bad; but why don't you call her Miss Muir?"

"She begged me not. She hates it, and loves to be called Jean, alone. I've imagined such a nice little romance about her, and someday I shall tell her, for I'm sure she has had a love trouble."

"Don't get such nonsense into your head, but follow Miss Muir's well-bred example and don't be curious about other people's affairs. Ask her to sing tonight; it amuses me."

"She won't come down, I think. We've planned to read and work in my boudoir, which is to be our study now. Mamma will stay in her room, so you and Lucia can have the drawing room all to yourselves."

"Thank you. What will Ned do?"

"He will amuse Mamma, he says. Dear old Ned! I wish you'd stir about and get him his commission. He is so impatient to be doing something and yet so proud he won't ask again, after you have neglected it so many times and refused Uncle's help."

"I'll attend to it very soon; don't worry me, child. He will do very well for a time, quietly here with us."

"You always say that, yet you know he chafes and is unhappy at being dependent on you. Mamma and I don't mind; but he is a man, and it frets him. He said he'd take matters into his own hands soon, and then you may be sorry you were so slow in helping him."

"Miss Muir is looking out of the window. You'd better go and take your run, else she will scold."

"Not she. I'm not a bit afraid of her, she's so gentle and sweet. I'm fond of her already. You'll get as brown as Ned, lying here in the sun. By the way, Miss Muir agrees with me in thinking him handsomer than you."

"I admire her taste and quite agree with her."

"She said he was manly, and that was more attractive than beauty in a man. She does express things so nicely. Now I'm off." And away danced Bella, humming the burden of Miss Muir's sweetest song.

"'Energy is more attractive than beauty in a man.' She is right, but how the deuce *can* a man be energetic, with nothing to expend his energies upon?" mused Coventry, with his hat over his eyes.

A few moments later, the sweep of a dress caught his ear. Without stirring, a sidelong glance showed him Miss Muir coming across the terrace, as if to join Bella. Two stone steps led down to the lawn. He lay near them, and Miss Muir did not see him till close upon him. She started and slipped on the last step, recovered herself, and glided on, with a glance of unmistakable contempt as she passed the recumbent figure of the apparent sleeper. Several things in Bella's report had nettled him, but this look made him angry, though he would not own it, even to himself.

"Gerald, come here, quick!" presently called Bella, from the rustic seat where she stood beside her governess, who sat with her hand over her face as if in pain.

Gathering himself up, Coventry slowly obeyed, but involuntarily quickened his pace as he heard Miss Muir say, "Don't call him; *he* can do nothing"; for the emphasis on the word "he" was very significant.

"What is it, Bella?" he asked, looking rather wider awake than usual.

"You startled Miss Muir and made her turn her ankle. Now help her to the house, for she is in great pain; and don't lie there anymore to frighten people like a snake in the grass," said his sister petulantly.

"I beg your pardon. Will you allow me?" And Coventry offered his arm.

Miss Muir looked up with the expression which annoyed him and answered coldly, "Thank you, Miss Bella will do as well."

"Permit me to doubt that." And with a gesture too decided to be resisted, Coventry drew her arm through his and led her into the house. She submitted quietly, said the pain would soon be over, and when settled on the couch in Bella's room dismissed him with the briefest thanks. Considering the unwonted exertion he had made, he thought she might have been a little more grateful, and went away to Lucia, who always brightened when he came.

No more was seen of Miss Muir till teatime; for now, while the family were in retirement, they dined early and saw no company. The governess had excused herself at dinner, but came down in the evening a little paler than usual and with a slight limp in her gait. Sir John was there, talking with his nephew, and they merely acknowledged her presence by the sort of bow which gentlemen bestow on governesses. As she slowly made her way to her place behind the urn, Coventry said to his brother, "Take her a footstool, and ask her how she is, Ned." Then, as if necessary to account for his politeness to his uncle, he explained how he was the cause of the accident.

"Yes, yes. I understand. Rather a nice little person, I fancy. Not exactly a beauty, but accomplished and well-bred, which is better for one of her class."

"Some tea, Sir John?" said a soft voice at his elbow, and there was Miss Muir, offering cups to the gentlemen.

"Thank you, thank you," said Sir John, sincerely hoping she had overheard him.

As Coventry took his, he said graciously, "You are very forgiving, Miss Muir, to wait upon me, after I have caused you so much pain."

"It is my duty, sir" was her reply, in a tone which plainly said, "but not my pleasure." And she returned to her place, to smile, and chat, and be charming, with Bella and her brother.

Lucia, hovering near her uncle and Gerald, kept them to herself, but was disturbed to find that their eyes often wandered to the cheerful group about the table, and that their attention seemed distracted by the frequent bursts of laughter and fragments of animated conversation which reached them. In the midst of an account of a tragic affair which she endeavored to make as interesting and pathetic as possible, Sir John burst into a hearty laugh, which betrayed that he had been listening to a livelier story than her own. Much annoyed, she said hastily, "I knew it would be so! Bella has no idea of the proper manner in which to treat a governess. She and Ned will forget the difference of rank and spoil that person for her work. She is inclined to be presumptuous already, and if my aunt won't trouble herself to give Miss Muir a hint in time, I shall."

"Wait till she has finished that story, I beg of you," said Coventry, for Sir John was already off.

"If you find that nonsense so entertaining, why don't you follow Uncle's example? I don't need you."

"Thank you. I will." And Lucia was deserted.

But Miss Muir had ended and, beckoning to Bella, left the room, as if quite unconscious of the honor conferred upon her or the dullness she left behind her. Ned went up to his mother, Gerald returned to make his peace with Lucia, and, bidding them good-night, Sir John turned homeward. Strolling along the terrace, he came to the lighted window of Bella's study, and wishing to say a word to her, he half pushed aside the curtain and looked in. A pleasant little scene. Bella working busily, and near her in a low chair, with the light falling on her fair hair and delicate profile, sat Miss Muir, reading aloud. "Novels!" thought Sir John, and smiled at them for a pair of romantic girls. But pausing to listen a moment before he spoke, he found it was no novel, but history, read with a fluency which made every fact interesting, every sketch of character memorable, by the dramatic effect given to it. Sir John was fond of history, and failing eyesight often curtailed his favorite amusement. He had tried readers, but none suited him, and he had given up the plan. Now as he listened, he thought how pleasantly the smoothly flowing voice would wile away his evenings, and he envied Bella her new acquisition.

A bell rang, and Bella sprang up, saying, "Wait for me a minute. I must run to Mamma, and then we will go on with this charming prince."

Away she went, and Sir John was about to retire as quietly as he came, when Miss Muir's peculiar behavior arrested him for an instant. Dropping the book, she threw her arms across the table, laid her head down upon them, and broke into a passion of tears, like one who could bear restraint no longer. Shocked and amazed, Sir John stole away; but all that night the kindhearted gentleman puzzled his brains with conjectures about his niece's interesting young governess, quite unconscious that she intended he should do so.

≋ *chapter III* ≋

PASSION AND PIQUE

FOR several weeks the most monotonous tranquillity seemed to
reign at Coventry House, and yet, unseen, unsuspected, a storm
was gathering. The arrival of Miss Muir seemed to produce a
change in everyone, though no one could have explained how or why.
Nothing could be more unobtrusive and retiring than her manners.
She was devoted to Bella, who soon adored her, and was only happy
when in her society. She ministered in many ways to Mrs. Coventry's
comfort, and that lady declared there never was such a nurse. She
amused, interested and won Edward with her wit and womanly sympathy. She made Lucia respect and envy her for her accomplishments,
and piqued indolent Gerald by her persistent avoidance of him, while
Sir John was charmed with her respectful deference and the graceful
little attentions she paid him in a frank and artless way, very winning
to the lonely old man. The very servants liked her; and instead of
being, what most governesses are, a forlorn creature hovering between
superiors and inferiors, Jean Muir was the life of the house, and the
friend of all but two.

Lucia disliked her, and Coventry distrusted her; neither could
exactly say why, and neither owned the feeling, even to themselves.
Both watched her covertly yet found no shortcoming anywhere. Meek,
modest, faithful, and invariably sweet-tempered—they could complain
of nothing and wondered at their own doubts, though they could not
banish them.

It soon came to pass that the family was divided, or rather that two members were left very much to themselves. Pleading timidity, Jean Muir kept much in Bella's study and soon made it such a pleasant little nook that Ned and his mother, and often Sir John, came in to enjoy the music, reading, or cheerful chat which made the evenings so gay. Lucia at first was only too glad to have her cousin to herself, and he too lazy to care what went on about him. But presently he wearied of her society, for she was not a brilliant girl, and possessed few of those winning arts which charm a man and steal into his heart. Rumors of the merrymakings that went on reached him and made him curious to share them; echoes of fine music went sounding through the house, as he lounged about the empty drawing room; and peals of laughter reached him while listening to Lucia's grave discourse.

She soon discovered that her society had lost its charm, and the more eagerly she tried to please him, the more signally she failed. Before long Coventry fell into a habit of strolling out upon the terrace of an evening, and amusing himself by passing and repassing the window of Bella's room, catching glimpses of what was going on and reporting the result of his observations to Lucia, who was too proud to ask admission to the happy circle or to seem to desire it.

"I shall go to London tomorrow, Lucia," Gerald said one evening, as he came back from what he called "a survey," looking very much annoyed.

"To London?" exclaimed his cousin, surprised.

"Yes, I must bestir myself and get Ned his commission, or it will be all over with him."

"How do you mean?"

"He is falling in love as fast as it is possible for a boy to do it. That girl has bewitched him, and he will make a fool of himself very soon, unless I put a stop to it."

"I was afraid she would attempt a flirtation. These persons always do, they are such a mischief-making race."

"Ah, but there you are wrong, as far as little Muir is concerned. She does not flirt, and Ned has too much sense and spirit to be caught by a silly coquette. She treats him like an elder sister, and mingles the most attractive friendliness with a quiet dignity that captivates the boy. I've been watching them, and there he is, devouring her with his eyes, while she reads a fascinating novel in the most fascinating style.

Bella and Mamma are absorbed in the tale, and see nothing; but Ned makes himself the hero, Miss Muir the heroine, and lives the love scene with all the ardor of a man whose heart has just waked up. Poor lad! Poor lad!"

Lucia looked at her cousin, amazed by the energy with which he spoke, the anxiety in his usually listless face. The change became him, for it showed what he might be, making one regret still more what he was. Before she could speak, he was gone again, to return presently, laughing, yet looking a little angry.

"What now?" she asked.

"'Listeners never hear any good of themselves' is the truest of proverbs. I stopped a moment to look at Ned, and heard the following flattering remarks. Mamma is gone, and Ned was asking little Muir to sing that delicious barcarole she gave us the other evening.

"'Not now, not here,' she said.

"'Why not? You sang it in the drawing room readily enough,' said Ned, imploringly.

"'That is a very different thing,' and she looked at him with a little shake of the head, for he was folding his hands and doing the passionate pathetic.

"'Come and sing it there then,' said innocent Bella. 'Gerald likes your voice so much, and complains that you will never sing to him.'

"'He never asks me,' said Muir, with an odd smile.

"'He is too lazy, but he wants to hear you.'

"'When he asks me, I will sing—if I feel like it.' And she shrugged her shoulders with a provoking gesture of indifference.

"'But it amuses him, and he gets so bored down here,' began stupid little Bella. 'Don't be shy or proud, Jean, but come and entertain the poor old fellow.'

"'No, thank you. I engaged to teach Miss Coventry, not to amuse Mr. Coventry' was all the answer she got.

"'You amuse Ned, why not Gerald? Are you afraid of him?' asked Bella.

"Miss Muir laughed, such a scornful laugh, and said, in that peculiar tone of hers, 'I cannot fancy anyone being *afraid* of your elder brother.'

"'I am, very often, and so would you be, if you ever saw him angry.' And Bella looked as if I'd beaten her.

"'Does he ever wake up enough to be angry?' asked that girl, with an air of surprise. Here Ned broke into a fit of laughter, and they are at it now, I fancy, by the sound."

"Their foolish gossip is not worth getting excited about, but I certainly would send Ned away. It's no use trying to get rid of 'that girl,' as you say, for my aunt is as deluded about her as Ned and Bella, and she really does get the child along splendidly. Dispatch Ned, and then she can do no harm," said Lucia, watching Coventry's altered face as he stood in the moonlight, just outside the window where she sat.

"Have you no fears for me?" he asked smiling, as if ashamed of his momentary petulance.

"No, have you for yourself?" And a shade of anxiety passed over her face.

"I defy the Scotch witch to enchant me, except with her music," he added, moving down the terrace again, for Jean was singing like a nightingale.

As the song ended, he put aside the curtain, and said, abruptly, "Has anyone any commands for London? I am going there tomorrow."

"A pleasant trip to you," said Ned carelessly, though usually his brother's movements interested him extremely.

"I want quantities of things, but I must ask Mamma first." And Bella began to make a list.

"May I trouble you with a letter, Mr. Coventry?"

Jean Muir turned around on the music stool and looked at him with the cold keen glance which always puzzled him.

He bowed, saying, as if to them all, "I shall be off by the early train, so you must give me your orders tonight."

"Then come away, Ned, and leave Jean to write her letter."

And Bella took her reluctant brother from the room.

"I will give you the letter in the morning," said Miss Muir, with a curious quiver in her voice, and the look of one who forcibly suppressed some strong emotion.

"As you please." And Coventry went back to Lucia, wondering who Miss Muir was going to write to. He said nothing to his brother of the purpose which took him to town, lest a word should produce the catastrophe which he hoped to prevent; and Ned, who now lived in a sort of dream, seemed to forget Gerald's existence altogether.

With unwonted energy Coventry was astir seven next morning. Lucia gave him his breakfast, and as he left the room to order the carriage, Miss Muir came gliding downstairs, very pale and heavy-eyed (with a sleepless, tearful night, he thought) and, putting a delicate little letter into his hand, said hurriedly, "Please leave this at Lady Sydney's, and if you see her, say 'I have remembered.'"

Her peculiar manner and peculiar message struck him. His eye involuntarily glanced at the address of the letter and read young Sydney's name. Then, conscious of his mistake, he thrust it into his pocket with a hasty "Good morning," and left Miss Muir standing with one hand pressed on her heart, the other half extended as if to recall the letter.

All the way to London, Coventry found it impossible to forget the almost tragical expression of the girl's face, and it haunted him through the bustle of two busy days. Ned's affair was put in the way of being speedily accomplished, Bella's commissions were executed, his mother's pet delicacies provided for her, and a gift for Lucia, whom the family had given him for his future mate, as he was too lazy to choose for himself.

Jean Muir's letter he had not delivered, for Lady Sydney was in the country and her townhouse closed. Curious to see how she would receive his tidings, he went quietly in on his arrival at home. Everyone had dispersed to dress for dinner except Miss Muir, who was in the garden, the servant said.

"Very well, I have a message for her"; and, turning, the "young master," as they called him, went to seek her. In a remote corner he saw her sitting alone, buried in thought. As his step roused her, a look of surprise, followed by one of satisfaction, passed over her face, and, rising, she beckoned to him with an almost eager gesture. Much amazed, he went to her and offered the letter, saying kindly, "I regret that I could not deliver it. Lady Sydney is in the country, and I did not like to post it without your leave. Did I do right?"

"Quite right, thank you very much—it is better so." And with an air of relief, she tore the letter to atoms, and scattered them to the wind.

More amazed than ever, the young man was about to leave her when she said, with a mixture of entreaty and command, "Please stay a moment. I want to speak to you."

He paused, eyeing her with visible surprise, for a sudden color dyed her cheeks, and her lips trembled. Only for a moment, then she was quite self-possessed again. Motioning him to the seat she had left, she remained standing while she said, in a low, rapid tone full of pain and of decision:

"Mr. Coventry, as the head of the house I want to speak to you, rather than to your mother, of a most unhappy affair which has occurred during your absence. My month of probation ends today; your mother wishes me to remain; I, too, wish it sincerely, for I am happy here, but I ought not. Read this, and you will see why."

She put a hastily written note into his hand and watched him intently while he read it. She saw him flush with anger, bite his lips, and knit his brows, then assume his haughtiest look, as he lifted his eyes and said in his most sarcastic tone, "Very well for a beginning. The boy has eloquence. Pity that it should be wasted. May I ask if you have replied to this rhapsody?"

"I have."

"And what follows? He begs you 'to fly with him, to share his fortunes, and be the good angel of his life.' Of course you consent?"

There was no answer, for, standing erect before him, Miss Muir regarded him with an expression of proud patience, like one who expected reproaches, yet was too generous to resent them. Her manner had its effect. Dropping his bitter tone, Coventry asked briefly, "Why do you show me this? What can I do?"

"I show it that you may see how much in earnest 'the boy' is, and how open I desire to be. You can control, advise, and comfort your brother, and help me to see what is my duty."

"You love him?" demanded Coventry bluntly.

"No!" was the quick, decided answer.

"Then why make him love you?"

"I never tried to do it. Your sister will testify that I have endeavored to avoid him as I—" And he finished the sentence with an unconscious tone of pique, "As you have avoided me."

She bowed silently, and he went on:

"I will do you the justice to say that nothing can be more blameless than your conduct toward myself; but why allow Ned to haunt you evening after evening? What could you expect of a romantic boy who had nothing to do but lose his heart to the first attractive woman he met?"

A momentary glisten shone in Jean Muir's steel-blue eyes as the last words left the young man's lips; but it was gone instantly, and her voice was full of reproach, as she said, steadily, impulsively, "If the 'romantic boy' had been allowed to lead the life of a man, as he longed to do, he would have had no time to lose his heart to the first sorrowful girl whom he pitied. Mr. Coventry, the fault is yours. Do not blame your brother, but generously own your mistake and retrieve it in the speediest, kindest manner."

For an instant Gerald sat dumb. Never since his father died had anyone reproved him; seldom in his life had he been blamed. It was a new experience, and the very novelty added to the effect. He saw his fault, regretted it, and admired the brave sincerity of the girl in telling him of it. But he did not know how to deal with the case, and was forced to confess not only past negligence but present incapacity. He was as honorable as he was proud, and with an effort he said frankly, "You are right, Miss Muir. I *am* to blame, yet as soon as I saw the danger, I tried to avert it. My visit to town was on Ned's account; he will have his commission very soon, and then he will be sent out of harm's way. Can I do more?"

"No, it is too late to send him away with a free and happy heart. He must bear his pain as he can, and it may help to make a man of him," she said sadly.

"He'll soon forget," began Coventry, who found the thought of gay Ned suffering an uncomfortable one.

"Yes, thank heaven, that is possible, for men."

Miss Muir pressed her hands together, with a dark expression on her half-averted face. Something in her tone, her manner, touched Coventry; he fancied that some old wound bled, some bitter memory awoke at the approach of a new lover. He was young, heart-whole, and romantic, under all his cool nonchalance of manner. This girl, who he fancied loved his friend and who was beloved by his brother, became an object of interest to him. He pitied her, desired to help her, and regretted his past distrust, as a chivalrous man always regrets injustice to a woman. She was happy here, poor, homeless soul, and she should stay. Bella loved her, his mother took comfort in her, and when Ned was gone, no one's peace would be endangered by her winning ways, her rich accomplishments. These thoughts swept through his mind during a brief pause, and when he spoke, it was to say gently:

"Miss Muir, I thank you for the frankness which must have been

painful to you, and I will do my best to be worthy of the confidence
which you repose in me. You were both discreet and kind to speak
only to me. This thing would have troubled my mother extremely, and
have done no good. I shall see Ned, and try and repair my long neglect
as promptly as possible. I know you will help me, and in return let me
beg of you to remain, for he will soon be gone."

She looked at him with eyes full of tears, and there was no
coolness in the voice that answered softly, "You are too kind, but I
had better go; it is not wise to stay."

"Why not?"

She colored beautifully, hesitated, then spoke out in the clear,
steady voice which was her greatest charm, "If I had known there
were sons in this family, I never should have come. Lady Sydney
spoke only of your sister, and when I found two gentlemen, I was
troubled, because—I am so unfortunate—or rather, people are so kind
as to like me more than I deserve. I thought I could stay a month, at
least, as your brother spoke of going away, and you were already affianced, but—"

"I am not affianced."

Why he said that, Coventry could not tell, but the words passed
his lips hastily and could not be recalled. Jean Muir took the announcement oddly enough. She shrugged her shoulders with an air
of extreme annoyance, and said almost rudely, "Then you should be;
you will be soon. But that is nothing to me. Miss Beaufort wishes me
gone, and I am too proud to remain and become the cause of disunion
in a happy family. No, I will go, and go at once."

She turned away impetuously, but Edward's arm detained her,
and Edward's voice demanded, tenderly, "Where will you go, my
Jean?"

The tender touch and name seemed to rob her of her courage
and calmness, for, leaning on her lover, she hid her face and sobbed
audibly.

"Now don't make a scene, for heaven's sake," began Coventry
impatiently, as his brother eyed him fiercely, divining at once what
had passed, for his letter was still in Gerald's hand and Jean's last words
had reached her lover's ear.

"Who gave you the right to read that, and to interfere in my
affairs?" demanded Edward hotly.

"Miss Muir" was the reply, as Coventry threw away the paper.

"And you add to the insult by ordering her out of the house," cried Ned with increasing wrath.

"On the contrary, I beg her to remain."

"The deuce you do! And why?"

"Because she is useful and happy here, and I am unwilling that your folly should rob her of a home which she likes."

"You are very thoughtful and devoted all at once, but I beg you will not trouble yourself. Jean's happiness and home will be my care now."

"My dear boy, do be reasonable. The thing is impossible. Miss Muir sees it herself; she came to tell me, to ask how best to arrange matters without troubling my mother. I've been to town to attend to your affairs, and you may be off now very soon."

"I have no desire to go. Last month it was the wish of my heart. Now I'll accept nothing from you." And Edward turned moodily away from his brother.

"What folly! Ned, you *must* leave home. It is all arranged and cannot be given up now. A change is what you need, and it will make a man of you. We shall miss you, of course, but you will be where you'll see something of life, and that is better for you than getting into mischief here."

"Are you going away, Jean?" asked Edward, ignoring his brother entirely and bending over the girl, who still hid her face and wept. She did not speak, and Gerald answered for her.

"No, why should she if you are gone?"

"Do you mean to stay?" asked the lover eagerly of Jean.

"I wish to remain, but—" She paused and looked up. Her eyes went from one face to the other, and she added, decidedly, "Yes, I must go, it is not wise to stay even when you are gone."

Neither of the young men could have explained why that hurried glance affected them as it did, but each felt conscious of a willful desire to oppose the other. Edward suddenly felt that his brother loved Miss Muir, and was bent on removing her from his way. Gerald had a vague idea that Miss Muir feared to remain on his account, and he longed to show her that he was quite safe. Each felt angry, and each showed it in a different way, one being violent, the other satirical.

"You are right, Jean, this is not the place for you; and you must let me see you in a safer home before I go," said Ned, significantly.

"It strikes me that this will be a particularly safe home when your dangerous self is removed," began Coventry, with an aggravating smile of calm superiority.

"And *I* think that I leave a more dangerous person than myself behind me, as poor Lucia can testify."

"Be careful what you say, Ned, or I shall be forced to remind you that I am master here. Leave Lucia's name out of this disagreeable affair, if you please."

"You *are* master here, but not of me, or my actions, and you have no right to expect obedience or respect, for you inspire neither. Jean, I asked you to go with me secretly; now I ask you openly to share my fortune. In my brother's presence I ask, and *will* have an answer."

He caught her hand impetuously, with a defiant look at Coventry, who still smiled, as if at boy's play, though his eyes were kindling and his face changing with the still, white wrath which is more terrible than any sudden outburst. Miss Muir looked frightened; she shrank away from her passionate young lover, cast an appealing glance at Gerald, and seemed as if she longed to claim his protection yet dared not.

"Speak!" cried Edward, desperately. "Don't look to him, tell me truly, with your own lips, do you, can you love me, Jean?"

"I have told you once. Why pain me by forcing another hard reply," she said pitifully, still shrinking from his grasp and seeming to appeal to his brother.

"You wrote a few lines, but I'll not be satisfied with that. You shall answer; I've seen love in your eyes, heard it in your voice, and I know it is hidden in your heart. You fear to own it; do not hesitate, no one can part us—speak, Jean, and satisfy me."

Drawing her hand decidedly away, she went a step nearer Coventry, and answered, slowly, distinctly, though her lips trembled, and she evidently dreaded the effect of her words, "I will speak, and speak truly. You have seen love in my face; it is in my heart, and I do not hesitate to own it, cruel as it is to force the truth from me, but this love is not for you. Are you satisfied?"

He looked at her with a despairing glance and stretched his hand toward her beseechingly. She seemed to fear a blow, for suddenly she clung to Gerald with a faint cry. The act, the look of fear, the protecting gesture Coventry involuntarily made were too much for Edward, already excited by conflicting passions. In a paroxysm of blind wrath, he caught up a large pruning knife left there by the gardener, and would have dealt his brother a fatal blow had he not warded it off with his arm. The stroke fell, and another might have followed had not Miss Muir with unexpected courage and strength wrested the knife from Edward and flung it into the little pond near by. Coventry dropped down upon the seat, for the blood poured from a deep wound in his arm, showing by its rapid flow that an artery had been severed. Edward stood aghast, for with the blow his fury passed, leaving him overwhelmed with remorse and shame.

Gerald looked up at him, smiled faintly, and said, with no sign of reproach or anger, "Never mind, Ned. Forgive and forget. Lend me a hand to the house, and don't disturb anyone. It's not much, I dare say." But his lips whitened as he spoke, and his strength failed him. Edward sprang to support him, and Miss Muir, forgetting her terrors, proved herself a girl of uncommon skill and courage.

"Quick! Lay him down. Give me your handkerchief, and bring some water," she said, in a tone of quiet command. Poor Ned obeyed and watched her with breathless suspense while she tied the handkerchief tightly around the arm, thrust the handle of his riding whip underneath, and pressed it firmly above the severed artery to stop the dangerous flow of blood.

"Dr. Scott is with your mother, I think. Go and bring him here" was the next order; and Edward darted away, thankful to do anything to ease the terror which possessed him. He was gone some minutes, and while they waited Coventry watched the girl as she knelt beside him, bathing his face with one hand while with the other she held the bandage firmly in its place. She was pale, but quite steady and self-possessed, and her eyes shone with a strange brilliancy as she looked down at him. Once, meeting his look of grateful wonder, she smiled a reassuring smile that made her lovely, and said, in a soft, sweet tone never used to him before, "Be quiet. There is no danger. I will stay by you till help comes."

Help did come speedily, and the doctor's first words were "Who improvised that tourniquet?"

"She did," murmured Coventry.

"Then you may thank her for saving your life. By Jove! It was capitally done"; and the old doctor looked at the girl with as much admiration as curiosity in his face.

"Never mind that. See to the wound, please, while I run for bandages, and salts, and wine."

Miss Muir was gone as she spoke, so fleetly that it was in vain to call her back or catch her. During her brief absence, the story was told by repentant Ned and the wound examined.

"Fortunately I have my case of instruments with me," said the doctor, spreading on the bench a long array of tiny, glittering implements of torture. "Now, Mr. Ned, come here, and hold the arm in that way, while I tie the artery. Hey! That will never do. Don't tremble so, man, look away and hold it steadily."

"I can't!" And poor Ned turned faint and white, not at the sight but with the bitter thought that he had longed to kill his brother.

"I will hold it," and a slender white hand lifted the bare and bloody arm so firmly, steadily, that Coventry sighed a sigh of relief, and Dr. Scott fell to work with an emphatic nod of approval.

It was soon over, and while Edward ran in to bid the servants beware of alarming their mistress, Dr. Scott put up his instruments and Miss Muir used salts, water, and wine so skillfully that Gerald was able to walk to his room, leaning on the old man, while the girl supported the wounded arm, as no sling could be made on the spot. As he entered the chamber, Coventry turned, put out his left hand, and with much feeling in his fine eyes said simply, "Miss Muir, I thank you."

The color came up beautifully in her pale cheeks as she pressed the hand and without a word vanished from the room. Lucia and the housekeeper came bustling in, and there was no lack of attendance on the invalid. He soon wearied of it, and sent them all away but Ned, who remorsefully haunted the chamber, looking like a comely young Cain and feeling like an outcast.

"Come here, lad, and tell me all about it. I was wrong to be domineering. Forgive me, and believe that I care for your happiness more sincerely than for my own."

These frank and friendly words healed the breach between the two brothers and completely conquered Ned. Gladly did he relate his love passages, for no young lover ever tires of that amusement if he has a sympathizing auditor, and Gerald *was* sympathetic now. For an hour did he lie listening patiently to the history of the growth of his brother's passion. Emotion gave the narrator eloquence, and Jean Muir's character was painted in glowing colors. All her unsuspected kindness to those about her was dwelt upon; all her faithful care, her sisterly interest in Bella, her gentle attentions to their mother, her sweet forbearance with Lucia, who plainly showed her dislike, and most of all, her friendly counsel, sympathy, and regard for Ned himself.

"She would make a man of me. She puts strength and courage into me as no one else can. She is unlike any girl I ever saw; there's no sentimentality about her; she is wise, and kind, and sweet. She says what she means, looks you straight in the eye, and is as true as steel. I've tried her, I know her, and—ah, Gerald, I love her so!"

Here the poor lad leaned his face into his hands and sighed a sigh that made his brother's heart ache.

"Upon my soul, Ned, I feel for you; and if there was no obstacle on her part, I'd do my best for you. She loves Sydney, and so there is nothing for it but to bear your fate like a man."

"Are you sure about Sydney? May it not be some one else?" and Ned eyed his brother with a suspicious look.

Coventry told him all he knew and surmised concerning his friend, not forgetting the letter. Edward mused a moment, then seemed relieved, and said frankly, "I'm glad it's Sydney and not you. I can bear it better."

"Me!" ejaculated Gerald, with a laugh.

"Yes, you; I've been tormented lately with a fear that you cared for her, or rather, she for you."

"You jealous young fool! We never see or speak to one another scarcely, so how could we get up a tender interest?"

"What do you lounge about on that terrace for every evening? And why does she get fluttered when your shadow begins to come and go?" demanded Edward.

"I like the music and don't care for the society of the singer, that's why I walk there. The fluttering is all your imagination; Miss Muir isn't a woman to be fluttered by a man's shadow." And Coventry glanced at his useless arm.

"Thank you for that, and for not saying 'little Muir,' as you generally do. Perhaps it was my imagination. But she never makes fun of you now, and so I fancied she might have lost her heart to the 'young master.' Women often do, you know."

"She used to ridicule me, did she?" asked Coventry, taking no notice of the latter part of his brother's speech, which was quite true nevertheless.

"Not exactly, she was too well-bred for that. But sometimes when

Bella and I joked about you, she'd say something so odd or witty that it was irresistible. You're used to being laughed at, so you don't mind, I know, just among ourselves."

"Not I. Laugh away as much as you like," said Gerald. But he did mind, and wanted exceedingly to know what Miss Muir had said, yet was too proud to ask. He turned restlessly and uttered a sigh of pain.

"I'm talking too much; it's bad for you. Dr. Scott said you must be quiet. Now go to sleep, if you can."

Edward left the bedside but not the room, for he would let no one take his place. Coventry tried to sleep, found it impossible, and after a restless hour called his brother back.

"If the bandage was loosened a bit, it would ease my arm and then I could sleep. Can you do it, Ned?"

"I dare not touch it. The doctor gave orders to leave it till he came in the morning, and I shall only do harm if I try."

"But I tell you it's too tight. My arm is swelling and the pain is intense. It can't be right to leave it so. Dr. Scott dressed it in a hurry and did it too tight. Common sense will tell you that," said Coventry impatiently.

"I'll call Mrs. Morris; she will understand what's best to be done." And Edward moved toward the door, looking anxious.

"Not she, she'll only make a stir and torment me with her chatter. I'll bear it as long as I can, and perhaps Dr. Scott will come tonight. He said he would if possible. Go to your dinner, Ned. I can ring for Neal if I need anything. I shall sleep if I'm alone, perhaps."

Edward reluctantly obeyed, and his brother was left to himself. Little rest did he find, however, for the pain of the wounded arm grew unbearable, and, taking a sudden resolution, he rang for his servant.

"Neal, go to Miss Coventry's study, and if Miss Muir is there, ask her to be kind enough to come to me. I'm in great pain, and she understands wounds better than anyone else in the house."

With much surprise in his face, the man departed and a few moments after the door noiselessly opened and Miss Muir came in. It had been a very warm day, and for the first time she had left off her plain black dress. All in white, with no ornament but her fair hair, and a fragrant posy of violets in her belt, she looked a different woman from the meek, nunlike creature one usually saw about the house. Her face was as altered as her dress, for now a soft color glowed in her cheeks, her eyes smiled shyly, and her lips no longer wore the firm look of one who forcibly repressed every emotion. A fresh, gentle, and charming woman she seemed, and Coventry found the dull room suddenly brightened by her presence. Going straight to him, she said simply, and with a happy, helpful look very comforting to see, "I'm glad you sent for me. What can I do for you?"

He told her, and before the complaint was ended, she began loosening the bandages with the decision of one who understood what was to be done and had faith in herself.

"Ah, that's relief, that's comfort!" ejaculated Coventry, as the last tight fold fell away. "Ned was afraid I should bleed to death if he touched me. What will the doctor say to us?"

"I neither know nor care. I shall say to him that he is a bad surgeon to bind it so closely, and not leave orders to have it untied if necessary. Now I shall make it easy and put you to sleep, for that is what you need. Shall I? May I?"

"I wish you would, if you can."

And while she deftly rearranged the bandages, the young man watched her curiously. Presently he asked, "How came you to know so much about these things?"

"In the hospital where I was ill, I saw much that interested me, and when I got better, I used to sing to the patients sometimes."

"Do you mean to sing to me?" he asked, in the submissive tone men unconsciously adopt when ill and in a woman's care.

"If you like it better than reading aloud in a dreamy tone," she answered, as she tied the last knot.

"I do, much better," he said decidedly.

"You are feverish. I shall wet your forehead, and then you will be quite comfortable." She moved about the room in the quiet way which made it a pleasure to watch her, and, having mingled a little cologne with water, bathed his face as unconcernedly as if he had been a child. Her proceedings not only comforted but amused Coventry, who mentally contrasted her with the stout, beer-drinking matron who had ruled over him in his last illness.

"A clever, kindly little woman," he thought, and felt quite at his ease, she was so perfectly easy herself.

"There, now you look more like yourself," she said with an approving nod as she finished, and smoothed the dark locks off his forehead with a cool, soft hand. Then seating herself in a large chair near by, she began to sing, while tidily rolling up the fresh bandages which had been left for the morning. Coventry lay watching her by the dim light that burned in the room, and she sang on as easily as a bird, a dreamy, low-toned lullaby, which soothed the listener like a spell. Presently, looking up to see the effect of her song, she found the young man wide awake, and regarding her with a curious mixture of pleasure, interest, and admiration.

"Shut your eyes, Mr. Coventry," she said, with a reproving shake of the head, and an odd little smile.

He laughed and obeyed, but could not resist an occasional covert glance from under his lashes at the slender white figure in the great velvet chair. She saw him and frowned.

"You are very disobedient; why won't you sleep?"

"I can't, I want to listen. I'm fond of nightingales."

"Then I shall sing no more, but try something that has never failed yet. Give me your hand, please."

Much amazed, he gave it, and, taking it in both her small ones, she sat down behind the curtain and remained as mute and motionless as a statue. Coventry smiled to himself at first, and wondered which would tire first. But soon a subtle warmth seemed to steal from the soft palms that enclosed his own, his heart beat quicker, his breath grew unequal, and a thousand fancies danced through his brain. He sighed, and said dreamily, as he turned his face toward her, "I like this." And in the act of speaking, seemed to sink into a soft cloud which encompassed him about with an atmosphere of perfect repose. More than this he could not remember, for sleep, deep and dreamless, fell upon him, and when he woke, daylight was shining in between the curtains, his hand lay alone on the coverlet, and his fair-haired enchantress was gone.

⚹ *chapter IV* ⚹

A DISCOVERY

FOR several days Coventry was confined to his room, much against his will, though everyone did their best to lighten his irksome captivity. His mother petted him, Bella sang, Lucia read, Edward was devoted, and all the household, with one exception, were eager to serve the young master. Jean Muir never came near him, and Jean Muir alone seemed to possess the power of amusing him. He soon tired of the others, wanted something new; recalled the piquant character of the girl and took a fancy into his head that she would lighten his ennui. After some hesitation, he carelessly spoke of her to Bella, but nothing came of it, for Bella only said Jean was well, and very busy doing something lovely to surprise Mamma with. Edward complained that he never saw her, and Lucia ignored her existence altogether. The only intelligence the invalid received was from the gossip of two housemaids over their work in the next room. From them he learned that the governess had been "scolded" by Miss Beaufort for going to Mr. Coventry's room; that she had taken it very sweetly and kept herself carefully out of the way of both young gentlemen, though it was plain to see that Mr. Ned was dying for her.

Mr. Gerald amused himself by thinking over this gossip, and quite annoyed his sister by his absence of mind.

"Gerald, do you know Ned's commission has come?"

"Very interesting. Read on, Bella."

"You stupid boy! You don't know a word I say," and she put down the book to repeat her news.

"I'm glad of it; now we must get him off as soon as possible—that is, I suppose he will want to be off as soon as possible." And Coventry woke up from his reverie.

"You needn't check yourself, I know all about it. I think Ned was very foolish, and that Miss Muir has behaved beautifully. It's quite impossible, of course, but I wish it wasn't, I do so like to watch lovers. You and Lucia are so cold you are not a bit interesting."

"You'll do me a favor if you'll stop all that nonsense about Lucia and me. We are not lovers, and never shall be, I fancy. At all events, I'm tired of the thing, and wish you and Mamma would let it drop, for the present at least."

"Oh Gerald, you know Mamma has set her heart upon it, that Papa desired it, and poor Lucia loves you so much. How can you speak of dropping what will make us all so happy?"

"It won't make me happy, and I take the liberty of thinking that this is of some importance. I'm not bound in any way, and don't intend to be till I am ready. Now we'll talk about Ned."

Much grieved and surprised, Bella obeyed, and devoted herself to Edward, who very wisely submitted to his fate and prepared to leave home for some months. For a week the house was in a state of excitement about his departure, and everyone but Jean was busied for him. She was scarcely seen; every morning she gave Bella her lessons, every afternoon drove out with Mrs. Coventry, and nearly every evening went up to the Hall to read to Sir John, who found his wish granted without exactly knowing how it had been done.

The day Edward left, he came down from bidding his mother good-bye, looking very pale, for he had lingered in his sister's little room with Miss Muir as long as he dared.

"Good-bye, dear. Be kind to Jean," he whispered as he kissed his sister.

"I will, I will," returned Bella, with tearful eyes.

"Take care of Mamma, and remember Lucia," he said again, as he touched his cousin's beautiful cheek.

"Fear nothing. I will keep them apart," she whispered back, and Coventry heard it.

Edward offered his hand to his brother, saying, significantly, as he looked him in the eye, "I trust you, Gerald."

"You may, Ned."

Then he went, and Coventry tired himself with wondering what Lucia meant. A few days later he understood.

Now Ned is gone, little Muir will appear, I fancy, he said to himself; but "little Muir" did not appear, and seemed to shun him more carefully than she had done her lover. If he went to the drawing room in the evening hoping for music, Lucia alone was there. If he tapped at Bella's door, there was always a pause before she opened it, and no sign of Jean appeared though her voice had been audible when he knocked. If he went to the library, a hasty rustle and the sound of flying feet betrayed that the room was deserted at his approach. In the garden Miss Muir never failed to avoid him, and if by chance they met in hall or breakfast room, she passed him with downcast eyes and the briefest, coldest greeting. All this annoyed him intensely, and the more she eluded him, the more he desired to see her—from a spirit of opposition, he said, nothing more. It fretted and yet it entertained him, and he found a lazy sort of pleasure in thwarting the girl's little maneuvers. His patience gave out at last, and he resolved to know what was the meaning of this peculiar conduct. Having locked and taken away the key of one door in the library, he waited till Miss Muir went in to get a book for his uncle. He had heard her speak to Bella of it, knew that she believed him with his mother, and smiled to himself as he stole after her. She was standing in a chair, reaching up, and he had time to see a slender waist, a pretty foot, before he spoke.

"Can I help you, Miss Muir?"

She started, dropped several books, and turned scarlet, as she said hurriedly, "Thank you, no; I can get the steps."

"My long arm will be less trouble. I've got but one, and that is tired of being idle, so it is very much at your service. What will you have?"

"I—I—you startled me so I've forgotten." And Jean laughed, nervously, as she looked about her as if planning to escape.

"I beg your pardon, wait till you remember, and let me thank you for the enchanted sleep you gave me ten days ago. I've had no chance yet, you've shunned me so pertinaciously."

"Indeed I try not to be rude, but—" She checked herself, and turned her face away, adding, with an accent of pain in her voice, "It is not my fault, Mr. Coventry. I only obey orders."

"Whose orders?" he demanded, still standing so that she could not escape.

"Don't ask; it is one who has a right to command where you are concerned. Be sure that it is kindly meant, though it may seem folly to us. Nay, don't be angry, laugh at it, as I do, and let me run away, please."

She turned, and looked down at him with tears in her eyes, a smile on her lips, and an expression half sad, half arch, which was altogether charming. The frown passed from his face, but he still looked grave and said decidedly, "No one has a right to command in this house but my mother or myself. Was it she who bade you avoid me as if I was a madman or a pest?"

"Ah, don't ask. I promised not to tell, and you would not have me break my word, I know." And still smiling, she regarded him with a look of merry malice which made any other reply unnecessary. It was Lucia, he thought, and disliked his cousin intensely just then. Miss Muir moved as if to step down; he detained her, saying earnestly, yet with a smile, "Do you consider me the master here?"

"Yes," and to the word she gave a sweet, submissive intonation which made it expressive of the respect, regard, and confidence which men find pleasantest when women feel and show it. Unconsciously his face softened, and he looked up at her with a different glance from any he had ever given her before.

"Well, then, will you consent to obey me if I am not tyrannical or unreasonable in my demands?"

"I'll try."

"Good! Now frankly, I want to say that all this sort of thing is very disagreeable to me. It annoys me to be a restraint upon anyone's liberty or comfort, and I beg you will go and come as freely as you like, and not mind Lucia's absurdities. She means well, but hasn't a particle of penetration or tact. Will you promise this?"

"No."

"Why not?"

"It is better as it is, perhaps."

"But you called it folly just now."

"Yes, it seems so, and yet—" She paused, looking both confused and distressed.

Coventry lost patience, and said hastily, "You women are such enigmas I never expect to understand you! Well, I've done my best to make you comfortable, but if you prefer to lead this sort of life, I beg you will do so."

"I *don't* prefer it; it is hateful to me. I like to be myself, to have my liberty, and the confidence of those about me. But I cannot think it kind to disturb the peace of anyone, and so I try to obey. I've promised Bella to remain, but I will go rather than have another scene with Miss Beaufort or with you."

Miss Muir had burst out impetuously, and stood there with a sudden fire in her eyes, sudden warmth and spirit in her face and voice that amazed Coventry. She was angry, hurt, and haughty, and the change only made her more attractive, for not a trace of her former meek self remained. Coventry was electrified, and still more surprised when she added, imperiously, with a gesture as if to put him aside, "Hand me that book and move away. I wish to go."

He obeyed, even offered his hand, but she refused it, stepped lightly down, and went to the door. There she turned, and with the same indignant voice, the same kindling eyes and glowing cheeks, she said rapidly, "I know I have no right to speak in this way. I restrain myself as long as I can, but when I can bear no more, my true self breaks loose, and I defy everything. I am tired of being a cold, calm machine; it is impossible with an ardent nature like mine, and I shall try no longer. I cannot help it if people love me. I don't want their love. I only ask to be left in peace, and why I am tormented so I cannot see. I've neither beauty, money, nor rank, yet every foolish boy mistakes my frank interest for something warmer, and makes me miserable. It is my misfortune. Think of me what you will, but beware of me in time, for against my will I may do you harm."

Almost fiercely she had spoken, and with a warning gesture she hurried from the room, leaving the young man feeling as if a sudden thunder-gust had swept through the house. For several minutes he sat in the chair she left, thinking deeply. Suddenly he rose, went to his sister, and said, in his usual tone of indolent good nature, "Bella, didn't I hear Ned ask you to be kind to Miss Muir?"

"Yes, and I try to be, but she is so odd lately."

"Odd! How do you mean?"

"Why, she is either as calm and cold as a statue, or restless and queer; she cries at night, I know, and sighs sadly when she thinks I don't hear. Something is the matter."

"She frets for Ned perhaps," began Coventry.

"Oh dear, no; it's a great relief to her that he is gone. I'm afraid that she likes someone very much, and someone don't like her. Can it be Mr. Sydney?"

"She called him a 'titled fool' once, but perhaps that didn't mean anything. Did you ever ask her about him?" said Coventry, feeling rather ashamed of his curiosity, yet unable to resist the temptation of questioning unsuspecting Bella.

"Yes, but she only looked at me in her tragical way, and said, so pitifully, 'My little friend, I hope you will never have to pass through the scenes I've passed through, but keep your peace unbroken all your life.' After that I dared say no more. I'm very fond of her, I want to make her happy, but I don't know how. Can you propose anything?"

"I was going to propose that you make her come among us more, now Ned is gone. It must be dull for her, moping about alone. I'm sure it is for me. She is an entertaining little person, and I enjoy her music very much. It's good for Mamma to have gay evenings; so you bestir yourself, and see what you can do for the general good of the family."

"That's all very charming, and I've proposed it more than once, but Lucia spoils all my plans. She is afraid you'll follow Ned's example, and that is so silly."

"Lucia is a—no, I won't say fool, because she has sense enough when she chooses; but I wish you'd just settle things with Mamma, and then Lucia can do nothing but submit," said Gerald angrily.

"I'll try, but she goes up to read to Uncle, you know, and since he has had the gout, she stays later, so I see little of her in the evening. There she goes now. I think she will captivate the old one as well as the young one, she is so devoted."

Coventry looked after her slender black figure, just vanishing through the great gate, and an uncomfortable fancy took possession of him, born of Bella's careless words. He sauntered away, and after eluding his cousin, who seemed looking for him, he turned toward the Hall, saying to himself, I will see what is going on up here. Such things have happened. Uncle is the simplest soul alive, and if the girl is ambitious, she can do what she will with him.

Here a servant came running after him and gave him a letter, which he thrust into his pocket without examining it. When he reached the Hall, he went quietly to his uncle's study. The door was ajar, and looking in, he saw a scene of tranquil comfort, very pleasant to watch. Sir John leaned in his easy chair with one foot on a cushion. He was dressed with his usual care and, in spite of the gout, looked like a handsome, well-preserved old gentleman. He was smiling as he listened, and his eyes rested complacently on Jean Muir, who sat near him reading in her musical voice, while the sunshine glittered on her hair and the soft rose of her cheek. She read well, yet Coventry thought her heart was not in her task, for once when she paused, while Sir John spoke, her eyes had an absent expression, and she leaned her head upon her hand, with an air of patient weariness.

Poor girl! I did her great injustice; she has no thought of captivating the old man, but amuses him from simple kindness. She is tired. I'll put an end to her task; and Coventry entered without knocking.

Sir John received him with an air of polite resignation, Miss Muir with a perfectly expressionless face.

"Mother's love, and how are you today, sir?"

"Comfortable, but dull, so I want you to bring the girls over this evening, to amuse the old gentleman. Mrs. King has got out the antique costumes and trumpery, as I promised Bella she should have them, and tonight we are to have a merrymaking, as we used to do when Ned was here."

"Very well, sir, I'll bring them. We've all been out of sorts since the lad left, and a little jollity will do us good. Are you going back, Miss Muir?" asked Coventry.

"No, I shall keep her to give me my tea and get things ready. Don't read anymore, my dear, but go and amuse yourself with the pictures, or whatever you like," said Sir John; and like a dutiful daughter she obeyed, as if glad to get away.

"That's a very charming girl, Gerald," began Sir John as she left the room. "I'm much interested in her, both on her own account and on her mother's."

"Her mother's! What do you know of her mother?" asked Coventry, much surprised.

"Her mother was Lady Grace Howard, who ran away with a poor Scotch minister twenty years ago. The family cast her off, and she lived and died so obscurely that very little is known of her except that she left an orphan girl at some small French pension. This is the girl, and a fine girl, too. I'm surprised that you did not know this."

"So am I, but it is like her not to tell. She is a strange, proud creature. Lady Howard's daughter! Upon my word, that is a discovery," and Coventry felt his interest in his sister's governess much increased by this fact; for, like all wellborn Englishmen, he valued rank and gentle blood even more than he cared to own.

"She has had a hard life of it, this poor little girl, but she has a brave spirit, and will make her way anywhere," said Sir John admiringly.

"Did Ned know this?" asked Gerald suddenly.

"No, she only told me yesterday. I was looking in the *Peerage* and chanced to speak of the Howards. She forgot herself and called Lady Grace her mother. Then I got the whole story, for the lonely little thing was glad to make a confidant of someone."

"That accounts for her rejection of Sydney and Ned: she knows she is their equal and will not snatch at the rank which is hers by right. No, she's not mercenary or ambitious."

"What do you say?" asked Sir John, for Coventry had spoken more to himself than to his uncle.

"I wonder if Lady Sydney was aware of this?" was all Gerald's answer.

"No, Jean said she did not wish to be pitied, and so told nothing to the mother. I think the son knew, but that was a delicate point, and I asked no questions."

"I shall write to him as soon as I discover his address. We have been so intimate I can venture to make a few inquiries about Miss Muir, and prove the truth of her story."

"Do you mean to say that you doubt it?" demanded Sir John angrily.

"I beg your pardon, Uncle, but I must confess I have an instinctive distrust of that young person. It is unjust, I dare say, yet I cannot banish it."

"Don't annoy me by expressing it, if you please. I have some penetration and experience, and I respect and pity Miss Muir heartily. This dislike of yours may be the cause of her late melancholy, hey, Gerald?" And Sir John looked suspiciously at his nephew.

Anxious to avert the rising storm, Coventry said hastily as he turned away, "I've neither time nor inclination to discuss the matter now, sir, but will be careful not to offend again. I'll take your message to Bella, so good-bye for an hour, Uncle."

And Coventry went his way through the park, thinking within himself, The dear old gentleman is getting fascinated, like poor Ned. How the deuce does the girl do it? Lady Howard's daughter, yet never told us; I don't understand that.

≈ *chapter V* ≈

HOW THE GIRL DID IT

AT home he found a party of young friends, who hailed with delight the prospect of a revel at the Hall. An hour later, the blithe company trooped into the great saloon, where preparations had already been made for a dramatic evening.

Good Sir John was in his element, for he was never so happy as when his house was full of young people. Several persons were chosen, and in a few moments the curtains were withdrawn from the first of these impromptu tableaux. A swarthy, darkly bearded man lay asleep on a tiger skin, in the shadow of a tent. Oriental arms and drapery surrounded him; an antique silver lamp burned dimly on a table where fruit lay heaped in costly dishes, and wine shone redly in half-emptied goblets. Bending over the sleeper was a woman robed with barbaric splendor. One hand turned back the embroidered sleeve from the arm which held a scimitar; one slender foot in a scarlet sandal was visible under the white tunic; her purple mantle swept down from snowy shoulders; fillets of gold bound her hair, and jewels shone on neck and arms. She was looking over her shoulder toward the entrance of the tent, with a steady yet stealthy look, so effective that for a moment the spectators held their breath, as if they also heard a passing footstep.

"Who is it?" whispered Lucia, for the face was new to her.

"Jean Muir," answered Coventry, with an absorbed look.

"Impossible! She is small and fair," began Lucia, but a hasty "Hush, let me look!" from her cousin silenced her.

Impossible as it seemed, he was right nevertheless; for Jean Muir it was. She had darkened her skin, painted her eyebrows, disposed some wild black locks over her fair hair, and thrown such an intensity of expression into her eyes that they darkened and dilated till they were as fierce as any southern eyes that ever flashed. Hatred, the deepest and bitterest, was written on her sternly beautiful face, courage glowed in her glance, power spoke in the nervous grip of the slender hand that held the weapon, and the indomitable will of the woman was expressed—even the firm pressure of the little foot half hidden in the tiger skin.

"Oh, isn't she splendid?" cried Bella under her breath.

"She looks as if she'd use her sword well when the time comes," said someone admiringly.

"Good night to Holofernes; his fate is certain," added another.

"He is the image of Sydney, with that beard on."

"'Doesn't she look as if she really hated him?"

"Perhaps she does."

Coventry uttered the last exclamation, for the two which preceded it suggested an explanation of the marvelous change in Jean. It was not all art: the intense detestation mingled with a savage joy that the object of her hatred was in her power was too perfect to be feigned; and having the key to a part of her story, Coventry felt as if he caught a glimpse of the truth. It was but a glimpse, however, for the curtain dropped before he had half analyzed the significance of that strange face.

"Horrible! I'm glad it's over," said Lucia coldly.

"Magnificent! Encore! Encore!" cried Gerald enthusiastically.

But the scene was over, and no applause could recall the actress. Two or three graceful or gay pictures followed, but Jean was in none, and each lacked the charm which real talent lends to the simplest part.

"Coventry, you are wanted," called a voice. And to everyone's surprise, Coventry went, though heretofore he had always refused to exert himself when handsome actors were in demand.

"What part am I to spoil?" he asked, as he entered the green room, where several excited young gentlemen were costuming and attitudinizing.

"A fugitive cavalier. Put yourself into this suit, and lose no time asking questions. Miss Muir will tell you what to do. She is in the tableau, so no one will mind you," said the manager pro tem, throwing a rich old suit toward Coventry and resuming the painting of a moustache on his own boyish face.

A gallant cavalier was the result of Gerald's hasty toilet, and when he appeared before the ladies a general glance of admiration was bestowed upon him.

"Come along and be placed; Jean is ready on the stage." And Bella ran before him, exclaiming to her governess, "Here he is, quite splendid. Wasn't he good to do it?"

Miss Muir, in the charmingly prim and puritanical dress of a Roundhead damsel, was arranging some shrubs, but turned suddenly and dropped the green branch she held, as her eye met the glittering figure advancing toward her.

"You!" she said with a troubled look, adding low to Bella, "Why did you ask *him*? I begged you not."

"He is the only handsome man here, and the best actor if he likes. He won't play usually, so make the most of him." And Bella was off to finish powdering her hair for "The Marriage à la Mode."

"I was sent for and I came. Do you prefer some other person?" asked Coventry, at a loss to understand the half-anxious, half-eager expression of the face under the little cap.

It changed to one of mingled annoyance and resignation as she said, "It is too late. Please kneel here, half behind the shrubs; put down your hat, and—allow me—you are too elegant for a fugitive."

As he knelt before her, she disheveled his hair, pulled his lace collar awry, threw away his gloves and sword, and half untied the cloak that hung about his shoulders.

"That is better; your paleness is excellent—nay, don't spoil it. We are to represent the picture which hangs in the Hall. I need tell you no more. Now, Roundheads, place yourselves, and then ring up the curtain."

With a smile, Coventry obeyed her; for the picture was of two lovers, the young cavalier kneeling, with his arm around the waist of the girl, who tries to hide him with her little mantle, and presses his head to her bosom in an ecstasy of fear, as she glances back at the approaching pursuers. Jean hesitated an instant and shrank a little as his hand touched her; she blushed deeply, and her eyes fell before his. Then, as the bell rang, she threw herself into her part with sudden spirit. One arm half covered him with her cloak, the other pillowed his head on the muslin kerchief folded over her bosom, and she looked backward with such terror in her eyes that more than one chivalrous young spectator longed to hurry to the rescue. It lasted but a moment; yet in that moment Coventry experienced another new sensation. Many women had smiled on him, but he had remained heart-whole, cool, and careless, quite unconscious of the power which a woman possesses and knows how to use, for the weal or woe of man. Now, as he knelt there with a soft arm about him, a slender waist yielding to his touch, and a maiden heart throbbing against his cheek, for the first time in his life he felt the indescribable spell of womanhood, and looked the ardent lover to perfection. Just as his face assumed this new and most becoming aspect, the curtain dropped, and clamorous encores recalled him to the fact that Miss Muir was trying to escape from his hold, which had grown painful in its unconscious pressure. He sprang up, half bewildered, and looking as he had never looked before.

"Again! Again!" called Sir John. And the young men who played the Roundheads, eager to share in the applause begged for a repetition in new attitudes.

"A rustle has betrayed you, we have fired and shot the brave girl, and she lies dying, you know. That will be effective; try it, Miss Muir," said one. And with a long breath, Jean complied.

The curtain went up, showing the lover still on his knees, unmindful of the captors who clutched him by the shoulder, for at his feet the girl lay dying. Her head was on his breast, now, her eyes looked full into his, no longer wild with fear, but eloquent with the love which even death could not conquer. The power of those tender eyes thrilled Coventry with a strange delight, and set his heart beating as rapidly as hers had done. She felt his hands tremble, saw the color flash into his cheek, knew that she had touched him at last, and when she rose it was with a sense of triumph which she found it hard to conceal. Others thought it fine acting; Coventry tried to believe so; but Lucia set her teeth, and, as the curtain fell on that second picture, she left her place to hurry behind the scenes, bent on putting an end to such dangerous play. Several actors were complimenting the mimic lovers. Jean took it merrily, but Coventry, in spite of himself, betrayed that he was excited by something deeper than mere gratified vanity.

As Lucia appeared, his manner changed to its usual indifference; but he could not quench the unwonted fire of his eyes, or keep all trace of emotion out of his face, and she saw this with a sharp pang.

"I have come to offer my help. You must be tired, Miss Muir. Can I relieve you?" said Lucia hastily.

"Yes, thank you. I shall be very glad to leave the rest to you, and enjoy them from the front."

So with a sweet smile Jean tripped away, and to Lucia's dismay Coventry fellowed.

"I want you, Gerald; please stay," she cried.

"I've done my part—no more tragedy for me tonight." And he was gone before she could entreat or command.

There was no help for it; she must stay and do her duty, or expose her jealousy to the quick eyes about her. For a time she bore it; but the sight of her cousin leaning over the chair she had left and chatting with the governess, who now filled it, grew unbearable, and she dispatched a little girl with a message to Miss Muir.

"Please, Miss Beaufort wants you for Queen Bess, as you are the only lady with red hair. Will you come?" whispered the child, quite unconscious of any hidden sting in her words.

"Yes, dear, willingly though I'm not stately enough for Her Majesty, nor handsome enough," said Jean, rising with an untroubled face, though she resented the feminine insult.

"Do you want an Essex? I'm all dressed for it," said Coventry, following to the door with a wistful look.

"No, Miss Beaufort said *you* were not to come. She doesn't want you both together," said the child decidedly.

Jean gave him a significant look, shrugged her shoulders, and went away smiling her odd smile, while Coventry paced up and down the hall in a curious state of unrest, which made him forgetful of everything till the young people came gaily out to supper.

"Come, bonny Prince Charlie, take me down, and play the lover as charmingly as you did an hour ago. I never thought you had so much warmth in you," said Bella, taking his arm and drawing him on against his will.

"Don't be foolish, child. Where is—Lucia?"

Why he checked Jean's name on his lips and substituted another's, he could not tell; but a sudden shyness in speaking of her possessed him, and though he saw her nowhere, he would not ask for her. His cousin came down looking lovely in a classical costume; but Gerald scarcely saw her, and, when the merriment was at its height, he slipped away to discover what had become of Miss Muir.

Alone in the deserted drawing room he found her, and paused to watch her a moment before he spoke; for something in her attitude and face struck him. She was leaning wearily back in the great chair which had served for a throne. Her royal robes were still unchanged, though the crown was off and all her fair hair hung about her shoulders. Excitement and exertion made her brilliant, the rich dress became her wonderfully, and an air of luxurious indolence changed the meek governess into a charming woman. She leaned on the velvet cushions as if she were used to such support; she played with the jewels which had crowned her as carelessly as if she were born to wear them; her attitude was full of negligent grace, and the expression of her face half proud, half pensive, as if her thoughts were bittersweet.

One would know she was wellborn to see her now. Poor girl, what a burden a life of dependence must be to a spirit like hers! I wonder what she is thinking of so intently. And Coventry indulged in another look before he spoke.

"Shall I bring you some supper, Miss Muir?"

"Supper!" she ejaculated, with a start. "Who thinks of one's body when one's soul is—" She stopped there, knit her brows, and laughed faintly as she added, "No, thank you. I want nothing but advice, and that I dare not ask of anyone."

"Why not?"

"Because I have no right."

"Everyone has a right to ask help, especially the weak of the strong. Can I help you? Believe me, I most heartily offer my poor services."

"Ah, you forget! This dress, the borrowed splendor of these jewels, the freedom of this gay evening, the romance of the part you played, all blind you to the reality. For a moment I cease to be a servant, and for a moment you treat me as an equal."

It was true; he *had* forgotten. That soft, reproachful glance touched him, his distrust melted under the new charm, and he answered with real feeling in voice and face, "I treat you as an equal because you *are* one; and when I offer help, it is not to my sister's governess alone, but to Lady Howard's daughter."

"Who told you that?" she demanded, sitting erect.

"My uncle. Do not reproach him. It shall go no further, if you forbid it. Are you sorry that I know it?"

"Yes."

"Why?"

"Because I will not be pitied!" And her eyes flashed as she made a half-defiant gesture.

"Then, if I may not pity the hard fate which has befallen an innocent life, may I admire the courage which meets adverse fortune so bravely, and conquers the world by winning the respect and regard of all who see and honor it?"

Miss Muir averted her face, put up her hand, and answered hastily, "No, no, not that! Do not be kind; it destroys the only barrier now left between us. Be cold to me as before, forget what I am, and let me go on my way, unknown, unpitied, and unloved!"

Her voice faltered and failed as the last word was uttered, and she bent her face upon her hand. Something jarred upon Coventry in this speech, and moved him to say, almost rudely, "You need have no fears for me. Lucia will tell you what an iceberg I am."

"Then Lucia would tell me wrong. I have the fatal power of reading character; I know you better than she does, and I see—" There she stopped abruptly.

"What? Tell me and prove your skill," he said eagerly.

Turning, she fixed her eyes on him with a penetrating power that made him shrink as she said slowly, "Under the ice I see fire, and warn you to beware lest it prove a volcano."

For a moment he sat dumb, wondering at the insight of the girl; for she was the first to discover the hidden warmth of a nature too proud to confess its tender impulses, or the ambitions that slept till some potent voice awoke them. The blunt, almost stern manner in which she warned him away from her only made her more attractive; for there was no conceit or arrogance in it, only a foreboding fear emboldened by past suffering to be frank. Suddenly he spoke impetuously:

"You are right! I am not what I seem, and my indolent indifference is but the mask under which I conceal my real self. I could be as passionate, as energetic and aspiring as Ned, if I had any aim in life. I have none, and so I am what you once called me, a thing to pity and despise."

"I never said that!" cried Jean indignantly.

"Not in those words, perhaps; but you looked it and thought it, though you phrased it more mildly. I deserved it, but I shall deserve it no longer. I am beginning to wake from my disgraceful idleness, and long for some work that shall make a man of me. Why do you go? I annoy you with my confessions. Pardon me. They are the first I ever made; they shall be the last."

"No, oh no! I am too much honored by your confidence; but is it wise, is it loyal to tell *me* your hopes and aims? Has not Miss Beaufort the first right to be your confidante?"

Coventry drew back, looking intensely annoyed, for the name recalled much that he would gladly have forgotten in the novel excitement of the hour. Lucia's love, Edward's parting words, his own reserve so strangely thrown aside, so difficult to resume. What he would have said was checked by the sight of a half-open letter which fell from Jean's dress as she moved away. Mechanically he took it up to return it, and, as he did so, he recognized Sydney's handwriting. Jean snatched it from him, turning pale to the lips as she cried, "Did you read it? What did you see? Tell me, tell me, on your honor!"

"On my honor, I saw nothing but this single sentence, 'By the love I bear you, believe what I say.' No more, as I am a gentleman. I know the hand, I guess the purport of the letter, and as a friend of Sydney, I earnestly desire to help you, if I can. Is this the matter upon which you want advice?"

"Yes."

"Then let me give it?"

"You cannot, without knowing all, and it is so hard to tell!"

"Let me guess it, and spare you the pain of telling. May I?" And Coventry waited eagerly for her reply, for the spell was still upon him.

Holding the letter fast, she beckoned him to follow, and glided before him to a secluded little nook, half boudoir, half conservatory. There she paused, stood an instant as if in doubt, then looked up at him with confiding eyes and said decidedly, "I will do it; for, strange as it may seem, you are the only person to whom I *can* speak. You know Sydney, you have discovered that I am an equal, you have offered your help. I accept it; but oh, do not think me unwomanly!

Remember how alone I am, how young, and how much I rely upon your sincerity, your sympathy!"

"Speak freely. I am indeed your friend." And Coventry sat down beside her, forgetful of everything but the soft-eyed girl who confided in him so entirely.

Speaking rapidly, Jean went on, "You know that Sydney loved me, that I refused him and went away. But you do not know that his importunities nearly drove me wild, that he threatened to rob me of my only treasure, my good name, and that, in desperation, I tried to kill myself. Yes, mad, wicked as it was, I did long to end the life which was, at best, a burden, and under his persecution had become a torment. You are shocked, yet what I say is the living truth. Lady Sydney will confirm it, the nurses at the hospital will confess that it was not a fever which brought me there; and here, though the external wound is healed, my heart still aches and burns with the shame and indignation which only a proud woman can feel."

She paused and sat with kindling eyes, glowing cheeks, and both hands pressed to her heaving bosom, as if the old insult roused her spirit anew. Coventry said not a word, for surprise, anger, incredulity, and admiration mingled so confusedly in his mind that he forgot to speak, and Jean went on, "That wild act of mine convinced him of my indomitable dislike. He went away, and I believed that this stormy love of his would be cured by absence. It is not, and I live in daily fear of fresh entreaties, renewed persecution. His mother promised not to betray where I had gone, but he found me out and wrote to me. The letter I asked you to take to Lady Sydney was a reply to his, imploring him to leave me in peace. You failed to deliver it, and I was glad, for I thought silence might quench hope. All in vain; this is a more passionate appeal than ever, and he vows he will never desist from his endeavors till I give another man the right to protect me. I *can* do this—I am sorely tempted to do it, but I rebel against the cruelty. I love my freedom, I have no wish to marry at this man's bidding. What can I do? How can I free myself? Be my friend, and help me!"

Tears streamed down her cheeks, sobs choked her words, and she clasped her hands imploringly as she turned toward the young man in all the abandonment of sorrow, fear, and supplication. Coventry found it hard to meet those eloquent eyes and answer calmly, for he had no experience in such scenes and knew not how to play his part. It is this absurd dress and that romantic nonsense which makes me feel so unlike myself, he thought, quite unconscious of the dangerous power which the dusky room, the midsummer warmth and fragrance, the memory of the "romantic nonsense," and, most of all, the presence of a beautiful, afflicted woman had over him. His usual self-possession deserted him, and he could only echo the words which had made the strongest impression upon him:

"You *can* do this, you are tempted to do it. Is Ned the man who can protect you?"

"No" was the soft reply.

"Who then?"

"Do not ask me. A good and honorable man; one who loves me well, and would devote his life to me; one whom once it would have been happiness to marry, but now—"

There her voice ended in a sigh, and all her fair hair fell down about her face, hiding it in a shining veil.

"Why not now? This is a sure and speedy way of ending your distress. Is it impossible?"

In spite of himself, Gerald leaned nearer, took one of the little hands in his, and pressed it as he spoke, urgently, compassionately, nay, almost tenderly. From behind the veil came a heavy sigh, and the brief answer, "It is impossible."

"Why, Jean?"

She flung her hair back with a sudden gesture, drew away her hand, and answered, almost fiercely, "Because I do not love him! Why do you torment me with such questions? I tell you I am in a sore strait and cannot see my way. Shall I deceive the good man, and secure peace at the price of liberty and truth? Or shall I defy Sydney and lead a life of dread? If he menaced my life, I should not fear; but he menaces that which is dearer than life—my good name. A look, a word can tarnish it; a scornful smile, a significant shrug can do me more harm than any blow; for I am a woman—friendless, poor, and at the mercy of his tongue. Ah, better to have died, and so have been saved the bitter pain that has come now!"

She sprang up, clasped her hands over her head, and paced despairingly through the little room, not weeping, but wearing an expression more tragical than tears. Still feeling as if he had suddenly stepped into a romance, yet finding a keen pleasure in the part assigned him, Coventry threw himself into it with spirit, and heartily did his best to console the poor girl who needed help so much. Going to her, he said as impetuously as Ned ever did, "Miss Muir—nay, I will say Jean, if that will comfort you—listen, and rest assured that no harm shall touch you if I can ward it off. You are needlessly alarmed. Indignant you may well be, but, upon my life, I think you wrong Sydney. He is violent, I know, but he is too honorable a man to injure you by a light word, an unjust act. He did but threaten, hoping to soften you. Let me see him, or write to him. He is my friend; he will listen to me. Of that I am sure."

"Be sure of nothing. When a man like Sydney loves and is thwarted in his love, nothing can control his headstrong will. Promise me you will not see or write to him. Much as I fear and despise him, I will submit, rather than any harm should befall you—or your brother. You promise me, Mr. Coventry?"

He hesitated. She clung to his arm with unfeigned solicitude in her eager, pleading face, and he could not resist it.

"I promise; but in return you must promise to let me give what help I can; and, Jean, never say again that you are friendless."

"You are so kind! God bless you for it. But I dare not accept your friendship; *she* will not permit it, and I have no right to mar her peace."

"Who will not permit it?" he demanded hotly.

"Miss Beaufort."

"Hang Miss Beaufort!" exclaimed Coventry, with such energy that Jean broke into a musical laugh, despite her trouble. He joined in it, and, for an instant they stood looking at one another as if the last barrier were down, and they were friends indeed. Jean paused suddenly, with the smile on her lips, the tears still on her cheek, and made a warning gesture. He listened: the sound of feet mingled with calls and laughter proved that they were missed and sought.

"That laugh betrayed us. Stay and meet them. I cannot." And Jean darted out upon the lawn. Coventry followed; for the thought of confronting so many eyes, so many questions, daunted him, and he fled like a coward. The sound of Jean's flying footsteps guided him, and he overtook her just as she paused behind a rose thicket to take breath.

"Fainthearted knight! You should have stayed and covered my retreat. Hark! they are coming! Hide! Hide!" she panted, half in fear, half in merriment, as the gay pursuers rapidly drew nearer.

"Kneel down; the moon is coming out and the glitter of your embroidery will betray you," whispered Jean, as they cowered behind the roses.

"Your arms and hair will betray you. 'Come under my plaiddie,' as the song says." And Coventry tried to make his velvet cloak cover the white shoulders and fair locks.

"We are acting our parts in reality now. How Bella will enjoy the thing when I tell her!" said Jean as the noises died away.

"Do not tell her," whispered Coventry.

"And why not?" she asked, looking up into the face so near her own, with an artless glance.

"Can you not guess why?"

"Ah, you are so proud you cannot bear to be laughed at."

"It is not that. It is because I do not want you to be annoyed by silly tongues; you have enough to pain you without that. I am your friend, now, and I do my best to prove it."

"So kind, so kind! How can I thank you?" murmured Jean. And she involuntarily nestled closer under the cloak that sheltered both.

Neither spoke for a moment, and in the silence the rapid beating of two hearts was heard. To drown the sound, Coventry said softly, "Are you frightened?"

"No, I like it," she answered, as softly, then added abruptly, "But why do we hide? There is nothing to fear. It is late. I must go. You are kneeling on my train. Please rise."

"Why in such haste? This flight and search only adds to the charm of the evening. I'll not get up yet. Will you have a rose, Jean?"

"No, I will not. Let me go, Mr. Coventry, I insist. There has been enough of this folly. You forget yourself."

She spoke imperiously, flung off the cloak, and put him from her. He rose at once, saying, like one waking suddenly from a pleasant dream, "I do indeed forget myself."

Here the sound of voices broke on them, nearer than before. Pointing to a covered walk that led to the house, he said, in his usually cool, calm tone, "Go in that way; I will cover your retreat." And turning, he went to meet the merry hunters.

Half an hour later, when the party broke up, Miss Muir joined them in her usual quiet dress, looking paler, meeker, and sadder than usual. Coventry saw this, though he neither looked at her nor addressed her. Lucia saw it also, and was glad that the dangerous girl had fallen back into her proper place again, for she had suffered much that night. She appropriated her cousin's arm as they went through the park, but he was in one of his taciturn moods, and all her attempts at conversation were in vain. Miss Muir walked alone, singing softly to herself as she followed in the dusk. Was Gerald so silent because he listened to that fitful song? Lucia thought so, and felt her dislike rapidly deepening to hatred.

When the young friends were gone, and the family were exchanging good-nights among themselves, Jean was surprised by Coventry's offering his hand, for he had never done it before, and whispering, as he held it, though Lucia watched him all the while, "I have not given my advice, yet."

"Thanks, I no longer need it. I have decided for myself."

"May I ask how?"

"To brave my enemy."

"Good! But what decided you so suddenly?"

"The finding of a friend." And with a grateful glance she was gone.

❧ *chapter VI* ❧

ON THE WATCH

"IF you please, Mr. Coventry, did you get the letter last night?" were the first words that greeted the "young master" as he left his room next morning.

"What letter, Dean? I don't remember any," he answered, pausing, for something in the maid's manner struck him as peculiar.

"It came just as you left for the Hall, sir. Benson ran after you with it, as it was marked 'Haste.' Didn't you get it, sir?" asked the woman, anxiously.

"Yes, but upon my life, I forgot all about it till this minute. It's in my other coat, I suppose, if I've not lost it. That absurd masquerading put everything else out of my head." And speaking more to himself than to the maid, Coventry turned back to look for the missing letter.

Dean remained where she was, apparently busy about the arrangement of the curtains at the hall window, but furtively watching meanwhile with a most unwonted air of curiosity.

"Not there, I thought so!" she muttered, as Coventry impatiently thrust his hand into one pocket after another. But as she spoke, an expression of amazement appeared in her face, for suddenly the letter was discovered.

"I'd have sworn it wasn't there! I don't understand it, but she's a deep one, or I'm much deceived." And Dean shook her head like one perplexed, but not convinced.

Coventry uttered an exclamation of satisfaction on glancing at the address and, standing where he was, tore open the letter.

> *Dear C:*
>   *I'm off to Baden. Come and join me, then you'll be out of harm's way; for if you fall in love with J. M. (and you can't escape if you stay where she is), you will incur the trifling inconvenience of having your brains blown out by*
>   *Yours truly, F. R. Sydney*

"The man is mad!" ejaculated Coventry, staring at the letter while an angry flush rose to his face. "What the deuce does he mean by writing to me in that style? Join him—not I! And as for the threat, I laugh at it. Poor Jean! This headstrong fool seems bent on tormenting her. Well, Dean, what are you waiting for?" he demanded, as if suddenly conscious of her presence.

"Nothing, sir; I only stopped to see if you found the letter. Beg pardon, sir."

And she was moving on when Coventry asked, with a suspicious look, "What made you think it was lost? You seem to take an uncommon interest in my affairs today."

"Oh dear, no, sir. I felt a bit anxious, Benson is so forgetful, and it was me who sent him after you, for I happened to see you go out, so I felt responsible. Being marked that way, I thought it might be important so I asked about it."

"Very well, you can go, Dean. It's all right, you see."

"I'm not so sure of that," muttered the woman, as she curtsied respectfully and went away, looking as if the letter had *not* been found.

Dean was Miss Beaufort's maid, a grave, middle-aged woman with keen eyes and a somewhat grim air. Having been long in the family, she enjoyed all the privileges of a faithful and favorite servant. She loved her young mistress with an almost jealous affection. She watched over her with the vigilant care of a mother and resented any attempt at interference on the part of others. At first she had pitied and liked Jean Muir, then distrusted her, and now heartily hated her, as the cause of the increased indifference of Coventry toward his cousin. Dean knew the depth of Lucia's love, and though no man, in her eyes, was worthy of her mistress, still, having honored him with her regard, Dean felt bound to like him, and the late change in his manner disturbed the maid almost as much as it did the mistress. She watched Jean narrowly, causing that amiable creature much amusement but little annoyance, as yet, for Dean's slow English wit was no match for the subtle mind of the governess. On the preceding night, Dean had been sent up to the Hall with costumes and had there seen something which much disturbed her. She began to speak of it while undressing her mistress, but Lucia, being in an unhappy mood, had so sternly ordered her not to gossip that the tale remained untold, and she was forced to bide her time.

Now I'll see how *she* looks after it; though there's not much to be got out of *her* face, the deceitful hussy, thought Dean, marching down the corridor and knitting her black brows as she went.

"Good morning, Mrs. Dean. I hope you are none the worse for last night's frolic. You had the work and we the play," said a blithe voice behind her; and turning sharply, she confronted Miss Muir. Fresh and smiling, the governess nodded with an air of cordiality which would have been irresistible with anyone but Dean.

"I'm quite well, thank you, miss," she returned coldly, as her keen eye fastened on the girl as if to watch the effect of her words. "I had a good rest when the young ladies and gentlemen were at supper, for while the maids cleared up, I sat in the 'little anteroom.'"

"Yes, I saw you, and feared you'd take cold. Very glad you didn't. How is Miss Beaufort? She seemed rather poorly last night" was the tranquil reply, as Jean settled the little frills about her delicate wrists. The cool question was a return shot for Dean's hint that she had been where she could oversee the interview between Coventry and Miss Muir.

"She is a bit tired, as any *lady* would be after such an evening. People who are *used* to *play-acting* wouldn't mind it, perhaps, but Miss Beaufort don't enjoy *romps* as much as *some* do."

The emphasis upon certain words made Dean's speech as impertinent as she desired. But Jean only laughed, and as Coventry's step was heard behind them, she ran downstairs, saying blandly, but with a wicked look, "I won't stop to thank you now, lest Mr. Coventry should bid me good-morning, and so increase Miss Beaufort's indisposition."

Dean's eyes flashed as she looked after the girl with a wrathful face, and went her way, saying grimly, "I'll bide my time, but I'll get the better of her yet."

Fancying himself quite removed from "last night's absurdity," yet curious to see how Jean would meet him, Coventry lounged into the breakfast room with his usual air of listless indifference. A languid nod and murmur was all the reply he vouchsafed to the greetings of cousin, sister, and governess as he sat down and took up his paper.

"Have you had a letter from Ned?" asked Bella, looking at the note which her brother still held.

"No" was the brief answer.

"Who then? You look as if you had received bad news."

There was no reply, and, peeping over his arm, Bella caught sight of the seal and exclaimed, in a disappointed tone, "It is the Sydney crest. I don't care about the note now. Men's letters to each other are not interesting."

Miss Muir had been quietly feeding one of Edward's dogs, but at the name she looked up and met Coventry's eyes, coloring so distressfully that he pitied her. Why he should take the trouble to cover her confusion, he did not stop to ask himself, but seeing the curl of Lucia's lip, he suddenly addressed her with an air of displeasure, "Do you know that Dean is getting impertinent? She presumes too much on her age and your indulgence, and forgets her place."

"What has she done?" asked Lucia coldly.

"She troubles herself about my affairs and takes it upon herself to keep Benson in order."

Here Coventry told about the letter and the woman's evident curiosity.

"Poor Dean, she gets no thanks for reminding you of what you had forgotten. Next time she will leave your letters to their fate, and perhaps it will be as well, if they have such a bad effect upon your temper, Gerald."

Lucia spoke calmly, but there was an angry color in her cheek as she rose and left the room. Coventry looked much annoyed, for on Jean's face he detected a faint smile, half pitiful, half satirical, which disturbed him more than his cousin's insinuation. Bella broke the awkward silence by saying, with a sigh, "Poor Ned! I do so long to hear again from him. I thought a letter had come for some of us. Dean said she saw one bearing his writing on the hall table yesterday."

"She seems to have a mania for inspecting letters. I won't allow it. Who was the letter for, Bella?" said Coventry, putting down his paper.

"She wouldn't or couldn't tell, but looked very cross and told me to ask you."

"Very odd! I've had none," began Coventry.

"But I had one several days ago. Will you please read it, and my reply?" And as she spoke, Jean laid two letters before him.

"Certainly not. It would be dishonorable to read what Ned intended for no eyes but your own. You are too scrupulous in one way, and not enough so in another, Miss Muir." And Coventry offered both the letters with an air of grave decision, which could not conceal the interest and surprise he felt.

"You are right. Mr. Edward's note *should* be kept sacred, for in it the poor boy has laid bare his heart to me. But mine I beg you will read, that you may see how well I try to keep my word to you. Oblige me in this, Mr. Coventry; I have a right to ask it of you."

So urgently she spoke, so wistfully she looked, that he could not refuse and, going to the window, read the letter. It was evidently an answer to a passionate appeal from the young lover, and was written with consummate skill. As he read, Gerald could not help thinking, If this girl writes in this way to a man whom she does *not* love, with what a world of power and passion would she write to one whom she *did* love. And this thought kept returning to him as his eye went over line after line of wise argument, gentle reproof, good counsel, and friendly regard. Here and there a word, a phrase, betrayed what she had already confessed, and Coventry forgot to return the letter, as he stood wondering who was the man whom Jean loved.

The sound of Bella's voice recalled him, for she was saying, half kindly, half petulantly, "Don't look so sad, Jean. Ned will outlive it, I dare say. You remember you said once men never died of love, though women might. In his one note to me, he spoke so beautifully of you, and begged me to be kind to you for his sake, that I try to be with all my heart, though if it was anyone but you, I really think I should hate them for making my dear boy so unhappy."

"You are too kind, Bella, and I often think I'll go away to relieve you of my presence; but unwise and dangerous as it is to stay, I haven't the courage to go. I've been so happy here." And as she spoke, Jean's head dropped lower over the dog as it nestled to her affectionately.

Before Bella could utter half the loving words that sprang to her lips, Coventry came to them with all languor gone from face and mien, and laying Jean's letter before her, he said, with an undertone of deep feeling in his usually emotionless voice, "A right womanly and eloquent letter, but I fear it will only increase the fire it was meant to quench. I pity my brother more than ever now."

"Shall I send it?" asked Jean, looking straight up at him, like one who had entire reliance on his judgment.

"Yes, I have not the heart to rob him of such a sweet sermon upon self-sacrifice. Shall I post it for you?"

"Thank you; in a moment." And with a grateful look, Jean dropped her eyes. Producing her little purse, she selected a penny, folded it in a bit of paper, and then offered both letter and coin to Coventry, with such a pretty air of business, that he could not control a laugh.

"So you won't be indebted to me for a penny? What a proud woman you are, Miss Muir."

"I am; it's a family failing." And she gave him a significant glance, which recalled to him the memory of who she was. He understood her feeling, and liked her the better for it, knowing that he would have done the same had he been in her place. It was a little thing, but if done for effect, it answered admirably, for it showed a quick insight into his character on her part, and betrayed to him the existence of a pride in which he sympathized heartily. He stood by Jean a moment, watching her as she burnt Edward's letter in the blaze of the spirit lamp under the urn.

"Why do you do that?" he asked involuntarily.

"Because it is my duty to forget" was all her answer.

"Can you always forget when it becomes a duty?"

"I wish I could! I wish I could!"

She spoke passionately, as if the words broke from her against her will, and, rising hastily, she went into the garden, as if afraid to stay.

"Poor, dear Jean is very unhappy about something, but I can't discover what it is. Last night I found her crying over a rose, and now she runs away, looking as if her heart was broken. I'm glad I've got no lessons."

"What kind of a rose?" asked Coventry from behind his paper as Bella paused.

"A lovely white one. It must have come from the Hall; we have none like it. I wonder if Jean was ever going to be married, and lost her lover, and felt sad because the flower reminded her of bridal roses."

Coventry made no reply, but felt himself change countenance as he recalled the little scene behind the rose hedge, where he gave Jean the flower which she had refused yet taken. Presently, to Bella's surprise, he flung down the paper, tore Sydney's note to atoms, and rang for his horse with an energy which amazed her.

"Why, Gerald, what has come over you? One would think Ned's restless spirit had suddenly taken possession of you. What are you going to do?"

"I'm going to work" was the unexpected answer, as Coventry turned toward her with an expression so rarely seen on his fine face.

"What has waked you up all at once?" asked Bella, looking more and more amazed.

"You did," he said, drawing her toward him.

"I! When? How?"

"Do you remember saying once that energy was better than beauty in a man, and that no one could respect an idler?"

"I never said anything half so sensible as that. Jean said something like it once, I believe, but I forgot. Are you tired of doing nothing, at last, Gerald?"

"Yes, I neglected my duty to Ned, till he got into trouble, and now I reproach myself for it. It's not too late to do other neglected tasks, so I'm going at them with a will. Don't say anything about it to anyone, and don't laugh at me, for I'm in earnest, Bell."

"I know you are, and I admire and love you for it, my dear old boy," cried Bella enthusiastically, as she threw her arms about his neck and kissed him heartily. "What will you do first?" she asked, as he stood thoughtfully smoothing the bright head that leaned upon his shoulder, with that new expression still clear and steady in his face.

"I'm going to ride over the whole estate, and attend to things as a master should; not leave it all to Bent, of whom I've heard many complaints, but have been too idle to inquire about them. I shall consult Uncle, and endeavor to be all that my father was in his time. Is that a worthy ambition, dear?"

"Oh, Gerald, let me tell Mamma. It will make her so happy. You are her idol, and to hear you say these things, to see you look so like dear Papa, would do more for her spirits than all the doctors in England."

"Wait till I prove what my resolution is worth. When I have

really done something, then I'll surprise Mamma with a sample of my work."

"Of course you'll tell Lucia?"

"Not on any account. It is a little secret between us, so keep it till I give you leave to tell it."

"But Jean will see it at once; she knows everything that happens, she is so quick and wise. Do you mind her knowing?"

"I don't see that I can help it if she is so wonderfully gifted. Let her see what she can, I don't mind her. Now I'm off." And with a kiss to his sister, a sudden smile on his face, Coventry sprang upon his horse and rode away at a pace which caused the groom to stare after him in blank amazement.

Nothing more was seen of him till dinnertime, when he came in so exhilarated by his brisk ride and busy morning that he found some difficulty in assuming his customary manner, and more than once astonished the family by talking animatedly on various subjects which till now had always seemed utterly uninteresting to him. Lucia was amazed, his mother delighted, and Bella could hardly control her desire to explain the mystery; but Jean took it very calmly and regarded him with the air of one who said, "I understand, but you will soon tire of it." This nettled him more than he would confess, and he exerted himself to silently contradict that prophecy.

"Have you answered Mr. Sydney's letter?" asked Bella, when they were all scattered about the drawing room after dinner.

"No," answered her brother, who was pacing up and down with restless steps, instead of lounging near his beautiful cousin.

"I ask because I remembered that Ned sent a message for him in my last note, as he thought you would know Sydney's address. Here it is, something about a horse. Please put it in when you write," and Bella laid the note on the writing table nearby.

"I'll send it at once and have done with it," muttered Coventry and, seating himself, he dashed off a few lines, sealed and sent the letter, and then resumed his march, eyeing the three young ladies with three different expressions, as he passed and repassed. Lucia sat apart, feigning to be intent upon a book, and her handsome face looked almost stern in its haughty composure, for though her heart ached, she was too proud to own it. Bella now lay on the sofa, half asleep, a rosy little creature, as unconsciously pretty as a child. Miss Muir sat in the recess of a deep window, in a low lounging chair, working at an embroidery frame with a graceful industry pleasant to see. Of late she had worn colors, for Bella had been generous in gifts, and the pale blue muslin which flowed in soft waves about her was very becoming to her fair skin and golden hair. The close braids were gone, and loose curls dropped here and there from the heavy coil wound around her well-shaped head. The tip of one dainty foot was visible, and a petulant litle gesture which now and then shook back the falling sleeve gave glimpses of a round white arm. Ned's great hound lay nearby, the sunshine flickered on her through the leaves, and as she sat smiling to herself, while the dexterous hands shaped leaf and flower, she made a charming picture of all that is most womanly and winning; a picture which few men's eyes would not have liked to rest upon.

Another chair stood near her, and as Coventry went up and down, a strong desire to take it possessed him. He was tired of his thoughts and wished to be amused by watching the changes of the girl's expressive face, listening to the varying tones of her voice, and trying to discover the spell which so strongly attracted him in spite of himself. More than once he swerved from his course to gratify his whim, but Lucia's presence always restrained him, and with a word to the dog, or a glance from the window, as pretext for a pause, he resumed his walk again. Something in his cousin's face reproached him, but her manner of late was so repellent that he felt no desire to resume their former familiarity, and, wishing to show that he did not consider himself bound, he kept aloof. It was a quiet test of the power of each woman over this man; they instinctively felt it, and both tried to conquer. Lucia spoke several times, and tried to speak frankly and affably; but her manner was constrained, and Coventry, having answered politely, relapsed into silence. Jean said nothing, but silently appealed to eye and ear by the pretty picture she made of herself, the snatches of song she softly sang, as if forgetting that she was not alone, and a shy glance now and then, half wistful, half merry, which was more alluring than graceful figure or sweet voice. When she had tormented Lucia and tempted Coventry long enough, she quietly asserted her supremacy in a way which astonished her rival, who knew nothing of the secret of her birth, which knowledge did much to attract and charm the young man. Letting a ball of silk escape from her lap, she watched it roll toward the promenader, who caught and returned it with an alacrity which added grace to the trifling service.

As she took it, she said, in the frank way that never failed to win him, "I think you must be tired; but if exercise is necessary, employ your energies to some purpose and put your mother's basket of silks in order. They are in a tangle, and it will please her to know that you did it, as your brother used to do."

"Hercules at the distaff," said Coventry gaily, and down he sat in the long-desired seat. Jean put the basket on his knee, and as he surveyed it, as if daunted at his task, she leaned back, and indulged in a musical little peal of laughter charming to hear. Lucia sat dumb with surprise, to see her proud, indolent cousin obeying the commands of a governess, and looking as if he heartily enjoyed it. In ten minutes she was as entirely forgotten as if she had been miles away; for Jean seemed in her wittiest, gayest mood, and as she now treated the "young master" like an equal, there was none of the former meek timidity. Yet often her eyes fell, her color changed, and the piquant sallies faltered on her tongue, as Coventry involuntarily looked deep into the fine eyes which had once shone on him so tenderly in that mimic tragedy. He could not forget it, and though neither alluded to it, the memory of the previous evening seemed to haunt both and lend a secret charm to the present moment. Lucia bore this as long as she could, and then left the room with the air of an insulted princess; but Coventry did not, and Jean feigned not to see her go. Bella was fast asleep, and before he knew how it came to pass, the young man was listening to the story of his companion's life. A sad tale, told with wonderful skill, for soon he was absorbed in it. The basket slid unobserved from his knee, the dog was pushed away, and, leaning forward, he listened eagerly as the girl's low voice recounted all the hardships, loneliness, and grief of her short life. In the midst of a touching episode she started, stopped, and looked straight before her, with an intent expression which changed to one of intense contempt, and her eye turned to Coventry's, as she said, pointing to the window behind him, "We are watched."

"By whom?" he demanded, starting up angrily.

"Hush, say nothing, let it pass. I am used to it."

"But *I* am not, and I'll not submit to it. Who was it, Jean?" he answered hotly.

She smiled significantly at a knot of rose-colored ribbon, which a little gust was blowing toward them along the terrace. A black frown darkened the young man's face as he sprang out of the long window and went rapidly out of sight, scrutinizing each green nook as he passed. Jean laughed quietly as she watched him, and said softly to herself, with her eyes on the fluttering ribbon, "That was a fortunate accident, and a happy inspiration. Yes, my dear Mrs. Dean, you will find that playing the spy will only get your mistress as well as yourself into trouble. You would not be warned, and you must take the consequences, reluctant as I am to injure a worthy creature like yourself."

Soon Coventry was heard returning. Jean listened with suspended breath to catch his first words, for he was not alone.

"Since you insist that it was you and not your mistress, I let it pass, although I still have my suspicions. Tell Miss Beaufort I desire to see her for a few moments in the library. Now go, Dean, and be careful for the future, if you wish to stay in my house."

The maid retired, and the young man came in looking both ireful and stern.

"I wish I had said nothing, but I was startled, and spoke involuntarily. Now you are angry, and I have made fresh trouble for poor Miss Lucia. Forgive me as I forgive her, and let it pass. I have learned to bear this surveillance, and pity her causeless jealousy," said Jean, with a self-reproachful air.

"I will forgive the dishonorable act, but I cannot forget it, and I intend to put a stop to it. I am not betrothed to my cousin, as I told you once, but you, like all the rest, seem bent on believing that I am. Hitherto I have cared too little about the matter to settle it, but now I shall prove beyond all doubt that I am free."

As he uttered the last word, Coventry cast on Jean a look that affected her strangely. She grew pale, her work dropped on her lap, and her eyes rose to his, with an eager, questioning expression, which slowly changed to one of mingled pain and pity, as she turned her face away, murmuring in a tone of tender sorrow, "Poor Lucia, who will comfort her?"

For a moment Coventry stood silent, as if weighing some fateful purpose in his mind. As Jean's rapt sigh of compassion reached his ear, he had echoed it within himself, and half repented of his resolution; then his eye rested on the girl before him looking so lonely in her sweet sympathy for another that his heart yearned toward her. Sudden fire shot into his eye, sudden warmth replaced the cold sternness of his face, and his steady voice faltered suddenly, as he said, very low, yet very earnestly, "Jean, I have tried to love her, but I cannot. Ought I to deceive her, and make myself miserable to please my family?"

"She is beautiful and good, and loves you tenderly; is there no hope for her?" asked Jean, still pale, but very quiet, though she held one hand against her heart, as if to still or hide its rapid beating.

"None," answered Coventry.

"But can you not learn to love her? Your will is strong, and most men would not find it a hard task."

"I cannot, for something stronger than my own will controls me."

"What is that?" And Jean's dark eyes were fixed upon him, full of innocent wonder.

His fell, and he said hastily, "I dare not tell you yet."

"Pardon! I should not have asked. Do not consult me in this matter; I am not the person to advise you. I can only say that it seems to me as if any man with an empty heart would be glad to have so beautiful a woman as your cousin."

"My heart is not empty," began Coventry, drawing a step nearer, and speaking in a passionate voice. "Jean, I *must* speak; hear me. I cannot love my cousin, because I love you."

"Stop!" And Jean sprang up with a commanding gesture. "I will not hear you while any promise binds you to another. Remember your mother's wishes, Lucia's hopes, Edward's last words, your own pride, my humble lot. You forget yourself, Mr. Coventry. Think well before you speak, weigh the cost of this act, and recollect who I am before you insult me by any transient passion, any false vows."

"I have thought, I do weigh the cost, and I swear that I desire to woo you as humbly, honestly as I would any lady in the land. You speak of my pride. Do I stoop in loving my equal in rank? You speak of your lowly lot, but poverty is no disgrace, and the courage with which you bear it makes it beautiful. I should have broken with Lucia before I spoke, but I could not control myself. My mother loves you, and will be happy in my happiness. Edward must forgive me, for I have tried to do my best, but love is irresistible. Tell me, Jean, is there any hope for me?"

He had seized her hand and was speaking impetuously, with ardent face and tender tone, but no answer came, for as Jean turned her eloquent countenance toward him, full of maiden shame and timid love, Dean's prim figure appeared at the door, and her harsh voice broke the momentary silence, saying, sternly, "Miss Beaufort is waiting for you, sir."

"Go, go at once, and be kind, for my sake, Gerald," whispered

Jean, for he stood as if deaf and blind to everything but her voice, her face.

As she drew his head down to whisper, her cheek touched his, and regardless of Dean, he kissed it, passionately, whispering back, "My little Jean! For your sake I can be anything."

"Miss Beaufort is waiting. Shall I say you will come, sir?" demanded Dean, pale and grim with indignation.

"Yes, yes, I'll come. Wait for me in the garden, Jean." And Coventry hurried away, in no mood for the interview but anxious to have it over.

As the door closed behind him, Dean walked up to Miss Muir, trembling with anger, and laying a heavy hand on her arm, she said below her breath, "I've been expecting this, you artful creature. I saw your game and did my best to spoil it, but you are too quick for me. You think you've got him. There you are mistaken; for as sure as my name is Hester Dean, I'll prevent it, or Sir John shall."

"Take your hand away and treat me with proper respect, or you will be dismissed from this house. Do you know who I am?" And Jean drew herself up with a haughty air, which impressed the woman more deeply than her words. "I am the daughter of Lady Howard and, if I choose it, can be the wife of Mr. Coventry."

Dean drew back amazed, yet not convinced. Being a well-trained servant, as well as a prudent woman, she feared to overstep the bounds of respect, to go too far, and get her mistress as well as herself into trouble. So, though she still doubted Jean, and hated her more than ever, she controlled herself. Dropping a curtsy, she assumed her usual air of deference, and said, meekly, "I beg pardon, miss. If I'd known, I should have conducted myself differently, of course, but ordinary governesses make so much mischief in a house, one can't help mistrusting them. I don't wish to meddle or be overbold, but being fond of my dear young lady, I naturally take her part, and must say that Mr. Coventry has not acted like a gentleman."

"Think what you please, Dean, but I advise you to say as little as possible if you wish to remain. I have not accepted Mr. Coventry yet, and if he chooses to set aside the engagement his family made for him, I think he has a right to do so. Miss Beaufort would hardly care to marry him against his will, because he pities her for her unhappy love," and with a tranquil smile, Miss Muir walked away.

≈ *chapter VII* ≈

THE LAST CHANCE

"SHE will tell Sir John, will she? Then I must be before her, and hasten events. It will be as well to have all sure before there can be any danger. My poor Dean, you are no match for me, but you may prove annoying, nevertheless."

These thoughts passed through Miss Muir's mind as she went down the hall, pausing an instant at the library door, for the murmur of voices was heard. She caught no word, and had only time for an instant's pause as Dean's heavy step followed her. Turning, Jean drew a chair before the door, and, beckoning to the woman, she said, smiling still, "Sit here and play watchdog. I am going to Miss Bella, so you can nod if you will."

"Thank you, miss. I will wait for my young lady. She may need me when this hard time is over." And Dean seated herself with a resolute face.

Jean laughed and went on; but her eyes gleamed with sudden malice, and she glanced over her shoulder with an expression which boded ill for the faithful old servant.

"I've got a letter from Ned, and here is a tiny note for you," cried Bella as Jean entered the boudoir. "Mine is a very odd, hasty letter, with no news in it, but his meeting with Sydney. I hope yours is better, or it won't be very satisfactory."

As Sydney's name passed Bella's lips, all the color died out of Miss Muir's face, and the note shook with the tremor of her hand.

Her very lips were white, but she said calmly, "Thank you. As you are busy, I'll go and read my letter on the lawn." And before Bella could speak, she was gone.

Hurrying to a quiet nook, Jean tore open the note and read the few blotted lines it contained.

> *I have seen Sydney; he has told me all; and, hard as I found it to believe, it was impossible to doubt, for he has discovered proofs which cannot be denied. I make no reproaches, shall demand no confession or atonement, for I cannot forget that I once loved you. I give you three days to find another home, before I return to tell the family who you are. Go at once, I beseech you, and spare me the pain of seeing your disgrace.*

Slowly, steadily she read it twice over, then sat motionless, knitting her brows in deep thought. Presently she drew a long breath, tore up the note, and rising, went slowly toward the Hall, saying to herself, "Three days, only three days! Can it be accomplished in so short a time? It shall be, if wit and will can do it, for it is my last chance. If this fails, I'll not go back to my old life, but end all at once."

Setting her teeth and clenching her hands, as if some memory stung her, she went on through the twilight, to find Sir John waiting to give her a hearty welcome.

"You look tired, my dear. Never mind the reading tonight; rest yourself, and let the book go," he said kindly, observing her worn look.

"Thank you, sir. I am tired, but I'd rather read, else the book will not be finished before I go."

"Go, child! Where are you going?" demanded Sir John, looking anxiously at her as she sat down.

"I will tell you by-and-by, sir." And opening the book, Jean read for a little while.

But the usual charm was gone; there was no spirit in the voice of the reader, no interest in the face of the listener, and soon he said, abruptly, "My dear, pray stop! I cannot listen with a divided mind. What troubles you? Tell your friend, and let him comfort you."

As if the kind words overcame her, Jean dropped the book, covered up her face, and wept so bitterly that Sir John was much alarmed; for such a demonstration was doubly touching in one who usually was all gaiety and smiles. As he tried to soothe her, his words grew tender, his solicitude full of a more than paternal anxiety, and his kind heart overflowed with pity and affection for the weeping girl. As she grew calmer, he urged her to be frank, promising to help and counsel her, whatever the affliction or fault might be.

"Ah, you are too kind, too generous! How can I go away and leave my one friend?" sighed Jean, wiping the tears away and looking up at him with grateful eyes.

"Then you do care a little for the old man?" said Sir John with an eager look, an involuntary pressure of the hand he held.

Jean turned her face away, and answered, very low, "No one ever was so kind to me as you have been. Can I help caring for you more than I can express?"

Sir John was a little deaf at times, but he heard that, and looked well pleased. He had been rather thoughtful of late, had dressed with unusual care, been particularly gallant and gay when the young ladies visited him, and more than once, when Jean paused in the reading to ask a question, he had been forced to confess that he had not been listening; though, as she well knew, his eyes had been fixed upon her. Since the discovery of her birth, his manner had been peculiarly benignant, and many little acts had proved his interest and goodwill. Now, when Jean spoke of going, a panic seized him, and desolation seemed about to fall upon the old Hall. Something in her unusual agitation struck him as peculiar and excited his curiosity. Never had she seemed so interesting as now, when she sat beside him with tearful eyes, and some soft trouble in her heart which she dared not confess.

"Tell me everything, child, and let your friend help you if he can." Formerly he said "father" or "the old man," but lately he always spoke of himself as her "friend."

"I will tell you, for I have no one else to turn to. I must go away because Mr. Coventry has been weak enough to love me."

"What, Gerald?" cried Sir John, amazed.

"Yes; today he told me this, and left me to break with Lucia; so I ran to you to help me prevent him from disappointing his mother's hopes and plans."

Sir John had started up and paced down the room, but as Jean paused he turned toward her, saying, with an altered face, "Then you do not love him? Is it possible?"

"No, I do not love him," she answered promptly.

"Yet he is all that women usually find attractive. How is it that you have escaped, Jean?"

"I love someone else" was the scarcely audible reply.

Sir John resumed his seat with the air of a man bent on getting at a mystery, if possible.

"It will be unjust to let you suffer for the folly of these boys, my little girl. Ned is gone, and I was sure that Gerald was safe; but now that his turn has come, I am perplexed, for he cannot be sent away."

"No, it is I who must go; but it seems so hard to leave this safe and happy home, and wander away into the wide, cold world again. You have all been too kind to me, and now separation breaks my heart."

A sob ended the speech, and Jean's head went down upon her hands again. Sir John looked at her a moment, and his fine old face was full of genuine emotion, as he said slowly, "Jean, will you stay and be a daughter to the solitary old man?"

"No, sir" was the unexpected answer.

"And why not?" asked Sir John, looking surprised, but rather pleased than angry.

"Because I could not be a daughter to you; and even if I could, it would not be wise, for the gossips would say you were not old enough to be the adopted father of a girl like me. Sir John, young as I am, I know much of the world, and am sure that this kind plan is impractical; but I thank you from the bottom of my heart."

"Where will you go, Jean?" asked Sir John, after a pause.

"To London, and try to find another situation where I can do no harm."

"Will it be difficult to find another home?"

"Yes. I cannot ask Mrs. Coventry to recommend me, when I have innocently brought so much trouble into her family; and Lady Sydney is gone, so I have no friend."

"Except John Coventry. I will arrange all that. When will you go, Jean?"

"Tomorrow."

"So soon!" And the old man's voice betrayed the trouble he was trying to conceal.

Jean had grown very calm, but it was the calmness of desperation. She had hoped that the first tears would produce the avowal for which she waited. It had not, and she began to fear that her last chance was slipping from her. Did the old man love her? If so, why did he not speak? Eager to profit by each moment, she was on the alert for any hopeful hint, any propitious word, look, or act, and every nerve was strung to the utmost.

"Jean, may I ask one question?" said Sir John.

"Anything of me, sir."

"This man whom you love—can he not help you?"

"He could if he knew, but he must not."

"If he knew what? Your present trouble?"

"No. My love."

"He does know this, then?"

"No, thank heaven! And he never will."

"Why not?"

"Because I am too proud to own it."

"He loves you, my child?"

"I do not know—I dare not hope it," murmured Jean.

"Can I not help you here? Believe me, I desire to see you safe and happy. Is there nothing I can do?"

"Nothing, nothing."

"May I know the name?"

"No! No! Let me go; I cannot bear this questioning!" And Jean's distressful face warned him to ask no more.

"Forgive me, and let me do what I may. Rest here quietly. I'll write a letter to a good friend of mine, who will find you a home, if you leave us."

As Sir John passed into his inner study, Jean watched him with despairing eyes and wrung her hands, saying to herself, Has all my skill deserted me when I need it most? How can I make him understand, yet not overstep the bounds of maiden modesty? He is so blind, so timid, or so dull he will not see, and time is going fast. What shall I do to open his eyes?

Her own eyes roved about the room, seeking for some aid from inanimate things, and soon she found it. Close behind the couch where she sat hung a fine miniature of Sir John. At first her eye rested on it as she contrasted its placid comeliness with the unusual pallor and disquiet of the living face seen through the open door, as the old man sat at his desk trying to write and casting covert glances at the girlish figure he had left behind him. Affecting unconsciousness of this, Jean gazed on as if forgetful of everything but the picture, and suddenly, as if obeying an irresistible impulse, she took it down, looked long and fondly at it, then, shaking her curls about her face, as if to hide the act, pressed it to her lips and seemed to weep over it in an uncontrollable paroxysm of tender grief. A sound startled her, and like a guilty thing, she turned to replace the picture; but it dropped from her hand as she uttered a faint cry and hid her face, for Sir John stood before her, with an expression which she could not mistake.

"Jean, why did you do that?" he asked, in an eager, agitated voice.

No answer, as the girl sank lower, like one overwhelmed with shame. Laying his hand on the bent head, and bending his own, he whispered, "Tell me, is the name John Coventry?"

Still no answer, but a stifled sound betrayed that his words had gone home.

"Jean, shall I go back and write the letter, or may I stay and tell you that the old man loves you better than a daughter?"

She did not speak, but a little hand stole out from under the falling hair, as if to keep him. With a broken exclamation he seized it, drew her up into his arms, and laid his gray head on her fair one, too happy for words. For a moment Jean Muir enjoyed her success; then, fearing lest some sudden mishap should destroy it, she hastened to make all secure. Looking up with well-feigned timidity and half-confessed affection, she said softly, "Forgive me that I could not hide this better. I meant to go away and never tell it, but you were so kind it made the parting doubly hard. Why did you ask such dangerous questions? Why did you look, when you should have been writing my dismissal?"

"How could I dream that you loved me, Jean, when you refused the only offer I dared make? Could I be presumptuous enough to fancy you would reject young lovers for an old man like me?" asked Sir John, caressing her.

"You are not old, to me, but everything I love and honor!" interrupted Jean, with a touch of genuine remorse, as this generous, honorable gentleman gave her both heart and home, unconscious of deceit. "It is I who am presumptuous, to dare to love one so far above me. But I did not know how dear you were to me till I felt that I must go. I ought not to accept this happiness. I am not worthy of it; and you will regret your kindness when the world blames you for giving a home to one so poor, and plain, and humble as I."

"Hush, my darling. I care nothing for the idle gossip of the world. If you are happy here, let tongues wag as they will. I shall be too busy enjoying the sunshine of your presence to heed anything that goes on about me. But, Jean, you are sure you love me? It seems incredible that I should win the heart that has been so cold to younger, better men than I."

"Dear Sir John, be sure of this, I love you truly. I will do my best to be a good wife to you, and prove that, in spite of my many faults, I possess the virtue of gratitude."

If he had known the strait she was in, he would have understood the cause of the sudden fervor of her words, the intense thankfulness that shone in her face, the real humility that made her stoop and kiss the generous hand that gave so much. For a few moments she enjoyed and let him enjoy the happy present, undisturbed. But the anxiety which devoured her, the danger which menaced her, soon recalled her, and forced her to wring yet more from the unsuspicious heart she had conquered.

"No need of letters now," said Sir John, as they sat side by side, with the summer moonlight glorifying all the room. "You have found a home for life; may it prove a happy one."

"It is not mine yet, and I have a strange foreboding that it never will be," she answered sadly.

"Why, my child?"

"Because I have an enemy who will try to destroy my peace, to poison your mind against me, and to drive me out from my paradise, to suffer again all I have suffered this last year."

"You mean that mad Sydney of whom you told me?"

"Yes. As soon as he hears of this good fortune to poor little Jean, he will hasten to mar it. He is my fate; I cannot escape him, and wherever he goes my friends desert me; for he has the power and uses it for my destruction. Let me go away and hide before he comes, for, having shared your confidence, it will break my heart to see you distrust and turn from me, instead of loving and protecting."

"My poor child, you are superstitious. Be easy. No one can harm you now, no one would dare attempt it. And as for my deserting you, that will soon be out of my power, if I have my way."

"How, dear Sir John?" asked Jean, with a flutter of intense relief at her heart, for the way seemed smoothing before her.

"I will make you my wife at once, if I may. This will free you from Gerald's love, protect you from Sydney's persecution, give you a safe home, and me the right to cherish and defend with heart and hand. Shall it be so, my child?"

"Yes; but oh, remember that I have no friend but you! Promise me to be faithful to the last—to believe in me, to trust me, protect and love me, in spite of all misfortunes, faults, and follies. I will be true as steel to you, and make your life as happy as it deserves to be. Let us promise these things now, and keep the promises unbroken to the end."

Her solemn air touched Sir John. Too honorable and upright himself to suspect falsehood in others, he saw only the natural impulse of a lovely girl in Jean's words, and, taking the hand she gave him in both of his, he promised all she asked, and kept that promise to the end. She paused an instant, with a pale, absent expression, as if she searched herself, then looked up clearly in the confiding face above her, and promised what she faithfully performed in afteryears.

"When shall it be, little sweetheart? I leave all to you, only let it be soon, else some gay young lover will appear, and take you from me," said Sir John, playfully, anxious to chase away the dark expression which had stolen over Jean's face.

"Can you keep a secret?" asked the girl, smiling up at him, all her charming self again.

"Try me."

"I will. Edward is coming home in three days. I must be gone before he comes. Tell no one of this; he wishes to surprise them. And if you love me, tell nobody of your approaching marriage. Do not betray that you care for me until I am really yours. There will be such a stir, such remonstrances, explanations, and reproaches that I shall be worn out, and run away from you all to escape the trial. If I could have my wish, I would go to some quiet place tomorrow and wait till you come for me. I know so little of such things, I cannot tell how soon we may be married; not for some weeks, I think."

"Tomorrow, if we like. A special license permits people to marry when and where they please. My plan is better than yours. Listen, and tell me if it can be carried out. I will go to town tomorrow, get the license, invite my friend, the Reverend Paul Fairfax, to return with me, and tomorrow evening you come at your usual time, and, in the presence of my discreet old servants, make me the happiest man in England. How does this suit you, my little Lady Coventry?"

The plan which seemed made to meet her ends, the name which was the height of her ambition, and the blessed sense of safety which came to her filled Jean Muir with such intense satisfaction that tears of real feeling stood in her eyes, and the glad assent she gave was the truest word that had passed her lips for months.

"We will go abroad or to Scotland for our honeymoon, till the storm blows over," said Sir John, well knowing that this hasty marriage would surprise or offend all his relations, and feeling as glad as Jean to escape the first excitement.

"To Scotland, please. I long to see my father's home," said Jean, who dreaded to meet Sydney on the continent.

They talked a little longer, arranging all things, Sir John so intent on hurrying the event that Jean had nothing to do but give a ready assent to all his suggestions. One fear alone disturbed her. If Sir John went to town, he might meet Edward, might hear and believe his statements. Then all would be lost. Yet this risk must be incurred, if the marriage was to be speedily and safely accomplished; and to guard against the meeting was Jean's sole care. As they went through the park—for Sir John insisted upon taking her home—she said, clinging to his arm:

"Dear friend, bear one thing in mind, else we shall be much annoyed, and all our plans disarranged. Avoid your nephews; you are so frank your face will betray you. They both love me, are both hot-tempered, and in the first excitement of the discovery might be violent. You must incur no danger, no disrespect for my sake; so shun them both till we are safe—particularly Edward. He will feel that his brother has wronged him, and that you have succeeded where he failed. This will irritate him, and I fear a stormy scene. Promise to avoid both for a day or two; do not listen to them, do not see them, do not write to or receive letters from them. It is foolish, I know; but you are all I have, and I am haunted by a strange foreboding that I am to lose you."

Touched and flattered by her tender solicitude, Sir John promised everything, even while he laughed at her fears. Love blinded the good gentleman to the peculiarity of the request; the novelty, romance, and secrecy of the affair rather bewildered though it charmed him; and the knowledge that he had outrivaled three young and ardent lovers gratified his vanity more than he would confess. Parting from the girl at the garden gate, he turned homeward, feeling like a boy again, and loitered back, humming a love lay, quite forgetful of evening damps, gout, and the five-and-fifty years which lay so lightly on his shoulders since Jean's arms had rested there. She hurried toward the house, anxious to escape Coventry; but he was waiting for her, and she was forced to meet him.

"How could you linger so long, and keep me in suspense?" he said reproachfully, as he took her hand and tried to catch a glimpse of her face in the shadow of her hat brim. "Come and rest in the grotto. I have so much to say, to hear and enjoy."

"Not now; I am too tired. Let me go in and sleep. Tomorrow we will talk. It is damp and chilly, and my head aches with all this worry." Jean spoke wearily, yet with a touch of petulance, and Coventry, fancying that she was piqued at his not coming for her, hastened to explain with eager tenderness.

"My poor little Jean, you do need rest. We wear you out, among us, and you never complain. I should have come to bring you home, but Lucia detained me, and when I got away I saw my uncle had forestalled me. I shall be jealous of the old gentleman, if he is so devoted. Jean, tell me one thing before we part; I am free as air, now, and have a right to speak. Do you love me? Am I the happy man who has won your heart? I dare to think so, to believe that this telltale face of yours has betrayed you, and to hope that I have gained what poor Ned and wild Sydney have lost."

"Before I answer, tell me of your interview with Lucia. I have a right to know," said Jean.

Coventry hesitated, for pity and remorse were busy at his heart when he recalled poor Lucia's grief. Jean was bent on hearing the humiliation of her rival. As the young man paused, she frowned, then lifted up her face wreathed in softest smiles, and laying her hand on his arm, she said, with most effective emphasis, half shy, half fond, upon his name, "Please tell me, Gerald!"

He could not resist the look, the touch, the tone, and taking the little hand in his, he said rapidly, as if the task was distasteful to him, "I told her that I did not, could not love her; that I had submitted to my mother's wish, and, for a time, had felt tacitly bound to her, though no words had passed between us. But now I demanded my liberty, regretting that the separation was not mutually desired."

"And she—what did she say? How did she bear it?" asked Jean, feeling in her own woman's heart how deeply Lucia's must have been wounded by that avowal.

"Poor girl! It was hard to bear, but her pride sustained her to the end. She owned that no pledge tied me, fully relinquished any claim my past behavior had seemed to have given her, and prayed that I might find another woman to love me as truly, tenderly as she had done. Jean, I felt like a villain; and yet I never plighted my word to her, never really loved her, and had a perfect right to leave her, if I would."

"Did she speak of me?"

"Yes."

"What did she say?"

"Must I tell you?"

"Yes, tell me everything. I know she hates me and I forgive her, knowing that I should hate any woman whom *you* loved."

"Are you jealous, dear?"

"Of you, Gerald?" And the fine eyes glanced up at him, full of a brilliancy that looked like the light of love.

"You make a slave of me already. How do you do it? I never obeyed a woman before. Jean, I think you are a witch. Scotland is the home of weird, uncanny creatures, who take lovely shapes for the bedevilment of poor weak souls. Are you one of those fair deceivers?"

"You are complimentary," laughed the girl. "I *am* a witch, and one day my disguise will drop away and you will see me as I am, old, ugly, bad and lost. Beware of me in time. I've warned you. Now love me at your peril."

Coventry had paused as he spoke, and eyed her with an unquiet look, conscious of some fascination which conquered yet brought no happiness. A feverish yet pleasurable excitement possessed him; a reckless mood, making him eager to obliterate the past by any rash act, any new experience which his passion brought. Jean regarded him with a wistful, almost woeful face, for one short moment; then a strange smile broke over it, as she spoke in a tone of malicious mockery, under which lurked the bitterness of a sad truth. Coventry looked half bewildered, and his eye went from the girl's mysterious face to a dimly lighted window, behind whose curtains poor Lucia hid her aching heart, praying for him the tender prayers that loving women give to those whose sins are all forgiven for love's sake. His heart smote him, and a momentary feeling of repulsion came over him, as he looked at Jean. She saw it, felt angry, yet conscious of a sense of relief; for now that her own safety was so nearly secured, she felt no wish to do mischief, but rather a desire to undo what was already done, and be at peace with all the world. To recall him to his allegiance, she sighed and walked on, saying gently yet coldly, "Will you tell me what I ask before I answer your question, Mr. Coventry?"

"What Lucia said of you? Well, it was this. 'Beware of Miss Muir. We instinctively distrusted her when we had no cause. I believe in instincts, and mine have never changed, for she has not tried to delude me. Her art is wonderful; I feel yet cannot explain or detect it, except in the working of events which her hand seems to guide. She has brought sorrow and dissension into this hitherto happy family. We are all changed, and this girl has done it. Me she can harm no further; you she will ruin, if she can. Beware of her in time, or you will bitterly repent your blind infatuation!'"

"And what answer did you make?" asked Jean, as the last words came reluctantly from Coventry's lips.

"I told her that I loved you in spite of myself, and would make you my wife in the face of all opposition. Now, Jean, your answer."

"Give me three days to think of it. Good night." And gliding from him, she vanished into the house, leaving him to roam about half the night, tormented with remorse, suspense, and the old distrust which would return when Jean was not there to banish it by her art.

❧ *chapter VIII* ❧

SUSPENSE

ALL the next day, Jean was in a state of the most intense anxiety, as every hour brought the crisis nearer, and every hour might bring defeat, for the subtlest human skill is often thwarted by some unforeseen accident. She longed to assure herself that Sir John was gone, but no servants came or went that day, and she could devise no pretext for sending to glean intelligence. She dared not go herself, lest the unusual act should excite suspicion, for she never went till evening. Even had she determined to venture, there was no time, for Mrs. Coventry was in one of her nervous states, and no one but Miss Muir could amuse her; Lucia was ill, and Miss Muir must give orders; Bella had a studious fit, and Jean must help her. Coventry lingered about the house for several hours, but Jean dared not send him, lest some hint of the truth might reach him. He had ridden away to his new duties when Jean did not appear, and the day dragged on wearisomely. Night came at last, and as Jean dressed for the late dinner, she hardly knew herself when she stood before her mirror, excitement lent such color and brilliancy to her countenance. Remembering the wedding which was to take place that evening, she put on a simple white dress and added a cluster of white roses in bosom and hair. She often wore flowers, but in spite of her desire to look and seem as usual, Bella's first words as she entered the drawing room were

"Why, Jean, how like a bride you look; a veil and gloves would make you quite complete!"

"You forget one other trifle, Bell," said Gerald, with eyes that brightened as they rested on Miss Muir.

"What is that?"asked his sister.

"A bridegroom."

Bella looked to see how Jean received this, but she seemed quite composed as she smiled one of her sudden smiles, and merely said, "That trifle will doubtless be found when the time comes. Is Miss Beaufort too ill for dinner?"

"She begs to be excused, and said you would be willing to take her place, she thought."

As innocent Bella delivered this message, Jean glanced at Coventry, who evaded her eye and looked ill at ease.

A little remorse will do him good, and prepare him for repentance after the grand *coup,* she said to herself, and was particularly gay at dinnertime, though Coventry looked often at Lucia's empty seat, as if he missed her. As soon as they left the table, Miss Muir sent Bella to her mother; and, knowing that Coventry would not linger long at his wine, she hurried away to the Hall. A servant was lounging at the door, and of him she asked, in a tone which was eager in spite of all efforts to be calm, "Is Sir John at home?"

"No, miss, he's just gone to town."

"Just gone! When do you mean?" cried Jean, forgetting the relief she felt in hearing of his absence in surprise at his late departure.

"He went half an hour ago, in the last train, miss."

"I thought he was going early this morning; he told me he should be back this evening."

"I believe he did mean to go, but was delayed by company. The steward came up on business, and a load of gentlemen called, so Sir John could not get off till night, when he wasn't fit to go, being worn out, and far from well."

"Do you think he will be ill? Did he look so?" And as Jean spoke, a thrill of fear passed over her, lest death should rob her of her prize.

"Well, you know, miss, hurry of any kind is bad for elderly gentlemen inclined to apoplexy. Sir John was in a worry all day, and not like himself. I wanted him to take his man, but he wouldn't; and drove off looking flushed and excited like. I'm anxious about him, for I know something is amiss to hurry him off in this way."

"When will he be back, Ralph?"

"Tomorrow noon, if possible; at night, certainly, he bid me tell anyone that called."

"Did he leave no note or message for Miss Coventry, or someone of the family?"

"No, miss, nothing."

"Thank you." And Jean walked back to spend a restless night and rise to meet renewed suspense.

The morning seemed endless, but noon came at last, and under the pretense of seeking coolness in the grotto, Jean stole away to a slope whence the gate to the Hall park was visible. For two long hours she watched, and no one came. She was just turning away when a horseman dashed through the gate and came galloping toward the Hall. Heedless of everything but the uncontrollable longing to gain some tidings, she ran to meet him, feeling assured that he brought ill news. It was a young man from the station, and as he caught sight of her, he drew bridle, looking agitated and undecided.

"Has anything happened?" she cried breathlessly.

"A dreadful accident on the railroad, just the other side of Croydon. News telegraphed half an hour ago," answered the man, wiping his hot face.

"The noon train? Was Sir John in it? Quick, tell me all!"

"It was that train, miss, but whether Sir John was in it or not, we don't know; for the guard is killed, and everything is in such confusion that nothing can be certain. They are at work getting out the dead and wounded. We heard that Sir John was expected, and I came up to tell Mr. Coventry, thinking he would wish to go down. A train leaves in fifteen minutes; where shall I find him? I was told he was at the Hall."

"Ride on, ride on! And find him if he is there. I'll run home and look for him. Lose no time. Ride! Ride!" And turning, Jean sped back like a deer, while the man tore up the avenue to rouse the Hall.

Coventry was there, and went off at once, leaving both Hall and house in dismay. Fearing to betray the horrible anxiety that possessed her, Jean shut herself up in her room and suffered untold agonies as the day wore on and no news came. At dark a sudden cry rang through the house, and Jean rushed down to learn the cause. Bella was standing in the hall, holding a letter, while a group of excited servants hovered near her.

"What is it?" demanded Miss Muir, pale and steady, though her heart died within her as she recognized Gerald's handwriting. Bella gave her the note, and hushed her sobbing to hear again the heavy tidings that had come.

> *Dear Bella:*
>
>   *Uncle is safe; he did not go in the noon train. But several persons are sure that Ned was there. No trace of him as yet, but many bodies are in the river, under the ruins of the bridge, and I am doing my best to find the poor lad, if he is there. I have sent to all his haunts in town, and as he has not been seen, I hope it is a false report and he is safe with his regiment. Keep this from my mother till we are sure. I write you, because Lucia is ill. Miss Muir will comfort and sustain you. Hope for the best, dear.*
>
>   *Yours, G. C.*

Those who watched Miss Muir as she read these words wondered at the strange expressions which passed over her face, for the joy which appeared there as Sir John's safety was made known did not change to grief or horror at poor Edward's possible fate. The smile died on her lips, but her voice did not falter, and in her downcast eyes shone an inexplicable look of something like triumph. No wonder, for if this was true, the danger which menaced her was averted for a time, and the marriage might be consummated without such desperate haste. This sad and sudden event seemed to her the mysterious fulfilment of a secret wish; and though startled she was not daunted but inspirited, for fate seemed to favor her designs. She did comfort Bella, control the excited household, and keep the rumors from Mrs. Coventry all that dreadful night.

At dawn Gerald came home exhausted, and bringing no tiding of the missing man. He had telegraphed to the headquarters of the regiment and received a reply, stating that Edward had left for London the previous day, meaning to go home before returning. The fact of his having been at the London station was also established, but whether he left by the train or not was still uncertain. The ruins were still being searched, and the body might yet appear.

"Is Sir John coming at noon?" asked Jean, as the three sat together in the rosy hush of dawn, trying to hope against hope.

"No, he had been ill, I learned from young Gower, who is just from town, and so had not completed his business. I sent him word to wait till night, for the bridge won't be passable till then. Now I must try and rest an hour; I've worked all night and have no strength left. Call me the instant any messenger arrives."

With that Coventry went to his room, Bella followed to wait on him, and Jean roamed through house and grounds, unable to rest. The morning was far spent when the messenger arrived. Jean went to receive his tidings, with the wicked hope still lurking at her heart.

"Is he found?" she asked calmly, as the man hesitated to speak.

"Yes, ma'am."

"You are sure?"

"I am certain, ma'am, though some won't say till Mr. Coventry comes to look."

"Is he alive?" And Jean's white lips trembled as she put the question.

"Oh no, ma'am, that warn't possible, under all them stones and water. The poor young gentleman is so wet, and crushed, and torn, no one would know him, except for the uniform, and the white hand with the ring on it."

Jean sat down, very pale, and the man described the finding of the poor shattered body. As he finished, Coventry appeared, and with one look of mingled remorse, shame, and sorrow, the elder brother went away, to find and bring the younger home. Jean crept into the garden like a guilty thing, trying to hide the satisfaction which struggled with a woman's natural pity, for so sad an end for this brave young life.

"Why waste tears or feign sorrow when I must be glad?" she muttered, as she paced to and fro along the terrace. "The poor boy is out of pain, and I am out of danger."

She got no further, for, turning as she spoke, she stood face to face with Edward! Bearing no mark of peril on dress or person, but stalwart and strong as ever, he stood there looking at her, with contempt and compassion struggling in his face. As if turned to stone, she remained motionless, with dilated eyes, arrested breath, and paling cheek. He did not speak but watched her silently till she put out a trembling hand, as if to assure herself by touch that it was really he. Then he drew back, and as if the act convinced as fully as words, she said slowly, "They told me you were dead."

"And you were glad to believe it. No, it was my comrade, young Courtney, who unconsciously deceived you all, and lost his life, as I should have done, if I had not gone to Ascot after seeing him off yesterday."

"To Ascot?" echoed Jean, shrinking back, for Edward's eye was on her, and his voice was stern and cold.

"Yes; you know the place. I went there to make inquiries concerning you and was well satisfied. Why are you still here?"

"The three days are not over yet. I hold you to your promise. Before night I shall be gone; till then you will be silent, if you have honor enough to keep your word."

"I have." Edward took out his watch and, as he put it back, said with cool precision, "It is now two, the train leaves for London at half-past six; a carriage will wait for you at the side door. Allow me to advise you to go then, for the instant dinner is over I shall speak." And with a bow he went into the house, leaving Jean nearly suffocated with a throng of contending emotions.

For a few minutes she seemed paralyzed; but the native energy of the woman forbade utter despair, till the last hope was gone. Frail as that now was, she still clung to it tenaciously, resolving to win the game in defiance of everything. Springing up, she went to her room, packed her few valuables, dressed herself with care, and then sat down to wait. She heard a joyful stir below, saw Coventry come hurrying back, and from a garrulous maid learned that the body was that of young Courtney. The uniform being the same as Edward's and the ring, a gift from him, had caused the men to believe the disfigured corpse to be that of the younger Coventry. No one but the maid came near her; once Bella's voice called her, but some one checked the girl, and the call was not repeated. At five an envelope was brought her, directed in Edward's hand, and containing a check which more than paid a year's salary. No word accompanied the gift, yet the generosity of it touched her, for Jean Muir had the relics of a once honest nature, and despite her falsehood could still admire nobleness and respect virtue. A tear of genuine shame dropped on the paper, and real gratitude filled her heart, as she thought that even if all else failed, she was not thrust out penniless into the world, which had no pity for poverty.

As the clock struck six, she heard a carriage drive around and went down to meet it. A servant put on her trunk, gave the order, "To the station, James," and she drove away without meeting anyone, speaking to anyone, or apparently being seen by anyone. A sense of utter weariness came over her, and she longed to lie down and forget. But the last chance still remained, and till that failed, she would not give up. Dismissing the carriage, she seated herself to watch for the quarter-past-six train from London, for in that Sir John would come if he came at all that night. She was haunted by the fear that Edward had met and told him. The first glimpse of Sir John's frank face would betray the truth. If he knew all, there was no hope, and she would go her way alone. If he knew nothing, there was yet time for the marriage; and once his wife, she knew she was safe, because for the honor of his name he would screen and protect her.

Up rushed the train, out stepped Sir John, and Jean's heart died within her. Grave, and pale, and worn he looked, and leaned heavily on the arm of a portly gentleman in black. The Reverend Mr. Fairfax, why has he come, if the secret is out? thought Jean, slowly advancing to meet them and fearing to read her fate in Sir John's face. He saw her, dropped his friend's arm, and hurried forward with the ardor of a young man, exclaiming, as he seized her hand with a beaming face, a glad voice, "My little girl! Did you think I would never come?"

She could not answer, the reaction was too strong, but she clung to him, regardless of time or place, and felt that her last hope had not failed. Mr. Fairfax proved himself equal to the occasion. Asking no questions, he hurried Sir John and Jean into a carriage and stepped in after them with a bland apology. Jean was soon herself again, and, having told her fears at his delay, listened eagerly while he related the various mishaps which had detained him.

"Have you seen Edward?" was her first question.

"Not yet, but I know he has come, and have heard of his narrow escape. I should have been in that train, if I had not been delayed by the indisposition which I then cursed, but now bless. Are you ready, Jean? Do you repent your choice, my child?"

"No, nô! I am ready, I am only too happy to become your wife, dear, generous Sir John," cried Jean, with a glad alacrity, which touched the old man to the heart, and charmed the Reverend Mr. Fairfax, who concealed the romance of a boy under his clerical suit.

They reached the Hall. Sir John gave orders to admit no one and after a hasty dinner sent for his old housekeeper and his steward, told them of his purpose, and desired them to witness his marriage. Obedience had been the law of their lives, and Master could do nothing wrong in their eyes, so they played their parts willingly, for Jean was a favorite at the Hall. Pale as her gown, but calm and steady, she stood beside Sir John, uttering her vows in a clear tone and taking upon herself the vows of a wife with more than a bride's usual docility. When the ring was fairly on, a smile broke over her face. When Sir John kissed and called her his "little wife," she shed a tear or two of sincere happiness; and when Mr. Fairfax addressed her as "my lady," she laughed her musical laugh, and glanced up at a picture of Gerald with eyes full of exultation. As the servants left the room, a message was brought from Mrs. Coventry, begging Sir John to come to her at once.

"You will not go and leave me so soon?" pleaded Jean, well knowing why he was sent for.

"My darling, I must." And in spite of its tenderness, Sir John's manner was too decided to be withstood.

"Then I shall go with you," cried Jean, resolving that no earthly power should part them.

❧ *chapter IX* ❧

LADY COVENTRY

W HEN the first excitement of Edward's return had subsided, and before they could question him as to the cause of this unexpected visit, he told them that after dinner their curiosity should be gratified, and meantime he begged them to leave Miss Muir alone, for she had received bad news and must not be disturbed. The family with difficulty restrained their tongues and waited impatiently. Gerald confessed his love for Jean and asked his brother's pardon for betraying his trust. He had expected an outbreak, but Edward only looked at him with pitying eyes, and said sadly, "You too! I have no reproaches to make, for I know what you will suffer when the truth is known."

"What do you mean?" demanded Coventry.

"You will soon know, my poor Gerald, and we will comfort one another."

Nothing more could be drawn from Edward till dinner was over, the servants gone, and all the family alone together. Then pale and grave, but very self-possessed, for trouble had made a man of him, he produced a packet of letters, and said, addressing himself to his brother, "Jean Muir has deceived us all. I know her story; let me tell it before I read her letters."

"Stop! I'll not listen to any false tales against her. The poor girl has enemies who belie her!" cried Gerald, starting up.

"For the honor of the family, you must listen, and learn what fools she has made of us. I can prove what I say, and convince you that she has the art of a devil. Sit still ten minutes, then go, if you will."

Edward spoke with authority, and his brother obeyed him with a foreboding heart.

"I met Sydney, and he begged me to beware of her. Nay, listen, Gerald! I know she has told her story, and that you believe it; but her own letters convict her. She tried to charm Sydney as she did us, and nearly succeeded in inducing him to marry her. Rash and wild as he is, he is still a gentleman, and when an incautious word of hers roused his suspicions, he refused to make her his wife. A stormy scene ensued, and, hoping to intimidate him, she feigned to stab herself as if in despair. She did wound herself, but failed to gain her point and insisted upon going to a hospital to die. Lady Sydney, good, simple soul, believed the girl's version of the story, thought her son was in the wrong, and when he was gone, tried to atone for his fault by finding Jean Muir another home. She thought Gerald was soon to marry Lucia, and that I was away, so sent her here as a safe and comfortable retreat."

"But, Ned, are you sure of all this? Is Sydney to be believed?" began Coventry, still incredulous.

"To convince you, I'll read Jean's letters before I say more. They were written to an accomplice and were purchased by Sydney. There was a compact between the two women, that each should keep the other informed of all adventures, plots and plans, and share whatever good fortune fell to the lot of either. Thus Jean wrote freely, as you shall judge. The letters concern us alone. The first was written a few days after she came.

"Dear Hortense:

"Another failure. Sydney was more wily than I thought. All was going well, when one day my old fault beset me, I took too much wine, and I carelessly owned that I had been an actress. He was shocked, and retreated. I got up a scene, and gave myself a safe little wound, to frighten him. The brute was not frightened, but coolly left me to my fate. I'd have died to spite him, if I dared, but as I didn't, I lived to torment him. As yet, I have had no chance, but I will not forget him. His mother is a poor, weak creature, whom I could use as I would, and through her I found an excellent place. A sick mother, silly daughter, and two eligible

sons. One is engaged to a handsome iceberg, but that only renders him more interesting in my eyes, rivalry adds so much to the charm of one's conquests. Well, my dear, I went, got up in the meek style, intending to do the pathetic; but before I saw the family, I was so angry I could hardly control myself. Through the indolence of Monsieur the young master, no carriage was sent for me, and I intend he shall atone for that rudeness by-and-by. The younger son, the mother, and the girl received me patronizingly, and I understood the simple souls at once. Monsieur (as I shall call him, as names are unsafe) was unapproachable, and took no pains to conceal his dislike of governesses. The cousin was lovely, but detestable with her pride, her coldness, and her very visible adoration of Monsieur, who let her worship him, like an inanimate idol as he is. I hated them both, of course, and in return for their insolence shall torment her with jealousy, and teach him how to woo a woman by making his heart ache. They are an intensely proud family, but I can humble them all, I think, by captivating the sons, and when they have committed themselves, cast them off, and marry the old uncle, whose title takes my fancy."

"She never wrote that! It is impossible. A woman could not do it," cried Lucia indignantly, while Bella sat bewildered and Mrs. Coventry supported herself with salts and fan. Coventry went to his brother, examined the writing, and returned to his seat, saying, in a tone of suppressed wrath, "She did write it. I posted some of those letters myself. Go on, Ned."

"I made myself useful and agreeable to the amiable ones, and overheard the chat of the lovers. It did not suit me, so I fainted away to stop it, and excite interest in the provoking pair. I thought I had succeeded, but Monsieur suspected me and showed me that he did. I forgot my meek role and gave him a stage look. It had a good effect, and I shall try it again. The man is well worth winning, but I prefer the title, and as the uncle is a hale, handsome gentleman, I can't wait for him to die, though Monsieur is very charming, with his elegant languor, and his heart so fast asleep no woman has had power to wake it yet. I told my story, and they believed it, though I had the audacity to say I was but nineteen, to talk Scotch, and bashfully confess that Sydney wished to marry me. Monsieur knows S. and evidently suspects something. I must watch him and keep the truth from him, if possible.

"I was very miserable that night when I got alone. Something in the atmosphere of this happy home made me wish I was anything but what I am. As I sat there trying to pluck up my spirits, I thought of the days when I was lovely and young, good and gay. My glass showed me an old woman of thirty, for my false locks were off, my paint gone, and my face was without its mask. Bah! how I hate sentiment! I drank your health from your own little flask, and went to bed to dream that I was playing Lady Tartuffe—as I am. Adieu, more soon."

No one spoke as Edward paused, and taking up another letter, he read on:

"My Dear Creature:

"All goes well. Next day I began my task, and having caught a hint of the character of each, tried my power over them. Early in the morning I ran over to see the Hall. Approved of it highly, and took the first step toward becoming its mistress, by piquing the curiosity and flattering the pride of its master. His estate is his idol; I praised it with a few artless compliments to himself, and he was charmed. The cadet of the family adores horses. I risked my neck to pet his beast, and he was charmed. The little girl is romantic about flowers; I made a posy and was sentimental, and she was charmed. The fair icicle loves her departed mamma, I had raptures over an old picture, and she thawed. Monsieur is used to being worshipped. I took no notice of him, and by the natural perversity of human nature, he began to take notice of me. He likes music; I sang, and stopped when he'd listened long enough to want more. He is lazily fond of being amused; I showed him my skill, but refused to exert it in his behalf. In short, I gave him no peace till he began to wake up. In order to get rid of the boy, I fascinated him, and he was sent away. Poor lad, I rather liked him, and if the title had been nearer would have married him.

"Many thanks for the honor." And Edward's lip curled with intense scorn. But Gerald sat like a statue, his teeth set, his eyes fiery, his brows bent, waiting for the end.

"The passionate boy nearly killed his brother, but I turned the affair to good account, and bewitched Monsieur by playing nurse, till Vashti (the icicle) interfered. Then I enacted injured virtue, and kept out of his way, knowing that he would miss me. I mystified him about S. by sending a letter where S. would not get it, and got up all manner of soft scenes to win this proud

creature. I get on well and meanwhile privately fascinate Sir J.
by being daughterly and devoted. He is a worthy old man, simple
as a child, honest as the day, and generous as a prince. I shall be
a happy woman if I win him, and you shall share my good fortune; so wish me success.

"This is the third, and contains something which will surprise
you," Edward said, as he lifted another paper.

"Hortense:

"I've done what I once planned to do on another occasion.
You know my handsome, dissipated father married a lady of rank
for his second wife. I never saw Lady H_____d but once, for
I was kept out of the way. Finding that this good Sir J. knew
something of her when a girl, and being sure that he did not
know of the death of her little daughter, I boldly said I was the
child, and told a pitiful tale of my early life. It worked like a
charm; he told Monsieur, and both felt the most chivalrous compassion for Lady Howard's daughter, though before they had
secretly looked down on me, and my real poverty and my lowli-
ness. That boy pitied me with an honest warmth and never waited
to learn my birth. I don't forget that and shall repay it if I can.
Wishing to bring Monsieur's affair to a successful crisis, I got up
a theatrical evening and was in my element. One little event I
must tell you, because I committed an actionable offense and was
nearly discovered. I did not go down to supper, knowing that the
moth would return to flutter about the candle, and preferring that
the fluttering should be done in private, as Vashti's jealousy is
getting uncontrollable. Passing through the gentlemen's dressing
room, my quick eye caught sight of a letter lying among the costumes. It was no stage affair, and an odd sensation of fear ran
through me as I recognized the hand of S. I had feared this, but
I believe in chance; and having found the letter, I examined it.
You know I can imitate almost any hand. When I read in this
paper the whole story of my affair with S., truly told, and also
that he had made inquiries into my past life and discovered the
truth, I was in a fury. To be so near success and fail was terrible,
and I resolved to risk everything. I opened the letter by means of
a heated knife blade under the seal, therefore the envelope was
perfect; imitating S.'s hand, I penned a few lines in his hasty
style, saying he was at Baden, so that if Monsieur answered, the
reply would not reach him, for he is in London, it seems. This
letter I put into the pocket whence the other must have fallen,

and was just congratulating myself on this narrow escape, when Dean, the maid of Vashti, appeared as if watching me. She had evidently seen the letter in my hand, and suspected something. I took no notice of her, but must be careful, for she is on the watch. After this the evening closed with strictly private theatricals, in which Monsieur and myself were the only actors. To make sure that he received my version of the story first, I told him a romantic story of S.'s persecution, and he believed it. This I followed up by a moonlight episode behind a rose hedge, and sent the young gentleman home in a half-dazed condition. What fools men are!"

"She is right!" muttered Coventry, who had flushed scarlet with shame and anger, as his folly became known and Lucia listened in astonished silence.

"Only one more, and my distasteful task will be nearly over," said Edward, unfolding the last of the papers. "This is not a letter, but a copy of one written three nights ago. Dean boldly ransacked Jean Muir's desk while she was at the Hall, and, fearing to betray the deed by keeping the letter, she made a hasty copy which she gave me today, begging me to save the family from disgrace. This makes the chain complete. Go now, if you will, Gerald. I would gladly spare you the pain of hearing this."

"I will not spare myself; I deserve it. Read on," replied Coventry, guessing what was to follow and nerving himself to hear it. Reluctantly his brother read these lines:

"The enemy has surrendered! Give me joy, Hortense; I can be the wife of this proud monsieur, if I will. Think what an honor for the divorced wife of a disreputable actor. I laugh at the farce and enjoy it, for I only wait till the prize I desire is fairly mine, to turn and reject this lover who has proved himself false to brother, mistress, and his own conscience. I resolved to be revenged on both, and I have kept my word. For my sake he cast off the beautiful woman who truly loved him; he forgot his promise to his brother, and put by his pride to beg of me the worn-out heart that is not worth a good man's love. Ah well, I am satisfied, for Vashti has suffered the sharpest pain a proud woman can endure, and will feel another pang when I tell her that I scorn her recreant lover, and give him back to her, to deal with as she will."

Coventry started from his seat with a fierce exclamation, but

Lucia bowed her face upon her hands, weeping, as if the pang had been sharper than even Jean foresaw.

"Send for Sir John! I am mortally afraid of this creature. Take her away; do something to her. My poor Bella, what a companion for you! Send for Sir John at once!" cried Mrs. Coventry incoherently, and clasped her daughter in her arms, as if Jean Muir would burst in to annihilate the whole family. Edward alone was calm.

"I have already sent, and while we wait, let me finish this story. It is true that Jean is the daughter of Lady Howard's husband, the pretended clergyman, but really a worthless man who married her for her money. Her own child died, but this girl, having beauty, wit and a bold spirit, took her fate into her own hands, and became an actress. She married an actor, led a reckless life for some years; quarreled with her husband, was divorced, and went to Paris; left the stage, and tried to support herself as governess and companion. You know how she fared with the Sydneys, how she has duped us, and but for this discovery would have duped Sir John. I was in time to prevent this, thank heaven. She is gone; no one knows the truth but Sydney and ourselves; he will be silent, for his own sake; we will be for ours, and leave this dangerous woman to the fate which will surely overtake her."

"Thank you, it has overtaken her, and a very happy one she finds it."

A soft voice uttered the words, and an apparition appeared at the door, which made all start and recoil with amazement—Jean Muir leaning on the arm of Sir John.

"How dare you return?" began Edward, losing the self-control so long preserved. "How dare you insult us by coming back to enjoy the mischief you have done? Uncle, you do not know that woman!"

"Hush, boy, I will not listen to a word, unless you remember where you are," said Sir John, with a commanding gesture.

"Remember your promise: love me, forgive me, protect me, and do not listen to their accusations," whispered Jean, whose quick eye had discovered the letters.

"I will; have no fears, my child," he answered, drawing her nearer as he took his accustomed place before the fire, always lighted when Mrs. Coventry was down.

Gerald, who had been pacing the room excitedly, paused behind Lucia's chair as if to shield her from insult; Bella clung to her mother;

and Edward, calming himself by a strong effort, handed his uncle the letters, saying briefly, "Look at those, sir, and let them speak."

"I will look at nothing, hear nothing, believe nothing which can in any way lessen my respect and affection for this young lady. She has prepared me for this. I know the enemy who is unmanly enough to belie and threaten her. I know that you both are unsuccessful lovers, and this explains your unjust, uncourteous treatment now. We all have committed faults and follies. I freely forgive Jean hers, and desire to know nothing of them from your lips. If she has innocently offended, pardon it for my sake, and forget the past."

"But, Uncle, we have proofs that this woman is not what she seems. Her own letters convict her. Read them, and do not blindly deceive yourself," cried Edward, indignant at his uncle's words.

A low laugh startled them all, and in an instant they saw the cause of it. While Sir John spoke, Jean had taken the letters from the hand which he had put behind him, a favorite gesture of his, and, unobserved, had dropped them on the fire. The mocking laugh, the sudden blaze, showed what had been done. Both young men sprang forward, but it was too late; the proofs were ashes, and Jean Muir's bold, bright eyes defied them, as she said, with a disdainful little gesture, "Hands off, gentlemen! You may degrade yourselves to the work of detectives, but I am not a prisoner yet. Poor Jean Muir you might harm, but Lady Coventry is beyond your reach."

"Lady Coventry!" echoed the dismayed family, in varying tones of incredulity, indignation, and amazement.

"Aye, my dear and honored wife," said Sir John, with a protecting arm about the slender figure at his side; and in the act, the words, there was a tender dignity that touched the listeners with pity and respect for the deceived man. "Receive her as such, and for my sake, forbear all further accusation," he continued steadily. "I know what I have done. I have no fear that I shall repent it. If I am blind, let me remain so till time opens my eyes. We are going away for a little while, and when we return, let the old life return again, unchanged, except that Jean makes sunshine for me as well as for you."

No one spoke, for no one knew what to say. Jean broke the silence, saying coolly, "May I ask how those letters came into your possession?"

"In tracing out your past life, Sydney found your friend Hortense.

She was poor, money bribed her, and your letters were given up to him as soon as received. Traitors are always betrayed in the end," replied Edward sternly.

Jean shrugged her shoulders, and shot a glance at Gerald, saying with her significant smile, "Remember that, monsieur, and allow me to hope that in wedding you will be happier than in wooing. Receive my congratulations, Miss Beaufort, and let me beg of you to follow my example, if you would keep your lovers."

Here all the sarcasm passed from her voice, the defiance from her eye, and the one unspoiled attribute which still lingered in this woman's artful nature shone in her face, as she turned toward Edward and Bella at their mother's side.

"You have been kind to me," she said, with grateful warmth. "I thank you for it, and will repay it if I can. To you I will acknowledge that I am not worthy to be this good man's wife, and to you I will solemnly promise to devote my life to his happiness. For his sake forgive me, and let there be peace between us."

There was no reply, but Edward's indignant eyes fell before hers. Bella half put out her hand, and Mrs. Coventry sobbed as if some regret mingled with her resentment. Jean seemed to expect no friendly demonstration, and to understand that they forbore for Sir John's sake, not for hers, and to accept their contempt as her just punishment.

"Come home, love, and forget all this," said her husband, ringing the bell, and eager to be gone. "Lady Coventry's carriage."

And as he gave the order, a smile broke over her face, for the sound assured her that the game was won. Pausing an instant on the threshold before she vanished from their sight, she looked backward, and fixing on Gerald the strange glance he remembered well, she said in her penetrating voice, "Is not the last scene better than the first?"

Pauline's Passion

~ *and* ~

PUNISHMENT

≱ *chapter I* ≰

TO and fro, like a wild creature in its cage, paced that handsome woman, with bent head, locked hands, and restless steps. Some mental storm, swift and sudden as a tempest of the tropics, had swept over her and left its marks behind. As if in anger at the beauty now proved powerless, all ornaments had been flung away, yet still it shone undimmed, and filled her with a passionate regret. A jewel glittered at her feet, leaving the lace rent to shreds on the indignant bosom that had worn it; the wreaths of hair that had crowned her with a woman's most womanly adornment fell disordered upon shoulders that gleamed the fairer for the scarlet of the pomegranate flowers clinging to the bright meshes that had imprisoned them an hour ago; and over the face, once so affluent in youthful bloom, a stern pallor had fallen like a blight, for pride was slowly conquering passion, and despair had murdered hope.

Pausing in her troubled march, she swept away the curtain swaying in the wind and looked out, as if imploring help from Nature, the great mother of us all. A summer moon rode high in a cloudless heaven, and far as eye could reach stretched the green wilderness of a Cuban *cafetal*. No forest, but a tropical orchard, rich in lime, banana, plantain, palm, and orange trees, under whose protective shade grew the evergreen coffee plant, whose dark-red berries are the fortune of their possessor, and the luxury of one-half the world. Wide avenues diverging from the mansion, with its belt of brilliant shrubs and

flowers, formed shadowy vistas, along which, on the wings of the wind, came a breath of far-off music, like a wooing voice; for the magic of night and distance lulled the cadence of a Spanish *contradanza* to a trance of sound, soft, subdued, and infinitely sweet. It was a southern scene, but not a southern face that looked out upon it with such unerring glance; there was no southern languor in the figure, stately and erect; no southern swarthiness on fairest cheek and arm; no southern darkness in the shadowy gold of the neglected hair; the light frost of northern snows lurked in the features, delicately cut, yet vividly alive, betraying a temperament ardent, dominant, and subtle. For passion burned in the deep eyes, changing their violet to black. Pride sat on the forehead, with its dark brows; all a woman's sweetest spells touched the lips, whose shape was a smile; and in the spirited carriage of the head appeared the freedom of an intellect ripened under colder skies, the energy of a nature that could wring strength from suffering, and dare to act where feebler souls would only dare desire.

Standing thus, conscious only of the wound that bled in that high heart of hers, and the longing that gradually took shape and deepened to a purpose, an alien presence changed the tragic atmosphere of that still room and woke her from her dangerous mood. A wonderfully winning guise this apparition wore, for youth, hope, and love endowed it with the charm that gives beauty to the plainest, while their reign endures. A boy in any other climate, in this his nineteen years had given him the stature of a man; and Spain, the land of romance, seemed embodied in this figure, full of the lithe slenderness of the whispering palms overhead, the warm coloring of the deep-toned flowers sleeping in the room, the native grace of the tame antelope lifting its human eyes to his as he lingered on the threshold in an attitude eager yet timid, watching that other figure as it looked into the night and found no solace there.

"Pauline!"

She turned as if her thought had taken voice and answered her, regarded him a moment, as if hesitating to receive the granted wish, then beckoned with the one word.

"Come!"

Instantly the fear vanished, the ardor deepened, and with an imperious "Lie down!" to his docile attendant, the young man obeyed with equal docility, looking as wistfully toward his mistress as the brute toward her master, while he waited proudly humble for her commands.

"Manuel, why are you here?"

"Forgive me! I saw Dolores bring a letter; you vanished, an hour passed, I could wait no longer, and I came."

"I am glad, I needed my one friend. Read that."

She offered a letter, and with her steady eyes upon him, her purpose strengthening as she looked, stood watching the changes of that expressive countenance. This was the letter:

> *Pauline—*
>
> *Six months ago I left you, promising to return and take you home my wife; I loved you, but I deceived you; for though my heart was wholly yours, my hand was not mine to give. This it was that haunted me through all that blissful summer, this that marred my happiness when you owned you loved me, and this drove me from you, hoping I could break the tie with which I had rashly bound myself. I could not, I am married, and there all ends. Hate me, forget me, solace your pride with the memory that none knew your wrong, assure your peace with the knowledge that mine is destroyed forever, and leave my punishment to remorse and time.*
>
> *Gilbert*

With a gesture of wrathful contempt, Manuel flung the paper from him as he flashed a look at his companion, muttering through his teeth, "Traitor! Shall I kill him?"

Pauline laughed low to herself, a dreary sound, but answered with a slow darkening of the face that gave her words an ominous significance. "Why should you? Such revenge is brief and paltry, fit only for mock tragedies or poor souls who have neither the will to devise nor the will to execute a better. There are fates more terrible than death; weapons more keen than poniards, more noiseless than pistols. Women use such, and work out a subtler vengeance than men can conceive. Leave Gilbert to remorse—and me."

She paused an instant, and by some strong effort banished the black frown from her brow, quenched the baleful fire of her eyes, and left nothing visible but the pale determination that made her beautiful face more eloquent than her words.

"Manuel, in a week I leave the island."

"Alone, Pauline?"

"No, not alone."

A moment they looked into each other's eyes, each endeavoring to read the other. Manuel saw some indomitable purpose, bent on conquering all obstacles. Pauline saw doubt, desire, and hope; knew that a word would bring the ally she needed; and, with a courage as native to her as her pride, resolved to utter it.

Seating herself, she beckoned her companion to assume the place beside her, but for the first time he hesitated. Something in the unnatural calmness of her manner troubled him, for his southern temperament was alive to influences whose presence would have been unfelt by one less sensitive. He took the cushion at her feet, saying, half tenderly, half reproachfully, "Let me keep my old place till I know in what character I am to fill the new. The man you trusted has deserted you; the boy you pitied will prove loyal. Try him, Pauline."

"I will."

And with the bitter smile unchanged upon her lips, the low voice unshaken in its tones, the deep eyes unwavering in their gaze, Pauline went on:

"You know my past, happy as a dream till eighteen. Then all was swept away, home, fortune, friends, and I was left, like an unfledged bird, without even the shelter of a cage. For five years I have made my life what I could, humble, honest, but never happy, till I came here, for here I saw Gilbert. In the poor companion of your guardian's daughter he seemed to see the heiress I had been, and treated me as such. This flattered my pride and touched my heart. He was kind, I grateful; then he loved me, and God knows how utterly I loved him! A few months of happiness the purest, then he went to make home ready for me, and I believed him; for where I wholly love I wholly trust. While my own peace was undisturbed, I learned to read the language of your eyes, Manuel, to find the boy grown into the man, the friend warmed into a lover. Your youth had kept me blind too long. Your society had grown dear to me, and I loved you like a sister for your unvarying kindness to the solitary woman who earned her bread and found it bitter. I told you my secret to prevent the utterance of your own. You remember the promise you made me then, keep it still, and bury the knowledge of my lost happiness deep in your pitying heart, as I shall in my proud one. Now the storm is over, and I am ready for my work again, but it must be a new task in a new scene. I hate this house, this room, the faces I must meet, the duties

I must perform, for the memory of that traitor haunts them all. I see a future full of interest, a stage whereon I could play a stirring part. I long for it intensely, yet cannot make it mine alone. Manuel, do you love me still?"

Bending suddenly, she brushed back the dark hair that streaked his forehead and searched the face that in an instant answered her. Like a swift rising light, the eloquent blood rushed over swarthy cheek and brow, the slumberous softness of the eyes kindled with a flash, and the lips, sensitive as any woman's, trembled yet broke into a rapturous smile as he cried, with fervent brevity, "I would die for you!"

A look of triumph swept across her face, for with this boy, as chivalrous as ardent, she knew that words were not mere breath. Still, with her stern purpose uppermost, she changed the bitter smile into one half-timid, half-tender, as she bent still nearer, "Manuel, in a week I leave the island. Shall I go alone?"

"No, Pauline."

He understood her now. She saw it in the sudden paleness that fell on him, heard it in the rapid beating of his heart, felt it in the strong grasp that fastened on her hand, and knew that the first step was won. A regretful pang smote her, but the dark mood which had taken possession of her stifled the generous warnings of her better self and drove her on.

"Listen, Manuel. A strange spirit rules me tonight, but I will have no reserves from you, all shall be told; then, if you will come, be it so; if not, I shall go my way as solitary as I came. If you think that this loss has broken my heart, undeceive yourself, for such as I live years in an hour and show no sign. I have shed no tears, uttered no cry, asked no comfort; yet, since I read that letter, I have suffered more than many suffer in a lifetime. I am not one to lament long over any hopeless sorrow. A single paroxysm, sharp and short, and it is over. Contempt has killed my love, I have buried it, and no power can make it live again, except as a pale ghost that will not rest till Gilbert shall pass through an hour as bitter as the last."

"Is that the task you give yourself, Pauline?"

The savage element that lurks in southern blood leaped up in the boy's heart as he listened, glittered in his eye, and involuntarily found expression in the nervous grip of the hands that folded a fairer one between them. Alas for Pauline that she had roused the sleeping devil, and was glad to see it!

"Yes, it is weak, wicked, and unwomanly; yet I persist as relentlessly as any Indian on a war trail. See me as I am, not the gay girl you have known, but a revengeful woman with but one tender spot now left in her heart, the place you fill. I have been wronged, and I long to right myself at once. Time is too slow; I cannot wait, for that man must be taught that two can play at the game of hearts, taught soon and sharply. I can do this, can wound as I have been wounded, can sting him with contempt, and prove that I too can forget."

"Go on, Pauline. Show me how I am to help you."

"Manuel, I want fortune, rank, splendor, and power; you can give me all these, and a faithful friend beside. I desire to show Gilbert the creature he deserted no longer poor, unknown, unloved, but lifted higher than himself, cherished, honored, applauded, her life one of royal pleasure, herself a happy queen. Beauty, grace, and talent you tell me I possess; wealth gives them luster, rank exalts them, power makes them irresistible. Place these worldly gifts in my hand and that hand is yours. See, I offer it."

She did so, but it was not taken. Manuel had left his seat and now stood before her, awed by the undertone of strong emotion in her calmly spoken words, bewildered by the proposal so abruptly made, longing to ask the natural question hovering on his lips, yet too generous to utter it. Pauline read his thought, and answered it with no touch of pain or pride in the magical voice that seldom spoke in vain.

"I know your wish; it is as just as your silence is generous, and I reply to it in all sincerity. You would ask, 'When I have given all that I possess, what do I receive in return?' This—a wife whose friendship is as warm as many a woman's love; a wife who will give you all the heart still left her, and cherish the hope that time may bring a harvest of real affection to repay you for the faithfulness of years; who, though she takes the retribution of a wrong into her hands and executes it in the face of heaven, never will forget the honorable name you give into her keeping or blemish it by any act of hers. I can promise no more. Will this content you, Manuel?"

Before she ended his face was hidden in his hands, and tears streamed through them as he listened, for like a true child of the south each emotion found free vent and spent itself as swiftly as it rose. The reaction was more than he could bear, for in a moment his life was changed, months of hopeless longing were banished with a word, a blissful yes canceled the hard no that had been accepted as inexorable, and Happiness, lifting her full cup to his lips, bade him drink. A moment he yielded to the natural relief, then dashed his tears away and threw himself at Pauline's feet in that attitude fit only for a race as graceful as impassioned.

"Forgive me! Take all I have—fortune, name, and my poor self; use us as you will, we are proud and happy to be spent for you! No service will be too hard, no trial too long if in the end you learn to love me with one tithe of the affection I have made my life. Do you mean it? Am I to go with you? To be near you always, to call you wife, and know we are each other's until death? What have I ever done to earn a fate like this?"

Fast and fervently he spoke, and very winsome was the glad abandonment of this young lover, half boy, half man, possessing the simplicity of the one, the fervor of the other. Pauline looked and listened with a soothing sense of consolation in the knowledge that this loyal heart was all her own, a sweet foretaste of the devotion which henceforth was to shelter her from poverty, neglect, and wrong, and turn life's sunnicst side to one who had so long seen only its most bleak and barren. Still at her feet, his arms about her waist, his face flushed and proud, lifted to hers, Manuel saw the cold mask soften, the stern eyes melt with a sudden dew as Pauline watched him, saying, "Dear Manuel, love me less; I am not worth such ardent and entire faith. Pause and reflect before you take this step. I will not bind you to my fate too soon lest you repent too late. We both stand alone in the world, free to make or mar our future as we will. I have chosen my lot. Recall all it may cost you to share it and be sure the price is not too high a one. Remember I am poor, you the possessor of one princely fortune, the sole heir to another."

"The knowledge of this burdened me before; now I glory in it because I have the more for you."

"Remember, I am older than yourself, and may early lose the beauty you love so well, leaving an old wife to burden your youth."

"What are a few years to me? Women like you grow lovelier with age, and you shall have a strong young husband to lean on all your life."

"Remember, I am not of your faith, and the priests will shut me out from your heaven."

"Let them prate as they will. Where you go I will go; Santa Paula shall be my madonna!"

"Remember, I am a deserted woman, and in the world we are

going to my name may become the sport of that man's cruel tongue. Could you bear that patiently, and curb your fiery pride if I desired it?"

"Anything for you, Pauline!"

"One thing more. I give you my liberty; for a time give me forbearance in return, and though wed in haste woo me slowly, lest this sore heart of mine find even your light yoke heavy. Can you promise this, and wait till time has healed my wound, and taught me to be meek?"

"I swear to obey you in all things; make me what you will, for soul and body I am wholly yours henceforth."

"Faithful and true! I knew you would not fail me. Now go, Manuel. Tomorrow do your part resolutely as I shall do mine, and in a week we will begin the new life together. Ours is a strange betrothal, but it shall not lack some touch of tenderness from me. Love, good night."

Pauline bent till her bright hair mingled with the dark, kissed the boy on lips and forehead as a fond sister might have done, then put him gently from her; and like one in a blessed dream he went away to pace all night beneath her window, longing for the day.

As the echo of his steps died along the corridor, Pauline's eye fell on the paper lying where her lover flung it. At this sight all the softness vanished, the stern woman reappeared, and, crushing it in her hand with slow significance, she said low to herself, "This is an old, old story, but it shall have a new ending."

≥ *chapter II* ≤

"WHAT jewels will the señora wear tonight?"
"None, Dolores. Manuel has gone for flowers—he likes them best. You may go."

"But the señora's toilette is not finished; the sandals, the gloves, the garland yet remain."

"Leave them all; I shall not go down. I am tired of this endless folly. Give me that book and go."

The pretty Creole obeyed; and careless of Dolores' work, Pauline sank into the deep chair with a listless mien, turned the pages for a little, then lost herself in thoughts that seemed to bring no rest.

Silently the young husband entered and, pausing, regarded his wife with mingled pain and pleasure—pain to see her so spiritless, pleasure to see her so fair. She seemed unconscious of his presence till the fragrance of his floral burden betrayed him, and looking up to smile a welcome she met a glance that changed the sad dreamer into an excited actor, for it told her that the object of her search was found. Springing erect, she asked eagerly, "Manuel, is he here?"

"Yes."

"Alone?"

"His wife is with him."

"Is she beautiful?"

"Pretty, petite, and petulant."

"And he?"

"Unchanged: the same imposing figure and treacherous face, the same restless eye and satanic mouth. Pauline, let me insult him!"

"Not yet. Were they together?"

"Yes. He seemed anxious to leave her, but she called him back imperiously, and he came like one who dared not disobey."

"Did he see you?"

"The crowd was too dense, and I kept in the shadow."

"The wife's name? Did you learn it?"

"Barbara St. Just."

"Ah! I knew her once and will again. Manuel, am I beautiful tonight?"

"How can you be otherwise to me?"

"That is not enough. I must look my fairest to others, brilliant and blithe, a happy-hearted bride whose honeymoon is not yet over."

"For his sake, Pauline?"

"For yours. I want him to envy you your youth, your comeliness, your content; to see the man he once sneered at the husband of the woman he once loved; to recall impotent regret. I know his nature, and can stir him to his heart's core with a look, revenge myself with a word, and read the secrets of his life with a skill he cannot fathom."

"And when you have done all this, shall you be happier, Pauline?"

"Infinitely; our three weeks' search is ended, and the real interest of the plot begins. I have played the lover for your sake, now play the man of the world for mine. This is the moment we have waited for. Help me to make it successful. Come! Crown me with your garland, give me the bracelets that were your wedding gift—none can be too brilliant for tonight. Now the gloves and fan. Stay, my sandals—you shall play Dolores and tie them on."

With an air of smiling coquetry he had never seen before, Pauline stretched out a truly Spanish foot and offered him its dainty covering. Won by the animation of her manner, Manuel forgot his misgivings and played his part with boyish spirit, hovering about his stately wife as no assiduous maid had ever done; for every flower was fastened with a word sweeter than itself, the white arms kissed as the ornaments went on, and when the silken knots were deftly accomplished, the lighthearted bridegroom performed a little dance of triumph about his idol, till she arrested him, beckoning as she spoke.

"Manuel, I am waiting to assume the last best ornament you have given me, my handsome husband." Then, as he came to her laughing with frank pleasure at her praise, she added, "You, too, must look your best and bravest now, and remember you must enact the man tonight. Before Gilbert wear your stateliest aspect, your tenderest to me, your courtliest to his wife. You possess dramatic skill. Use it for my sake, and come for your reward when this night's work is done."

The great hotel was swarming with life, ablaze with light, resonant with the tread of feet, the hum of voices, the musical din of the band, and full of the sights and sounds which fill such human hives at a fashionable watering place in the height of the season. As Manuel led his wife along the grand hall thronged with promenaders, his quick ear caught the whispered comments of the passers-by, and the fragmentary rumors concerning themselves amused him infinitely.

"*Mon ami!* There are five bridal couples here tonight, and there is the handsomest, richest, and most enchanting of them all. The groom is not yet twenty, they tell me, and the bride still younger. Behold them!"

Manuel looked down at Pauline with a mirthful glance, but she had not heard.

"See, Belle! Cubans; own half the island between them. Splendid, aren't they? Look at the diamonds on her lovely arms, and his ravishing moustache. Isn't he your ideal of Prince Djalma, in *The Wandering Jew?*"

A pretty girl, forgetting propriety in interest, pointed as they passed. Manuel half-bowed to the audible compliment, and the blushing damsel vanished, but Pauline had not seen.

"Jack, there's the owner of the black span you fell into raptures over. My lord and lady look as highbred as their stud. We'll patronize them!"

Manuel muttered a disdainful *"Impertinente!"* between his teeth as he surveyed a brace of dandies with an air that augured ill for the patronage of Young America, but Pauline was unconscious of both criticism and reproof. A countercurrent held them stationary for a moment, and close behind them sounded a voice saying, confidentially, to some silent listener, "The Redmonds are here tonight, and I am curious to see how he bears his disappointment. You know he married for money, and was outwitted in the bargain; for his wife's fortune not only proves to be much less than he was led to believe, but is so tied up that he is entirely dependent upon her, and the bachelor debts he sold himself to liquidate still harass him, with a wife's reproaches to augment the affliction. To be ruled by a spoiled child's whims is a fit punishment for a man whom neither pride nor principle could curb before. Let us go and look at the unfortunate."

Pauline heard now. Manuel felt her start, saw her flush and pale, then her eye lit, and the dark expression he dreaded to see settled on her face as she whispered, like a satanic echo, "Let us also go and look at this unfortunate."

A jealous pang smote the young man's heart as he recalled the past.

"You pity him, Pauline, and pity is akin to love."

"I only pity what I respect. Rest content, my husband."

Steadily her eyes met his, and the hand whose only ornament was a wedding ring went to meet the one folded on his arm with a confiding gesture that made the action a caress.

"I will try to be, yet mine is a hard part," Manuel answered with a sigh, then silently they both paced on.

Gilbert Redmond lounged behind his wife's chair, looking intensely bored.

"Have you had enough of this folly, Babie?"

"No, we have but just come. Let us dance."

"Too late; they have begun."

"Then go about with me. It's very tiresome sitting here."

"It is too warm to walk in all that crowd, child."

"You are so indolent! Tell me who people are as they pass. I know no one here."

"Nor I."

But his act belied the words, for as they passed his lips he rose erect, with a smothered exclamation and startled face, as if a ghost had suddenly confronted him. The throng had thinned, and as his wife followed the direction of his glance, she saw no uncanny apparition to cause such evident dismay, but a woman fair-haired, violet-eyed, blooming and serene, sweeping down the long hall with noiseless grace. An air of sumptuous life pervaded her, the shimmer of bridal snow surrounded her, bridal gifts shone on neck and arms, and bridal happiness seemed to touch her with its tender charm as she looked up at her companion, as if there were but one human being in the world to her. This companion, a man slender and tall, with a face delicately dark as a fine bronze, looked back at her with eyes as eloquent as her own, while both spoke rapidly and low in the melodious language which seems made for lover's lips.

"Gilbert, who are they?"

There was no answer, and before she could repeat the question the approaching pair paused before her, and the beautiful woman offered her hand, saying, with inquiring smiles, "Barbara, have you forgotten your early friend, Pauline?"

Recognition came with the familiar name, and Mrs. Redmond welcomed the newcomer with a delight as unrestrained as if she were still the schoolgirl, Babie. Then, recovering herself, she said, with a pretty attempt at dignity, "Let me present my husband. Gilbert, come and welcome my friend Pauline Valary."

Scarlet with shame, dumb with conflicting emotions, and utterly deserted by self-possession, Redmond stood with downcast eyes and agitated mien, suffering a year's remorse condensed into a moment. A mute gesture was all the greeting he could offer. Pauline slightly bent her haughty head as she answered, in a voice frostily sweet, "Your wife mistakes. Pauline Valary died three weeks ago, and Pauline Laroche rose from her ashes. Manuel, my schoolmate, Mrs. Redmond; Gilbert you already know."

With the manly presence he could easily assume and which was henceforth to be his role in public, Manuel bowed courteously to the lady, coldly to the gentleman, and looked only at his wife. Mrs. Redmond, though childish, was observant; she glanced from face to face, divined a mystery, and spoke out at once.

"Then you have met before? Gilbert, you have never told me this."

"It was long ago—in Cuba. I believed they had forgotten me."

"I never forget." And Pauline's eye turned on him with a look he dared not meet.

Unsilenced by her husband's frown, Mrs. Redmond, intent on pleasing herself, drew her friend to the seat beside her as she said petulantly, "Gilbert tells me nothing, and I am constantly discovering things which might have given me pleasure had he only chosen to be frank. I've spoken of you often, yet he never betrayed the least knowledge of you, and I take it very ill of him, because I am sure he has not forgotten you. Sit here, Pauline, and let me tease you with questions, as I used to do so long ago. You were always patient with me, and though far more beautiful, your face is still the same kind one that comforted the little child at school. Gilbert, enjoy your friend, and leave us to ourselves until the dance is over."

Pauline obeyed; but as she chatted, skillfully leading the young wife's conversation to her own affairs, she listened to the two voices behind her, watched the two figures reflected in the mirror before her, and felt a secret pride in Manuel's address, for it was evident that the former positions were renewed.

The timid boy who had feared the sarcastic tongue of his guardian's guest, and shrunk from his presence to conceal the jealousy that was his jest, now stood beside his formal rival, serene and self-possessed, by far the manliest man of the two, for no shame daunted him, no fear oppressed him, no dishonorable deed left him at the mercy of another's tongue.

Gilbert Redmond felt this keenly, and cursed the falsehood which had placed him in such an unenviable position. It was vain to assume the old superiority that was forfeited; but too much a man of the world to be long discomforted by any contretemps like this, he rapidly regained his habitual ease of manner, and avoiding the perilous past clung to the safer present, hoping, by some unguarded look or word, to fathom the purpose of his adversary, for such he knew the husband of Pauline must be at heart. But Manuel schooled his features, curbed his tongue, and when his hot blood tempted him to point his smooth speech with a taunt, or offer a silent insult with the eye, he remembered Pauline, looked down on the graceful head below, and forgot all other passions in that of love.

"Gilbert, my shawl. The sea air chills me."

"I forgot it, Babie."

"Allow me to supply the want."

Mindful of his wife's commands, Manuel seized this opportunity to win a glance of commendation from her. And taking the downy mantle that hung upon his arm, he wrapped the frail girl in it with a care that made the act as cordial as courteous. Mrs. Redmond felt the charm of his manner with the quickness of a woman, and sent a reproachful glance at Gilbert as she said plantively, "Ah! It is evident that my honeymoon is over, and the assiduous lover replaced by the negligent husband. Enjoy your midsummer night's dream while you may, Pauline, and be ready for the awakening that must come."

"Not to her, madame, for our honeymoon shall last till the golden wedding day comes round. Shall it not, *cariña?*"

"There is no sign of waning yet, Manuel," and Pauline looked up into her husband's face with a genuine affection which made her own more beautiful and filled his with a visible content. Gilbert read the glance, and in that instant suffered the first pang of regret that Pauline had foretold. He spoke abruptly, longing to be away.

"Babie, we may dance now, if you will."

"I am going, but not with you—so give me my fan, and entertain Pauline till my return."

He unclosed his hand, but the delicately carved fan fell at his feet in a shower of ivory shreds—he had crushed it as he watched his first love with the bitter thought "It might have been!"

"Forgive me, Babie, it was too frail for use; you should choose a stronger."

"I will next time, and a gentler hand to hold it. Now, Monsieur Laroche, I am ready."

Mrs. Redmond rose in a small bustle of satisfaction, shook out her flounces, glanced at the mirror, then Manuel led her away; and the other pair were left alone. Both felt a secret agitation quicken their breath and thrill along their nerves, but the woman concealed it best. Gilbert's eye wandered restlessly to and fro, while Pauline fixed her own on his as quietly as if he were the statue in the niche behind him. For a moment he tried to seem unconscious of it, then essayed to meet and conquer it, but failed signally and, driven to his last resources by that steady gaze, resolved to speak out and have all over before his wife's return. Assuming the seat beside her, he said, impetuously, "Pauline, take off your mask as I do mine—we are alone now, and may see each other as we are."

Leaning deep into the crimson curve of the couch, with the indolent grace habitual to her, yet in strong contrast to the vigilant gleam of her eye, she swept her hand across her face as if obeying him, yet no change followed, as she said with a cold smile, "It is off; what next?"

"Let me understand you. Did my letter reach your hands?"

"A week before my marriage."

He drew a long breath of relief, yet a frown gathered as he asked, like one loath and eager to be satisfied, "Your love died a natural death, then, and its murder does not lie at my door?"

Pointing to the shattered toy upon the ground, she only echoed his own words. "It was too frail for use—I chose a stronger."

It wounded, as she meant it should; and the evil spirit to whose guidance she had yielded herself exulted to see his self-love bleed, and pride vainly struggle to conceal the stab. He caught the expression in her averted glance, bent suddenly a fixed and scrutinizing gaze upon her, asking, below his breath, "Then why are you here to tempt me with the face that tempted me a year ago?"

"I came to see the woman to whom you sold yourself. I have seen her, and am satisfied."

Such quiet contempt iced her tones, such pitiless satisfaction shone through the long lashes that swept slowly down, after her eye had met and caused his own to fall again, that Gilbert's cheek burned as if the words had been a blow, and mingled shame and anger trembled in his voice.

"Ah, you are quick to read our secret, for you possess the key. Have you no fear that I may read your own, and tell the world you sold your beauty for a name and fortune? Your bargain is a better one than mine, but I know you too well, though your fetters are diamonds and your master a fond boy."

She had been prepared for this, and knew she had a shield in the real regard she bore her husband, for though sisterly, it was sincere. She felt its value now, for it gave her courage to confront the spirit of retaliation she had roused, and calmness to answer the whispered taunt with an unruffled mien, as lifting her white arm she let its single decoration drop glittering to her lap.

"You see my 'fetters' are as loose as they are light, and nothing binds me but my will. Read my heart, if you can. You will find there contempt for a love so poor that it feared poverty; pity for a man who dared not face the world and conquer it, as a girl had done before him, and gratitude that I have found my 'master' in a truehearted boy, not a falsehearted man. If I am a slave, I never know it. Can you say as much?"

Her woman's tongue avenged her, and Gilbert owned his defeat. Pain quenched the ire of his glance, remorse subdued his pride, self-condemnation compelled him to ask, imploringly, "Pauline, when may I hope for pardon?"

"Never."

The stern utterance of the word dismayed him, and, like one shut

out from hope, he rose, as if to leave her, but paused irresolutely, looked back, then sank down again, as if constrained against his will by a longing past control. If she had doubted her power this action set the doubt at rest, as the haughtiest nature she had known confessed it by a bittersweet complaint. Eyeing her wistfully, tenderly, Gilbert murmured, in the voice of long ago, "Why do I stay to wound and to be wounded by the hand that once caressed me? Why do I find more pleasure in your contempt than in another woman's praise, and feel myself transported into the delights of that irrecoverable past, now grown the sweetest, saddest memory of my life? Send me away, Pauline, before the old charm asserts its power, and I forget that I am not the happy lover of a year ago."

"Leave me then, Gilbert. Good night."

Half unconsciously, the former softness stole into her voice as it lingered on his name. The familiar gesture accompanied the words, the old charm did assert itself, and for an instant changed the cold woman into the ardent girl again. Gilbert did not go but, with a hasty glance down the deserted hall behind him, captured and kissed the hand he had lost, passionately whispering, "Pauline, I love you still, and that look assures me that you have forgiven, forgotten, and kept a place for me in that deep heart of yours. It is too late to deny it. I have seen the tender eyes again, and the sight has made me the proudest, happiest man that walks the world tonight, slave though I am."

Over cheek and forehead rushed the treacherous blood as the violet eyes filled and fell before his own, and in the glow of mingled pain and fear that stirred her blood, Pauline, for the first time, owned the peril of the task she had set herself, saw the dangerous power she possessed, and felt the buried passion faintly moving in its grave. Indignant at her own weakness, she took refuge in the memory of her wrong, controlled the rebel color, steeled the front she showed him, and with feminine skill mutely conveyed the rebuke she would not trust herself to utter, by stripping the glove from the hand he had touched and dropping it disdainfully as if unworthy of its place. Gilbert had not looked for such an answer, and while it baffled him it excited his man's spirit to rebel against her silent denial. With a bitter laugh he snatched up the glove.

"I read a defiance in your eye as you flung this down. I accept the challenge, and will keep gage until I prove myself the victor. I have asked for pardon. You refuse it. I have confessed my love. You scorn it. I have possessed myself of your secret, yet you deny it. Now we will try our strength together, and leave those children to their play."

"We are the children, and we play with edge tools. There has been enough of this, there must be no more." Pauline rose with her haughtiest mien, and the brief command, "Take me to Manuel."

Silently Gilbert offered his arm, and silently she rejected it.

"Will you accept nothing from me?"

"Nothing."

Side by side they passed through the returning throng till Mrs. Redmond joined them, looking blithe and bland with the exhilaration of gallantry and motion. Manuel's first glance was at Pauline, his second at her companion; there was a shadow upon the face of each, which seemed instantly to fall upon his own as he claimed his wife with a masterful satisfaction as novel as becoming, and which prompted her to whisper, "You enact your role to the life, and shall enjoy a foretaste of your reward at once. I want excitement; let us show these graceless, frozen people the true art of dancing, and electrify them with the life and fire of a Cuban valse."

Manuel kindled at once, and Pauline smiled stealthily as she glanced over her shoulder from the threshold of the dancing hall, for her slightest act, look, and word had their part to play in that night's drama.

"Gilbert, if you are tired I will go now."

"Thank you, I begin to find it interesting. Let us watch the dancers."

Mrs. Redmond accepted the tardy favor, wondering at his unwonted animation, for never had she seen such eagerness in his countenance, such energy in his manner as he pressed through the crowd and won a place where they could freely witness one of those exhibitions of fashionable figurante which are nightly to be seen at such resorts. Many couples were whirling around the white hall, but among them one pair circled with slowly increasing speed, in perfect time to the inspiring melody of trumpet, flute, and horn, that seemed to sound for them alone. Many paused to watch them, for they gave to the graceful pastime the enchantment which few have skill enough to lend it, and made it a spectacle of life-enjoying youth, to be remembered long after the music ceased and the agile feet were still.

Gilbert's arm was about his little wife to shield her from the pressure of the crowd, and as they stood his hold unconsciously tightened, till, marveling at this unwonted care, she looked up to thank him with a happy glance and discovered that his eye rested on a single pair, kindling as they approached, keenly scanning every gesture as they floated by, following them with untiring vigilance through the many-colored mazes they threaded with such winged steps, while his breath quickened, his hand kept time, and every sense seemed to own the intoxication of the scene. Sorrowfully she too watched this pair, saw their grace, admired their beauty, envied their happiness; for, short as her wedded life had been, the thorns already pierced her through the roses, and with each airy revolution of those figures, dark and bright, her discontent increased, her wonder deepened, her scrutiny grew keener, for she knew no common interest held her husband there, fascinated, flushed, and excited as if his heart beat responsive to the rhythmic rise and fall of that booted foot and satin slipper. The music ended with a crash, the crowd surged across the floor, and the spell was broken. Like one but half disenchanted, Gilbert stood a moment, then remembered his wife, and looking down met brown eyes, full of tears, fastened on his face.

"Tired so soon, Babie? Or in a pet because I cannot change myself into a thistledown and float about with you, like Manuel and Pauline?"

"Neither; I was only wishing that you loved me as he loves her, and hoping he would never tire of her, they are so fond and charming now. How long have you known them—and where?"

"I shall have no peace until I tell you. I passed a single summer with them in a tropical paradise, where we swung half the day in hammocks, under tamarind and almond trees; danced half the night to music, of which this seems but a faint echo; and led a life of luxurious delight in an enchanted climate, where all is so beautiful and brilliant that its memory haunts a life as pressed flowers sweeten the leaves of a dull book."

"Why did you leave it then?"

"To marry you, child."

"That was a regretful sigh, as if I were not worth the sacrifice. Let us go back and enjoy it together."

"If you were dying for it, I would not take you to Cuba. It would be purgatory, not paradise, now."

"How stern you look, how strangely you speak. Would you not go to save your own life, Gilbert?"

"I would not cross the room to do that much, less the sea."

"Why do you both love and dread it? Don't frown, but tell me. I have a right to know."

"Because the bitterest blunder of my life was committed there—a blunder that I never can repair in this world, and may be damned for in the next. Rest satisfied with this, Babie, lest you prove like Bluebeard's wife, and make another skeleton in my closet, which has enough already."

Strange regret was in his voice, strange gloom fell upon his face; but though rendered doubly curious by the change, Mrs. Redmond dared not question further and, standing silent, furtively scanned the troubled countenance beside her. Gilbert spoke first, waking out of his sorrowful reverie with a start.

"Pauline is coming. Say adieu, not au revoir, for tomorrow we must leave this place."

His words were a command, his aspect one of stern resolve, though the intensest longing mingled with the dark look he cast on the approaching pair. The tone, the glance displeased his willful wife, who loved to use her power and exact obedience where she had failed to win affection, often ruling imperiously when a tender word would have made her happy to submit.

"Gilbert, you take no thought for my pleasures though you pursue your own at my expense. Your neglect forces me to find solace and satisfaction where I can, and you have forfeited your right to command or complain. I love Pauline, I am happy with her, therefore I shall stay until we tire of one another. I am a burden to you; go if you will."

"You know I cannot without you, Babie. I ask it as a favor. For my sake, for your own, I implore you to come away."

"Gilbert, do you love her?"

She seized his arm and forced an answer by the energy of her sharply whispered question. He saw that it was vain to dissemble, yet replied with averted head, "I did and still remember it."

"And she? Did she return your love?"

"I believed so; but she forgot me when I went. She married Manuel and is happy. Babie, let me go!"

"No! you shall stay and feel a little of the pain I feel when I look into your heart and find I have no place there. It is this which has stood between us and made all my efforts vain. I see it now and despise you for the falsehood you have shown me, vowing you loved no one but me until I married you, then letting me so soon discover that I was only an encumbrance to your enjoyment of the fortune I possessed. You treat me like a child, but I suffer like a woman, and you shall share my suffering, because you might have spared me, and you did not. Gilbert, you shall stay."

"Be it so, but remember I have warned you."

An exultant expression broke through the gloom of her husband's face as he answered with the grim satisfaction of one who gave restraint to the mind, and stood ready to follow whatever impulse should sway him next. His wife trembled inwardly at what she had done, but was too proud to recall her words and felt a certain bitter pleasure in the excitement of the new position she had taken, the new interest given to her listless life.

Pauline and Manuel found them standing silently together, for a moment had done the work of years and raised a barrier between them never to be swept away.

Mrs. Redmond spoke first, and with an air half resentful, half triumphant:

"Pauline, this morose husband of mine says we must leave tomorrow. But in some things I rule; this is one of them. Therefore we remain and go with you to the mountains when we are tired of the gay life here. So smile and submit, Gilbert, else these friends will count your society no favor. Would you not fancy, from the aspect he thinks proper to assume, that I had sentenced him to a punishment, not a pleasure?"

"Perhaps you have unwittingly, Babie. Marriage is said to cancel the follies of the past, but not those of the future, I believe; and, as there are many temptations to an idle man in a place like this, doubtless your husband is wise enough to own that he dares not stay but finds discretion the better part of valor."

Nothing could be softer than the tone in which these words were uttered, nothing sharper than the hidden taunt conveyed, but Gilbert only laughed a scornful laugh as he fixed his keen eyes full upon her and took her bouquet with the air of one assuming former rights.

"My dear Pauline, discretion is the last virtue I should expect to be accused of by you; but if valor consists in daring all things, I may lay claim to it without its 'better part,' for temptation is my delight—the stronger the better. Have no fears for me, my friend. I gladly accept Babie's decree and, ignoring the last ten years, intend to begin life anew, having discovered a *sauce piquante* which will give the stalest pleasures a redoubled zest. I am unfortunate tonight, and here is a second wreck; this I can rebuild happily. Allow me to do so, for I remember you once praised my skill in floral architecture."

With an air of eager gallantry in strange contrast to the malign expression of his countenance, Gilbert knelt to regather the flowers which a careless gesture of his own had scattered from their jeweled holder. His wife turned to speak to Manuel, and, yielding to the unconquerable anxiety his reckless manner awoke, Pauline whispered below her breath as she bent as if to watch the work, "Gilbert, follow your first impulse, and go tomorrow."

"Nothing shall induce me to."

"I warn you harm will come of it."

"Let it come; I am past fear now."

"Shun me for Babie's sake, if not for your own."

"Too late for that; she is headstrong—let her suffer."

"Have you no power, Gilbert?"

"None over her, much over you."

"We will prove that!"

"We will!"

Rapidly as words could shape them, these questions and answers fell, and with their utterance the last generous feeling died in Pauline's breast; for as she received the flowers, now changed from a love token to a battle gage, she saw the torn glove still crushed in Gilbert's hand, and silently accepted his challenge to the tournament so often held between man and woman—a tournament where the keen tongue is the lance, pride the shield, passion the fiery steed, and the hardest heart the winner of the prize, which seldom fails to prove a barren honor, ending in remorse.

≫ *chapter III* ≪

FOR several days the Cubans were almost invisible, appearing only for a daily drive, a twilight saunter on the beach, or a brief visit to the ballroom, there to enjoy the excitement of the pastime in which they both excelled. Their apartments were in the quietest wing of the hotel, and from the moment of their occupancy seemed to acquire all the charms of home. The few guests admitted felt the atmosphere of poetry and peace that pervaded the nest which Love, the worker of miracles, had built himself even under that tumultuous roof. Strollers in the halls or along the breezy verandas often paused to listen to the music of instrument or voice which came floating out from these sequestered rooms. Frequent laughter and the murmur of conversation proved that ennui was unknown, and a touch of romance inevitably enhanced the interest wakened by the beautiful young pair, always together, always happy, never weary of the *dolce far niente* of this summer life.

In a balcony like a hanging garden, sheltered from the sun by blossoming shrubs and vines that curtained the green nook with odorous shade, Pauline lay indolently swinging in a gaily fringed hammock as she had been wont to do in Cuba, then finding only pleasure in the luxury of motion which now failed to quiet her unrest. Manuel had put down the book to which she no longer listened and, leaning his head upon his hand, sat watching her as she swayed to and fro with thoughtful eyes intent upon the sea, whose murmurous

voice possessed a charm more powerful than his own. Suddenly he spoke:

"Pauline, I cannot understand you! For three weeks we hurried east and west to find this man, yet when found you shun him and seem content to make my life a heaven upon earth. I sometimes fancy that you have resolved to let the past sleep, but the hope dies as soon as born, for in moments like this I see that, though you devote yourself to me, the old purpose is unchanged, and I marvel why you pause."

Her eyes came back from their long gaze and settled on him full of an intelligence which deepened his perplexity. "You have not learned to know me yet; death is not more inexorable or time more tireless than I. This week has seemed one of indolent delight to you. To me it has been one of constant vigilance and labor, for scarcely a look, act, or word of mine has been without effect. At first I secluded myself that Gilbert might contrast our life with his and, believing us all and all to one another, find impotent regret his daily portion. Three days ago accident placed an unexpected weapon in my hand which I have used in silence, lest in spite of promises you should rebel and end his trial too soon. Have you no suspicion of my meaning?"

"None. You are more mysterious than ever, and I shall, in truth, believe you are the enchantress I have so often called you if your spells work invisibly."

"They do not, and I use no supernatural arts, as I will prove to you. Take my lorgnette that lies behind you, part the leaves where the green grapes hang thickest, look up at the little window in the shadowy angle of the low roof opposite, and tell me what you see."

"Nothing but a half-drawn curtain."

"Ah! I must try the ruse that first convinced me. Do not show yourself, but watch, and if you speak, let it be in Spanish."

Leaving her airy cradle, Pauline bent over the balcony as if to gather the climbing roses that waved their ruddy clusters in the wind. Before the third stem was broken Manuel whispered, "I see the curtain move; now comes the outline of a head, and now a hand, with some bright object in it. Santo Pablo! It is a man staring at you as coolly as if you were a lady in a balcony. What prying rascal is it?"

"Gilbert."

"Impossible! He is a gentleman."

"If gentlemen play the traitor and the spy, then he is one. I am not mistaken; for since the glitter of his glass first arrested me I have watched covertly, and several trials as successful as the present have confirmed the suspicion which Babie's innocent complaints of his long absences aroused. Now do you comprehend why I remained in these rooms with the curtains seldom drawn? Why I swung the hammock here and let you sing and read to me while I played with your hair or leaned upon your shoulder? Why I have been all devotion and made this balcony a little stage for the performance of our version of the honeymoon for one spectator?"

Still mindful of the eager eyes upon her, Pauline had been fastening the roses in her bosom as she spoke, and ended with a silvery laugh that made the silence musical with its heartsome sound. As she paused, Manuel flung down the lorgnette and was striding past her with ireful impetuosity, but the white arms took him captive, adding another figure to the picture framed by the green arch as she whispered decisively, "No farther! There must be no violence. You promised obedience and I exact it. Do you think detection to a man so lost to honor would wound as deeply as the sights which make his daily watch a torment? Or that a blow would be as hard to bear as the knowledge that his own act has placed you where you are and made him what he is? Silent contempt is the law now, so let this insult pass, unclench your hand and turn that defiant face to me, while I console you for submission with a kiss."

He yielded to the command enforced by the caress but drew her jealously from sight, and still glanced rebelliously through the leaves, asking with a frown, "Why show me this if I may not resent it? How long must I bear with this man? Tell me your design, else I shall mar it in some moment when hatred of him conquers love of you."

"I will, for it is time, because though I have taken the first step you must take the second. I showed you this that you might find action pleasanter than rest, and you must bear with this man a little longer for my sake, but I will give you an amusement to beguile the time. Long ago you told me that Gilbert was a gambler. I would not believe it then, now I can believe anything, and you can convince the world of this vice of his as speedily as you will."

"Do you wish me to become a gambler that I may prove him one? I also told you that he was suspected of dishonorable play—shall I load the dice and mark the cards to catch him in his own snares?"

Manuel spoke bitterly, for his high spirit chafed at the task as-

signed him; womanly wiles seemed more degrading than the mascu-
line method of retaliation, in which strength replaces subtlety and
speedier vengeance brings speedier satisfaction. But Pauline, fast
learning to play upon that mysterious instrument, the human heart,
knew when to stimulate and when to soothe.

"Do not reproach me that I point out a safer mode of operation
than your own. You would go to Gilbert and by a hot word, a rash
act, put your life and my happiness into his hands, for though dueling
is forbidden here, he would not hesitate to break all laws, human or
divine, if by so doing he could separate us. What would you gain by
it? If you kill him he is beyond our reach forever, and a crime remains
to be atoned for. If he kill you your blood will be upon my head, and
where should I find consolation for the loss of the one heart always
true and tender?"

With the inexplicable prescience which sometimes foreshadows
coming ills, she clung to him as if a vision of the future dimly swept
before her, but he only saw the solicitude it was a sweet surprise to
find he had awakened, and in present pleasure forgot past pain.

"You shall not suffer from this man any grief that I can shield
you from, rest assured of that, my heart. I will be patient, though your
ways are not mine, for the wrong was yours, and the retribution shall
be such as you decree."

"Then hear your task and see the shape into which circumstances
have molded my design. I would have you exercise a self-restraint that
shall leave Gilbert no hold upon you, accept all invitations like that
which you refused when we passed him on the threshold of the bil-
liard room an hour ago, and seem to find in such amusements the
same fascination as himself. Your skill in games of chance excels his,
as you proved at home where these pastimes lose their disreputable
aspect by being openly enjoyed. Therefore I would have you whet
this appetite of his by losing freely at first—he will take a grim delight
in lessening the fortune he covets—then exert all your skill till he is
deeply in your debt. He has nothing but what is doled out to him by
Babie's father, I find; he dare not ask help there for such a purpose;
other resources have failed else he would not have married; and if
the sum be large enough, it lays him under an obligation which will
be a thorn in his flesh, the sharper for your knowledge of his impo-
tence to draw it out. When this is done, or even while it is in progress,
I would have you add the pain of a new jealousy to the old. He ne-

glects this young wife of his, and she is eager to recover the affections she believes she once possessed. Help her, and teach Gilbert the value of what he now despises. You are young, comely, accomplished, and possessed of many graces more attractive than you are conscious of; your southern birth and breeding gift you with a winning warmth of manners in strong contrast to the colder natures around you; and your love for me lends an almost tender deference to your intercourse with all womankind. Amuse, console this poor girl, and show her husband what he should be; I have no fear of losing your heart nor need you fear for hers; she is one of those spaniel-like creatures who love the hand that strikes them and fawn upon the foot that spurns them."

"Am I to be the sole actor in the drama of deceit? While I woo Babie, what will you do, Pauline?"

"Let Gilbert woo me—have patience till you understand my meaning; he still loves me and believes I still return that love. I shall not undeceive him yet, but let silence seem to confess what I do not own in words. He fed me with false promises, let me build my life's happiness on baseless hopes, and rudely woke me when he could delude no longer, leaving me to find I had pursued a shadow. I will do the same. He shall follow me undaunted, undeterred by all obstacles, all ties; shall stake his last throw and lose it, for when the crowning moment comes I shall show him that through me he is made bankrupt in love, honor, liberty, and hope, tell him I am yours entirely and forever, then vanish like an *ignis-fatuus,* leaving him to the darkness of despair and defeat. Is not this a better retribution than the bullet that would give him peace at once?"

Boy, lover, husband though he was, Manuel saw and stood aghast at the baleful spirit which had enslaved this woman, crushing all generous impulses, withering all gentle charities, and making her the saddest spectacle this world can show—one human soul rebelling against Providence, to become the nemesis of another. Involuntarily he recoiled from her, exclaiming, "Pauline! Are you possessed of a devil?"

"Yes! One that will not be cast out till every sin, shame, and sorrow mental ingenuity can conceive and inflict has been heaped on that man's head. I thought I should be satisfied with one accusing look, one bitter word; I am not, for the evil genii once let loose cannot be recaptured. Once I ruled it, now it rules me, and there is no turning

back. I have come under the law of fate, and henceforth the powers
I possess will ban, not bless, for I am driven to whet and wield them
as weapons which may win me success at the price of my salvation.
It is not yet too late for you to shun the spiritual contagion I bear
about me. Choose now, and abide by that choice without a shadow
of turning, as I abide by mine. Take me as I am; help me willingly
and unwillingly; and in the end receive the promised gift—years like
the days you have called heaven upon earth. Or retract the vows you
plighted, receive again the heart and name you gave me, and live
unvexed by the stormy nature time alone can tame. Here is the ring.
Shall I restore or keep it, Manuel?"

Never had she looked more beautiful as she stood there, an image
of will, daring, defiant, and indomitable, with eyes darkened by intensity of emotion, voice half sad, half stern, and outstretched hand
on which the wedding ring no longer shone. She felt her power, yet
was wary enough to assure it by one bold appeal to the strongest
element of her husband's character: passions, not principles, were the
allies she desired, and before the answer came she knew that she had
gained them at the cost of innocence and self-respect.

As Manuel listened, an expression like a dark reflection of her
own settled on his face; a year of youth seemed to drop away; and
with the air of one who puts fear behind him, he took the hand,
replaced the ring, resolutely accepted the hard conditions, and gave
all to love, only saying as he had said before, "Soul and body, I belong
to you; do with me as you will."

A fortnight later Pauline sat alone, waiting for her husband.
Under the pretext of visiting a friend, she had absented herself a week,
that Manuel might give himself entirely to the distasteful task she set
him. He submitted to the separation, wrote daily, but sent no tidings
of his progress, told her nothing when they met that night, and had
left her an hour before asking her to have patience till he could show
his finished work. Now, with her eye upon the door, her ear alert
to catch the coming step, her mind disturbed by contending hopes
and fears, she sat waiting with the vigilant immobility of an Indian
on the watch. She had not long to look and listen. Manuel entered
hastily, locked the door, closed the windows, dropped the curtains,
then paused in the middle of the room and broke into a low, triumphant laugh as he eyed his wife with an expression she had never seen

in those dear eyes before. It startled her, and, scarcely knowing what to desire or dread, she asked eagerly, "You are come to tell me you have prospered."

"Beyond your hopes, for the powers of darkness seem to help us, and lead the man to his destruction faster than any wiles of ours can do. I am tired, let me lie here and rest. I have earned it, so when I have told all say, 'Love, you have done well,' and I am satisfied."

He threw himself along the couch where she still sat and laid his head in her silken lap, her cool hand on his hot forehead, and continued in a muffled voice.

"You know how eagerly Gilbert took advantage of my willingness to play, and soon how recklessly he pursued it, seeming to find the satisfaction you foretold, till, obeying your commands, I ceased losing and won sums which surprised me. Then you went, but I was not idle, and in the effort to extricate himself, Gilbert plunged deeper into debt; for my desire to please you seemed to gift me with redoubled skill. Two days ago I refused to continue the unequal conflict, telling him to give himself no uneasiness, for I could wait. You were right in thinking it would oppress him to be under any obligation to me, but wrong in believing he would endure, and will hardly be prepared for the desperate step he took to free himself. That night he played falsely, was detected, and though his opponent generously promised silence for Babie's sake, the affair stole out—he is shunned and this resource has failed. I thought he had no other, but yesterday he came to me with a strange expression of relief, discharged the debt to the last farthing, then hinted that my friendship with his wife was not approved by him and must cease. This proves that I have obeyed you in all things, though the comforting of Babie was an easy task, for, both loving you, our bond of sympathy and constant theme has been Pauline and her perfections."

"Hush! No praise—it is a mockery. I am what one man's perfidy has made; I may yet learn to be worthy of another man's devotion. What more, Manuel?"

"I thought I should have only a defeat to show you, but today has given me a strange success. At noon a gentleman arrived and asked for Gilbert. He was absent, but upon offering information relative to the time of his return, which proved my intimacy with him, this Seguin entered into conversation with me. His evident desire to avoid Mrs. Redmond and waylay her husband interested me, and when he

questioned me somewhat closely concerning Gilbert's habits and movements of late, my suspicions were roused; and on mentioning the debt
so promptly discharged, I received a confidence that startled me. In
a moment of despair Gilbert had forged the name of his former friend,
whom he believed abroad, had drawn the money and freed himself
from my power, but not for long. The good fortune which has led him
safely through many crooked ways seems to have deserted him in this
strait. For the forgery was badly executed, inspection raised doubts,
and Seguin, just returned, was at his banker's an hour after Gilbert,
to prove the fraud; he came hither at once to accuse him of it and
made me his confidant. What would you have had me do, Pauline?
Time was short, and I could not wait for you."

"How can I tell at once? Why pause to ask? What did you do?"

"Took a leaf from your book and kept accusation, punishment,
and power in my own hands, to be used in your behalf. I returned
the money, secured the forged check, and prevailed on Seguin to leave
the matter in my hands, while he departed as quietly as he had come.
Babie's presence when we met tonight prevented my taking you into
my counsels. I had prepared this surprise for you and felt a secret pride
in working it out alone. An hour ago I went to watch for Gilbert. He
came, I took him to his rooms, told him what I had done, added that
compassion for his wife had actuated me. I left him saying the possession of the check was a full equivalent for the money, which I now
declined to receive from such dishonorable hands. Are you satisfied,
Pauline?"

With countenance and gestures full of exultation she sprang up
to pace the room, exclaiming, as she seized the forged paper, "Yes, that
stroke was superb! How strangely the plot thickens. Surely the powers
of darkness are working with us and have put this weapon in our hands
when that I forged proved useless. By means of this we have a hold
upon him which nothing can destroy unless he escape by death. Will
he, Manuel?"

"No; there was more wrath than shame in his demeanor when I
accused him. He hates me too much to die yet, and had I been the only
possessor of this fatal fact, I fancy it might have gone hard with me;
for if ever there was murder in a man's heart it was in his when I
showed him that paper and then replaced it next the little poniard
you smile at me for wearing. This is over. What next, my queen?"

There was energy in the speaker's tone but none in attitude or aspect, as, still lying where she had left him, he pillowed his head upon his arm and turned toward her a face already worn and haggard with the feverish weariness that had usurped the blithe serenity which had been his chiefest charm a month ago. Pausing in her rapid walk, as if arrested by the change that seemed to strike her suddenly, she recalled her thoughts from the dominant idea of her life and, remembering the youth she was robbing of its innocent delights, answered the wistful look which betrayed the hunger of a heart she had never truly fed, as she knelt beside her husband and, laying her soft cheek to his, whispered in her tenderest accents, "I am not wholly selfish or ungrateful, Manuel. You shall rest now while I sing to you, and tomorrow we will go away among the hills and leave behind us for a time the dark temptation which harms you through me."

"No! Finish what you have begun. I will have all or nothing, for if we pause now you will bring me a divided mind, and I shall possess only the shadow of a wife. Take Gilbert and Babie with us, and end this devil's work without delay. Hark! What is that?"

Steps came flying down the long hall, a hand tried the lock, then beat impetuously upon the door, and a low voice whispered with shrill importunity, "Let me in! Oh, let me in!"

Manuel obeyed the urgent summons, and Mrs. Redmond, half dressed, with streaming hair and terror-stricken face, fled into Pauline's arms, crying incoherently, "Save me! Keep me! I never can go back to him; he said I was a burden and a curse, and wished I never had been born!"

"What has happened, Babie? We are your friends. Tell us, and let us comfort and protect you if we can."

But for a time speech was impossible, and the poor girl wept with a despairing vehemence sad to see, till their gentle efforts soothed her; and, sitting by Pauline, she told her trouble, looking oftenest at Manuel, who stood before them, as if sure of redress from him.

"When I left here an hour or more ago I found my rooms still empty, and, though I had not seen my husband since morning, I knew he would be displeased to find me waiting, so I cried myself to sleep and dreamed of the happy time when he was kind, till the sound of voices woke me. I heard Gilbert say, 'Babie is with your wife, her maid tells me; therefore we are alone here. What is this mysterious affair, Laroche?' That tempted me to listen, and then, Manuel, I learned all the shame and misery you so generously tried to spare me. How can I ever repay you, ever love and honor you enough for such care of one so helpless and forlorn as I?"

"I am repaid already. Let that pass, and tell what brings you here with such an air of fright and fear?"

"When you were gone he came straight to the inner room in search of something, saw me, and knew I must have heard all he had concealed from me so carefully. If you have ever seen him when that fierce temper of his grows ungovernable, you can guess what I endured. He said such cruel things I could not bear it, and cried out that I would come to you, for I was quite wild with terror, grief, and shame, that seemed like oil to fire. He swore I should not, and oh, Pauline, he struck me! See, if I do not tell the living truth!"

Trembling with excitement, Mrs. Redmond pushed back the wide sleeve of her wrapper and showed the red outline of a heavy hand. Manuel set his teeth and stamped his foot into the carpet with an indignant exclamation and the brief question, "Then you left him, Babie?"

"Yes, although he locked me in my room, saying the law gave him the right to teach obedience. I flung on these clothes, crept noiselessly along the balcony till the hall window let me in, and then I ran to you. He will come for me. Can he take me away? Must I go back to suffer any more?"

In the very act of uttering the words, Mrs. Redmond clung to Manuel with a cry of fear, for on the threshold stood her husband. A comprehensive glance seemed to stimulate his wrath and lend the hardihood wherewith to confront the three, saying sternly as he beckoned, "Babie, I am waiting for you."

She did not speak, but still clung to Manuel as if he were her only hope. A glance from Pauline checked the fiery words trembling on his lips, and he too stood silent while she answered with a calmness that amazed him:

"Your wife has chosen us her guardians, and I think you will scarcely venture to use force again with two such witnesses as these to prove that you have forfeited your right to her obedience and justify the step she has taken."

With one hand she uncovered the discolored arm, with the other held the forgery before him. For a moment Gilbert stood daunted by these mute accusations, but just then his ire burned hottest against Manuel; and believing that he could deal a double blow by wounding

Pauline through her husband, he ignored her presence and, turning to the young man, asked significantly, "Am I to understand that you refuse me my wife, and prefer to abide by the consequences of such an act?"

Calmed by Pauline's calmness, Manuel only drew the trembling creature closer, and answered with his haughtiest mien, "I do; spare yourself the labor of insulting me, for having placed yourself beyond the reach of a gentleman's weapon, I shall accept no challenge from a——"

A soft hand at his lips checked the opprobrious word, as Babie, true woman through it all, whispered with a broken sob, "Spare him, for I loved him once."

Gilbert Redmond had a heart, and, sinful though it was, this generous forbearance wrung it with a momentary pang of genuine remorse, too swiftly followed by a selfish hope that all was not lost if through his wife he could retain a hold upon the pair which now possessed for him the strong attraction of both love and hate. In that brief pause this thought came, was accepted and obeyed, for, as if yielding to an uncontrollable impulse of penitent despair, he stretched his arms to his wife, saying humbly, imploringly, "Babie, come back to me, and teach me how I may retrieve the past. I freely confess I bitterly repent my manifold transgressions, and submit to your decree alone; but in executing justice, oh, remember mercy! Remember that I was too early left fatherless, motherless, and went astray for want of some kind heart to guide and cherish me. There is still time. Be compassionate and save me from myself. Am I not punished enough? Must death be my only comforter? Babie, when all others cast me off, will you too forsake me?"

"No, I will not! Only love me, and I can forgive, forget, and still be happy!"

Pauline was right. The spaniel-like nature still loved the hand that struck it, and Mrs. Redmond joyfully returned to the arms from which she had so lately fled. The tenderest welcome she had ever received from him welcomed the loving soul whose faith was not yet dead, for Gilbert felt the value this once neglected possession had suddenly acquired, and he held it close; yet as he soothed with gentle touch and tone, could not forbear a glance of triumph at the spectators of the scene.

Pauline met it with that inscrutable smile of hers, and a look of intelligence toward her husband, as she said, "Did I not prophesy truly, Manuel? Be kind to her, Gilbert, and when next we meet show us a happier wife than the one now sobbing on your shoulder. Babie, good night and farewell, for we are off to the mountains in the morning."

"Oh, let us go with you as you promised! You know our secret, you pity me and will help Gilbert to be what he should. I cannot live at home, and places like this will seem so desolate when you and Manuel are gone. May we, can we be with you a little longer?"

"If Gilbert wishes it and Manuel consents, we will bear and forbear much for your sake, my poor child."

Pauline's eye said, "Dare you go?" and Gilbert's answered, "Yes," as the two met with a somber fire in each; but his lips replied, "Anywhere with you, Babie," and Manuel took Mrs. Redmond's hand with a graceful warmth that touched her deeper than his words.

"Your example teaches me the beauty of compassion, and Pauline's friends are mine."

"Always so kind to me! Dear Manuel, I never can forget it, though I have nothing to return but this," and, like a grateful child, she lifted up her innocent face so wistfully he could only bend his tall head to receive the kiss she offered.

Gilbert's black brows lowered ominously at the sight, but he never spoke; and, when her good-nights were over, bowed silently and carried his little wife away, nestling to him as if all griefs and pains were banished by returning love.

"Poor little heart! She should have a smoother path to tread. Heaven grant she may hereafter; and this sudden penitence prove no sham." Manuel paused suddenly, for as if obeying an unconquerable impulse, Pauline laid a hand on either shoulder and searched his face with an expression which baffled his comprehension, though he bore it steadily till her eyes fell before his own, when he asked smilingly:

"Is the doubt destroyed, *cariña?*"

"No; it is laid asleep."

Then as he drew her nearer, as if to make his peace for his unknown offense, she turned her cheek away and left him silently. Did she fear to find Babie's kiss upon his lips?

≥ *chapter IV* ≤

THE work of weeks is soon recorded, and when another month was gone these were the changes it had wrought. The four so strangely bound together by ties of suffering and sin went on their way, to the world's eye, blessed with every gracious gift, but below the tranquil surface rolled that undercurrent whose mysterious tides ebb and flow in human hearts unfettered by race or rank or time. Gilbert was a good actor, but, though he curbed his fitful temper, smoothed his mien, and sweetened his manner, his wife soon felt the vanity of hoping to recover that which never had been hers. Silently she accepted the fact and, uttering no complaint, turned to others for the fostering warmth without which she could not live. Conscious of a hunger like her own, Manuel could offer her sincerest sympathy, and soon learned to find a troubled pleasure in the knowledge that she loved him and her husband knew it, for his life of the emotions was rapidly maturing the boy into the man, as the fierce ardors of his native skies quicken the growth of wondrous plants that blossom in a night. Mrs. Redmond, as young in character as in years, felt the attraction of a nature generous and sweet, and yielded to it as involuntarily as an unsupported vine yields to the wind that blows it to the strong arms of a tree, still unconscious that a warmer sentiment than gratitude made his companionship the sunshine of her life. Pauline saw this, and sometimes owned within herself that she had evoked spirits which she could not rule, but her purpose drove her on, and in it she found a charm more perilously potent than before. Gilbert watched the three with a smile darker than a frown, yet no reproach warned his wife of the danger which she did not see; no jealous demonstration roused Manuel to rebel against the oppression of a presence so distasteful to him; no rash act or word gave Pauline power to banish him, though the one desire of his soul became the discovery of the key to the inscrutable expression of her eyes as they followed the young pair, whose growing friendship left their mates alone. Slowly her manner softened toward him, pity seemed to bridge across the gulf that lay between them, and in rare moments time appeared to have retraced its steps, leaving the tender woman of a year ago. Nourished by such unexpected hope, the early passion throve and strengthened until it became the mastering ambition of his life, and, only pausing to make assurance doubly sure, he waited the advent of the hour when he could "put his fortune to the touch and win or lose it all."

"Manuel, are you coming?"

He was lying on the sward at Mrs. Redmond's feet, and, waking from the reverie that held him, while his companion sang the love lay he was teaching her, he looked up to see his wife standing on the green slope before him. A black lace scarf lay over her blonde hair as Spanish women wear their veils, below it the violet eyes shone clear, the cheek glowed with the color fresh winds had blown upon their paleness, the lips parted with a wistful smile, and a knot of bright-hued leaves upon her bosom made a mingling of snow and fire in the dress, whose white folds swept the grass. Against a background of hoary cliffs and somber pines, this figure stood out like a picture of blooming womanhood, but Manuel saw three blemishes upon it—Gilbert had sketched her with that shadowy veil upon her head, Gilbert had swung himself across a precipice to reach the scarlet nosegay for her breast, Gilbert stood beside her with her hand upon his arm; and troubled by the fear that often haunted him since Pauline's manner to himself had grown so shy and sad, Manuel leaned and looked forgetful of reply, but Mrs. Redmond answered blithely:

"He is coming, but with me. You are too grave for us, so go your ways, talking wisely of heaven and earth, while we come after, enjoying both as we gather lichens, chase the goats, and meet you at the waterfall. Now señor, put away guitar and book, for I have learned my lesson; so help me with this unruly hair of mine and leave the Spanish for today."

They looked a pair of lovers as Manuel held back the long locks blowing in the wind, while Babie tied her hat, still chanting the burthen of the tender song she had caught so soon. A voiceless sigh stirred the ruddy leaves on Pauline's bosom as she turned away, but Gilbert embodied it in words, "They are happier without us. Let us go."

Neither spoke till they reached the appointed tryst. The others were not there, and, waiting for them, Pauline sat on a mossy stone, Gilbert leaned against the granite boulder beside her, and both silently surveyed a scene that made the heart glow, the eye kindle with delight as it swept down from that airy height, across valleys dappled with shadow and dark with untrodden forests, up ranges of majestic mountains, through gap after gap, each hazier than the last, far out into that sea of blue which rolls around all the world. Behind them roared the waterfall swollen with autumn rains and hurrying to pour itself into the rocky basin that lay boiling below, there to leave its legacy of shattered trees, then to dash itself into a deeper chasm, soon to be haunted by a tragic legend and go glittering away through forest, field, and intervale to join the river rolling slowly to the sea. Won by the beauty and the grandeur of the scene, Pauline forgot she was not alone, till turning, she suddenly became aware that while she scanned the face of nature her companion had been scanning hers. What he saw there she could not tell, but all restraint had vanished from his manner, all reticence from his speech, for with the old ardor in his eye, the old impetuosity in his voice, he said, leaning down as if to read her heart, "This is the moment I have waited for so long. For now you see what I see, that both have made a bitter blunder, and may yet repair it. Those children love each other; let them love, youth mates them, fortune makes them equals, fate brings them together that we may be free. Accept this freedom as I do, and come out into the world with me to lead the life you were born to enjoy."

With the first words he uttered Pauline felt that the time had come, and in the drawing of a breath was ready for it, with every sense alert, every power under full control, every feature obedient to the art which had become a second nature. Gilbert had seized her hand, and she did not draw it back; the sudden advent of the instant which must end her work sent an unwonted color to her cheek, and she did avert it;

the exultation which flashed into her eyes made it unsafe to meet his own, and they drooped before him as if in shame or fear, her whole face woke and brightened with the excitement that stirred her blood. She did not seek to conceal it, but let him cheat himself with the belief that love touched it with such light and warmth, as she softly answered in a voice whose accents seemed to assure his hope.

"You ask me to relinquish much. What do you offer in return, Gilbert, that I may not for a second time find love's labor lost?"

It was a wily speech, though sweetly spoken, for it reminded him how much he had thrown away, how little now remained to give, but her mien inspired him, and nothing daunted, he replied more ardently than ever:

"I can offer you a heart always faithful in truth though not in seeming, for I never loved that child. I would give years of happy life to undo that act and be again the man you trusted. I can offer you a name which shall yet be an honorable one, despite the stain an hour's madness cast upon it. You once taunted me with cowardice because I dared not face the world and conquer it. I dare do that now; I long to escape from this disgraceful servitude, to throw myself into the press, to struggle and achieve for your dear sake. I can offer you strength, energy, devotion—three gifts worthy any woman's acceptance who possesses power to direct, reward, and enjoy them as you do, Pauline. Because with your presence for my inspiration, I feel that I can retrieve my faultful past, and with time become God's noblest work—an honest man. Babie never could exert this influence over me. You can, you will, for now my earthly hope is in your hands, my soul's salvation in your love."

If that love had not died a sudden death, it would have risen up to answer him as the one sincere desire of an erring life cried out to her for help, and this man, as proud as sinful, knelt down before her with a passionate humility never paid at any other shrine, human or divine. It seemed to melt and win her, for he saw the color ebb and flow, heard the rapid beating of her heart, felt the hand tremble in his own, and received no denial but a lingering doubt, whose removal was a keen satisfaction to himself.

"Tell me, before I answer, are you sure that Manuel loves Babie?"

"I am; for every day convinces me that he has outlived the brief delusion, and longs for liberty, but dares not ask it. Ah! that pricks pride! But it is so. I have watched with jealous vigilance and let no sign escape me; because in his infidelity to you lay my chief hope. Has he not grown melancholy, cold, and silent? Does he not seek Babie and, of late, shun you? Will he not always yield his place to me without a token of displeasure or regret? Has he ever uttered reproach, warning, or command to you, although he knows I was and am your lover? Can you deny these proofs, or pause to ask if he will refuse to break the tie that binds him to a woman, whose superiority in all things keeps him a subject where he would be a king? You do not know the heart of man if you believe he will not bless you for his freedom."

Like the cloud which just then swept across the valley, blotting out its sunshine with a gloomy shadow, a troubled look flitted over Pauline's face. But if the words woke any sleeping fear she cherished, it was peremptorily banished, for scarcely had the watcher seen it than it was gone. Her eyes still shone upon the ground, and still she prolonged the bittersweet delight at seeing this humiliation of both soul and body by asking the one question whose reply would complete her sad success.

"Gilbert, do you believe I love you still?"

"I know it! Can I not read the signs that proved it to me once? Can I forget that, though you followed me to pity and despise, you have remained to pardon and befriend? Am I not sure that no other power could work the change you have wrought in me? I was learning to be content with slavery, and slowly sinking into that indolence of will which makes submission easy. I was learning to forget you, and be resigned to hold the shadow when the substance was gone, but you came, and with a look undid my work, with a word destroyed my hard-won peace, with a touch roused the passion which was not dead but sleeping, and have made this month of growing certainty to be the sweetest in my life—for I believed all lost, and you showed me that all was won. Surely that smile is propitious! and I may hope to hear the happy confirmation of my faith from lips that were formed to say 'I love!' "

She looked up then, and her eyes burned on him, with an expression which made his heart leap with expectant joy, as over cheek and forehead spread a glow of womanly emotion too genuine to be feigned, and her voice thrilled with the fervor of that sentiment which blesses life and outlives death.

"Yes, I love; not as of old, with a girl's blind infatuation, but with the warmth and wisdom of heart, mind, and soul—love made up of honor, penitence and trust, nourished in secret by the better self which lingers in the most tried and tempted of us, and now ready to blossom and bear fruit, if God so wills. I have been once deceived, but faith still endures, and I believe that I may yet earn this crowning gift of a woman's life for the man who shall make my happiness as I make his —who shall find me the prouder for past coldness, the humbler for past pride—whose life shall pass serenely loving. And that beloved is—my husband."

If she had lifted her white hand and stabbed him, with that smile upon her face, it would not have shocked him with a more pale dismay than did those two words as Pauline shook him off and rose up, beautiful and stern as an avenging angel. Dumb with an amazement too fathomless for words, he knelt there motionless and aghast. She did not speak. And, passing his hand across his eyes as if he felt himself the prey to some delusion, he rose slowly, asking, half incredulously, half imploringly, "Pauline, this is a jest?"

"To me it is; to you—a bitter earnest."

A dim foreboding of the truth fell on him then, and with it a strange sense of fear; for in this apparition of human judgment he seemed to receive a premonition of the divine. With a sudden gesture of something like entreaty, he cried out, as if his fate lay in her hands, "How will it end? how will it end?"

"As it began—in sorrow, shame and loss."

Then, in words that fell hot and heavy on the sore heart made desolate, she poured out the dark history of the wrong and the atonement wrung from him with such pitiless patience and inexorable will. No hard fact remained unrecorded, no subtle act unveiled, no hint of her bright future unspared to deepen the gloom of his. And when the final word of doom died upon the lips that should have awarded pardon, not punishment, Pauline tore away the last gift he had given, and dropping it to the rocky path, set her foot upon it, as if it were the scarlet badge of her subjection to the evil spirit which had haunted her so long, now cast out and crushed forever.

Gilbert had listened with a slowly gathering despair, which deepened to the blind recklessness that comes to those whose passions are their masters, when some blow smites but cannot subdue. Pale to his very lips, with the still white wrath, so much more terrible to witness than the fiercest ebullition of the ire that flames and feeds like a sudden fire, he waited till she ended, then used the one retaliation she had left

him. His hand went to his breast, a tattered glove flashed white against the cliff as he held it up before her, saying, in a voice that rose gradually till the last words sounded clear above the waterfall's wild song:

"It was well and womanly done, Pauline, and I could wish Manuel a happy life with such a tender, frank, and noble wife; but the future which you paint so well never shall be his. For, by the Lord that hears me! I swear I will end this jest of yours in a more bitter earnest than you prophesied. Look; I have worn this since the night you began the conflict, which has ended in defeat to me, as it shall to you. I do not war with women, but you shall have one man's blood upon your soul, for I will goad that tame boy to rebellion by flinging this in his face and taunting him with a perfidy blacker than my own. Will that rouse him to forget your commands and answer like a man?"

"Yes!"

The word rang through the air sharp and short as a pistol shot, a slender brown hand wrenched the glove away, and Manuel came between them. Wild with fear, Mrs. Redmond clung to him. Pauline sprang before him, and for a moment the two faced each other, with a year's smoldering jealousy and hate blazing in fiery eyes, trembling in clenched hands, and surging through set teeth in defiant speech.

"This is the gentleman who gambles his friend to desperation, and skulks behind a woman, like the coward he is," sneered Gilbert.

"Traitor and swindler, you lie!" shouted Manuel, and, flinging his wife behind him, he sent the glove, with a stinging blow, full in his opponent's face.

Then the wild beast that lurks in every strong man's blood leaped up in Gilbert Redmond's, as, with a single gesture of his sinewy right arm he swept Manuel to the verge of the narrow ledge, saw him hang poised there one awful instant, struggling to save the living weight that weighed him down, heard a heavy plunge into the black pool below, and felt that thrill of horrible delight which comes to murderers alone.

So swift and sure had been the act it left no time for help. A rush, a plunge, a pause, and then two figures stood where four had been—a man and woman staring dumbly at each other, appalled at the dread silence that made high noon more ghostly than the deepest night. And with that moment of impotent horror, remorse, and woe, Pauline's long punishment began.

The Mysterious Key

~ and ~

WHAT IT OPENED

BY L. M. ALCOTT

∗ *chapter I* ∗

THE PROPHECY

Trevlyn lands and Trevlyn gold,
Heir nor heiress e'er shall hold,
Undisturbed, till, spite of rust,
Truth is found in Trevlyn dust.

"THIS is the third time I've found you poring over that old rhyme. What is the charm, Richard? Not its poetry I fancy."

And the young wife laid a slender hand on the yellow, time-worn page where, in Old English text, appeared the lines she laughed at.

Richard Trevlyn looked up with a smile and threw by the book, as if annoyed at being discovered reading it. Drawing his wife's hand through his own, he led her back to her couch, folded the soft shawls about her, and, sitting in a low chair beside her, said in a cheerful tone, though his eyes betrayed some hidden care, "My love, that book is a history of our family for centuries, and that old prophecy has never yet been fulfilled, except the 'heir and heiress' line. I am the last Trevlyn, and as the time draws near when my child shall be born, I naturally think of his future, and hope he will enjoy his heritage in peace."

"God grant it!" softly echoed Lady Trevlyn, adding, with a look askance at the old book, "I read that history once, and fancied it must be a romance, such dreadful things are recorded in it. Is it all true, Richard?"

"Yes, dear. I wish it was not. Ours has been a wild, unhappy race till the last generation or two. The stormy nature came in with old Sir Ralph, the fierce Norman knight, who killed his only son in a fit of wrath, by a blow with his steel gauntlet, because the boy's strong will would not yield to his."

"Yes, I remember, and his daughter Clotilde held the castle during a siege, and married her cousin, Count Hugo. 'Tis a warlike race, and I like it in spite of the mad deeds."

"Married her cousin! That has been the bane of our family in times past. Being too proud to mate elsewhere, we have kept to ourselves till idiots and lunatics began to appear. My father was the first who broke the law among us, and I followed his example: choosing the freshest, sturdiest flower I could find to transplant into our exhausted soil."

"I hope it will do you honor by blossoming bravely. I never forget that you took me from a very humble home, and have made me the happiest wife in England."

"And I never forget that you, a girl of eighteen, consented to leave your hills and come to cheer the long-deserted house of an old man like me," returned her husband fondly.

"Nay, don't call yourself old, Richard; you are only forty-five, the boldest, handsomest man in Warwickshire. But lately you look worried; what is it? Tell me, and let me advise or comfort you."

"It is nothing, Alice, except my natural anxiety for you— Well, Kingston, what do you want?"

Trevlyn's tender tones grew sharp as he addressed the entering servant, and the smile on his lips vanished, leaving them dry and white as he glanced at the card he handed him. An instant he stood staring at it, then asked, "Is the man here?"

"In the library, sir."

"I'll come."

Flinging the card into the fire, he watched it turn to ashes before he spoke, with averted eyes: "Only some annoying business, love; I shall soon be with you again. Lie and rest till I come."

With a hasty caress he left her, but as he passed a mirror, his wife saw an expression of intense excitement in his face. She said nothing, and lay motionless for several minutes evidently struggling with some strong impulse.

"He is ill and anxious, but hides it from me; I have a right to know, and he'll forgive me when I prove that it does no harm."

As she spoke to herself she rose, glided noiselessly through the hall, entered a small closet built in the thickness of the wall, and, bending to the keyhole of a narrow door, listened with a half-smile on her lips at the trespass she was committing. A murmur of voices met her ear. Her husband spoke oftenest, and suddenly some word of his dashed the smile from her face as if with a blow. She started, shrank, and shivered, bending lower with set teeth, white cheeks, and panic-stricken heart. Paler and paler grew his lips, wilder and wilder her eyes, fainter and fainter her breath, till, with a long sigh, a vain effort to save herself, she sank prone upon the threshold of the door, as if struck down by death.

"Mercy on us, my lady, are you ill?" cried Hester, the maid, as her mistress glided into the room looking like a ghost, half an hour later.

"I am faint and cold. Help me to my bed, but do not disturb Sir Richard."

A shiver crept over her as she spoke, and, casting a wild, woeful look about her, she laid her head upon the pillow like one who never cared to lift it up again. Hester, a sharp-eyed, middle-aged woman, watched the pale creature for a moment, then left the room muttering, "Something is wrong, and Sir Richard must know it. That black-bearded man came for no good, I'll warrant."

At the door of the library she paused. No sound of voices came from within; a stifled groan was all she heard; and without waiting to knock she went in, fearing she knew not what. Sir Richard sat at his writing table pen in hand, but his face was hidden on his arm, and his whole attitude betrayed the presence of some overwhelming despair.

"Please, sir, my lady is ill. Shall I send for anyone?"

No answer. Hester repeated her words, but Sir Richard never stirred. Much alarmed, the woman raised his head, saw that he was unconscious, and rang for help. But Richard Trevlyn was past help, though he lingered for some hours. He spoke but once, murmuring faintly, "Will Alice come to say good-bye?"

"Bring her if she can come," said the physician.

Hester went, found her mistress lying as she left her, like a figure carved in stone. When she gave the message, Lady Trevlyn answered sternly, "Tell him I will not come," and turned her face to the wall, with an expression which daunted the woman too much for another word.

Hester whispered the hard answer to the physician, fearing to utter it aloud, but Sir Richard heard it, and died with a despairing prayer for pardon on his lips.

When day dawned Sir Richard lay in his shroud and his little daughter in her cradle, the one unwept, the other unwelcomed by the wife and mother, who, twelve hours before, had called herself the happiest woman in England. They thought her dying, and at her own command gave her the sealed letter bearing her address which her husband left behind him. She read it, laid it in her bosom, and, waking from the trance which seemed to have so strongly chilled and changed her, besought those about her with passionate earnestness to save her life.

For two days she hovered on the brink of the grave, and nothing but the indomitable will to live saved her, the doctors said. On the third day she rallied wonderfully, and some purpose seemed to gift her with unnatural strength. Evening came, and the house was very still, for all the sad bustle of preparation for Sir Richard's funeral was over, and he lay for the last night under his own roof. Hester sat in the darkened chamber of her mistress, and no sound broke the hush but the low lullaby the nurse was singing to the fatherless baby in the adjoining room. Lady Trevlyn seemed to sleep, but suddenly put back the curtain, saying abruptly, "Where does he lie?"

"In the state chamber, my lady," replied Hester, anxiously watching the feverish glitter of her mistress's eye, the flush on her cheek, and the unnatural calmness of her manner.

"Help me to go there; I must see him."

"It would be your death, my lady. I beseech you, don't think of it," began the woman; but Lady Trevlyn seemed not to hear her, and something in the stern pallor of her face awed the woman into submission.

Wrapping the slight form of her mistress in a warm cloak, Hester half-led, half-carried her to the state room, and left her on the threshold.

"I must go in alone; fear nothing, but wait for me here," she said, and closed the door behind her.

Five minutes had not elapsed when she reappeared with no sign of grief on her rigid face.

"Take me to my bed and bring my jewel box," she said, with a shuddering sigh, as the faithful servant received her with an exclamation of thankfulness.

When her orders had been obeyed, she drew from her bosom the portrait of Sir Richard which she always wore, and, removing the ivory oval from the gold case, she locked the former in a tiny drawer of the casket, replaced the empty locket in her breast, and bade Hester give the jewels to Watson, her lawyer, who would see them put in a safe place till the child was grown.

"Dear heart, my lady, you'll wear them yet, for you're too young to grieve all your days, even for so good a man as my blessed master. Take comfort, and cheer up, for the dear child's sake if no more."

"I shall never wear them again" was all the answer as Lady Trevlyn drew the curtains, as if to shut out hope.

Sir Richard was buried and, the nine days' gossip over, the mystery of his death died for want of food, for the only person who could have explained it was in a state which forbade all allusion to that tragic day.

For a year Lady Trevlyn's reason was in danger. A long fever left her so weak in mind and body that there was little hope of recovery, and her days were passed in a state of apathy sad to witness. She seemed to have forgotten everything, even the shock which had so sorely stricken her. The sight of her child failed to rouse her, and month after month slipped by, leaving no trace of their passage on her mind, and but slightly renovating her feeble body.

Who the stranger was, what his aim in coming, or why he never reappeared, no one discovered. The contents of the letter left by Sir Richard were unknown, for the paper had been destroyed by Lady Trevlyn and no clue could be got from her. Sir Richard had died of heart disease, the physicians said, though he might have lived years had no sudden shock assailed him. There were few relatives to make investigations, and friends soon forgot the sad young widow; so the years rolled on, and Lillian the heiress grew from infancy to childhood in the shadow of this mystery.

≈ *chapter II* ≈

PAUL

"COME, child, the dew is falling, and it is time we went in."
"No, no, Mamma is not rested yet, so I may run down
to the spring if I like." And Lillian, as willful as winsome,
vanished among the tall ferns where deer couched and rabbits hid.

Hester leisurely followed, looking as unchanged as if a day instead
of twelve years had passed since her arms received the little mistress,
who now ruled her like a tyrant. She had taken but a few steps when
the child came flying back, exclaiming in an excited tone, "Oh, come
quick! There's a man there, a dead man. I saw him and I'm frightened!"

"Nonsense, child, it's one of the keepers asleep, or some stroller
who has no business here. Take my hand and we'll see who it is."

Somewhat reassured, Lillian led her nurse to one of the old oaks
beside the path, and pointed to a figure lying half hidden in the fern.
A slender, swarthy boy of sixteen, with curly black hair, dark brows,
and thick lashes, a singularly stern mouth, and a general expression of
strength and pride, which added character to his boyish face and dignified his poverty. His dress betrayed that, being dusty and threadbare,
his shoes much worn, and his possessions contained in the little bundle
on which he pillowed his head. He was sleeping like one quite spent

with weariness, and never stirred, though Hester bent away the ferns and examined him closely.

"He's not dead, my deary; he's asleep, poor lad, worn out with his day's tramp, I dare say."

"I'm glad he's alive, and I wish he'd wake up. He's a pretty boy, isn't he? See what nice hands he's got, and his hair is more curly than mine. Make him open his eyes, Hester," commanded the little lady, whose fear had given place to interest.

"Hush, he's stirring. I wonder how he got in, and what he wants," whispered Hester.

"I'll ask him," and before her nurse could arrest her, Lillian drew a tall fern softly over the sleeper's face, laughing aloud as she did so.

The boy woke at the sound, and without stirring lay looking up at the lovely little face bent over him, as if still in a dream.

"Bella cara," he said, in a musical voice. Then, as the child drew back abashed at the glance of his large, bright eyes, he seemed to wake entirely and, springing to his feet, looked at Hester with a quick, searching glance. Something in his face and air caused the woman to soften her tone a little, as she said gravely, "Did you wish to see any one at the Hall?"

"Yes. Is Lady Trevlyn here?" was the boy's answer, as he stood cap in hand, with the smile fading already from his face.

"She is, but unless your business is very urgent you had better see Parks, the keeper; we don't trouble my lady with trifles."

"I've a note for her from Colonel Daventry; and as it is *not* a trifle, I'll deliver it myself, if you please."

Hester hesitated an instant, but Lillian cried out, "Mamma is close by, come and see her," and led the way, beckoning as she ran.

The lad followed with a composed air, and Hester brought up the rear, taking notes as she went with a woman's keen eye.

Lady Trevlyn, a beautiful, pale woman, delicate in health and melancholy in spirit, sat on a rustic seat with a book in her hand; not reading, but musing with an absent mind. As the child approached, she held out her hand to welcome her, but neither smiled nor spoke.

"Mamma, here is a—a person to see you," cried Lillian, rather at a loss how to designate the stranger, whose height and gravity now awed her.

"A note from Colonel Daventry, my lady," and with a bow the boy delivered the missive.

Scarcely glancing at him, she opened it and read:

My Dear Friend,

The bearer of this, Paul Jex, has been with me some months and has served me well. I brought him from Paris, but he is English born, and, though friendless, prefers to remain here, even after we leave, as we do in a week. When I last saw you you mentioned wanting a lad to help in the garden; Paul is accustomed to that employment, though my wife used him as a sort of page in the house. Hoping you may be able to give him shelter, I venture to send him. He is honest, capable, and trustworthy in all respects. Pray try him, and oblige,

Yours sincerely,

J. R. Daventry

"The place is still vacant, and I shall be very glad to give it to you, if you incline to take it," said Lady Trevlyn, lifting her eyes from the note and scanning the boy's face.

"I do, madam," he answered respectfully.

"The colonel says you are English," added the lady, in a tone of surprise.

The boy smiled, showing a faultless set of teeth, as he replied, "I am, my lady, though just now I may not look it, being much tanned and very dusty. My father was an Englishman, but I've lived abroad a good deal since he died, and got foreign ways, perhaps."

As he spoke without any accent, and looked full in her face with a pair of honest blue eyes under the dark lashes, Lady Trevlyn's momentary doubt vanished.

"Your age, Paul?"

"Sixteen, my lady."

"You understand gardening?"

"Yes, my lady."

"And what else?"

"I can break horses, serve at table, do errands, read aloud, ride after a young lady as groom, illuminate on parchment, train flowers, and make myself useful in any way."

The tone, half modest, half eager, in which the boy spoke, as well as the odd list of his accomplishments, brought a smile to Lady Trevlyn's lips, and the general air of the lad prepossessed her.

"I want Lillian to ride soon, and Roger is rather old for an escort to such a little horsewoman. Don't you think we might try Paul?" she said, turning to Hester.

The woman gravely eyed the lad from head to foot, and shook her head, but an imploring little gesture and a glance of the handsome eyes softened her heart in spite of herself.

"Yes, my lady, if he does well about the place, and Parks thinks he's steady enough, we might try it by-and-by."

Lillian clapped her hands and, drawing nearer, exclaimed confidingly, as she looked up at her new groom, "I know he'll do, Mamma. I like him very much, and I hope you'll let him train my pony for me. Will you, Paul?"

"Yes."

As he spoke very low and hastily, the boy looked away from the eager little face before him, and a sudden flush of color crossed his dark cheek.

Hester saw it and said within herself, "That boy has good blood in his veins. He's no clodhopper's son, I can tell by his hands and feet, his air and walk. Poor lad, it's hard for him, I'll warrant, but he's not too proud for honest work, and I like that."

"You may stay, Paul, and we will try you for a month. Hester, take him to Parks and see that he is made comfortable. Tomorrow we will see what he can do. Come, darling, I am rested now."

As she spoke, Lady Trevlyn dismissed the boy with a gracious gesture and led her little daughter away. Paul stood watching her, as if forgetful of his companion, till she said, rather tartly, "Young man, you'd better have thanked my lady while she was here than stare after her now it's too late. If you want to see Parks, you'd best come, for I'm going."

"Is that the family tomb yonder, where you found me asleep?" was the unexpected reply to her speech, as the boy quietly followed her, not at all daunted by her manner.

"Yes, and that reminds me to ask how you got in, and why you were napping there, instead of doing your errand properly?"

"I leaped the fence and stopped to rest before presenting myself, Miss Hester" was the cool answer, accompanied by a short laugh as he confessed his trespass.

"You look as if you'd had a long walk; where are you from?"

"London."

"Bless the boy! It's fifty miles away."

"So my shoes show; but it's a pleasant trip in summer time."

"But why did you walk, child! Had you no money?"

"Plenty, but not for wasting on coaches, when my own stout legs could carry me. I took a two days' holiday and saved my money for better things."

"I like that," said Hester, with an approving nod. "You'll get on, my lad, if that's your way, and I'll lend a hand, for laziness is my abomination, and one sees plenty nowadays."

"Thank you. That's friendly, and I'll prove that I am grateful. Please tell me, is my lady ill?"

"Always delicate since Sir Richard died."

"How long ago was that?"

"Ten years or more."

"Are there no young gentlemen in the family?"

"No, Miss Lillian is an only child, and a sweet one, bless her!"

"A proud little lady, I should say."

"And well she may be, for there's no better blood in England than the Trevlyns, and she's heiress to a noble fortune."

"Is that the Trevlyn coat of arms?" asked the boy abruptly, pointing to a stone falcon with the motto ME AND MINE carved over the gate through which they were passing.

"Yes. Why do you ask?"

"Mere curiosity; I know something of heraldry and often paint these things for my own pleasure. One learns odd amusements abroad," he added, seeing an expression of surprise on the woman's face.

"You'll have little time for such matters here. Come in and report yourself to the keeper, and if you'll take my advice ask no questions of him, for you'll get no answers."

"I seldom ask questions of men, as *they* are not fond of gossip." And the boy nodded with a smile of mischievous significance as he entered the keeper's lodge.

A sharp lad and a saucy, if he likes. I'll keep my eye on him, for my lady takes no more thought of such things than a child, and Lillian cares for nothing but her own will. He has a taking way with him, though, and knows how to flatter. It's well he does, poor lad, for life's a hard matter to a friendless soul like him.

As she thought these thoughts Hester went on to the house, leaving Paul to win the good graces of the keeper, which he speedily did by assuming an utterly different manner from that he had worn with the woman.

That night, when the boy was alone in his own room, he wrote a long letter in Italian describing the events of the day, enclosed a sketch of the falcon and motto, directed it to "Father Cosmo Carmela, Genoa," and lay down to sleep, muttering, with a grim look and a heavy sigh, "So far so well; I'll not let my heart be softened by pity, or my purpose change till my promise is kept. Pretty child, I wish I had never seen her!"

≽ *chapter III* ≼

SECRET SERVICE

IN a week Paul was a favorite with the household; even prudent
Hester felt the charm of his presence, and owned that Lillian
was happier for a young companion in her walks. Hitherto the
child had led a solitary life, with no playmates of her own age, such
being the will of my lady; therefore she welcomed Paul as a new
and delightful amusement, considering him her private property and
soon transferring his duties from the garden to the house. Satisfied
of his merits, my lady yielded to Lillian's demands, and Paul was
installed as page to the young lady. Always respectful and obedient,
he never forgot his place, yet seemed unconsciously to influence all
who approached him, and win the goodwill of everyone.

My lady showed unusual interest in the lad, and Lillian openly
displayed her admiration for his accomplishments and her affection
for her devoted young servitor. Hester was much flattered by the
confidence he reposed in her, for to her alone did he tell his story,
and of her alone asked advice and comfort in his various small straits.
It was as she suspected: Paul was a gentleman's son, but misfortune
had robbed him of home, friends, and parents, and thrown him upon
the world to shift for himself. This sad story touched the woman's
heart, and the boy's manly spirit won respect. She had lost a son years
ago, and her empty heart yearned over the motherless lad. Ashamed
to confess the tender feeling, she wore her usual severe manner to

him in public, but in private softened wonderfully and enjoyed the boy's regard heartily.

"Paul, come in. I want to speak with you a moment," said my lady, from the long window of the library to the boy who was training vines outside.

Dropping his tools and pulling off his hat, Paul obeyed, looking a little anxious, for the month of trial expired that day. Lady Trevlyn saw and answered the look with a gracious smile.

"Have no fears. You are to stay if you will, for Lillian is happy and I am satisfied with you."

"Thank you, my lady." And an odd glance of mingled pride and pain shone in the boy's downcast eyes.

"That is settled, then. Now let me say what I called you in for. You spoke of being able to illuminate on parchment. Can you restore this old book for me?"

She put into his hand the ancient volume Sir Richard had been reading the day he died. It had lain neglected in a damp nook for years till my lady discovered it, and, sad as were the associations connected with it, she desired to preserve it for the sake of the weird prophecy if nothing else. Paul examined it, and as he turned it to and fro in his hands it opened at the page oftenest read by its late master. His eye kindled as he looked, and with a quick gesture he turned as if toward the light, in truth to hide the flash of triumph that passed across his face. Carefully controlling his voice, he answered in a moment, as he looked up, quite composed, "Yes, my lady, I can retouch the faded colors on these margins and darken the pale ink of the Old English text. I like the work, and will gladly do it if you like."

"Do it, then, but be very careful of the book while in your hands. Provide what is needful, and name your own price for the work," said his mistress.

"Nay, my lady, I am already paid—"

"How so?" she asked, surprised.

Paul had spoken hastily, and for an instant looked embarrassed, but answered with a sudden flush on his dark cheeks, "You have been kind to me, and I am glad to show my gratitude in any way, my lady."

"Let that pass, my boy. Do this little service for me and we will see about the recompense afterward." And with a smile Lady Trevlyn left him to begin his work.

The moment the door closed behind her a total change passed over Paul. He shook his clenched hand after her with a gesture of menace, then tossed up the old book and caught it with an exclamation of delight, as he reopened it at the worn page and reread the inexplicable verse.

"Another proof, another proof! The work goes bravely on, Father Cosmo; and boy as I am, I'll keep my word in spite of everything," he muttered.

"What is that you'll keep, lad?" said a voice behind him.

"I'll keep my word to my lady, and do my best to restore this book, Mrs. Hester," he answered, quickly recovering himself.

"Ah, that's the last book poor Master read. I hid it away, but my lady found it in spite of me," said Hester, with a doleful sigh.

"Did he die suddenly, then?" asked the boy.

"Dear heart, yes; I found him dying in this room with the ink scarce dry on the letter he left for my lady. A mysterious business and a sad one."

"Tell me about it. I like sad stories, and I already feel as if I belonged to the family, a loyal retainer as in the old times. While you dust the books and I rub the mold off this old cover, tell me the tale, please, Mrs. Hester."

She shook her head, but yielded to the persuasive look and tone of the boy, telling the story more fully than she intended, for she loved talking and had come to regard Paul as her own, almost.

"And the letter? What was in it?" asked the boy, as she paused at the catastrophe.

"No one ever knew but my lady."

"She destroyed it, then?"

"I thought so, till a long time afterward, one of the lawyers came pestering me with questions, and made me ask her. She was ill at the time, but answered with a look I shall never forget, 'No, it's not burnt, but no one shall ever see it.' I dared ask no more, but I fancy she has it safe somewhere and if it's ever needed she'll bring it out. It was only some private matters, I fancy."

"And the stranger?"

"Oh, he vanished as oddly as he came, and has never been found. A strange story, lad. Keep silent, and let it rest."

"No fear of my tattling," and the boy smiled curiously to himself as he bent over the book, polishing the brassbound cover.

"What are you doing with that pretty white wax?" asked Lillian the next day, as she came upon Paul in a quiet corner of the garden and found him absorbed in some mysterious occupation.

With a quick gesture he destroyed his work, and, banishing a momentary expression of annoyance, he answered in his accustomed tone as he began to work anew, "I am molding a little deer for you, Miss Lillian. See, here is a rabbit already done, and I'll soon have a stag also."

"It's very pretty! How many nice things you can do, and how kind you are to think of my liking something new. Was this wax what you went to get this morning when you rode away so early?" asked the child.

"Yes, Miss Lillian. I was ordered to exercise your pony and I made him useful as well. Would you like to try this? It's very easy."

Lillian was charmed, and for several days wax modeling was her favorite play. Then she tired of it, and Paul invented a new amusement, smiling his inexplicable smile as he threw away the broken toys of wax.

"You are getting pale and thin, keeping such late hours, Paul. Go to bed, boy, go to bed, and get your sleep early," said Hester a week afterward, with a motherly air, as Paul passed her one morning.

"And how do you know I don't go to bed?" he asked, wheeling about.

"My lady has been restless lately, and I sit up with her till she sleeps. As I go to my room, I see your lamp burning, and last night I got as far as your door, meaning to speak to you, but didn't, thinking you'd take it amiss. But really you are the worse for late hours, child."

"I shall soon finish restoring the book, and then I'll sleep. I hope I don't disturb you. I have to grind my colors, and often make more noise than I mean to."

Paul fixed his eyes sharply on the woman as he spoke, but she seemed unconscious of it, and turned to go on, saying indifferently, "Oh, that's the odd sound, is it? No, it doesn't trouble me, so grind away, and make an end of it as soon as may be."

An anxious fold in the boy's forehead smoothed itself away as he left her, saying to himself with a sigh of relief, "A narrow escape; it's well I keep the door locked."

The boy's light burned no more after that, and Hester was content till a new worry came to trouble her. On her way to her room late one night, she saw a tall shadow flit down one of the side corridors that branched from the main one. For a moment she was startled, but, being a woman of courage, she followed noiselessly, till the shadow seemed to vanish in the gloom of the great hall.

"If the house ever owned a ghost I'd say that's it, but it never did, so I suspect some deviltry. I'll step to Paul. He's not asleep, I dare say. He's a brave and a sensible lad, and with him I'll quietly search the house."

Away she went, more nervous than she would own, and tapped at the boy's door. No one answered, and, seeing that it was ajar, Hester whisked in so hurriedly that her candle went out. With an impatient exclamation at her carelessness she glided to the bed, drew the curtain, and put forth her hand to touch the sleeper. The bed was empty. A disagreeable thrill shot through her, as she assured herself of the fact by groping along the narrow bed. Standing in the shadow of the curtain, she stared about the dusky room, in which objects were visible by the light of a new moon.

"Lord bless me, what is the boy about! I do believe it was him I saw in the—" She got no further in her mental exclamation for the sound of light approaching footsteps neared her. Slipping around the bed she waited in the shadow, and a moment after Paul appeared, looking pale and ghostly, with dark, disheveled hair, wide-open eyes, and a cloak thrown over his shoulders. Without a pause he flung it off, laid himself in bed, and seemed to sleep at once.

"Paul! Paul!" whispered Hester, shaking him, after a pause of astonishment at the whole proceeding.

"Hey, what is it?" And he sat up, looking drowsily about him.

"Come, come, no tricks, boy. What are you doing, trailing about the house at this hour and in such trim?"

"Why, Hester, is it you?" he exclaimed with a laugh, as he shook off her grip and looked up at her in surprise.

"Yes, and well it is me. If it had been any of those silly girls, the house would have been roused by this time. What mischief is afoot that you leave your bed and play ghost in this wild fashion?"

"Leave my bed! Why, my good soul, I haven't stirred, but have been dreaming with all my might these two hours. What do you mean, Hester?"

She told him as she relit her lamp, and stood eyeing him sharply the while. When she finished he was silent a minute, then said, looking half vexed and half ashamed, "I see how it is, and I'm glad you alone have found me out. I walk in my sleep sometimes, Hester, that's the truth. I thought I'd got over it, but it's come back, you see, and I'm sorry for it. Don't be troubled. I never do any mischief or come to any harm. I just take a quiet promenade and march back to bed again. Did I frighten you?"

"Just a trifle, but it's nothing. Poor lad, you'll have to have a bedfellow or be locked up; it's dangerous to go roaming about in this way," said Hester anxiously.

"It won't last long, for I'll get more tired and then I shall sleep sounder. Don't tell anyone, please, else they'll laugh at me, and that's not pleasant. I don't mind your knowing for you seem almost like a mother, and I thank you for it with all my heart."

He held out his hand with the look that was irresistible to Hester. Remembering only that he was a motherless boy, she stroked the curly hair off his forehead, and kissed him, with the thought of her own son warm at her heart.

"Good night, dear. I'll say nothing, but give you something that will ensure quiet sleep hereafter."

With that she left him, but would have been annoyed could she have seen the convulsion of boyish merriment which took possession of him when alone, for he laughed till the tears ran down his cheeks.

⇘ *chapter IV* ⇙

VANISHED

"HE'S a handsome lad, and one any woman might be proud to call her son," said Hester to Bedford, the stately butler, as they lingered at the hall door one autumn morning to watch their young lady's departure on her daily ride.

"You are right, Mrs. Hester, he's a fine lad, and yet he seems above his place, though he does look the very picture of a lady's groom," replied Bedford approvingly.

So he did, as he stood holding the white pony of his little mistress, for the boy gave an air to whatever he wore and looked like a gentleman even in his livery. The dark-blue coat with silver buttons, the silver band about his hat, his white-topped boots and bright spurs, spotless gloves, and tightly drawn belt were all in perfect order, all becoming, and his handsome, dark face caused many a susceptible maid to blush and simper as they passed him. "Gentleman Paul" as the servants called him, was rather lofty and reserved among his mates, but they liked him nonetheless, for Hester had dropped hints of his story and quite a little romance had sprung up about him. He stood leaning against the docile creature, sunk in thought, and quite unconscious of the watchers and whisperers close by. But as Lillian appeared he woke up, attended to his duties like a well-trained groom, and lingered over his task as if he liked it. Down the avenue he rode behind her, but as they turned into a shady lane Lillian

(172)

beckoned, saying, in the imperious tone habitual to her, "Ride near me. I wish to talk."

Paul obeyed, and amused her with the chat she liked till they reached a hazel copse; here he drew rein, and, leaping down, gathered a handful of ripe nuts for her.

"How nice. Let us rest a minute here, and while I eat a few, please pull some of those flowers for Mamma. She likes a wild nosegay better than any I can bring her from the garden."

Lillian ate her nuts till Paul came to her with a hatful of late flowers and, standing by her, held the impromptu basket while she made up a bouquet to suit her taste.

"You shall have a posy, too; I like you to wear one in your buttonhole as the ladies' grooms do in the Park," said the child, settling a scarlet poppy in the blue coat.

"Thanks, Miss Lillian, I'll wear your colors with all my heart, especially today, for it is my birthday." And Paul looked up at the blooming little face with unusual softness in his keen blue eyes.

"Is it? Why, then, you're seventeen; almost a man, aren't you?"

"Yes, thank heaven," muttered the boy, half to himself.

"I wish I was as old. I shan't be in my teens till autumn. I must give you something, Paul, because I like you very much, and you are always doing kind things for me. What shall it be?" And the child held out her hand with a cordial look and gesture that touched the boy.

With one of the foreign fashions which sometimes appeared when he forgot himself, he kissed the small hand, saying impulsively, "My dear little mistress, I want nothing but your goodwill—and your forgiveness," he added, under his breath.

"You have that already, Paul, and I shall find something to add to it. But what is that?" And she laid hold of a little locket which had slipped into sight as Paul bent forward in his salute.

He thrust it back, coloring so deeply that the child observed it, and exclaimed, with a mischievous laugh, "It is your sweetheart, Paul. I heard Bessy, my maid, tell Hester she was sure you had one because you took no notice of them. Let me see it. Is she pretty?"

"Very pretty," answered the boy, without showing the picture.

"Do you like her very much?" questioned Lillian, getting interested in the little romance.

"Very much," and Paul's black eyelashes fell.

"Would you die for her, as they say in the old songs?" asked the girl, melodramatically.

"Yes, Miss Lillian, or live for her, which is harder."

"Dear me, how very nice it must be to have anyone care for one so much," said the child innocently. "I wonder if anybody ever will for me?"

> "Love comes to all soon or late,
>   And maketh gay or sad;
> For every bird will find its mate,
>   And every lass a lad,"

sang Paul, quoting one of Hester's songs, and looking relieved that Lillian's thoughts had strayed from him. But he was mistaken.

"Shall you marry this sweetheart of yours someday?" asked Lillian, turning to him with a curious yet wistful look.

"Perhaps."

"You look as if there was no 'perhaps' about it," said the child, quick to read the kindling of the eye and the change in the voice that accompanied the boy's reply.

"She is very young and I must wait, and while I wait many things may happen to part us."

"Is she a lady?"

"Yes, a wellborn, lovely little lady, and I'll marry her if I live." Paul spoke with a look of decision, and a proud lift of the head that contrasted curiously with the badge of servitude he wore.

Lillian felt this, and asked, with a sudden shyness coming over her, "But you are a gentleman, and so no one will mind even if you are not rich."

"How do you know what I am?" he asked quickly.

"I heard Hester tell the housekeeper that you were not what you seemed, and one day she hoped you'd get your right place again. I asked Mamma about it, and she said she would not let me be with you so much if you were not a fit companion for me. I was not to speak of it, but she means to be your friend and help you by-and-by."

"Does she?"

And the boy laughed an odd, short laugh that jarred on Lillian's ear and made her say reprovingly, "You are proud, I know, but you'll let us help you because we like to do it, and I have no brother to share my money with."

"Would you like one, or a sister?" asked Paul, looking straight into her face with his piercing eyes.

"Yes, indeed! I long for someone to be with me and love me, as Mamma can't."

"Would you be willing to share everything with another person —perhaps have to give them a great many things you like and now have all to yourself?"

"I think I should. I'm selfish, I know, because everyone pets and spoils me, but if I loved a person dearly I'd give up anything to them. Indeed I would, Paul, pray believe me."

She spoke earnestly, and leaned on his shoulder as if to enforce her words. The boy's arm stole around the little figure in the saddle, and a beautiful bright smile broke over his face as he answered warmly, "I do believe it, dear, and it makes me happy to hear you say so. Don't be afraid, I'm your equal, but I'll not forget that you are my little mistress till I can change from groom to gentleman."

He added the last sentence as he withdrew his arm, for Lillian had shrunk a little and blushed with surprise, not anger, at this first breach of respect on the part of her companion. Both were silent for a moment, Paul looking down and Lillian busy with her nosegay. She spoke first, assuming an air of satisfaction as she surveyed her work.

"That will please Mamma, I'm sure, and make her quite forget my naughty prank of yesterday. Do you know I offended her dreadfully by peeping into the gold case she wears on her neck? She was asleep and I was sitting by her. In her sleep she pulled it out and said something about a letter and Papa. I wanted to see Papa's face, for I never did, because the big picture of him is gone from the gallery where the others are, so I peeped into the case when she let it drop and was so disappointed to find nothing but a key."

"A key! What sort of a key?" cried Paul in an eager tone.

"Oh, a little silver one like the key of my piano, or the black cabinet. She woke and was very angry to find me meddling."

"What did it belong to?" asked Paul.

"Her treasure box, she said, but I don't know where or what that is, and I dare not ask any more, for she forbade my speaking to her about it. Poor Mamma! I'm always troubling her in some way or other."

With a penitent sigh, Lillian tied up her flowers and handed them to Paul to carry. As she did so, the change in his face struck her.

"How grim and old you look," she exclaimed. "Have I said anything that troubles you?"

"No, Miss Lillian. I'm only thinking."

"Then I wish you wouldn't think, for you get a great wrinkle in your forehead, your eyes grow almost black, and your mouth looks fierce. You are a very odd person, Paul; one minute as gay as any boy, and the next as grave and stern as a man with a deal of work to do."

"I *have* got a deal of work to do, so no wonder I look old and grim."

"What work, Paul?"

"To make my fortune and win my lady."

When Paul spoke in that tone and wore that look, Lillian felt as if they had changed places, and he was the master and she the servant. She wondered over this in her childish mind, but proud and willful as she was, she liked it, and obeyed him with unusual meekness when he suggested that it was time to return. As he rode silently beside her, she stole covert glances at him from under her wide hat brim, and studied his unconscious face as she had never done before. His lips moved now and then but uttered no audible sound, his black brows were knit, and once his hand went to his breast as if he thought of the little sweetheart whose picture lay there.

He's got a trouble. I wish he'd tell me and let me help him if I can. I'll make him show me that miniature someday, for I'm interested in that girl, thought Lillian with a pensive sigh.

As he held his hand for her little foot in dismounting her at the hall door, Paul seemed to have shaken off his grave mood, for he looked up and smiled at her with his blithest expression. But Lillian appeared to be the thoughtful one now and with an air of dignity, very pretty and becoming, thanked her young squire in a stately manner and swept into the house, looking tall and womanly in her flowing skirts.

Paul laughed as he glanced after her and, flinging himself onto his horse, rode away to the stables at a reckless pace, as if to work off some emotion for which he could find no other vent.

"Here's a letter for you, lad, all the way from some place in Italy. Who do you know there?" said Bedford, as the boy came back.

With a hasty "Thank you," Paul caught the letter and darted away to his own room, there to tear it open and, after reading a single line, to drop into a chair as if he had received a sudden blow. Growing paler and paler he read on, and when the letter fell from his hands he exclaimed, in a tone of despair, "How could he die at such a time!"

For an hour the boy sat thinking intently, with locked door, curtained window, and several papers strewn before him. Letters, memoranda, plans, drawings, and bits of parchment, all of which he took from a small locked portfolio always worn about him. Over these he pored with a face in which hope, despondency, resolve, and regret alternated rapidly. Taking the locket out he examined a ring which lay in one side, and the childish face which smiled on him from the other. His eyes filled as he locked and put it by, saying tenderly, "Dear little heart! I'll not forget or desert her whatever happens. Time must help me, and to time I must leave my work. One more attempt and then I'm off."

"I'll go to bed now, Hester; but while you get my things ready I'll take a turn in the corridor. The air will refresh me."

As she spoke, Lady Trevlyn drew her wrapper about her and paced softly down the long hall lighted only by fitful gleams of moonlight and the ruddy glow of the fire. At the far end was the state chamber, never used now, and never visited except by Hester, who occasionally went in to dust and air it, and my lady, who always passed the anniversary of Sir Richard's death alone there. The gallery was very dark, and she seldom went farther than the last window in her restless walks, but as she now approached she was startled to see a streak of yellow light under the door. She kept the key herself and neither she nor Hester had been there that day. A cold shiver passed over her for, as she looked, the shadow of a foot darkened the light for a moment and vanished as if someone had noiselessly passed. Obeying a sudden impulse, my lady sprang forward and tried to open the door. It was locked, but as her hand turned the silver knob a sound as if a drawer softly closed met her ear. She stooped to the keyhole but it was dark, a key evidently being in the lock. She drew back and flew to her room, snatched the key from her dressing table, and, bidding Hester follow, returned to the hall.

"What is it, my lady?" cried the woman, alarmed at the agitation of her mistress.

"A light, a sound, a shadow in the state chamber. Come quick!" cried Lady Trevlyn, adding, as she pointed to the door, "There, there, the light shines underneath. Do you see it?"

"No, my lady, it's dark," returned Hester.

It was, but never pausing my lady thrust in the key, and to her surprise it turned, the door flew open, and the dim, still room was before them. Hester boldly entered, and while her mistress slowly followed, she searched the room, looking behind the tall screen by the hearth, up the wide chimney, in the great wardrobe, and under the ebony cabinet, where all the relics of Sir Richard were kept. Nothing appeared, not even a mouse, and Hester turned to my lady with an air of relief. But her mistress pointed to the bed shrouded in dark velvet hangings, and whispered breathlessly, "You forgot to look there."

Hester had not forgotten, but in spite of her courage and good sense she shrank a little from looking at the spot where she had last seen her master's dead face. She believed the light and sound to be phantoms of my lady's distempered fancy, and searched merely to satisfy her. The mystery of Sir Richard's death still haunted the minds of all who remembered it, and even Hester felt a superstitious dread of that room. With a nervous laugh she looked under the bed and, drawing back the heavy curtains, said soothingly, "You see, my lady, there's nothing there."

But the words died on her lips, for, as the pale glimmer of the candle pierced the gloom of that funeral couch, both saw a face upon the pillow: a pale face framed in dark hair and beard, with closed eyes and the stony look the dead wear. A loud, long shriek that roused the house broke from Lady Trevlyn as she fell senseless at the bedside, and dropping both curtain and candle Hester caught up her mistress and fled from the haunted room, locking the door behind her.

In a moment a dozen servants were about them, and into their astonished ears Hester poured her story while vainly trying to restore her lady. Great was the dismay and intense the unwillingness of anyone to obey when Hester ordered the men to search the room again, for she was the first to regain her self-possession.

"Where's Paul? He's the heart of a man, boy though he is," she said angrily as the men hung back.

"He's not here. Lord! Maybe it was him a-playing tricks, though it ain't like him," cried Bessy, Lillian's little maid.

"No, it can't be him, for I locked him in myself. He walks in his sleep sometimes, and I was afraid he'd startle my lady. Let him sleep; this would only excite him and set him to marching again. Follow me, Bedford and James, I'm not afraid of ghosts or rogues."

With a face that belied her words Hester led the way to the awful room, and flinging back the curtain resolutely looked in. The bed was empty, but on the pillow was plainly visible the mark of a head and a single scarlet stain, as of blood. At that sight Hester turned pale and caught the butler's arm, whispering with a shudder, "Do you remember the night we put him in his coffin, the drop of blood that fell from his white lips? Sir Richard has been here."

"Good Lord, ma'am, don't say that! We can never rest in our beds if such things are to happen," gasped Bedford, backing to the door.

"It's no use to look, we've found all we shall find so go your ways and tell no one of this," said the woman in a gloomy tone, and, having assured herself that the windows were fast, Hester locked the room and ordered everyone but Bedford and the housekeeper to bed. "Do you sit outside my lady's door till morning," she said to the butler, "and you, Mrs. Price, help me to tend my poor lady, for if I'm not mistaken this night's work will bring on the old trouble."

Morning came, and with it a new alarm; for, though his door was fast locked and no foothold for even a sparrow outside the window, Paul's room was empty, and the boy nowhere to be found.

❧ *chapter V* ❧

A HERO

FOUR years had passed, and Lillian was fast blooming into a lovely woman: proud and willful as ever, but very charming, and already a belle in the little world where she still reigned a queen. Owing to her mother's ill health, she was allowed more freedom than is usually permitted to an English girl of her age; and, during the season, often went into company with a friend of Lady Trevlyn's who was chaperoning two young daughters of her own. To the world Lillian seemed a gay, free-hearted girl; and no one, not even her mother, knew how well she remembered and how much she missed the lost Paul. No tidings of him had ever come, and no trace of him was found after his flight. Nothing was missed, he went without his wages, and no reason could be divined for his departure except the foreign letter. Bedford remembered it, but forgot what postmark it bore, for he had only been able to decipher "Italy." My lady made many inquiries and often spoke of him; but when month after month passed and no news came, she gave him up, and on Lillian's account feigned to forget him. Contrary to Hester's fear, she did not seem the worse for the nocturnal fright, but evidently connected the strange visitor with Paul, or, after a day or two of nervous exhaustion, returned to her usual state of health. Hester had her own misgivings, but, being forbidden to allude to the subject, she held her peace, after emphatically declaring that Paul would yet appear to set her mind at rest.

"Lillian, Lillian, I've such news for you! Come and hear a charming little romance, and prepare to see the hero of it!" cried Maud Churchill, rushing into her friend's pretty boudoir one day in the height of the season.

Lillian lay on a couch, rather languid after a ball, and listlessly begged Maud to tell her story, for she was dying to be amused.

"Well, my dear, just listen and you'll be as enthusiastic as I am," cried Maud. And throwing her bonnet on one chair, her parasol on another, and her gloves anywhere, she settled herself on the couch and began: "You remember reading in the papers, some time ago, that fine account of the young man who took part in the Italian revolution and did that heroic thing with the bombshell?"

"Yes, what of him?" asked Lillian, sitting up.

"He is my hero, and we are to see him tonight."

"Go on, go on! Tell all, and tell it quickly," she cried.

"You know the officers were sitting somewhere, holding a council, while the city (I forget the name) was being bombarded, and how a shell came into the midst of them, how they sat paralyzed, expecting it to burst, and how this young man caught it up and ran out with it, risking his own life to save theirs?"

"Yes, yes, I remember!" And Lillian's listless face kindled at the recollection.

"Well, an Englishman who was there was so charmed by the act that, finding the young man was poor and an orphan, he adopted him. Mr. Talbot was old, and lonely, and rich, and when he died, a year after, he left his name and fortune to this Paolo."

"I'm glad, I'm glad!" cried Lillian, clapping her hands with a joyful face. "How romantic and charming it is!"

"Isn't it? But, my dear creature, the most romantic part is to come. Young Talbot served in the war, and then came to England to take possession of his property. It's somewhere down in Kent, a fine place and good income, all his; and he deserves it. Mamma heard a deal about him from Mrs. Langdon, who knew old Talbot and has seen the young man. Of course all the girls are wild to behold him, for he is very handsome and accomplished, and a gentleman by birth. But the dreadful part is that he is already betrothed to a lovely Greek girl, who came over at the same time, and is living in London with a

companion; quite elegantly, Mrs. Langdon says, for she called and
was charmed. This girl has been seen by some of our gentlemen
friends, and they already rave about the 'fair Helene,' for that's her
name."

Here Maud was forced to stop for breath, and Lillian had a
chance to question her.

"How old is she?"

"About eighteen or nineteen, they say."

"Very pretty?"

"Ravishing, regularly Greek and divine, Fred Raleigh says."

"When is she to be married?"

"Don't know; when Talbot gets settled, I fancy."

"And he? Is he as charming as she?"

"Quite, I'm told. He's just of age, and is, in appearance as in
everything else, a hero of romance."

"How came your mother to secure him for tonight?"

"Mrs. Langdon is dying to make a lion of him, and begged to
bring him. He is very indifferent on such things and seems intent on
his own affairs. Is grave and old for his years, and doesn't seem to
care much for pleasure and admiration, as most men would after a
youth like his, for he has had a hard time, I believe. For a wonder, he
consented to come when Mrs. Langdon asked him, and I flew off at
once to tell you and secure you for tonight."

"A thousand thanks. I meant to rest, for Mamma frets about my
being so gay; but she won't object to a quiet evening with you. What
shall we wear?" And here the conversation branched off on the all-
absorbing topic of dress.

When Lillian joined her friend that evening, the hero had already arrived, and, stepping into a recess, she waited to catch a glimpse
of him. Maud was called away, and she was alone when the crowd
about the inner room thinned and permitted young Talbot to be
seen. Well for Lillian that no one observed her at that moment, for
she grew pale and sank into a chair, exclaiming below her breath,
"It is Paul—*my* Paul!"

She recognized him instantly, in spite of increased height, a dark
moustache, and martial bearing. It was Paul, older, graver, handsomer,
but still "her Paul," as she called him, with a flush of pride and delight as she watched him, and felt that of all there she knew him best

and loved him most. For the childish affection still existed, and this discovery added a tinge of romance that made it doubly dangerous as well as doubly pleasant.

Will he know me? she thought, glancing at a mirror which reflected a slender figure with bright hair, white arms, and brilliant eyes; a graceful little head, proudly carried, and a sweet mouth, just then very charming, as it smiled till pearly teeth shone between the ruddy lips.

I'm glad I'm not ugly, and I hope he'll like me, she thought, as she smoothed the golden ripples on her forehead, settled her sash, and shook out the folds of her airy dress in a flutter of girlish excitement. "I'll pretend not to know him, when we meet, and see what he will do," she said, with a wicked sense of power; for being forewarned she was forearmed, and, fearing no betrayal of surprise on her own part, was eager to enjoy any of which he might be guilty.

Leaving her nook, she joined a group of young friends and held herself prepared for the meeting. Presently she saw Maud and Mrs. Langdon approaching, evidently intent on presenting the hero to the heiress.

"Mr. Talbot, Miss Trevlyn," said the lady. And looking up with a well-assumed air of indifference, Lillian returned the gentleman's bow with her eyes fixed full upon his face.

Not a feature of that face changed, and so severely unconscious of any recognition was it that the girl was bewildered. For a moment she fancied she had been mistaken in his identity, and a pang of disappointment troubled her; but as he moved a chair for Maud, she saw on the one ungloved hand a little scar which she remembered well, for he received it in saving her from a dangerous fall. At the sight all the happy past rose before her, and if her telltale eyes had not been averted they would have betrayed her. A sudden flush of maidenly shame dyed her cheek as she remembered that last ride, and the childish confidences then interchanged. This Helen was the little sweetheart whose picture he wore, and now, in spite of all obstacles, he had won both fortune and ladylove. The sound of his voice recalled her thoughts, and glancing up she met the deep eyes fixed on her with the same steady look they used to wear. He had addressed her, but what he said she knew not, beyond a vague idea that it was some slight allusion to the music going on in the next room. With a smile which would serve for an answer to almost any remark, she hastily plunged into conversation with a composure that did her credit in the eyes of her friends, who stood in awe of the young hero, for all were but just out.

"Mr. Talbot hardly needs an introduction here, for his name is well-known among us, though this is perhaps his first visit to England?" she said, flattering herself that this artful speech would entrap him into the reply she wanted.

With a slight frown, as if the allusion to his adventure rather annoyed him, and a smile that puzzled all but Lillian, he answered very simply, "It is not my first visit to this hospitable island. I was here a few years ago, for a short time, and left with regret."

"Then you have old friends here?" And Lillian watched him as she spoke.

"I had. They have doubtless forgotten me now," he said, with a sudden shadow marring the tranquillity of his face.

"Why doubt them? If they were true friends, they will not forget."

The words were uttered impulsively, almost warmly, but Talbot made no response, except a polite inclination and an abrupt change in the conversation.

"That remains to be proved. Do you sing, Miss Trevlyn?"

"A little." And Lillian's tone was both cold and proud.

"A great deal, and very charmingly," added Maud, who took pride in her friend's gifts both of voice and beauty. "Come, dear, there are so few of us you will sing, I know. Mamma desired me to ask you when Edith had done."

To her surprise Lillian complied, and allowed Talbot to lead her to the instrument. Still hoping to win some sign of recognition from him, the girl chose an air he taught her and sang it with a spirit and skill that surprised the listeners who possessed no key to her mood. At the last verse her voice suddenly faltered, but Talbot took up the song and carried her safely through it with his well-tuned voice.

"You know the air then?" she said in a low tone, as a hum of commendation followed the music.

"All Italians sing it, though few do it like yourself," he answered quietly, restoring the fan he had held while standing beside her.

Provoking boy! why won't he know me? thought Lillian. And her tone was almost petulant as she refused to sing again.

Talbot offered his arm and led her to a seat, behind which stood a little statuette of a child holding a fawn by a daisy chain.

"Pretty, isn't it?" she said, as he paused to look at it instead of taking the chair before her. "I used to enjoy modeling tiny deer and hinds in wax, as well as making daisy chains. Is sculpture among the many accomplishments which rumor tells us you possess?"

"No. Those who, like me, have their own fortunes to mold find time for little else," he answered gravely, still examining the marble group.

Lillian broke her fan with an angry flirt, for she was tired of her trial, and wished she had openly greeted him at the beginning; feeling now how pleasant it would have been to sit chatting of old times, while her friends dared hardly address him at all. She was on the point of calling him by his former name, when the remembrance of what he had been arrested the words on her lips. He was proud; would he not dread to have it known that, in his days of adversity, he had been a servant? For if she betrayed her knowledge of his past, she would be forced to tell where and how that knowledge was gained. No, better wait till they met alone, she thought; he would thank her for her delicacy, and she could easily explain her motive. He evidently wished to seem a stranger, for once she caught a gleam of the old, mirthful mischief in his eye, as she glanced up unexpectedly. He did remember her, she was sure, yet was trying her, perhaps, as she tried him. Well, she would stand the test and enjoy the joke by-and-by. With this fancy in her head she assumed a gracious air and chatted away in her most charming style, feeling both gay and excited, so anxious was she to please, and so glad to recover her early friend. A naughty whim seized her as her eye fell on a portfolio of classical engravings which someone had left in disorder on a table near her. Tossing them over she asked his opinion of several, and then handed him one in which Helen of Troy was represented as giving her hand to the irresistible Paris.

"Do you think her worth so much bloodshed, and deserving so much praise?" she asked, vainly trying to conceal the significant smile that would break loose on her lips and sparkle in her eyes.

Talbot laughed the short, boyish laugh so familiar to her ears, as he glanced from the picture to the arch questioner, and answered in a tone that made her heart beat with a nameless pain and pleasure, so full of suppressed ardor was it:

"Yes! 'All for love or the world well lost' is a saying I heartily agree to. La belle Hélène is my favorite heroine, and I regard Paris as the most enviable of men."

"I should like to see her."

The wish broke from Lillian involuntarily, and she was too much confused to turn it off by any general expression of interest in the classical lady.

"You may sometime," answered Talbot, with an air of amusement; adding, as if to relieve her, "I have a poetical belief that all the lovely women of history or romance will meet, and know, and love each other in some charming hereafter."

"But I'm no heroine and no beauty, so I shall never enter your poetical paradise," said Lillian, with a pretty affectation of regret.

"Some women are beauties without knowing it, and the heroines of romances never given to the world. I think you and Helen will yet meet, Miss Trevlyn."

As he spoke, Mrs. Langdon beckoned, and he left her pondering over his last words, and conscious of a secret satisfaction in his implied promise that she should see his betrothed.

"How do you like him?" whispered Maud, slipping into the empty chair.

"Very well," was the composed reply; for Lillian enjoyed her little mystery too much to spoil it yet.

"What did you say to him? I longed to hear, for you seemed to enjoy yourselves very much, but I didn't like to be a marplot."

Lillian repeated a part of the conversation, and Maud professed to be consumed with jealousy at the impression her friend had evidently made.

"It is folly to try to win the hero, for he is already won, you know," answered Lillian, shutting the cover on the pictured Helen with a sudden motion as if glad to extinguish her.

"Oh dear, no; Mrs. Langdon just told Mamma that she was mistaken about their being engaged; for she asked him and he shook his head, saying Helen was his ward."

"But that is absurd, for he's only a boy himself. It's very odd, isn't it? Never mind, I shall soon know all about it."

"How?" cried Maud, amazed at Lillian's assured manner.

"Wait a day or two, and I'll tell you a romance in return for yours. Your mother beckons to me, so I know Hester has come. Good night. I've had a charming time."

And with this tantalizing adieu, Lillian slipped away. Hester was waiting in the carriage, but as Lillian appeared, Talbot put aside the footman and handed her in, saying very low, in the well-remembered tone:

"Good night, my little mistress."

❧ *chapter VI* ❧

FAIR HELEN

TO no one but her mother and Hester did Lillian confide the
discovery she had made. None of the former servants but old
Bedford remained with them, and till Paul chose to renew the
old friendship it was best to remain silent. Great was the surprise and
delight of our lady and Hester at the good fortune of their protégé, and
many the conjectures as to how he would explain his hasty flight.

"You will go and see him, won't you, Mamma, or at least inquire about him?" said Lillian, eager to assure the wanderer of a welcome, for those few words of his had satisfied her entirely.

"No, dear, it is for him to seek us, and till he does, I shall make
no sign. He knows where we are, and if he chooses he can renew
the acquaintance so strangely broken off. Be patient, and above all
things remember, Lillian, that you are no longer a child," replied my
lady, rather disturbed by her daughter's enthusiastic praises of Paul.

"I wish I was, for then I might act as I feel, and not be afraid
of shocking the proprieties." And Lillian went to bed to dream of her
hero.

For three days she stayed at home, expecting Paul, but he did
not come, and she went out for her usual ride in the Park, hoping to
meet him. An elderly groom now rode behind her, and she surveyed
him with extreme disgust, as she remembered the handsome lad who
had once filled that place. Nowhere did Paul appear, but in the

Ladies' Mile she passed an elegant brougham in which sat a very lovely girl and a mild old lady.

"That is Talbot's fiancée," said Maud Churchill, who had joined her. "Isn't she beautiful?"

"Not at all—yes, very," was Lillian's somewhat peculiar reply, for jealousy and truth had a conflict just then.

"He's so perfectly absorbed and devoted that I am sure that story is true, so adieu to our hopes," laughed Maud.

"Did you have any? Good-bye, I must go." And Lillian rode home at a pace which caused the stout groom great distress.

"Mamma, I've seen Paul's betrothed!" she cried, running into her mother's boudoir.

"And I have seen Paul himself," replied my lady, with a warning look, for there he stood, with half-extended hand, as if waiting to be acknowledged.

Lillian forgot her embarrassment in her pleasure, and made him an elaborate curtsy, saying, with a half-merry, half-reproachful glance, "Mr. Talbot is welcome in whatever guise he appears."

"I choose to appear as Paul, then, and offer you a seat, Miss Lillian," he said, assuming as much of his boyish manner as he could.

Lillian took it and tried to feel at ease, but the difference between the lad she remembered and the man she now saw was too great to be forgotten.

"Now tell us your adventures, and why you vanished away so mysteriously four years ago," she said, with a touch of the childish imperiousness in her voice, though her frank eyes fell before his.

"I was about to do so when you appeared with news concerning my cousin," he began.

"Your cousin!" exclaimed Lillian.

"Yes, Helen's mother and my own were sisters. Both married Englishmen, both died young, leaving us to care for each other. We were like a brother and sister, and always together till I left her to serve Colonel Daventry. The death of the old priest to whom I entrusted her recalled me to Genoa, for I was then her only guardian. I meant to have taken leave of you, my lady, properly, but the consequences of that foolish trick of mine frightened me away in the most unmannerly fashion."

"Ah, it was you, then, in the state chamber; I always thought so," and Lady Trevlyn drew a long breath of relief.

"Yes, I heard it whispered among the servants that the room was haunted, and I felt a wish to prove the truth of the story and my own courage. Hester locked me in, for fear of my sleepwalking; but I lowered myself by a rope and then climbed in at the closet window of the state chamber. When you came, my lady, I thought it was Hester, and slipped into the bed, meaning to give her a fright in return for her turning the key on me. But when your cry showed me what I had done, I was filled with remorse, and escaped as quickly and quietly as possible. I should have asked pardon before; I do now, most humbly, my lady, for it was sacrilege to play pranks *there*."

During the first part of his story Paul's manner had been frank and composed, but in telling the latter part, his demeanor underwent a curious change. He fixed his eyes on the ground and spoke as if repeating a lesson, while his color varied, and a half-proud, half-submissive expression replaced the former candid one. Lillian observed this, and it disturbed her, but my lady took it for shame at his boyish freak and received his confession kindly, granting a free pardon and expressing sincere pleasure at his amended fortunes. As he listened, Lillian saw him clench his hand hard and knit his brows, assuming the grim look she had often seen, as if trying to steel himself against some importunate emotion or rebellious thought.

"Yes, half my work is done, and I have a home, thanks to my generous benefactor, and I hope to enjoy it well and wisely," he said in a grave tone, as if the fortune had not yet brought him his heart's desire.

"And when is the other half of the work to be accomplished, Paul? That depends on your cousin, perhaps." And Lady Trevlyn regarded him with a gleam of womanly curiosity in her melancholy eyes.

"It does, but not in the way you fancy, my lady. Whatever Helen may be, she is not my fiancée yet, Miss Lillian." And the shadow lifted as he laughed, looking at the young lady, who was decidedly abashed, in spite of a sense of relief caused by his words.

"I merely accepted the world's report," she said, affecting a nonchalant air.

"The world is a liar, as you will find in time" was his abrupt reply.

"I hope to see this beautiful cousin, Paul. Will she receive us as old friends of yours?"

"Thanks, not yet, my lady. She is still too much a stranger here to enjoy new faces, even kind ones. I have promised perfect rest and freedom for a time, but you shall be the first whom she receives."

Again Lillian detected the secret disquiet which possessed him, and her curiosity was roused. It piqued her that this Helen felt no desire to meet her and chose to seclude herself, as if regardless of the interest and admiration she excited. "I *will* see her in spite of her refusal, for I only caught a glimpse in the Park. Something is wrong, and I'll discover it, for it evidently worries Paul, and perhaps I can help him."

As this purpose sprang up in the warm but willful heart of the girl, she regained her spirits and was her most charming self while the young man stayed. They talked of many things in a pleasant, confidential manner, though when Lillian recalled that hour, she was surprised to find how little Paul had really told them of his past life or future plans. It was agreed among them to say nothing of their former relations, except to old Bedford, who was discretion itself, but to appear to the world as new-made friends—thus avoiding unpleasant and unnecessary explanations which would only excite gossip. My lady asked him to dine, but he had business out of town and declined, taking his leave with a lingering look, which made Lillian steal away to study her face in the mirror and wonder if she looked her best, for in Paul's eyes she had read undisguised admiration.

Lady Trevlyn went to her room to rest, leaving the girl free to ride, drive, or amuse herself as she liked. As if fearing her courage would fail if she delayed, Lillian ordered the carriage, and, bidding Hester mount guard over her, she drove away to St. John's Wood.

"Now, Hester, don't lecture or be prim when I tell you that we are going on a frolic," she began, after getting the old woman into an amiable mood by every winning wile she could devise. "I think you'll like it, and if it's found out I'll take the blame. There is some mystery about Paul's cousin, and I'm going to find it out."

"Bless you, child, how?"

"She lives alone here, is seldom seen, and won't go anywhere or receive anyone. That's not natural in a pretty girl. Paul won't talk about her, and, though he's fond of her, he always looks grave and grim when I ask questions. That's provoking, and I won't hear it. Maud is engaged to Raleigh, you know; well, he confided to her that he and a friend had found out where Helen was, had gone to the next villa, which is empty, and under pretense of looking at it got a peep at the girl in her garden. I'm going to do the same."

"And what am *I* to do?" asked Hester, secretly relishing the prank, for she was dying with curiosity to behold Paul's cousin.

"You are to do the talking with the old woman, and give me a chance to look. Now say you will, and I'll behave myself like an angel in return."

Hester yielded, after a few discreet scruples, and when they reached Laburnum Lodge played her part so well that Lillian soon managed to stray away into one of the upper rooms which overlooked the neighboring garden. Helen was there, and with eager eyes the girl scrutinized her. She was very beautiful, in the classical style; as fair and finely molded as a statue, with magnificent dark hair and eyes, and possessed of that perfect grace which is as effective as beauty. She was alone, and when first seen was bending over a flower which she caressed and seemed to examine with great interest as she stood a long time motionless before it. Then she began to pace slowly around and around the little grass plot, her hands hanging loosely clasped before her, and her eyes fixed on vacancy as if absorbed in thought. But as the first effect of her beauty passed away, Lillian found something peculiar about her. It was not the somewhat foreign dress and ornaments she wore; it was in her face, her movements, and the tone of her voice, for as she walked she sang a low, monotonous song, as if unconsciously. Lillian watched her keenly, marking the aimless motions of the little hands, the apathy of the lovely face, and the mirthless accent of the voice; but most of all the vacant fixture of the great dark eyes. Around and around she went, with an elastic step and a mechanical regularity wearisome to witness.

What is the matter with her? thought Lillian anxiously, as this painful impression increased with every scrutiny of the unconscious girl. So abashed was she that Hester's call was unheard, and Hester was unseen as she came and stood beside her. Both looked a moment, and as they looked an old lady came from the house and led Helen in, still murmuring her monotonous song and moving her hands as if to catch and hold the sunshine.

"Poor dear, poor dear. No wonder Paul turns sad and won't talk of her, and that she don't see anyone," sighed Hester pitifully.

"What is it? I see, but don't understand," whispered Lillian.

"She's an innocent, deary, an idiot, though that's a hard word for a pretty creature like her."

"How terrible! Come away, Hester, and never breathe to anyone what we have seen." And with a shudder and sense of pain and pity lying heavy at her heart, she hurried away, feeling doubly guilty in the discovery of this affliction. The thought of it haunted her continually; the memory of the lonely girl gave her no peace; and a consciousness of deceit burdened her unspeakably, especially in Paul's presence. This lasted for a week, then Lillian resolved to confess, hoping that when he found she knew the truth he would let her share his cross and help to lighten it. Waiting her opportunity, she seized a moment when her mother was absent, and with her usual frankness spoke out impetuously.

"Paul, I've done wrong, and I can have no peace till I am pardoned. I have seen Helen."

"Where, when, and how?" he asked, looking disturbed and yet relieved.

She told him rapidly, and as she ended she looked up at him with her sweet face, so full of pity, shame, and grief it would have been impossible to deny her anything.

"Can you forgive me for discovering this affliction?"

"I think I could forgive you a far greater fault, Lillian," he answered, in a tone that said many things.

"But deceit is so mean, so dishonorable and contemptible, how can you so easily pardon it in me?" she asked, quite overcome by this forgiveness, granted without any reproach.

"Then you would find it hard to pardon such a thing in another?" he said, with the expression that always puzzled her.

"Yes, it would be hard; but in those I loved, I could forgive much for love's sake."

With a sudden gesture he took her hand saying, impulsively, "How little changed you are! Do you remember that last ride of ours nearly five years ago?"

"Yes, Paul," she answered, with averted eyes.

"And what we talked of?"

"A part of that childish gossip I remember well."

"Which part?"

"The pretty little romance you told me." And Lillian looked up now, longing to ask if Helen's childhood had been blighted like her youth.

Paul dropped her hand as if he read her thoughts, and his own hand went involuntarily toward his breast, betraying that the locket still hung there.

"What did I say?" he asked, smiling at her sudden shyness.

"You vowed you'd win and wed your fair little ladylove if you lived."

"And so I will," he cried, with sudden fire in his eyes.

"What, marry her?"

"Aye, that I will."

"Oh Paul, will you tie yourself for life to a—" The word died on her lips, but a gesture of repugnance finished the speech.

"A what?" he demanded, excitedly.

"An innocent, one bereft of reason," stammered Lillian, entirely forgetting herself in her interest for him.

"Of whom do you speak?" asked Paul, looking utterly bewildered.

"Of poor Helen."

"Good heavens, who told you that base lie?" And his voice deepened with indignant pain.

"I saw her, you did not deny her affliction; Hester said so, and I believed it. Have I wronged her, Paul?"

"Yes, cruelly. She is blind, but no idiot, thank God."

There was such earnestness in his voice, such reproach in his words, and such ardor in his eye, that Lillian's pride gave way, and with a broken entreaty for pardon, she covered up her face, weeping the bitterest tears she ever shed. For in that moment, and the sharp pang it brought her, she felt how much she loved Paul and how hard it was to lose him. The childish affection had blossomed into a woman's passion, and in a few short weeks had passed through many phases of jealousy, hope, despair, and self-delusion. The joy she felt on seeing him again, the pride she took in him, the disgust Helen caused her, the relief she had not dared to own even to herself, when she fancied fate had put an insurmountable barrier between Paul and his cousin, the despair at finding it only a fancy, and the anguish of hearing him declare his unshaken purpose to marry his first love—all these conflicting emotions had led to this hard moment, and now self-control deserted her in her need. In spite of her efforts the passionate tears would have their way, though Paul soothed her with assurances of entire forgiveness, promises of Helen's friendship, and every gentle device he could imagine. She commanded herself at last by a strong effort, murmuring eagerly as she shrank from the hand that put back her fallen hair, and the face so full of tender sympathy bending over her:

"I am so grieved and ashamed at what I have said and done. I shall never dare to see Helen. Forgive me, and forget this folly. I'm sad and heavyhearted just now; it's the anniversary of Papa's death, and Mamma always suffers so much at such times that I get nervous."

"It is your birthday also. I remembered it, and ventured to bring a little token in return for the one you gave me long ago. This is a talisman, and tomorrow I will tell you the legend concerning it. Wear it for my sake, and God bless you, dear."

The last words were whispered hurriedly; Lillian saw the glitter of an antique ring, felt the touch of bearded lips on her hand, and Paul was gone.

But as he left the house he set his teeth, exclaiming low to himself, "Yes, tomorrow there shall be an end of this! We must risk everything and abide the consequences now. I'll have no more torment for any of us."

≈ *chapter VII* ≈

THE SECRET KEY

"IS Lady Trevlyn at home, Bedford?" asked Paul, as he presented himself at an early hour next day, wearing the keen, stern expression which made him look ten years older than he was.

"No, sir, my lady and Miss Lillian went down to the Hall last night."

"No ill news, I hope?" And the young man's eye kindled as if he felt a crisis at hand.

"Not that I heard, sir. Miss Lillian took one of her sudden whims and would have gone alone, if my lady hadn't given in much against her will, this being a time when she is better away from the place."

"Did they leave no message for me?"

"Yes, sir. Will you step in and read the note at your ease. We are in sad confusion, but this room is in order."

Leading the way to Lillian's boudoir, the man presented the note and retired. A few hasty lines from my lady, regretting the necessity of this abrupt departure, yet giving no reason for it, hoping they might meet next season, but making no allusion to seeing him at the Hall, desiring Lillian's thanks and regards, but closing with no hint of Helen, except compliments. Paul smiled as he threw it into the fire, saying to himself, "Poor lady, she thinks she has escaped the danger by flying, and Lillian tries to hide her trouble from me. Tender little heart! I'll comfort it without delay."

He sat looking about the dainty room still full of tokens of her presence. The piano stood open with a song he liked upon the rack; a bit of embroidery, whose progress he had often watched, lay in her basket with the little thimble near it; there was a strew of papers on the writing table, torn notes, scraps of drawing, and ball cards; a pearl-colored glove lay on the floor; and in the grate the faded flowers he had brought two days before. As his eye roved to and fro, he seemed to enjoy some happy dream, broken too soon by the sound of servants shutting up the house. He arose but lingered near the table, as if longing to search for some forgotten hint of himself.

"No, there has been enough lock picking and stealthy work; I'll do no more for her sake. This theft will harm no one and tell no tales." And snatching up the glove, Paul departed.

"Helen, the time has come. Are you ready?" he asked, entering her room an hour later.

"I am ready." And rising, she stretched her hand to him with a proud expression, contrasting painfully with her helpless gesture.

"They have gone to the Hall, and we must follow. It is useless to wait longer; we gain nothing by it, and the claim must stand on such proof as we have, or fall for want of that one link. I am tired of disguise. I want to be myself and enjoy what I have won, unless I lose it all."

"Paul, whatever happens, remember we cling together and share good or evil fortune as we always have done. I am a burden, but I cannot live without you, for you are my world. Do not desert me."

She groped her way to him and clung to his strong arm as if it was her only stay. Paul drew her close, saying wistfully, as he caressed the beautiful sightless face leaning on his shoulder, "*Mia cara*, would it break your heart, if at the last hour I gave up all and let the word remain unspoken? My courage fails me, and in spite of the hard past I would gladly leave them in peace."

"No, no, you shall not give it up!" cried Helen almost fiercely, while the slumbering fire of her southern nature flashed into her face. "You have waited so long, worked so hard, suffered so much, you must not lose your reward. You promised, and you must keep the promise."

"But it is so beautiful, so noble to forgive, and return a blessing for a curse. Let us bury the old feud, and right the old wrong in a new way. Those two are so blameless, it is cruel to visit the sins of the dead on their innocent heads. My lady has suffered enough already, and Lillian is so young, so happy, so unfit to meet a storm like this. Oh, Helen, mercy is more divine than justice."

Something moved Paul deeply, and Helen seemed about to yield, when the name of Lillian wrought a subtle change in her. The color died out of her face, her black eyes burned with a gloomy fire, and her voice was relentless as she answered, while her frail hands held him fast, "I will not let you give it up. We are as innocent as they; we have suffered more; and we deserve our rights, for we have no sin to expiate. Go on, Paul, and forget the sentimental folly that unmans you."

Something in her words seemed to sting or wound him. His face darkened, and he put her away, saying briefly, "Let it be so then. In an hour we must go."

On the evening of the same day, Lady Trevlyn and her daughter sat together in the octagon room at the Hall. Twilight was falling and candles were not yet brought, but a cheery fire blazed in the wide chimney, filling the apartment with a ruddy glow, turning Lillian's bright hair to gold and lending a tinge of color to my lady's pallid cheeks. The girl sat on a low lounging chair before the fire, her head on her hand, her eyes on the red embers, her thoughts—where? My lady lay on her couch, a little in the shadow, regarding her daughter with an anxious air, for over the young face a somber change had passed which filled her with disquiet.

"You are out of spirits, love," she said at last, breaking the long silence, as Lillian gave an unconscious sigh and leaned wearily into the depths of her chair.

"Yes, Mamma, a little."

"What is it? Are you ill?"

"No, Mamma; I think London gaiety is rather too much for me. I'm too young for it, as you often say, and I've found it out."

"Then it is only weariness that makes you so pale and grave, and so bent on coming back here?"

Lillian was the soul of truth, and with a moment's hesitation answered slowly, "Not that alone, Mamma. I'm worried about other things. Don't ask me what, please."

"But I must ask. Tell me, child, what things? Have you seen any one? Had letters, or been annoyed in any way about—anything?"

My lady spoke with sudden energy and rose on her arm, eyeing the girl with unmistakable suspicion and excitement.

"No, Mamma, it's only a foolish trouble of my own," answered Lillian, with a glance of surprise and a shamefaced look as the words reluctantly left her lips.

"Ah, a love trouble, nothing more? Thank God for that!" And my lady sank back as if a load was off her mind. "Tell me all, my darling; there is no confidante like a mother."

"You are very kind, and perhaps you can cure my folly if I tell it, and yet I am ashamed," murmured the girl. Then yielding to an irresistible impulse to ask help and sympathy, she added, in an almost inaudible tone, "I came away to escape from Paul."

"Because he loves you, Lillian?" asked my lady, with a frown and a half smile.

"Because he does *not* love me, Mamma." And the poor girl hid her burning cheeks in her hands, as if overwhelmed with maidenly shame at the implied confession of her own affection.

"My child, how is this? I cannot but be glad that he does *not* love you; yet it fills me with grief to see that this pains you. He is not a mate for you, Lillian. Remember this, and forget the transient regard that has sprung up from that early intimacy of yours."

"He is wellborn, and now my equal in fortune, and oh, so much my superior in all gifts of mind and heart," sighed the girl, still with hidden face, for tears were dropping through her slender fingers.

"It may be, but there is a mystery about him; and I have a vague dislike to him in spite of all that has passed. But, darling, are you sure he does not care for you? I fancied I read a different story in his face, and when you begged to leave town so suddenly, I believed that you had seen this also, and kindly wished to spare him any pain."

"It was to spare myself. Oh, Mamma, he loves Helen, and will marry her although she is blind. He told me this, with a look I could not doubt, and so I came away to hide my sorrow," sobbed poor Lillian in despair.

Lady Trevlyn went to her and, laying the bright head on her motherly bosom, said soothingly as she caressed it, "My little girl, it is too soon for you to know these troubles, and I am punished for yielding to your entreaties for a peep at the gay world. It is now too late to spare you this; you have had your wish and must pay its price, dear. But, Lillian, call pride to aid you, and conquer this fruitless love. It cannot be very deep as yet, for you have known Paul, the man, too short a time to be hopelessly enamored. Remember, there are others, better, braver, more worthy of you; that life is long, and full of pleasure yet untried."

"Have no fears for me, Mamma. I'll not disgrace you or myself by any sentimental folly. I do love Paul, but I can conquer it, and I will. Give me a little time, and you shall see me quite myself again."

Lillian lifted her head with an air of proud resolve that satisfied her mother, and with a grateful kiss stole away to ease her full heart alone. As she disappeared Lady Trevlyn drew a long breath and, clasping her hands with a gesture of thanksgiving, murmured to herself in an accent of relief, "Only a love sorrow! I feared it was some new terror like the old one. Seventeen years of silence, seventeen years of secret dread and remorse for me," she said, pacing the room with tightly locked hands and eyes full of unspeakable anguish. "Oh, Richard, Richard! I forgave you long ago, and surely I have expiated my innocent offense by these years of suffering! For her sake I did it, and for her sake I still keep dumb. God knows I ask nothing for myself but rest and oblivion by your side."

Half an hour later, Paul stood at the hall door. It was ajar, for the family had returned unexpectedly, as was evident from the open doors and empty halls. Entering unseen, he ascended to the room my lady usually occupied. The fire burned low, Lillian's chair was empty, and my lady lay asleep, as if lulled by the sighing winds without and the deep silence that reigned within. Paul stood regarding her with a great pity softening his face as he marked the sunken eyes, pallid cheeks, locks too early gray, and restless lips muttering in dreams.

"I wish I could spare her this," he sighed, stooping to wake her with a word. But he did not speak, for, suddenly clutching the chain about her neck, she seemed to struggle with some invisible foe and beat it off, muttering audibly as she clenched her thin hands on the golden case. Paul leaned and listened as if the first word had turned him to stone, till the paroxysm had passed, and with a heavy sigh my lady sank into a calmer sleep. Then, with a quick glance over his shoulder, Paul skillfully opened the locket, drew out the silver key, replaced it with one from the piano close by, and stole from the house noiselessly as he had entered it.

That night, in the darkest hour before the dawn, a figure went gliding through the shadowy Park to its most solitary corner. Here stood the tomb of the Trevlyns, and here the figure paused. A dull spark of light woke in its hand, there was a clank of bars, the creak of rusty hinges, then light and figure both seemed swallowed up.

Standing in the tomb where the air was close and heavy, the pale glimmer of the lantern showed piles of moldering coffins in the niches, and everywhere lay tokens of decay and death. The man drew his hat lower over his eyes, pulled the muffler closer about his mouth, and surveyed the spot with an undaunted aspect, though the beating of his heart was heard in the deep silence. Nearest the door stood a long casket covered with black velvet and richly decorated with silver ornaments, tarnished now. The Trevlyns had been a stalwart race, and the last sleeper brought there had evidently been of goodly stature, for the modern coffin was as ponderous as the great oaken beds where lay the bones of generations. Lifting the lantern, the intruder brushed the dust from the shield-shaped plate, read the name RICHARD TREVLYN and a date, and, as if satisfied, placed a key in the lock, half-raised the lid, and, averting his head that he might not see the ruin seventeen long years had made, he laid his hand on the dead breast and from the folded shroud drew a mildewed paper. One glance sufficed, the casket was relocked, the door rebarred, the light extinguished, and the man vanished like a ghost in the darkness of the wild October night.

❧ *chapter VIII* ❧

WHICH?

"A GENTLEMAN, my lady."

Taking a card from the silver salver on which the servant offered it, Lady Trevlyn read, "Paul Talbot," and below the name these penciled words, "I beseech you to see me." Lillian stood beside her and saw the line. Their eyes met, and in the girl's face was such a sudden glow of hope, and love, and longing, that the mother could not doubt or disappoint her wish.

"I will see him," she said.

"Oh, Mamma, how kind you are!" cried the girl with a passionate embrace, adding breathlessly, "He did not ask for me. I cannot see him yet. I'll hide in the alcove, and can appear or run away as I like when we know why he comes."

They were in the library, for, knowing Lillian's fondness for the room which held no dark memories for her, my lady conquered her dislike and often sat there. As she spoke, the girl glided into the deep recess of a bay window and drew the heavy curtains just as Paul's step sounded at the door.

Hiding her agitation with a woman's skill, my lady rose with outstretched hand to welcome him. He bowed but did not take the hand, saying, in a voice of grave respect in which was audible an undertone of strong emotion, "Pardon me, Lady Trevlyn. Hear what I have to say; and then if you offer me your hand, I shall gratefully receive it."

She glanced at him, and saw that he was very pale, that his eye glittered with suppressed excitement, and his whole manner was that of a man who had nerved himself up to the performance of a difficult but intensely interesting task. Fancying these signs of agitation only natural in a young lover coming to woo, my lady smiled, reseated herself, and calmly answered, "I will listen patiently. Speak freely, Paul, and remember I am an old friend."

"I wish I could forget it. Then my task would be easier," he murmured in a voice of mingled regret and resolution, as he leaned on a tall chair opposite and wiped his damp forehead, with a look of such deep compassion that her heart sank with a nameless fear.

"I must tell you a long story, and ask your forgiveness for the offenses I committed against you when a boy. A mistaken sense of duty guided me, and I obeyed it blindly. Now I see my error and regret it," he said earnestly.

"Go on," replied my lady, while the vague dread grew stronger, and she braced her nerves as for some approaching shock. She forgot Lillian, forgot everything but the strange aspect of the man before her, and the words to which she listened like a statue. Still standing pale and steady, Paul spoke rapidly, while his eyes were full of mingled sternness, pity, and remorse.

"Twenty years ago, an English gentleman met a friend in a little Italian town, where he had married a beautiful wife. The wife had a sister as lovely as herself, and the young man, during that brief stay, loved and married her—in a very private manner, lest his father should disinherit him. A few months passed, and the Englishman was called home to take possession of his title and estates, the father being dead. He went alone, promising to send for the wife when all was ready. He told no one of his marriage, meaning to surprise his English friends by producing the lovely woman unexpectedly. He had been in England but a short time when he received a letter from the old priest of the Italian town, saying the cholera had swept through it, carrying off half its inhabitants, his wife and friend among others. This blow prostrated the young man, and when he recovered he hid his grief, shut himself up in his country house, and tried to forget. Accident threw in his way another lovely woman, and he married again. Before the first year was out, the friend whom he supposed was dead appeared, and told him that his wife still lived, and had borne him a child. In the terror and confusion of the plague, the priest had mistaken one sister for the other, as the elder did die."

"Yes, yes, I know; go on!" gasped my lady, with white lips, and eyes that never left the narrator's face.

"This friend had met with misfortune after flying from the doomed village with the surviving sister. They had waited long for letters, had written, and, when no answer came, had been delayed by illness and poverty from reaching England. At this time the child was born, and the friend, urged by the wife and his own interest, came here, learned that Sir Richard was married, and hurried to him in much distress. We can imagine the grief and horror of the unhappy man. In that interview the friend promised to leave all to Sir Richard, to preserve the secret till some means of relief could be found; and with this promise he returned, to guard and comfort the forsaken wife. Sir Richard wrote the truth to Lady Trevlyn, meaning to kill himself, as the only way of escape from the terrible situation between two women, both so beloved, both so innocently wronged. The pistol lay ready, but death came without its aid, and Sir Richard was spared the sin of suicide."

Paul paused for breath, but Lady Trevlyn motioned him to go on, still sitting rigid and white as the marble image near her.

"The friend only lived to reach home and tell the story. It killed the wife, and she died, imploring the old priest to see her child righted and its father's name secured to it. He promised; but he was poor, the child was a frail baby, and he waited. Years passed, and when the child was old enough to ask for its parents and demand its due, the proofs of the marriage were lost, and nothing remained but a ring, a bit of writing, and the name. The priest was very old, had neither friends, money, nor proofs to help him; but I was strong and hopeful, and though a mere boy I resolved to do the work. I made my way to England, to Trevlyn Hall, and by various stratagems (among which, I am ashamed to say, were false keys and feigned sleepwalking) I collected many proofs, but nothing which would satisfy a court, for no one but you knew where Sir Richard's confession was. I searched every nook and corner of the Hall, but in vain, and began to despair, when news of the death of Father Cosmo recalled me to Italy; for Helen was left to my care then. The old man had faithfully recorded the facts and left witnesses to prove the truth of his story; but for four years I never used it, never made any effort to secure the title or estates."

"Why not?" breathed my lady in a faint whisper, as hope suddenly revived.

"Because I was grateful," and for the first time Paul's voice faltered. "I was a stranger, and you took me in. I never could forget that, nor the many kindnesses bestowed upon the friendless boy. This afflicted me, even while I was acting a false part, and when I was away my heart failed me. But Helen gave me no peace; for my sake, she urged me to keep the vow made to that poor mother, and threatened to tell the story herself. Talbot's benefaction left me no excuse for delaying longer, and I came to finish the hardest task I can ever undertake. I feared that a long dispute would follow any appeal to law, and meant to appeal first to you, but fate befriended me, and the last proof was found."

"Found! Where?" cried Lady Trevlyn, springing up aghast.

"In Sir Richard's coffin, where you hid it, not daring to destroy, yet fearing to keep it."

"Who has betrayed me?" And her eye glanced wildly about the room, as if she feared to see some spectral accuser.

"Your own lips, my lady. Last night I came to speak of this. You lay asleep, and in some troubled dream spoke of the paper, safe in its writer's keeping, and your strange treasure here, the key of which you guarded day and night. I divined the truth. Remembering Hester's stories, I took the key from your helpless hand, found the paper on Sir Richard's dead breast, and now demand that you confess your part in this tragedy."

"I do, I do! I confess, I yield, I relinquish everything, and ask pity only for my child."

Lady Trevlyn fell upon her knees before him, with a submissive gesture, but imploring eyes, for, amid the wreck of womanly pride and worldly fortune, the mother's heart still clung to its idol.

"Who should pity her, if not I? God knows I would have spared her this blow if I could; but Helen would not keep silent, and I was driven to finish what I had begun. Tell Lillian this, and do not let her hate me."

As Paul spoke, tenderly, eagerly, the curtain parted, and Lillian appeared, trembling with the excitement of that interview, but conscious of only one emotion as she threw herself into his arms, crying in a tone of passionate delight, "Brother! Brother! Now I may love you!"

Paul held her close, and for a moment forgot everything but the joy of that moment. Lillian spoke first, looking up through tears of tenderness, her little hand laid caressingly against his cheek, as she whispered with sudden bloom in her own, "Now I know why I loved you so well, and now I can see you marry Helen without breaking my heart. Oh, Paul, you are still mine, and I care for nothing else."

"But, Lillian, I am not your brother."

"Then, in heaven's name, who are you?" she cried, tearing herself from his arms.

"Your lover, dear!"

"Who, then, is the heir?" demanded Lady Trevlyn, springing up, as Lillian turned to seek shelter with her mother.

"I am."

Helen spoke, and Helen stood on the threshold of the door, with a hard, haughty look upon her beautiful face.

"You told your story badly, Paul," she said, in a bitter tone. "You forgot me, forgot my affliction, my loneliness, my wrongs, and the natural desire of a child to clear her mother's honor and claim her father's name. I am Sir Richard's eldest daughter. I can prove my birth, and I demand my right with his own words to sustain me."

She paused, but no one spoke; and with a slight tremor in her proud voice, she added, "Paul has done the work; he shall have the reward. I only want my father's name. Title and fortune are nothing to one like me. I coveted and claimed them that I might give them to you, Paul, my one friend, always, so tender and so true."

"I'll have none of it," he answered, almost fiercely. "I have kept my promise, and am free. You chose to claim your own, although I offered all I had to buy your silence. It is yours by right—take it, and enjoy it if you can. I'll have no reward for work like this."

He turned from her with a look that would have stricken her to the heart could she have seen it. She felt it, and it seemed to augment some secret anguish, for she pressed her hands against her bosom with an expression of deep suffering, exclaiming passionately, "Yes, I *will* keep it, since I am to lose all else. I am tired of pity. Power is sweet, and I will use it. Go, Paul, and be happy if you can, with a nameless wife, and the world's compassion or contempt to sting your pride."

"Oh, Lillian, where shall we go? This is no longer our home, but who will receive us now?" cried Lady Trevlyn, in a tone of despair, for her spirit was utterly broken by the thought of the shame and sorrow in store for this beloved and innocent child.

"I will." And Paul's face shone with a love and loyalty they could not doubt. "My lady, you gave me a home when I was homeless; now let me pay my debt. Lillian, I have loved you from the time when, a romantic boy, I wore your little picture in my breast, and vowed to win you if I lived. I dared not speak before, but now, when other hearts may be shut against you, mine stands wide open to welcome you. Come, both. Let me protect and cherish you, and so atone for the sorrow I have brought you."

It was impossible to resist the sincere urgency of his voice, the tender reverence of his manner, as he took the two forlorn yet innocent creatures into the shelter of his strength and love. They clung to him instinctively, feeling that there still remained to them one staunch friend whom adversity could not estrange.

An eloquent silence fell upon the room, broken only by sobs, grateful whispers, and the voiceless vows that lovers plight with eyes, and hands, and tender lips. Helen was forgotten, till Lillian, whose elastic spirit threw off sorrow as a flower sheds the rain, looked up to thank Paul, with smiles as well as tears, and saw the lonely figure in the shadow. Her attitude was full of pathetic significance; she still stood on the threshold, for no one had welcomed her, and in the strange room she knew not where to go; her hands were clasped before her face, as if those sightless eyes had seen the joy she could not share, and at her feet lay the time-stained paper that gave her a barren title, but no love. Had Lillian known how sharp a conflict between passion and pride, jealousy and generosity, was going on in that young heart, she could not have spoken in a tone of truer pity or sincerer goodwill than that in which she softly said, "Poor girl! We must not forget her, for, with all her wealth, she is poor compared to us. We both had one father, and should love each other in spite of this misfortune. Helen, may I call you sister?"

"Not yet. Wait till I deserve it."

As if that sweet voice had kindled an answering spark of nobleness in her own heart, Helen's face changed beautifully, as she tore the paper to shreds, saying in a glad, impetuous tone, while the white flakes fluttered from her hands, "I, too, can be generous. I, too, can forgive. I bury the sad past. See! I yield my claim, I destroy my proofs, I promise eternal silence, and keep 'Paul's cousin' for my only title. Yes, you are happy, for you love one another!" she cried, with a sudden passion of tears. "Oh, forgive me, pity me, and take me in, for I am all alone and in the dark!"

There could be but one reply to an appeal like that, and they gave it, as they welcomed her with words that sealed a household league of mutual secrecy and sacrifice.

They *were* happy, for the world never knew the hidden tie that bound them so faithfully together, never learned how well the old prophecy had been fulfilled, or guessed what a tragedy of life and death the silver key unlocked.

The Abbot's Ghost

~ or ~

MAURICE TREHERNE'S TEMPTATION

A Christmas Story

BY A. M. BARNARD

≽ *chapter I* ≼

DRAMATIS PERSONAE

"HOW goes it, Frank? Down first, as usual."

"The early bird gets the worm, Major."

"Deuced ungallant speech, considering that the lovely Octavia is the worm," and with a significant laugh the major assumed an Englishman's favorite attitude before the fire.

His companion shot a quick glance at him, and an expression of anxiety passed over his face as he replied, with a well-feigned air of indifference, "You are altogether too sharp, Major. I must be on my guard while you are in the house. Any new arrivals? I thought I heard a carriage drive up not long ago."

"It was General Snowdon and his charming wife. Maurice Treherne came while we were out, and I've not seen him yet, poor fellow!"

"Aye, you may well say that; his is a hard case, if what I heard is true. I'm not booked up in the matter, and I should be, lest I make some blunder here, so tell me how things stand, Major. We've a good half hour before dinner. Sir Jasper is never punctual."

"Yes, you've a right to know, if you are going to try your fortune with Octavia."

The major marched through the three drawing rooms to see that no inquisitive servant was eavesdropping, and, finding all deserted, he resumed his place, while young Annon lounged on a couch as he listened with intense interest to the major's story.

"You know it was supposed that old Sir Jasper, being a bachelor, would leave his fortune to his two nephews. But he was an oddity, and as the title *must* go to young Jasper by right, the old man said Maurice should have the money. He was poor, young Jasper rich, and it seemed but just, though Madame Mère was very angry when she learned how the will was made."

"But Maurice didn't get the fortune. How was that?"

"There was some mystery there which I shall discover in time. All went smoothly till that unlucky yachting trip, when the cousins were wrecked. Maurice saved Jasper's life, and almost lost his own in so doing. I fancy he wishes he had, rather than remain the poor cripple he is. Exposure, exertion, and neglect afterward brought on paralysis of the lower limbs, and there he is—a fine, talented, spirited fellow tied to that cursed chair like a decrepit old man."

"How does he bear it?" asked Annon, as the major shook his gray head, with a traitorous huskiness in his last words.

"Like a philosopher or a hero. He is too proud to show his despair at such a sudden end to all his hopes, too generous to complain, for Jasper is desperately cut up about it, and too brave to be daunted by a misfortune which would drive many a man mad."

"Is it true that Sir Jasper, knowing all this, made a new will and left every cent to his namesake?"

"Yes, and there lies the mystery. Not only did he leave it away from poor Maurice, but so tied it up that Jasper cannot transfer it, and at his death it goes to Octavia."

"The old man must have been demented. What in heaven's name did he mean by leaving Maurice helpless and penniless after all his devotion to Jasper? Had he done anything to offend the old party?"

"No one knows; Maurice hasn't the least idea of the cause of this sudden whim, and the old man would give no reason for it. He died soon after, and the instant Jasper came to the title and estate he brought his cousin home, and treats him like a brother. Jasper is a noble fellow, with all his faults, and this act of justice increases my respect for him," said the major heartily.

"What will Maurice do, now that he can't enter the army as he intended?" asked Annon, who now sat erect, so full of interest was he.

"Marry Octavia, and come to his own, I hope."

"An excellent little arrangement, but Miss Treherne may object," said Annon, rising with sudden kindling of the eye.

"I think not, if no one interferes. Pity, with women, is akin to love, and she pities her cousin in the tenderest fashion. No sister could be more devoted, and as Maurice is a handsome, talented fellow, one can easily foresee the end, if, as I said before, no one interferes to disappoint the poor lad again."

"You espouse his cause, I see, and tell me this that I may stand aside. Thanks for the warning, Major; but as Maurice Treherne is a man of unusual power in many ways, I think we are equally matched, in spite of his misfortune. Nay, if anything, he has the advantage of me, for Miss Treherne pities him, and that is a strong ally for my rival. I'll be as generous as I can, but I'll *not* stand aside and relinquish the woman I love without a trial first."

With an air of determination Annon faced the major, whose keen eyes had read the truth which he had but newly confessed to himself. Major Royston smiled as he listened, and said briefly, as steps approached, "Do your best. Maurice will win."

"We shall see," returned Annon between his teeth.

Here their host entered, and the subject of course was dropped. But the major's words rankled in the young man's mind, and would have been doubly bitter had he known that their confidential conversation had been overheard. On either side of the great fireplace was a door leading to a suite of rooms which had been old Sir Jasper's. These apartments had been given to Maurice Treherne, and he had just returned from London, whither he had been to consult a certain famous physician. Entering quietly, he had taken possession of his rooms, and having rested and dressed for dinner, rolled himself into the library, to which led the curtained door on the right. Sitting idly in his light, wheeled chair, ready to enter when his cousin appeared, he had heard the chat of Annon and the major. As he listened, over his usually impassive face passed varying expressions of anger, pain, bitterness, and defiance, and when the young man uttered his almost fierce "We shall see," Treherne smiled a scornful smile and clenched his pale hand with a gesture which proved that a year of suffering had not conquered the man's spirit, though it had crippled his strong body.

A singular face was Maurice Treherne's; well-cut and somewhat haughty features; a fine brow under the dark locks that carelessly streaked it; and remarkably piercing eyes. Slight in figure and wasted by pain, he still retained the grace as native to him as the stern fortitude which enabled him to hide the deep despair of an ambitious

nature from every eye, and bear his affliction with a cheerful philos-
ophy more pathetic than the most entire abandonment to grief. Carefully dressed, and with no hint at invalidism but the chair, he bore
himself as easily and calmly as if the doom of lifelong helplessness
did not hang over him. A single motion of the hand sent him rolling
noiselessly to the curtained door, but as he did so, a voice exclaimed
behind him, "Wait for me, cousin." And as he turned, a young girl
approached, smiling a glad welcome as she took his hand, adding in a
tone of soft reproach, "Home again, and not let me know it, till I heard
the good news by accident."

"Was it good news, Octavia?" and Maurice looked up at the
frank face with a new expression in those penetrating eyes of his. His
cousin's open glance never changed as she stroked the hair off his forehead with the caress one often gives a child, and answered eagerly,
"The best to me; the house is dull when you are away, for Jasper
always becomes absorbed in horses and hounds, and leaves Mamma
and me to mope by ourselves. But tell me, Maurice, what they said
to you, since you would not write."

"A little hope, with time and patience. Help me to wait, dear,
help me to wait."

His tone was infinitely sad, and as he spoke, he leaned his cheek
against the kind hand he held, as if to find support and comfort
there. The girl's face brightened beautifully, though her eyes filled, for
to her alone did he betray his pain, and in her alone did he seek
consolation.

"I will, I will with heart and hand! Thank heaven for the hope,
and trust me it shall be fulfilled. You look very tired, Maurice. Why
go in to dinner with all those people? Let me make you cozy here,"
she added anxiously.

"Thanks, I'd rather go in, it does me good; and if I stay away,
Jasper feels that he must stay with me. I dressed in haste, am I right,
little nurse?"

She gave him a comprehensive glance, daintily settled his cravat,
brushed back a truant lock, and, with a maternal air that was charming, said, "My boy is always elegant, and I'm proud of him. Now we'll
go in." But with her hand on the curtain she paused, saying quickly,
as a voice reached her, "Who is that?"

"Frank Annon. Didn't you know he was coming?" Maurice eyed
her keenly.

"No, Jasper never told me. Why did he ask him?"

"To please you."

"Me! When he knows I detest the man. No matter, I've got on the color he hates, so he won't annoy me, and Mrs. Snowdon can amuse herself with him. The general has come, you know?"

Treherne smiled, well pleased, for no sign of maiden shame or pleasure did the girl's face betray, and as he watched her while she peeped, he thought with satisfaction, Annon is right, I have the advantage, and I'll keep it at all costs.

"Here is Mamma. We must go in," said Octavia, as a stately old lady made her appearance in the drawing room.

The cousins entered together and Annon watched them covertly, while seemingly intent on paying his respects to Madame Mère, as his hostess was called by her family.

"Handsomer than ever," he muttered, as his eye rested on the blooming girl, looking more like a rose than ever in the peach-colored silk which he had once condemned because a rival admired it. She turned to reply to the major, and Annon glanced at Treherne with an irrepressible frown, for sickness had not marred the charm of that peculiar face, so colorless and thin that it seemed cut in marble; but the keen eyes shone with a wonderful brilliancy, and the whole countenance was alive with a power of intellect and will which made the observer involuntarily exclaim, "That man must suffer a daily martyrdom, so crippled and confined; if it last long he will go mad or die."

"General and Mrs. Snowdon," announced the servant, and a sudden pause ensued as everyone looked up to greet the newcomers.

A feeble, white-haired old man entered, leaning on the arm of an indescribably beautiful woman. Not thirty yet, tall and nobly molded, with straight black brows over magnificent eyes; rippling dark hair gathered up in a great knot, and ornamented with a single band of gold. A sweeping dress of wine-colored velvet, set off with a dazzling neck and arms decorated like her stately head with ornaments of Roman gold. At the first glance she seemed a cold, haughty creature, born to dazzle but not to win. A deeper scrutiny detected lines of suffering in that lovely face, and behind the veil of reserve, which pride forced her to wear, appeared the anguish of a strong-willed woman burdened by a heavy cross. No one would dare express pity or offer sympathy, for her whole air repelled it, and in her gloomy eyes sat scorn of herself mingled with defiance of the scorn of others. A strange, almost tragical-looking woman, in spite of beauty, grace, and the cold sweetness of her manner. A faint smile parted her lips as she greeted those about her, and as her husband seated himself beside Lady Treherne, she lifted her head with a long breath, and a singular expression of relief, as if a burden was removed, and for the time being she was free. Sir Jasper was at her side, and as she listened, her eye glanced from face to face.

"Who is with you now?" she asked, in a low, mellow voice that was full of music.

"My sister and my cousin are yonder. You may remember Tavia as a child, she is little more now. Maurice is an invalid, but the finest fellow breathing."

"I understand," and Mrs. Snowdon's eyes softened with a sudden glance of pity for one cousin and admiration for the other, for she knew the facts.

"Major Royston, my father's friend, and Frank Annon, my own. Do you know him?" asked Sir Jasper.

"No."

"Then allow me to make him happy by presenting him, may I?"

"Not now. I'd rather see your cousin."

"Thanks, you are very kind. I'll bring him over."

"Stay, let me go to him," began the lady, with more feeling in face and voice than one would believe her capable of showing.

"Pardon, it will offend him, he will not be pitied, or relinquish any of the duties or privileges of a gentleman which he can possibly perform. He is proud, we can understand the feeling, so let us humor the poor fellow."

Mrs. Snowdon bowed silently, and Sir Jasper called out in his hearty, blunt way, as if nothing was amiss with his cousin, "Maurice, I've an honor for you. Come and receive it."

Divining what it was, Treherne noiselessly crossed the room, and with no sign of self-consciousness or embarrassment, was presented to the handsome woman. Thinking his presence might be a restraint, Sir Jasper went away. The instant his back was turned, a change came over both: an almost grim expression replaced the suavity of Treherne's face, and Mrs. Snowdon's smile faded suddenly, while a deep flush rose to her brow, as her eyes questioned his beseechingly.

"How dared you come?" he asked below his breath.

"The general insisted."

"And you could not change his purpose; poor woman!"

"You will not be pitied, neither will I," and her eyes flashed; then the fire was quenched in tears, and her voice lost all its pride in a pleading tone.

"Forgive me, I longed to see you since your illness, and so I 'dared' to come."

"You shall be gratified; look, quite helpless, crippled for life, perhaps."

The chair was turned from the groups about the fire, and as he spoke, with a bitter laugh Treherne threw back the skin which covered his knees, and showed her the useless limbs once so strong and fleet. She shrank and paled, put out her hand to arrest him, and cried in an indignant whisper, "No, no, not that! You know I never meant such cruel curiosity, such useless pain to both—"

"Be still, someone is coming," he returned inaudibly; adding aloud, as he adjusted the skin and smoothed the rich fur as if speaking of it, "Yes, it is a very fine one, Jasper gave it to me. He spoils me, like a dear, generous-hearted fellow as he is. Ah, Octavia, what can I do for you?"

"Nothing, thank you. I want to recall myself to Mrs. Snowdon's memory, if she will let me."

"No need of that; I never forget happy faces and pretty pictures. Two years ago I saw you at your first ball, and longed to be a girl again."

As she spoke, Mrs. Snowdon pressed the hand shyly offered, and smiled at the spirited face before her, though the shadow in her own eyes deepened as she met the bright glance of the girl.

"How kind you were that night! I remember you let me chatter away about my family, my cousin, and my foolish little affairs with the sweetest patience, and made me very happy by your interest. I was homesick, and Aunt could never bear to hear of those things. It was before your marriage, and all the kinder, for you were the queen of the night, yet had a word for poor little me."

Mrs. Snowdon was pale to the lips, and Maurice impatiently tapped the arm of his chair, while the girl innocently chatted on.

"I am sorry the general is such an invalid; yet I dare say you find great happiness in taking care of him. It is so pleasant to be of use to those we love." And as she spoke, Octavia leaned over her cousin to hand him the glove he had dropped.

The affectionate smile that accompanied the act made the color
deepen again in Mrs. Snowdon's cheek, and lit a spark in her softened
eyes. Her lips curled and her voice was sweetly sarcastic as she answered, "Yes, it is charming to devote one's life to these dear invalids,
and find one's reward in their gratitude. Youth, beauty, health, and
happiness are small sacrifices if one wins a little comfort for the poor
sufferers."

The girl felt the sarcasm under the soft words and drew back
with a troubled face.

Maurice smiled, and glanced from one to the other, saying significantly, "Well for me that my little nurse loves her labor, and finds
no sacrifice in it. I am fortunate in my choice."

"I trust it may prove so—" Mrs. Snowdon got no further, for at
that moment dinner was announced, and Sir Jasper took her away.
Annon approached with him and offered his arm to Miss Treherne,
but with an air of surprise, and a little gesture of refusal, she said
coldly:

"My cousin always takes me in to dinner. Be good enough to escort the major." And with her hand on the arm of the chair, she
walked away with a mischievous glitter in her eyes.

Annon frowned and fell back, saying sharply, "Come, Major,
what are you doing there?"

"Making discoveries."

❧ *chapter II* ❦

BYPLAY

A RIGHT splendid old dowager was Lady Treherne, in her black velvet and point lace, as she sat erect and stately on a couch by the drawing-room fire, a couch which no one dare occupy in her absence, or share uninvited. The gentlemen were still over their wine, and the three ladies were alone. My lady never dozed in public, Mrs. Snowdon never gossiped, and Octavia never troubled herself to entertain any guests but those of her own age, so long pauses fell, and conversation languished, till Mrs. Snowdon roamed away into the library. As she disappeared, Lady Treherne beckoned to her daughter, who was idly making chords at the grand piano. Seating herself on the ottoman at her mother's feet, the girl took the still handsome hand in her own and amused herself with examining the old-fashioned jewels that covered it, a pretext for occupying her telltale eyes, as she suspected what was coming.

"My dear, I'm not pleased with you, and I tell you so at once, that you may amend your fault," began Madame Mère in a tender tone, for though a haughty, imperious woman, she idolized her children.

"What have I done, Mamma?" asked the girl.

"Say rather, what have you left undone. You have been very rude to Mr. Annon. It must not occur again; not only because he is a guest, but because he is your—brother's friend."

My lady hesitated over the word "lover," and changed it, for to

(219)

her Octavia still seemed a child, and though anxious for the alliance, she forbore to speak openly, lest the girl should turn willful, as she inherited her mother's high spirit.

"I'm sorry, Mamma. But how can I help it, when he teases me so that I detest him?" said Octavia, petulantly.

"How tease, my love?"

"Why, he follows me about like a dog, puts on a sentimental look when I appear; blushes, and beams, and bows at everything I say, if I am polite; frowns and sighs if I'm not; and glowers tragically at every man I speak to, even poor Maurice. Oh, Mamma, what foolish creatures men are!" And the girl laughed blithely, as she looked up for the first time into her mother's face.

My mother smiled, as she stroked the bright head at her knee, but asked quickly, "Why say 'even poor Maurice,' as if it were impossible for anyone to be jealous of him?"

"But isn't it, Mamma? I thought strong, well men regarded him as one set apart and done with, since his sad misfortune."

"Not entirely; while women pity and pet the poor fellow, his comrades will be jealous, absurd as it is."

"No one pets him but me, and I have a right to do it, for he is my cousin," said the girl, feeling a touch of jealousy herself.

"Rose and Blanche Talbot outdo you, my dear, and there is no cousinship to excuse them."

"Then let Frank Annon be jealous of them, and leave me in peace. They promised to come today; I'm afraid something has happened to prevent them." And Octavia gladly seized upon the new subject. But my lady was not to be eluded.

"They said they could not come till after dinner. They will soon arrive. Before they do so, I must say a few words, Tavia, and I beg you to give heed to them. I desire you to be courteous and amiable to Mr. Annon, and before strangers to be less attentive and affectionate to Maurice. You mean it kindly, but it looks ill, and causes disagreeable remarks."

"Who blames me for being devoted to my cousin? Can I ever do enough to repay him for his devotion? Mamma, you forget he saved your son's life."

Indignant tears filled the girl's eyes, and she spoke passionately, forgetting that Mrs. Snowdon was within earshot of her raised voice. With a frown my lady laid her hand on her daughter's lips, saying coldly, "I do not forget, and I religiously discharge my every obligation by every care and comfort it is in my power to bestow. You are young, romantic, and tender-hearted. You think you must give your time and health, must sacrifice your future happiness to this duty. You are wrong, and unless you learn wisdom in season, you will find that you have done harm, not good."

"God forbid! How can I do that? Tell me, and I will be wise in time."

Turning the earnest face up to her own, Lady Treherne whispered anxiously, "Has Maurice ever looked or hinted anything of love during this year he has been with us, and you his constant companion?"

"Never, Mamma; he is too honorable and too unhappy to speak or think of that. I am his little nurse, sister, and friend, no more, nor ever shall be. Do not suspect us, or put such fears into my mind, else all our comfort will be spoiled."

Flushed and eager was the girl, but her clear eyes betrayed no tender confusion as she spoke, and all her thought seemed to be to clear her cousin from the charge of loving her too well. Lady Treherne looked relieved, paused a moment, then said, seriously but gently, "This is well, but, child, I charge you tell me at once, if ever he forgets himself, for this thing cannot be. Once I hoped it might, now it is impossible; remember that he continue a friend and cousin, nothing more. I warn you in time, but if you neglect the warning, Maurice must go. No more of this; recollect my wish regarding Mr. Annon, and let your cousin amuse himself without you in public."

"Mamma, do you wish me to like Frank Annon?"

The abrupt question rather disturbed my lady, but knowing her daughter's frank, impetuous nature, she felt somewhat relieved by this candor, and answered decidedly, "I do. He is your equal in all respects; he loves you, Jasper desires it, I approve, and you, being heart-whole, can have no just objection to the alliance."

"Has he spoken to you?"

"No, to your brother."

"You wish this much, Mamma?"

"Very much, my child."

"I will try to please you, then." And stifling a sigh, the girl kissed her mother with unwonted meekness in tone and manner.

"Now I am well pleased. Be happy, my love. No one will urge

or distress you. Let matters take their course, and if this hope of ours can be fulfilled, I shall be relieved of the chief care of my life."

A sound of girlish voices here broke on their ears, and springing up, Octavia hurried to meet her friends, exclaiming joyfully, "They have come! they have come!"

Two smiling, blooming girls met her at the door, and, being at an enthusiastic age, they gushed in girlish fashion for several minutes, making a pretty group as they stood in each other's arms, all talking at once, with frequent kisses and little bursts of laughter, as vents for their emotion. Madame Mère welcomed them and then went to join Mrs. Snowdon, leaving the trio to gossip unrestrained.

"My dearest creature, I thought we never should get here, for Papa had a tiresome dinner party, and we were obliged to stay, you know," cried Rose, the lively sister, shaking out the pretty dress and glancing at herself in the mirror as she fluttered about the room like a butterfly.

"We were dying to come, and so charmed when you asked us, for we haven't seen you this age, darling," added Blanche, the pensive one, smoothing her blond curls after a fresh embrace.

"I'm sorry the Ulsters couldn't come to keep Christmas with us, for we have no gentlemen but Jasper, Frank Annon, and the major. Sad, isn't it?" said Octavia, with a look of despair, which caused a fresh peal of laughter.

"One apiece, my dear, it might be worse." And Rose privately decided to appropriate Sir Jasper.

"Where is your cousin?" asked Blanche, with a sigh of sentimental interest.

"He is here, of course. I forget him, but he is not on the flirting list, you know. We must amuse him, and not expect him to amuse us, though really, all the capital suggestions and plans for merrymaking always come from him."

"He is better, I hope?" asked both sisters with real sympathy, making their young faces womanly and sweet.

"Yes, and has hopes of entire recovery. At least, they tell him so, though Dr. Ashley said there was no chance of it."

"Dear, dear, how sad! Shall we see him, Tavia?"

"Certainly; he is able to be with us now in the evening, and enjoys society as much as ever. But please take no notice of his infirmity, and make no inquiries beyond the usual 'How do you do.'

He is sensitive, and hates to be considered an invalid more than ever."

"How charming it must be to take care of him, he is so accomplished and delightful. I quite envy you," said Blanche pensively.

"Sir Jasper told us that the General and Mrs. Snowdon were coming. I hope they will, for I've a most intense curiosity to see her—" began Rose.

"Hush, she is here with Mamma! Why curious? What is the mystery? For you look as if there was one," questioned Octavia under her breath.

The three charming heads bent toward one another as Rose replied in a whisper, "If I knew, I shouldn't be inquisitive. There was a rumor that she married the old general in a fit of pique, and now repents. I asked Mamma once, but she said such matters were not for young girls to hear, and not a word more would she say. *N'importe*, I have wits of my own, and I can satisfy myself. The gentlemen are coming! Am I all right, dear?" And the three glanced at one another with a swift scrutiny that nothing could escape, then grouped themselves prettily, and waited, with a little flutter of expectation in each young heart.

In came the gentlemen, and instantly a new atmosphere seemed to pervade the drawing room, for with the first words uttered, several romances began. Sir Jasper was taken possession of by Rose, Blanche intended to devote herself to Maurice Treherne, but Annon intercepted her, and Octavia was spared any effort at politeness by this unexpected move on the part of her lover.

"He is angry, and wishes to pique me by devoting himself to Blanche. I wish he would, with all my heart, and leave me in peace. Poor Maurice, he expects me, and I long to go to him, but must obey Mamma." And Octavia went to join the group formed by my lady, Mrs. Snowdon, the general, and the major.

The two young couples flirted in different parts of the room, and Treherne sat alone, watching them all with eyes that pierced below the surface, reading the hidden wishes, hopes, and fears that ruled them. A singular expression sat on his face as he turned from Octavia's clear countenance to Mrs. Snowdon's gloomy one. He leaned his head upon his hand and fell into deep thought, for he was passing through one of those fateful moments which come to us all, and which may make or mar a life. Such moments come when least looked for: an unexpected meeting, a peculiar mood, some trivial circumstance, or careless word produces it, and often it is gone before we realize its presence, leaving aftereffects to show us what we have gained or lost. Treherne was conscious that the present hour, and the acts that filled it, possessed unusual interest, and would exert an unusual influence on his life. Before him was the good and evil genius of his nature in the guise of those two women. Edith Snowdon had already tried her power, and accident only had saved him. Octavia, all unconscious as she was, never failed to rouse and stimulate the noblest attributes of mind and heart. A year spent in her society had done much for him, and he loved her with a strange mingling of passion, reverence, and gratitude. He knew why Edith Snowdon came, he felt that the old fascination had not lost its charm, and though fear was unknown to him, he was ill pleased at the sight of the beautiful, dangerous woman. On the other hand, he saw that Lady Treherne desired her daughter to shun him and smile on Annon; he acknowledged that he had no right to win the young creature, crippled and poor as he was, and a pang of jealous pain wrung his heart as he watched her.

Then a sense of power came to him, for helpless, poor, and seemingly an object of pity, he yet felt that he held the honor, peace, and happiness of nearly every person present in his hands. It was a strong temptation to this man, so full of repressed passion and power, so set apart and shut out from the more stirring duties and pleasures of life. A few words from his lips, and the pity all felt for him would be turned to fear, respect, and admiration. Why not utter them, and enjoy all that was possible? He owed the Trehernes nothing; why suffer injustice, dependence, and the compassion that wounds a proud man deepest? Wealth, love, pleasure might be his with a breath. Why not secure them now?

His pale face flushed, his eye kindled, and his thin hand lay clenched like a vise as these thoughts passed rapidly through his mind. A look, a word at that moment would sway him; he felt it, and leaned forward, waiting in secret suspense for the glance, the speech which should decide him for good or ill. Who shall say what subtle instinct caused Octavia to turn and smile at him with a wistful, friendly look that warmed his heart? He met it with an answering glance, which thrilled her strangely, for love, gratitude, and some mysterious intelligence met and mingled in the brilliant yet soft expression which swiftly shone and faded in her face. What it was she could not tell;

she only felt that it filled her with an indescribable emotion never experienced before. In an instant it all passed, Lady Treherne spoke to her, and Blanche Talbot addressed Maurice, wondering, as she did so, if the enchanting smile he wore was meant for her.

"Mr. Annon having mercifully set me free, I came to try to cheer your solitude; but you look as if solitude made you happier than society does the rest of us," she said without her usual affectation, for his manner impressed her.

"You are very kind and very welcome. I do find pleasures to beguile my loneliness, which gayer people would not enjoy, and it is well that I can, else I should turn morose and tyrannical, and doom some unfortunate to entertain me all day long." He answered with a gentle courtesy which was his chief attraction to womankind.

"Pray tell me some of your devices. I'm often alone in spirit, if not so in the flesh, for Rose, though a dear girl, is not congenial, and I find no kindred soul."

A humorous glimmer came to Treherne's eyes, as the sentimental damsel beamed a soft sigh and drooped her long lashes effectively. Ignoring the topic of "kindred souls," he answered coldly, "My favorite amusement is studying the people around me. It may be rude, but tied to my corner, I cannot help watching the figures around me, and discovering their little plots and plans. I'm getting very expert, and really surprise myself sometimes by the depth of my researches."

"I can believe it; your eyes look as if they possessed that gift. Pray don't study *me*." And the girl shrank away with an air of genuine alarm.

Treherne smiled involuntarily, for he had read the secret of that shallow heart long ago, and was too generous to use the knowledge, however flattering it might be to him. In a reassuring tone he said, turning away the keen eyes she feared, "I give you my word I never will, charming as it might be to study the white pages of a maidenly heart. I find plenty of others to read, so rest tranquil, Miss Blanche."

"Who interests you most just now?" asked the girl, coloring with pleasure at his words. "Mrs. Snowdon looks like one who has a romance to be read, if you have the skill."

"I have read it. My lady is my study just now. I thought I knew her well, but of late she puzzles me. Human minds are more full of mysteries than any written book and more changeable than the cloud shapes in the air."

"A fine old lady, but I fear her so intensely I should never dare to try to read her, as you say." Blanche looked toward the object of discussion as she spoke, and added, "Poor Tavia, how forlorn she seems. Let me ask her to join us, may I?"

"With all my heart" was the quick reply.

Blanche glided away but did not return, for my lady kept her as well as her daughter.

"That test satisfies me; well, I submit for a time, but I think I can conquer my aunt yet." And with a patient sigh Treherne turned to observe Mrs. Snowdon.

She now stood by the fire, talking with Sir Jasper, a handsome, reckless, generous-hearted young gentleman, who very plainly showed his great admiration for the lady. When he came, she suddenly woke up from her listless mood and became as brilliantly gay as she had been unmistakably melancholy before. As she chatted, she absently pushed to and fro a small antique urn of bronze on the chimneypiece, and in doing so she more than once gave Treherne a quick, significant glance, which he answered at last by a somewhat haughty nod. Then, as if satisfied, she ceased toying with the ornament and became absorbed in Sir Jasper's gallant badinage.

The instant her son approached Mrs. Snowdon, Madame Mère grew anxious, and leaving Octavia to her friends and lover, she watched Jasper. But her surveillance availed little, for she could neither see nor hear anything amiss, yet could not rid herself of the feeling that some mutual understanding existed between them. When the party broke up for the night, she lingered till all were gone but her son and nephew.

"Well, Madame Ma Mère, what troubles you?" asked Sir Jasper, as she looked anxiously into his face before bestowing her good-night kiss.

"I cannot tell, yet I feel ill at ease. Remember, my son, that you are the pride of my heart, and any sin or shame of yours would kill me. Good night, Maurice." And with a stately bow she swept away.

Lounging with both elbows on the low chimneypiece, Sir Jasper smiled at his mother's fears, and said to his cousin, the instant they were alone, "She is worried about E. S. Odd, isn't it, what instinctive antipathies women take to one another?"

"Why did you ask E. S. here?" demanded Treherne.

"My dear fellow, how could I help it? My mother wanted the

general, my father's friend, and of course his wife must be asked also. I couldn't tell my mother that the lady had been a most arrant coquette, to put it mildly, and had married the old man in a pet, because my cousin and I declined to be ruined by her."

"You *could* have told her what mischief she makes wherever she goes, and for Octavia's sake have deferred the general's visit for a time. I warn you, Jasper, harm will come of it."

"To whom, you or me?"

"To both, perhaps, certainly to you. She was disappointed once when she lost us both by wavering between your title and my supposed fortune. She is miserable with the old man, and her only hope is in his death, for he is very feeble. You are free, and doubly attractive now, so beware, or she will entangle you before you know it."

"Thanks, Mentor. I've no fear, and shall merely amuse myself for a week—they stay no longer." And with a careless laugh, Sir Jasper strolled away.

"Much mischief may be done in a week, and this is the beginning of it," muttered Treherne, as he raised himself to look under the bronze vase for the note. It was gone!

≫ *chapter III* ≪

WHO WAS IT?

WHO had taken it? This question tormented Treherne all that sleepless night. He suspected three persons, for only these had approached the fire after the note was hidden. He had kept his eye on it, he thought, till the stir of breaking up. In that moment it must have been removed by the major, Frank Annon, or my lady; Sir Jasper was out of the question, for he never touched an ornament in the drawing room since he had awkwardly demolished a whole *étagère* of costly trifles, to his mother's and sister's great grief. The major evidently suspected something, Annon was jealous, and my lady would be glad of a pretext to remove her daughter from his reach. Trusting to his skill in reading faces, he waited impatiently for morning, resolving to say nothing to anyone but Mrs. Snowdon, and from her merely to inquire what the note contained.

Treherne usually was invisible till lunch, often till dinner; therefore, fearing to excite suspicion by unwonted activity, he did not appear till noon. The mailbag had just been opened, and everyone was busy over their letters, but all looked up to exchange a word with the newcomer, and Octavia impulsively turned to meet him, then checked herself and hid her suddenly crimsoned face behind a newspaper. Treherne's eye took in everything, and saw at once in the unusually late arrival of the mail a pretext for discovering the pilferer of the note.

"All have letters but me, yet I expected one last night. Major, have you got it among yours?" And as he spoke, Treherne fixed his penetrating eyes full on the person he addressed.

With no sign of consciousness, no trace of confusion, the major carefully turned over his pile, and replied in the most natural manner, "Not a trace of it; I wish there was, for nothing annoys me more than any delay or mistake about my letters."

He knows nothing of it, thought Treherne, and turned to Annon, who was deep in a long epistle from some intimate friend, with a talent for imparting news, to judge from the reader's interest.

"Annon, I appeal to you, for I *must* discover who has robbed me of my letter."

"I have but one, read it, if you will, and satisfy yourself" was the brief reply.

"No, thank you. I merely asked in joke; it is doubtless among my lady's. Jasper's letters and mine often get mixed, and my lady takes care of his for him. I think you must have it, Aunt."

Lady Treherne looked up impatiently. "My dear Maurice, what a coil about a letter! We none of us have it, so do not punish us for the sins of your correspondent or the carelessness of the post."

She was not the thief, for she is always intensely polite when she intends to thwart me, thought Treherne, and, apologizing for his rudeness in disturbing them, he rolled himself to his nook in a sunny window and became apparently absorbed in a new magazine.

Mrs. Snowdon was opening the general's letters for him, and, having finished her little task, she roamed away into the library, as if in search of a book. Presently returning with one, she approached Treherne, and, putting it into his hand, said, in her musically distinct voice, "Be so kind as to find for me the passage you spoke of last night. I am curious to see it."

Instantly comprehending her stratagem, he opened it with apparent carelessness, secured the tiny note laid among the leaves, and, selecting a passage at hazard, returned her book and resumed his own. Behind the cover of it he unfolded and read these words:

> *I understand, but do not be anxious; the line I left was merely this—"I must see you alone, tell me when and where." No one can make much of it, and I will discover the thief before*

*dinner. Do nothing, but watch to whom I speak first on entering,
when we meet in the evening, and beware of that person.*

Quietly transferring the note to the fire with the wrapper of the
magazine, he dismissed the matter from his mind and left Mrs. Snowdon to play detective as she pleased, while he busied himself about
his own affairs.

It was a clear, bright December day, and when the young people
separated to prepare for a ride, while the general and the major sunned
themselves on the terrace, Lady Treherne said to her nephew, "I am
going for an airing in the pony carriage. Will you be my escort,
Maurice?"

"With pleasure," replied the young man, well knowing what was
in store for him.

My lady was unusually taciturn and grave, yet seemed anxious
to say something which she found difficult to utter. Treherne saw this,
and ended an awkward pause by dashing boldly into the subject which
occupied both.

"I think you want to say something to me about Tavie, Aunt.
Am I right?"

"Yes."

"Then let me spare you the pain of beginning, and prove my
sincerity by openly stating the truth, as far as I am concerned. I love
her very dearly, but I am not mad enough to dream of telling her so.
I know that it is impossible, and I relinquish my hopes. Trust me. I
will keep silent and see her marry Annon without a word of complaint,
if you will it. I see by her altered manner that you have spoken to her,
and that my little friend and nurse is to be mine no longer. Perhaps
you are wise, but if you do this on my account, it is in vain—the mischief is done, and while I live I shall love my cousin. If you do it to
spare her, I am dumb, and will go away rather than cause her a care
or pain."

"Do you really mean this, Maurice?" And Lady Treherne looked
at him with a changed and softened face.

Turning upon her, Treherne showed her a countenance full of
suffering and sincerity, of resignation and resolve, as he said earnestly,
"I do mean it; prove me in any way you please. I am not a bad fellow,
Aunt, and I desire to be better. Since my misfortune I've had time

to test many things, myself among others, and in spite of many faults, I do cherish the wish to keep my soul honest and true, even though my body be a wreck. It is easy to say these things, but in spite of temptation, I think I can stand firm, if you trust me."

"My dear boy, I do trust you, and thank you gratefully for this frankness. I never forget that I owe Jasper's life to you, and never expect to repay that debt. Remember this when I seem cold or unkind, and remember also that I say now, had you been spared this affliction, I would gladly have given you my girl. But—"

"But, Aunt, hear one thing," broke in Treherne. "They tell me that any sudden and violent shock of surprise, joy, or sorrow may do for me what they hope time will achieve. I said nothing of this, for it is but a chance; yet, while there is any hope, need I utterly renounce Octavia?"

"It is hard to refuse, and yet I cannot think it wise to build upon a chance so slight. Once let her have you, and both are made unhappy, if the hope fail. No, Maurice, it is better to be generous, and leave her free to make her own happiness elsewhere. Annon loves her, she is heart-whole, and will soon learn to love him, if you are silent. My poor boy, it seems cruel, but I must say it."

"Shall I go away, Aunt?" was all his answer, very firmly uttered, though his lips were white.

"Not yet, only leave them to themselves, and hide your trouble if you can. Yet, if you prefer, you shall go to town, and Benson shall see that you are comfortable. Your health will be a reason, and I will come, or write often, if you are homesick. It shall depend on you, for I want to be just and kind in this hard case. You shall decide."

"Then I will stay. I can hide my love; and to see them together will soon cease to wound me, if Octavia is happy."

"So let it rest then, for a time. You shall miss your companion as little as possible, for I will try to fill her place. Forgive me, Maurice, and pity a mother's solicitude, for these two are the last of many children, and I am a widow now."

Lady Treherne's voice faltered, and if any selfish hope or plan lingered in her nephew's mind, that appeal banished it and touched his better nature. Pressing her hand he said gently, "Dear Aunt, do not lament over me. I am one set apart for afflictions, yet I will not be conquered by them. Let us forget my youth and be friendly counselors together for the good of the two whom we both love. I must say a word about Jasper, and you will not press me to explain more than I can without breaking my promise."

"Thank you, thank you! It is regarding that woman, I know. Tell me all you can; I will not be importunate, but I disliked her the instant I saw her, beautiful and charming as she seems."

"When my cousin and I were in Paris, just before my illness, we met her. She was with her father then, a gay old man who led a life of pleasure, and was no fit guardian for a lovely daughter. She knew our story and, having fascinated both, paused to decide which she would accept: Jasper, for his title, or me, for my fortune. This was before my uncle changed his will, and I believed myself his heir; but, before she made her choice, something (don't ask me what, if you please) occurred to send us from Paris. On our return voyage we were wrecked, and then came my illness, disinheritance, and helplessness. Edith Dubarry heard the story, but rumor reported it falsely, and she believed both of us had lost the fortune. Her father died penniless, and in a moment of despair she married the general, whose wealth surrounds her with the luxury she loves, and whose failing health will soon restore her liberty—"

"And then, Maurice?" interrupted my lady.

"She hopes to win Jasper, I think."

"Never! We must prevent that at all costs. I had rather see him dead before me, than the husband of such a woman. Why is she permitted to visit homes like mine? I should have been told this sooner," exclaimed my lady angrily.

"I should have told you had I known it, and I reproved Jasper for his neglect. Do not be needlessly troubled, Aunt. There is no blemish on Mrs. Snowdon's name, and, as the wife of a brave and honorable man, she is received without question; for beauty, grace, or tact like hers can make their way anywhere. She stays but a week, and I will devote myself to her; this will save Jasper, and, if necessary, convince Tavie of my indifference—" Then he paused to stifle a sigh.

"But yourself, have you no fears for your own peace, Maurice? You must not sacrifice happiness or honor, for me or mine."

"I am safe; I love my cousin, and that is my shield. Whatever happens remember that I tried to serve you, and sincerely endeavored to forget myself."

"God bless you, my son! Let me call you so, and feel that, though

I deny you my daughter, I give you heartily a mother's care and affection."

Lady Treherne was as generous as she was proud, and her nephew had conquered her by confidence and submission. He acted no part, yet, even in relinquishing all, he cherished a hope that he might yet win the heart he coveted. Silently they parted, but from that hour a new and closer bond existed between the two, and exerted an unsuspected influence over the whole household.

Maurice waited with some impatience for Mrs. Snowdon's entrance, not only because of his curiosity to see if she had discovered the thief, but because of the part he had taken upon himself to play. He was equal to it, and felt a certain pleasure in it for a threefold reason. It would serve his aunt and cousin, would divert his mind from its own cares, and, perhaps by making Octavia jealous, waken love; for, though he had chosen the right, he was but a man, and moreover a lover.

Mrs. Snowdon was late. She always was, for her toilet was elaborate, and she liked to enjoy its effects upon others. The moment she entered Treherne's eye was on her, and to his intense surprise and annoyance she addressed Octavia, saying blandly, "My dear Miss Treherne, I've been admiring your peacocks. Pray let me see you feed them tomorrow. Miss Talbot says it is a charming sight."

"If you are on the terrace just after lunch, you will find them there, and may feed them yourself, if you like" was the cool, civil reply.

"She looks like a peacock herself in that splendid green and gold dress, doesn't she?" whispered Rose to Sir Jasper, with a wicked laugh.

"Faith, so she does. I wish Tavie's birds had voices like Mrs. Snowdon's; their squalling annoys me intensely."

"I rather like it, for it is honest, and no malice or mischief is hidden behind it. I always distrust those smooth, sweet voices; they are insincere. I like a full, clear tone; sharp, if you please, but decided and true."

"Well said, Octavia. I agree with you, and your own is a perfect sample of the kind you describe." And Treherne smiled as he rolled by to join Mrs. Snowdon, who evidently waited for him, while Octavia turned to her brother to defend her pets.

"Are you sure? How did you discover?" said Maurice, affecting to admire the lady's bouquet, as he paused beside her.

"I suspected it the moment I saw her this morning. She is no actress; and dislike, distrust, and contempt were visible in her face when we met. Till you so cleverly told me my note was lost, I fancied she was disturbed about her brother—or you."

A sudden pause and a keen glance followed the last softly uttered word, but Treherne met it with an inscrutable smile and a quiet "Well, what next?"

"The moment I learned that you did not get the note I was sure she had it, and, knowing that she must have seen me put it there, in spite of her apparent innocence, I quietly asked her for it. This surprised her, this robbed the affair of any mystery, and I finished her perplexity by sending it to the major the moment she returned it to me, as if it had been intended for him. She begged pardon, said her brother was thoughtless, and she watched over him lest he should get into mischief; professed to think I meant the line for him, and behaved like a charming simpleton, as she is."

"Quite a tumult about nothing. Poor little Tavie! You doubtlessly frightened her so that we may safely correspond hereafter."

"You may give me an answer, now and here."

"Very well, meet me on the terrace tomorrow morning; the peacocks will make the meeting natural enough. I usually loiter away an hour or two there, in the sunny part of the day."

"But the girl?"

"I'll send her away."

"You speak as if it would be an easy thing to do."

"It will, both easy and pleasant."

"Now you are mysterious or uncomplimentary. You either care nothing for a tête-à-tête with her, or you will gladly send her out of my way. Which is it?"

"You shall decide. Can I have this?"

She looked at him as he touched a rose with a warning glance, for the flower was both an emblem of love and of silence. Did he mean to hint that he recalled the past, or to warn her that someone was near? She leaned from the shadow of the curtain where she sat, and caught a glimpse of a shadow gliding away.

"Who was it?" she asked, below her breath.

"A Rose," he answered, laughing. Then, as if the danger was over, he said, "How will you account to the major for the message you sent him?"

"Easily, by fabricating some interesting perplexity in which I want sage counsel. He will be flattered, and by seeming to take him into my confidence, I can hoodwink the excellent man to my heart's content, for he annoys me by his odd way of mounting guard over me at all times. Now take me in to dinner, and be your former delightful self."

"That is impossible," he said, yet proved that it was not.

↣ *chapter IV* ↢

FEEDING THE
PEACOCKS

IT was indeed a charming sight, the twelve stately birds perched on the broad stone balustrade, or prancing slowly along the terrace, with the sun gleaming on their green and golden necks and the glories of their gorgeous plumes, widespread, or sweeping like rich trains behind them. In pretty contrast to the splendid creatures was their young mistress, in her simple morning dress and fur-trimmed hood and mantle, as she stood feeding the tame pets from her hand, calling their fanciful names, laughing at their pranks, and heartily enjoying the winter sunshine, the fresh wind, and the girlish pastime. As Treherne slowly approached, he watched her with lover's eyes, and found her very sweet and blithe, and dearer in his sight than ever. She had shunned him carefully all the day before, had parted at night with a hasty handshake, and had not come as usual to bid him good-morning in the library. He had taken no notice of the change as yet, but now, remembering his promise to his aunt, he resolved to let the girl know that he fully understood the relation which henceforth was to exist between them.

"Good morning, cousin. Shall I drive you away, if I take a turn or two here?" he said, in a cheerful tone, but with a half-reproachful glance.

She looked at him an instant, then went to him with extended hand and cheeks rosier than before, while her frank eyes filled, and her voice had a traitorous tremor in it, as she said, impetuously: "I *will* be myself for a moment, in spite of everything. Maurice, don't think me unkind, don't reproach me, or ask my leave to come where I am. There is a reason for the change you see in me; it's not caprice, it is obedience."

"My dear girl, I know it. I meant to speak of it, and show you that I understand. Annon is a good fellow, as worthy of you as any man can be, and I wish you all the happiness you deserve."

"Do you?" And her eyes searched his face keenly.

"Yes; do you doubt it?" And so well did he conceal his love, that neither face, voice, nor manner betrayed a hint of it.

Her eyes fell, a cloud passed over her clear countenance, and she withdrew her hand, as if to caress the hungry bird that gently pecked at the basket she held. As if to change the conversation, she said playfully, "Poor Argus, you have lost your fine feathers, and so all desert you, except kind little Juno, who never forgets her friends. There, take it all, and share between you."

Treherne smiled, and said quickly, "I am a human Argus, and you have been a kind little Juno to me since I lost my plumes. Continue to be so, and you will find me a very faithful friend."

"I will." And as she answered, her old smile came back and her eyes met his again.

"Thanks! Now we shall get on happily. I don't ask or expect the old life—that is impossible. I knew that when lovers came, the friend would fall into the background; and I am content to be second, where I have so long been first. Do not think you neglect me; be happy with your lover, dear, and when you have no pleasanter amusement, come and see old Maurice."

She turned her head away, that he might not see the angry color in her cheeks, the trouble in her eyes, and when she spoke, it was to say petulantly, "I wish Jasper and Mamma would leave me in peace. I hate lovers and want none. If Frank teases, I'll go into a convent and so be rid of him."

Maurice laughed, and turned her face toward himself, saying, in his persuasive voice, "Give him a trial first, to please your mother. It can do no harm and may amuse you. Frank is already lost, and, as you are heart-whole, why not see what you can do for him? I shall have a new study, then, and not miss you so much."

"You are very kind; I'll do my best. I wish Mrs. Snowdon would come, if she is coming; I've an engagement at two, and Frank will look tragical if I'm not ready. He is teaching me billiards, and I really like the game, though I never thought I should."

"That looks well. I hope you'll learn a double lesson, and Annon find a docile pupil in both."

"You are very pale this morning; are you in pain, Maurice?" suddenly asked Octavia, dropping the tone of assumed ease and gaiety under which she had tried to hide her trouble.

"Yes, but it will soon pass. Mrs. Snowdon is coming. I saw her at the hall door a moment ago. I will show her the peacocks, if you want to go. She won't mind the change, I dare say, as you don't like her, and I do."

"No, I am sure of that. It was an arrangement, perhaps? I understand. I will not play Mademoiselle De Trop."

Sudden fire shone in the girl's eyes, sudden contempt curled her lip, and a glance full of meaning went from her cousin to the door, where Mrs. Snowdon appeared, waiting for her maid to bring her some additional wrappings.

"You allude to the note you stole. How came you to play that prank, Tavie?" asked Treherne tranquilly.

"I saw her put it under the urn. I thought it was for Jasper, and I took it," she said boldly.

"Why for Jasper?"

"I remembered his speaking of meeting her long ago, and describing her beauty enthusiastically—and so did you."

"You have a good memory."

"I have for everything concerning those I love. I observed her manner of meeting my brother, his devotion to her, and, when they stood laughing together before the fire, I felt sure that she wished to charm him again."

"Again? Then she did charm him once?" asked Treherne, anxious to know how much Jasper had told his sister.

"He always denied it, and declared that you were the favorite."

"Then why not think the note for me?" he asked.

"I do now" was the sharp answer.

"But she told you it was for the major, and sent it."

"She deceived me; I am not surprised. I am glad Jasper is safe, and I wish you a pleasant tête-à-tête."

Bowing with unwonted dignity, Octavia set down her basket,

and walked away in one direction as Mrs. Snowdon approached in another.

"I have done it now," sighed Treherne, turning from the girlish figure to watch the stately creature who came sweeping toward him with noiseless grace.

Brilliancy and splendor became Mrs. Snowdon; she enjoyed luxury, and her beauty made many things becoming which in a plainer woman would have been out of taste, and absurd. She had wrapped herself in a genuine Eastern burnous of scarlet, blue, and gold; the hood drawn over her head framed her fine face in rich hues, and the great gilt tassels shone against her rippling black hair. She wore it with grace, and the barbaric splendor of the garment became her well. The fresh air touched her cheeks with a delicate color; her usually gloomy eyes were brilliant now, and the smile that parted her lips was full of happiness.

"Welcome, Cleopatra!" cried Treherne, with difficulty repressing a laugh, as the peacocks screamed and fled before the rustling amplitude of her drapery.

"I might reply by calling you Thaddeus of Warsaw, for you look very romantic and Polish with your pale, pensive face, and your splendid furs," she answered, as she paused beside him with admiration very visibly expressed in her eyes.

Treherne disliked the look, and rather abruptly said, as he offered her the basket of bread, "I have disposed of my cousin, and offered to do the honors of the peacocks. Here they are—will you feed them?"

"No, thank you—I care nothing for the fowls, as you know; I came to speak to you," she said impatiently.

"I am at your service."

"I wish to ask you a question or two—is it permitted?"

"What man ever refused Mrs. Snowdon a request?"

"Nay, no compliments; from you they are only satirical evasions. I was deceived when abroad, and rashly married that old man. Tell me truly how things stand."

"Jasper has all. I have nothing."

"I am glad of it."

"Many thanks for the hearty speech. You at least speak sincerely," he said bitterly.

"I do, Maurice—I do; let me prove it."

Treherne's chair was close beside the balustrade. Mrs. Snowdon leaned on the carved railing, with her back to the house and her face screened by a tall urn. Looking steadily at him, she said rapidly and low, "You thought I wavered between you and Jasper, when we parted two years ago. I did; but it was not between title and fortune that I hesitated. It was between duty and love. My father, a fond, foolish old man, had set his heart on seeing me a lady. I was his all; my beauty was his delight, and no untitled man was deemed worthy of me. I loved him tenderly. You may doubt this, knowing how selfish, reckless, and vain I am, but I have a heart, and with better training had been a better woman. No matter, it is too late now. Next my father, I loved you. Nay, hear me—I *will* clear myself in your eyes. I mean no wrong to the general. He is kind, indulgent, generous; I respect him—I am grateful, and while he lives, I shall be true to him."

"Then be silent now. Do not recall the past, Edith; let it sleep, for both our sakes," began Treherne; but she checked him imperiously.

"It shall, when I am done. I loved you, Maurice; for, of all the gay, idle, pleasure-seeking men I saw about me, you were the only one who seemed to have a thought beyond the folly of the hour. Under the seeming frivolity of your life lay something noble, heroic, and true. I felt that you had a purpose, that your present mood was but transitory—a young man's holiday, before the real work of his life began. This attracted, this won me; for even in the brief regard you then gave me, there was an earnestness no other man had shown. I wanted your respect; I longed to earn your love, to share your life, and prove that even in my neglected nature slept the power of canceling a frivolous past by a noble future. Oh, Maurice, had you lingered one week more, I never should have been the miserable thing I am!"

There her voice faltered and failed, for all the bitterness of lost love, peace, and happiness sounded in the pathetic passion of that exclamation. She did not weep, for tears seldom dimmed those trag-ical eyes of hers; but she wrung her hands in mute despair, and looked down into the frost-blighted gardens below, as if she saw there a true symbol of her own ruined life. Treherne uttered not a word, but set his teeth with an almost fierce glance toward the distant figure of Sir Jasper, who was riding gaily away, like one unburdened by a memory or a care.

Hurriedly Mrs. Snowdon went on, "My father begged and com-manded me to choose your cousin. I could not break his heart, and asked for time, hoping to soften him. While I waited, that mysterious affair hurried you from Paris, and then came the wreck, the illness, and the rumor that old Sir Jasper had disinherited both nephews. They told me you were dying, and I became a passive instrument in my father's hands. I promised to recall and accept your cousin, but the old man died before it was done, and then I cared not what became of me.

"General Snowdon was my father's friend; he pitied me; he saw my desolate, destitute state, my despair and helplessness. He comforted, sustained, and saved me. I was grateful; and when he offered me his heart and home, I accepted them. He knew I had no love to give; but as a friend, a daughter, I would gladly serve him, and make his declining years as happy as I could. It was all over, when I heard that you were alive, afflicted, and poor. I longed to come and live for you. My new bonds became heavy fetters then, my wealth oppressed me, and I was doubly wretched—for I dared not tell my trouble, and it nearly drove me mad. I have seen you now; I know that you are happy; I read your cousin's love and see a peaceful life in store for you. This must content me, and I must learn to bear it as I can."

She paused, breathless and pale, and walked rapidly along the terrace, as if to hide or control the agitation that possessed her.

Treherne still sat silent, but his heart leaped within him, as he thought, "She sees that Octavia loves me! A woman's eye is quick to detect love in another, and she asserts what I begin to hope. My cousin's manner just now, her dislike of Annon, her new shyness with me; it may be true, and if it is— Heaven help me—what am I saying! I must not hope, nor wish, nor dream; I must renounce and forget."

He leaned his head upon his hand, and sat so till Mrs. Snowdon rejoined him, pale, but calm and self-possessed. As she drew near, she marked his attitude, the bitter sadness of his face, and hope sprang up within her. Perhaps she was mistaken; perhaps he did not love his cousin; perhaps he still remembered the past, and still regretted the loss of the heart she had just laid bare before him. Her husband was failing, and might die any day. And then, free, rich, beautiful, and young, what might she not become to Treherne, helpless, poor, and ambitious? With all her faults, she was generous, and this picture charmed her fancy, warmed her heart, and comforted her pain.

"Maurice," she said softly, pausing again beside him, "If I mistake you and your hopes, it is because I dare ask nothing for myself;

but if ever a time shall come when I have liberty to give or help, ask of me *anything,* and it is gladly yours."

He understood her, pitied her, and, seeing that she found consolation in a distant hope, he let her enjoy it while she might. Gravely, yet gratefully, he spoke, and pressed the hand extended to him with an impulsive gesture.

"Generous as ever, Edith, and impetuously frank. Thank you for your sincerity, your kindness, and the affection you once gave me. I say 'once,' for now duty, truth, and honor bar us from each other. My life must be solitary, yet I shall find work to do, and learn to be content. You owe all devotion to the good old man who loves you, and will not fail him, I am sure. Leave the future and the past, but let us make the present what it may be—a time to forgive and forget, to take heart and begin anew. Christmas is a fitting time for such resolves, and the birth of friendship such as ours may be."

Something in his tone and manner struck her, and, eyeing him with soft wonder, she exclaimed, "How changed you are!"

"Need you tell me that?" And he glanced at his helpless limbs with a bitter yet pathetic look of patience.

"No, no—not so! I mean in mind, not body. Once you were gay and careless, eager and fiery, like Jasper; now you are grave and quiet, or cheerful, and so very kind. Yet, in spite of illness and loss, you seem twice the man you were, and something wins respect, as well as admiration—and love."

Her dark eyes filled as the last word left her lips, and the beauty of a touched heart shone in her face. Maurice looked up quickly, asking with sudden earnestness, "Do you see it? Then it is true. Yes, I *am* changed, thank God! And she has done it."

"Who?" demanded his companion jealously.

"Octavia. Unconsciously, yet surely, she has done much for me, and this year of seeming loss and misery has been the happiest, most profitable of my life. I have often heard that afflictions were the best teachers, and I believe it now."

Mrs. Snowdon shook her head sadly.

"Not always; they are tormentors to some. But don't preach, Maurice. I am still a sinner, though you incline to sainthood, and I have one question more to ask. What was it that took you and Jasper so suddenly away from Paris?"

"That I can never tell you."

"I shall discover it for myself, then."

"It is impossible."

"Nothing is impossible to a determined woman."

"You can neither wring, surprise, nor bribe this secret from the two persons who hold it. I beg of you to let it rest," said Treherne earnestly.

"I have a clue, and I shall follow it; for I am convinced that something is wrong, and you are—"

"Dear Mrs. Snowdon, are you so charmed with the birds that you forget your fellow-beings, or so charmed with one fellow-being that you forget the birds?"

As the sudden question startled both, Rose Talbot came along the terrace, with hands full of holly and a face full of merry mischief, adding as she vanished, "I shall tell Tavie that feeding the peacocks is such congenial amusement for lovers, she and Mr. Annon had better try it."

"Saucy gypsy!" muttered Treherne.

But Mrs. Snowdon said, with a smile of double meaning, "Many a true word is spoken in jest."

❧ *chapter V* ❧

UNDER THE
MISTLETOE

U NUSUALLY gay and charming the three young friends looked,
dressed alike in fleecy white with holly wreaths in their hair,
as they slowly descended the wide oaken stairway arm in arm.
A footman was lighting the hall lamps, for the winter dusk gathered
early, and the girls were merrily chatting about the evening's festivity
when suddenly a loud, long shriek echoed through the hall. A heavy
glass shade fell from the man's hand with a crash, and the young
ladies clung to one another aghast, for mortal terror was in the cry,
and a dead silence followed it.

"What was it, John?" demanded Octavia, very pale, but steady in
a moment.

"I'll go and see, miss." And the man hurried away.

"Where did the dreadful scream come from?" asked Rose, col-
lecting her wits as rapidly as possible.

"Above us somewhere. Oh, let us go down among people; I am
frightened to death," whispered Blanche, trembling and faint.

Hurrying into the parlor, they found only Annon and the major,
both looking startled, and both staring out of the windows.

"Did you hear it? What could it be? Don't go and leave us!" cried
the girls in a breath, as they rushed in.

The gentlemen had heard, couldn't explain the cry, and were

quite ready to protect the pretty creatures who clustered about them like frightened fawns. John speedily appeared, looking rather wild, and as eager to tell his tale as they to listen.

"It's Patty, one of the maids, miss, in a fit. She went up to the north gallery to see that the fires was right, for it takes a power of wood to warm the gallery even enough for dancing, as you know, miss. Well, it was dark, for the fires was low and her candle went out as she whisked open the door, being flurried, as the maids always is when they go in there. Halfway down the gallery she says she heard a rustling, and stopped. She's the pluckiest of 'em all, and she called out, 'I see you!' thinking it was some of us trying to fright her. Nothing answered, and she went on a bit, when suddenly the fire flared up one flash, and there right before her was the ghost."

"Don't be foolish, John. Tell us what it was," said Octavia sharply, though her face whitened and her heart sank as the last word passed the man's lips.

"It was a tall, black figger, miss, with a dead-white face and a black hood. She see it plain, and turned to go away, but she hadn't gone a dozen steps when there it was again before her, the same tall, dark thing with the dead-white face looking out from the black hood. It lifted its arm as if to hold her, but she gave a spring and dreadful screech, and ran to Mrs. Benson's room, where she dropped in a fit."

"How absurd to be frightened by the shadows of the figures in armor that stand along the gallery!" said Rose, boldly enough, though she would have declined entering the gallery without a light.

"Nay, I don't wonder, it's a ghostly place at night. How is the poor thing?" asked Blanche, still hanging on the major's arm in her best attitude.

"If Mamma knows nothing of it, tell Mrs. Benson to keep it from her, please. She is not well, and such things annoy her very much," said Octavia, adding as the man turned away, "Did anyone look in the gallery after Patty told her tale?"

"No, miss. I'll go and do it myself; I'm not afraid of man, ghost, or devil, saving your presence, ladies," replied John.

"Where is Sir Jasper?" suddenly asked the major.

"Here I am. What a deuce of a noise someone has been making. It disturbed a capital dream. Why, Tavie, what is it?" And Sir Jasper came out of the library with a sleepy face and tumbled hair.

They told him the story, whereat he laughed heartily, and said the maids were a foolish set to be scared by a shadow. While he still laughed and joked, Mrs. Snowdon entered, looking alarmed, and anxious to know the cause of the confusion.

"How interesting! I never knew you kept a ghost. Tell me all about it, Sir Jasper, and soothe our nerves by satisfying our curiosity," she said in her half-persuasive, half-commanding way, as she seated herself on Lady Treherne's sacred sofa.

"There's not much to tell, except that this place used to be an abbey, in fact as well as in name. An ancestor founded it, and for years the monks led a jolly life here, as one may see, for the cellar is twice as large as the chapel, and much better preserved. But another ancestor, a gay and gallant baron, took a fancy to the site for his castle, and, in spite of prayers, anathemas, and excommunication, he turned the poor fellows out, pulled down the abbey, and built this fine old place. Abbot Boniface, as he left his abbey, uttered a heavy curse on all who should live here, and vowed to haunt us till the last Treherne vanished from the face of the earth. With this amiable threat the old party left Baron Roland to his doom, and died as soon as he could in order to begin his cheerful mission."

"Did he haunt the place?" asked Blanche eagerly.

"Yes, most faithfully from that time to this. Some say many of the monks still glide about the older parts of the abbey, for Roland spared the chapel and the north gallery which joined it to the modern building. Poor fellows, they are welcome, and once a year they shall have a chance to warm their ghostly selves by the great fires always kindled at Christmas in the gallery."

"Mrs. Benson once told me that when the ghost walked, it was a sure sign of a coming death in the family. Is that true?" asked Rose, whose curiosity was excited by the expression of Octavia's face, and a certain uneasiness in Sir Jasper's manner in spite of his merry mood.

"There is a stupid superstition of that sort in the family, but no one except the servants believes it, of course. In times of illness some silly maid or croaking old woman can easily fancy they see a phantom, and, if death comes, they are sure of the ghostly warning. Benson saw it before my father died, and old Roger, the night my uncle was seized with apoplexy. Patty will never be made to believe that this warning does not forebode the death of Maurice or myself, for the gallant spirit leaves the ladies of our house to depart in peace. How does it strike you, Cousin?"

Turning as he spoke, Sir Jasper glanced at Treherne, who had entered while he spoke.

"I am quite skeptical and indifferent to the whole affair, but I agree with Octavia that it is best to say nothing to my aunt if she is ignorant of the matter. Her rooms are a long way off, and perhaps she did not hear the confusion."

"You seem to hear everything; you were not with us when I said that." And Octavia looked up with an air of surprise.

Smiling significantly, Treherne answered, "I hear, see, and understand many things that escape others. Jasper, allow me to advise you to smooth the hair which your sleep has disarranged. Mrs. Snowdon, permit me. This rich velvet catches the least speck." And with his handkerchief he delicately brushed away several streaks of white dust which clung to the lady's skirt.

Sir Jasper turned hastily on his heel and went to remake his toilet; Mrs. Snowdon bit her lip, but thanked Treherne sweetly and begged him to fasten her glove. As he did so, she said softly, "Be more careful next time. Octavia has keen eyes, and the major may prove inconvenient."

"I have no fear that *you* will," he whispered back, with a malicious glance.

Here the entrance of my lady put an end to the ghostly episode, for it was evident that she knew nothing of it. Octavia slipped away to question John, and learn that no sign of a phantom was to be seen. Treherne devoted himself to Mrs. Snowdon, and the major entertained my lady, while Sir Jasper and the girls chatted apart.

It was Christmas Eve, and a dance in the great gallery was the yearly festival at the abbey. All had been eager for it, but the maid's story seemed to have lessened their enthusiasm, though no one would own it. This annoyed Sir Jasper, and he exerted himself to clear the atmosphere by affecting gaiety he did not feel. The moment the gentlemen came in after dinner he whispered to his mother, who rose, asked the general for his arm, and led the way to the north gallery, whence the sound of music now proceeded. The rest followed in a merry procession, even Treherne, for two footmen carried him up the great stairway, chair and all.

Nothing could look less ghostly now than the haunted gallery. Fires roared up a wide chimney at either end, long rows of figures clad in armor stood on each side, one mailed hand grasping a lance, the other bearing a lighted candle, a device of Sir Jasper's. Narrow windows pierced in the thick walls let in gleams of wintry moonlight; ivy, holly, and evergreen glistened in the ruddy glow of mingled firelight and candle shine. From the arched stone roof hung tattered banners, and in the midst depended a great bunch of mistletoe. Red-cushioned seats stood in recessed window nooks, and from behind a high-covered screen of oak sounded the blithe air of Sir Roger de Coverley.

With the utmost gravity and stateliness my lady and the general led off the dance, for, according to the good old fashion, the men and maids in their best array joined the gentlefolk and danced with their betters in a high state of pride and bashfulness. Sir Jasper twirled the old housekeeper till her head spun around and around and her decorous skirts rustled stormily; Mrs. Snowdon captivated the gray-haired butler by her condescension; and John was made a proud man by the hand of his young mistress. The major came out strong among the pretty maids, and Rose danced the footmen out of breath long before the music paused.

The merriment increased from that moment, and when the general surprised my lady by gallantly saluting her as she unconsciously stood under the mistletoe, the applause was immense. Everyone followed the old gentleman's example as fast as opportunities occurred, and the young ladies soon had as fine a color as the housemaids. More dancing, games, songs, and all manner of festival devices filled the evening, yet under cover of the gaiety more than one little scene was enacted that night, and in an hour of seeming frivolity the current of several lives was changed.

By a skillful maneuver Annon led Octavia to an isolated recess, as if to rest after a brisk game, and, taking advantage of the auspicious hour, pleaded his suit. She heard him patiently and, when he paused, said slowly, yet decidedly, and with no sign of maiden hesitation, "Thanks for the honor you do me, but I cannot accept it, for I do not love you. I think I never can."

"Have you tried?" he asked eagerly.

"Yes, indeed I have. I like you as a friend, but no more. I know Mamma desires it, that Jasper hopes for it, and I try to please them, but love will not be forced, so what can I do?" And she smiled in spite of herself at her own blunt simplicity.

"No, but it can be cherished, strengthened, and in time won, with patience and devotion. Let me try, Octavia; it is but fair, unless you have already learned from another the lesson I hope to teach. Is it so?"

"No, I think not. I do not understand myself as yet, I am so young, and this so sudden. Give me time, Frank."

She blushed and fluttered now, looked half angry, half beseeching, and altogether lovely.

"How much time shall I give? It cannot take long to read a heart like yours, dear." And fancying her emotion a propitious omen, he assumed the lover in good earnest.

"Give me time till the New Year. I will answer then, and, meantime, leave me free to study both myself and you. We have known each other long, I own, but, still, this changes everything, and makes you seem another person. Be patient, Frank, and I will try to make my duty a pleasure."

"I will. God bless you for the kind hope, Octavia. It has been mine for years, and if I lose it, it will go hardly with me."

Later in the evening General Snowdon stood examining the antique screen. In many places carved oak was pierced quite through, so that voices were audible from behind it. The musicians had gone down to supper, the young folk were quietly busy at the other end of the hall, and as the old gentleman admired the quaint carving, the sound of his own name caught his ear. The housekeeper and butler still remained, though the other servants had gone, and sitting cosily behind the screen chatted in low tones believing themselves secure.

"It *was* Mrs. Snowdon, Adam, as I'm a living woman, though I wouldn't say it to anyone but you. She and Sir Jasper were here wrapped in cloaks, and up to mischief, I'll be bound. She is a beauty, but I don't envy her, and there'll be trouble in the house if she stays long."

"But how do you know, Mrs. Benson, she was here? Where's your proof, mum?" asked the pompous butler.

"Look at this, and then look at the outlandish trimming of the lady's dress. You men are so dull about such matters you'd never observe these little points. Well, I was here first after Patty, and my light shone on this jet ornament lying near where she saw the spirit. No one has any such tasty trifles but Mrs. Snowdon, and these are all over her gown. If that ain't proof, what is?"

"Well, admitting it, I then say what on earth should she and master be up here for, at such a time?" asked the slow-witted butler.

"Adam, we are old servants of the family, and to you I'll say what tortures shouldn't draw from to another. Master has been wild, as you know, and it's my belief that he loved this lady abroad. There was a talk of some mystery, or misdeed, or misfortune, more than a year ago, and she was in it. I'm loath to say it, but I think Master loves her still, and she him. The general is an old man, she is but young, and so spirited and winsome she can't in reason care for him as for a fine, gallant gentleman like Sir Jasper. There's trouble brewing, Adam, mark my words. There's trouble brewing for the Trehernes."

So low had the voices fallen that the listener could not have caught the words had not his ear been strained to the utmost. He did hear all, and his wasted face flashed with the wrath of a young man, then grew pale and stern as he turned to watch his wife. She stood apart from the others talking to Sir Jasper, who looked unusually handsome and debonair as he fanned her with a devoted air.

Perhaps it is true, thought the old man bitterly. They are well matched, were lovers once, no doubt, and long to be so again. Poor Edith, I was very blind. And with his gray head bowed upon his breast the general stole away, carrying an arrow in his brave old heart.

"Blanche, come here and rest, you will be ill tomorrow; and I promised Mamma to take care of you." With which elder-sisterly command Rose led the girl to an immense old chair, which held them both. "Now listen to me and follow my advice, for I am wise in my generation, though not yet gray. They are all busy, so leave them alone and let me show you what is to be done."

Rose spoke softly, but with great resolution, and nodded her pretty head so energetically that the holly berries came rolling over her white shoulders.

"We are not as rich as we might be, and must establish ourselves as soon and as well as possible. I intend to be Lady Treherne. You can be the Honorable Mrs. Annon, if you give your mind to it."

"My dear child, are you mad?" whispered Blanche.

"Far from it, but you will be if you waste your time on Maurice. He is poor, and a cripple, though very charming, I admit. He loves Tavie, and she will marry him, I am sure. She can't endure Frank, but tries to because my lady commands it. Nothing will come of it, so try your fascinations and comfort the poor man; sympathy now will foster love hereafter."

"Don't talk so here, Rose, someone will hear us," began her sister, but the other broke in briskly.

"No fear, a crowd is the best place for secrets. Now remember what I say, and make your game while the ball is rolling. Other people are careful not to put their plans into words, but I'm no hypocrite, and say plainly what I mean. Bear my sage counsel in mind and act wisely. Now come and begin."

Treherne was sitting alone by one of the great fires, regarding the gay scene with serious air. For him there was neither dancing nor games; he could only roam about catching glimpses of forbidden pleasures, impossible delights, and youthful hopes forever lost to him. Sad but not morose was his face, and to Octavia it was a mute reproach which she could not long resist. Coming up as if to warm herself, she spoke to him in her usually frank and friendly way, and felt her heart beat fast when she saw how swift a change her cordial manner wrought in him.

"How pretty your holly is! Do you remember how we used to go and gather it for festivals like this, when we were happy children?" he asked, looking up at her with eyes full of tender admiration.

"Yes, I remember. Everyone wears it tonight as a badge, but you have none. Let me get you a bit, I like to have you one of us in all things."

She leaned forward to break a green sprig from the branch over the chimneypiece; the strong draft drew in her fleecy skirt, and in an instant she was enveloped in flames.

"Maurice, save me, help me!" cried a voice of fear and agony, and before anyone could reach her, before he himself knew how the deed was done, Treherne had thrown himself from his chair, wrapped the tiger skin tightly about her, and knelt there clasping her in his arms heedless of fire, pain, or the incoherent expressions of love that broke from his lips.

❧ *chapter VI* ❧

MIRACLES

GREAT was the confusion and alarm which reigned for many minutes, but when the panic subsided two miracles appeared.

Octavia was entirely uninjured, and Treherne was standing on his feet, a thing which for months he had not done without crutches. In the excitement of the moment, no one observed the wonder; all were crowding about the girl, who, pale and breathless but now self-possessed, was the first to exclaim, pointing to her cousin, who had drawn himself up, with the help of his chair, and leaned there smiling, with a face full of intense delight.

"Look at Maurice! Oh, Jasper, help him or he'll fall!"

Sir Jasper sprung to his side and put a strong arm about him, while a chorus of wonder, sympathy, and congratulations rose about them.

"Why, lad, what does it mean? Have you been deceiving us all this time?" cried Jasper, as Treherne leaned on him, looking exhausted but truly happy.

"It means that I am not to be a cripple all my life; that they did not deceive me when they said a sudden shock might electrify me with a more potent magnetism than any they could apply. It *has,* and if I am cured I owe it all to you, Octavia."

He stretched his hands to her with a gesture of such passionate gratitude that the girl covered her face to hide its traitorous tenderness, and my lady went to him, saying brokenly, as she embraced him with maternal warmth, "God bless you for this act, Maurice, and reward you with a perfect cure. To you I owe the lives of both my children; how can I thank you as I ought?"

"I dare not tell you yet," he whispered eagerly, then added, "I am growing faint, Aunt. Get me away before I make a scene."

This hint recalled my lady to her usual state of dignified self-possession. Bidding Jasper and the major help Treherne to his room without delay, she begged Rose to comfort her sister, who was sobbing hysterically, and as they all obeyed her, she led her daughter away to her own apartment, for the festivities of the evening were at an end.

At the same time Mrs. Snowdon and Annon bade my lady good-night, as if they also were about to retire, but as they reached the door of the gallery Mrs. Snowdon paused and beckoned Annon back. They were alone now, and, standing before the fire which had so nearly made that Christmas Eve a tragical one, she turned to him with a face full of interest and sympathy as she said, nodding toward the blackened shreds of Octavia's dress, and the scorched tiger skin which still lay at their feet, "That was both a fortunate and an unfortunate little affair, but I fear Maurice's gain will be your loss. Pardon my frankness for Octavia's sake; she is a fine creature, and I long to see her given to one worthy of her. I am a woman to read faces quickly; I know that your suit does not prosper as you would have it, and I desire to help you. May I?"

"Indeed you may, and command any service of me in return. But to what do I owe this unexpected friendliness?" cried Annon, both grateful and surprised.

"To my regard for the young lady, my wish to save her from an unworthy man."

"Do you mean Treherne?" asked Annon, more and more amazed.

"I do. Octavia must not marry a gambler!"

"My dear lady, you labor under some mistake; Treherne is by no means a gambler. I owe him no goodwill, but I cannot hear him slandered."

"You are generous, but I am not mistaken. Can you, on your honor, assure me that Maurice never played?"

Mrs. Snowdon's keen eyes were on him, and he looked embarrassed for a moment, but answered with some hesitation, "Why, no, I cannot say that, but I can assure you that he is not an habitual gambler. All young men of his rank play more or less, especially abroad. It is merely an amusement with most, and among men is not considered dishonorable or dangerous. Ladies think differently, I believe, at least in England."

At the word "abroad," Mrs. Snowdon's face brightened, and she suddenly dropped her eyes, as if afraid of betraying some secret purpose.

"Indeed we do, and well we may, many of us having suffered from this pernicious habit. I have had special cause to dread and condemn it, and the fear that Octavia should in time suffer what I have suffered as a girl urges me to interfere where otherwise I should be dumb. Mr. Annon, there was a rumor that Maurice was forced to quit Paris, owing to some dishonorable practices at the gaming table. Is this true?"

"Nay, don't ask me; upon my soul I cannot tell you. I only know that something was amiss, but what I never learned. Various tales were whispered at the clubs, and Sir Jasper indignantly denied them all. The bravery with which Maurice saved his cousin, and the sad affliction which fell upon him, silenced the gossip, and it was soon forgotten."

Mrs. Snowdon remained silent for a moment, with brows knit in deep thought, while Annon uneasily watched her. Suddenly she glanced over her shoulder, drew nearer, and whispered cautiously, "Did the rumors of which you speak charge him with—" and the last word was breathed into Annon's ear almost inaudibly.

He started, as if some new light broke on him, and stared at the speaker with a troubled face for an instant, saying hastily, "No, but now you remind me that when an affair of that sort was discussed the other day Treherne looked very odd, and rolled himself away, as if it didn't interest him. I can't believe it, and yet it may be something of the kind. That would account for old Sir Jasper's whim, and Treherne's steady denial of any knowledge of the cause. How in heaven's name did you learn this?"

"My woman's wit suggested it, and my woman's will shall confirm or destroy the suspicion. My lady and Octavia evidently know nothing, but they shall if there is any danger of the girl's being won by him."

"You would not tell her!" exclaimed Annon.

"I will, unless you do it" was the firm answer.

"Never! To betray a friend, even to gain the woman I love, is a thing I cannot do; my honor forbids it."

Mrs. Snowdon smiled scornfully.

"Men's code of honor is a strong one, and we poor women suffer from it. Leave this to me; do your best, and if all other means fail, you may be glad to try my device to prevent Maurice from marrying his cousin. Gratitude and pity are strong allies, and if he recovers, his strong will will move heaven and earth to gain her. Good night." And leaving her last words to rankle in Annon's mind, Mrs. Snowdon departed to endure sleepless hours full of tormenting memories, newborn hopes, and alternations of determination and despair.

Treherne's prospect of recovery filled the whole house with delight, for his patient courage and unfailing cheerfulness had endeared him to all. It was no transient amendment, for day by day he steadily gained strength and power, passing rapidly from chair to crutches, from crutches to a cane and a friend's arm, which was always ready for him. Pain returned with returning vitality, but he bore it with a fortitude that touched all who witnessed it. At times motion was torture, yet motion was necessary lest the torpidity should return, and Treherne took his daily exercise with unfailing perseverance, saying with a smile, though great drops stood upon his forehead, "I have something dearer even than health to win. Hold me up, Jasper, and let me stagger on, in spite of everything, till my twelve turns are made."

He remembered Lady Treherne's words, "If you were well, I'd gladly give my girl to you." This inspired him with strength, endurance, and a happiness which could not be concealed. It overflowed in looks, words, and acts; it infected everyone, and made these holidays the blithest the old abbey had seen for many a day.

Annon devoted himself to Octavia, and in spite of her command to be left in peace till the New Year, she was very kind—so kind that hope flamed up in his heart, though he saw that something like compassion often shone on him from her frank eyes, and her compliance had no touch of the tender docility which lovers long to see. She still avoided Treherne, but so skillfully that few observed the change but Annon and himself. In public Sir Jasper appeared to worship at the sprightly Rose's shrine, and she fancied her game was prospering well.

But had any one peeped behind the scenes it would have been

discovered that during the half hour before dinner, when everyone was in their dressing rooms and the general taking his nap, a pair of ghostly black figures flitted about the haunted gallery, where no servant ventured without orders. The major fancied himself the only one who had made this discovery, for Mrs. Snowdon affected Treherne's society in public, and was assiduous in serving and amusing the "dear convalescent," as she called him. But the general did not sleep; he too watched and waited, longing yet dreading to speak, and hoping that this was but a harmless freak of Edith's, for her caprices were many, and till now he had indulged them freely. This hesitation disgusted the major, who, being a bachelor, knew little of women's ways, and less of their powers of persuasion. The day before New Year he took a sudden resolution, and demanded a private interview with the general.

"I have come on an unpleasant errand, sir," he abruptly began, as the old man received him with an expression which rather daunted the major. "My friendship for Lady Treherne, and my guardianship of her children, makes me jealous of the honor of the family. I fear it is in danger, sir; pardon me for saying it, but your wife is the cause."

"May I trouble you to explain, Major Royston" was all the general's reply, as his old face grew stern and haughty.

"I will, sir, briefly. I happen to know from Jasper that there were love passages between Miss Dubarry and himself a year or more ago in Paris. A whim parted them, and she married. So far no reproach rests upon either, but since she came here it has been evident to others as well as myself that Jasper's affection has revived, and that Mrs. Snowdon does not reject and reprove it as she should. They often meet, and from Jasper's manner I am convinced that mischief is afloat. He is ardent, headstrong, and utterly regardless of the world's opinion in some cases. I have watched them, and what I tell you is true."

"Prove it."

"I will. They meet in the north gallery, wrapped in dark cloaks, and play ghost if anyone comes. I concealed myself behind the screen last evening at dusk, and satisfied myself that my suspicions were correct. I heard little of their conversation, but that little was enough."

"Repeat it, if you please."

"Sir Jasper seemed pleading for some promise which she reluctantly gave, saying, 'While you live I will be true to my word with everyone but him. He will suspect, and it will be useless to keep it from him.'

" 'He will shoot me for this if he knows I am the traitor,' expostulated Jasper.

" 'He shall not know that; I can hoodwink him easily, and serve my purpose also.'

" 'You are mysterious, but I leave all to you and wait for my reward. When shall I have it, Edith?' She laughed, and answered so low I could not hear, for they left the gallery as they spoke. Forgive me, General, for the pain I inflict. You are the only person to whom I have spoken, and you are the only person who can properly and promptly prevent this affair from bringing open shame and scandal on an honorable house. To you I leave it, and will do my part with this infatuated young man if you will withdraw the temptation which will ruin him."

"I will. Thank you, Major. Trust to me, and by tomorrow I will prove that I can act as becomes me."

The grief and misery in the general's face touched the major; he silently wrung his hand and went away, thanking heaven more fervently than ever that no cursed coquette of a woman had it in her power to break his heart.

While this scene was going on above, another was taking place in the library. Treherne sat there alone, thinking happy thoughts evidently, for his eyes shone and his lips smiled as he mused, while watching the splendors of a winter sunset. A soft rustle and the faint scent of violets warned him of Mrs. Snowdon's approach, and a sudden foreboding told him that danger was near. The instant he saw her face his fear was confirmed, for exultation, resolve, and love met and mingled in the expression it wore. Leaning in the window recess, where the red light shone full on her lovely face and queenly figure, she said, softly yet with a ruthless accent below the softness, "Dreaming dreams, Maurice, which will never come to pass, unless I will it. I know your secret, and I shall use it to prevent the fulfillment of the foolish hope you cherish."

"Who told you?" he demanded, with an almost fierce flash of the eye and an angry flush.

"I discovered it, as I warned you I should. My memory is good, I recall the gossip of long ago, I observe the faces, words, and acts of those whom I suspect, and unconscious hints from them give me the truth."

"I doubt it," and Treherne smiled securely.

She stooped and whispered one short sentence into his ear. Whatever it was it caused him to start up with a pale, panic-stricken face, and eye her as if she had pronounced his doom.

"Do you doubt it now?" she asked coldly.

"He told you! Even your skill and craft could not discover it alone," he muttered.

"Nay, I told you nothing was impossible to a determined woman. I needed no help, for I knew more than you think."

He sank down again in a despairing attitude and hid his face, saying mournfully, "I might have known you would hunt me down and dash my hopes when they were surest. How will you use this unhappy secret?"

"I will tell Octavia, and make her duty less hard. It will be kind to both of you, for even with her this memory would mar your happiness; and it saves her from the shame and grief of discovering, when too late, that she has given herself to a——"

"Stop!" he cried, in a tone that made her start and pale, as he rose out of his chair white with a stern indignation which awed her for a moment. "You shall not utter that word—you know but half the truth, and if you wrong me or trouble the girl I will turn traitor also, and tell the general the game you are playing with my cousin. You feign to love me as you feigned before, but his title is the bait now as then, and you fancy that by threatening to mar my hopes you will secure my silence, and gain your end."

"Wrong, quite wrong. Jasper is nothing to me; I use *him* as a tool, not you. If I threaten, it is to keep you from Octavia, who cannot forgive the past and love you for yourself, as I have done all these miserable months. You say I know but half the truth. Tell me the whole and I will spare you."

If ever a man was tempted to betray a trust it was Treherne then. A word, and Octavia might be his; silence, and she might be lost; for this woman was in earnest, and possessed the power to ruin his good name forever. The truth leaped to his lips and would have passed them, had not his eye fallen on the portrait of Jasper's father. This man had loved and sheltered the orphan all his life, had made of him a son, and, dying, urged him to guard and serve and save the rebellious youth he left, when most needing a father's care.

"I promised, and I will keep my promise at all costs," sighed Treherne, and with a gesture full of pathetic patience he waved the fair tempter from him, saying steadily, "I will never tell you, though you rob me of that which is dearer than my life. Go and work your will, but remember that when you might have won the deepest gratitude of the man you profess to love, you chose instead to earn his hatred and contempt."

Waiting for no word of hers, he took refuge in his room, and Edith Snowdon sank down upon the couch, struggling with contending emotions of love and jealousy, remorse and despair. How long she sat there she could not tell; an approaching step recalled her to herself, and looking up she saw Octavia. As the girl approached down the long vista of the drawing rooms, her youth and beauty, innocence and candor touched that fairer and more gifted woman with an envy she had never known before. Something in the girl's face struck her instantly: a look of peace and purity, a sweet serenity more winning than loveliness, more impressive than dignity or grace. With a smile on her lips, yet a half-sad, half-tender light in her eyes, and a cluster of pale winter roses in her hand, she came on till she stood before her rival and, offering the flowers, said, in words as simple as sincere, "Dear Mrs. Snowdon, I cannot let the last sun of the old year set on any misdeeds of mine for which I may atone. I have disliked, distrusted, and misjudged you, and now I come to you in all humility to say forgive me."

With the girlish abandon of her impulsive nature Octavia knelt down before the woman who was plotting to destroy her happiness, laid the roses like a little peace offering on her lap, and with eloquently pleading eyes waited for pardon. For a moment Mrs. Snowdon watched her, fancying it a well-acted ruse to disarm a dangerous rival; but in that sweet face there was no art; one glance showed her that. The words smote her to the heart and won her in spite of pride or passion, as she suddenly took the girl into her arms, weeping repentant tears. Neither spoke, but in the silence each felt the barrier which had stood between them vanishing, and each learned to know the other better in that moment than in a year of common life. Octavia rejoiced that the instinct which had prompted her to make this appeal had not misled her, but assured her that behind the veil of coldness, pride, and levity which this woman wore there was a heart aching for sympathy and help and love. Mrs. Snowdon felt her worser self slip from her, leaving all that was true and noble to make her worthy of the test applied. Art she could meet with equal art, but nature conquered her. For spite of her misspent life and faulty character, the germ of virtue, which lives in the worst, was there, only waiting for the fostering sun and dew of love to strengthen it, even though the harvest be a late one.

"Forgive you!" she cried, brokenly. "It is I who should ask forgiveness of you—I who should atone, confess, and repent. Pardon *me*, pity me, love me, for I am more wretched than you know."

"Dear, I do with heart and soul. Believe it, and let me be your friend" was the soft answer.

"God knows I need one!" sighed the poor woman, still holding fast the only creature who had wholly won her. "Child, I am not good, but not so bad that I dare not look in your innocent face and call you friend. I never had one of my own sex. I never knew my mother; and no one ever saw in me the possibility of goodness, truth, and justice but you. Trust and love and help me, Octavia, and I will reward you with a better life, if I can do no more."

"I will, and the new year shall be happier than the old."

"God bless you for that prophecy; may I be worthy of it."

Then as a bell warned them away, the rivals kissed each other tenderly, and parted friends. As Mrs. Snowdon entered her room, she saw her husband sitting with his gray head in his hands, and heard him murmur despairingly to himself, "My life makes her miserable. But for the sin of it I'd die to free her."

"No, live for me, and teach me to be happy in your love." The clear voice startled him, but not so much as the beautiful changed face of the wife who laid the gray head on her bosom, saying tenderly, "My kind and patient husband, you have been deceived. From me you shall know all the truth, and when you have forgiven my faulty past, you shall see how happy I will try to make your future."

❧ *chapter VII* ❧

A GHOSTLY REVEL

"**B**LESS me, how dull we all are tonight!" exclaimed Rose, as the younger portion of the party wandered listlessly about the drawing rooms that evening, while my lady and the major played an absorbing game of piquet, and the general dozed peacefully at last.

"It is because Maurice is not here; he always keeps us going, for he is a fellow of infinite resources," replied Sir Jasper, suppressing a yawn.

"Have him out then," said Annon.

"He won't come. The poor lad is blue tonight, in spite of his improvement. Something is amiss, and there is no getting a word from him."

"Sad memories afflict him, perhaps," sighed Blanche.

"Don't be absurd, dear, sad memories are all nonsense; melancholy is always indigestion, and nothing is so sure a cure as fun," said Rose briskly. "I'm going to send in a polite invitation begging him to come and amuse us. He'll accept, I haven't a doubt."

The message was sent, but to Rose's chagrin a polite refusal was returned.

"He *shall* come. Sir Jasper, do you and Mr. Annon go as a deputation from us, and return without him at your peril" was her command.

They went, and while waiting their reappearance the sisters spoke of what all had observed.

"How lovely Mrs. Snowdon looks tonight. I always thought she owed half her charms to her skill in dress, but she never looked so beautiful as in that plain black silk, with those roses in her hair," said Rose.

"What has she done to herself?" replied Blanche. "I see a change, but can't account for it. She and Tavie have made some beautifying discovery, for both look altogether uplifted and angelic all of a sudden."

"Here come the gentlemen, and, as I'm a Talbot, they haven't got him!" cried Rose as the deputation appeared, looking very crestfallen. "Don't come near me," she added, irefully, "you are disloyal cowards, and I doom you to exile till I want you. I am infinite in resources as well as this recreant man, and come he shall. Mrs. Snowdon, would you mind asking Mr. Treherne to suggest something to wile away the rest of this evening? We are in despair, and can think of nothing, and you are all-powerful with him."

"I must decline, since he refuses you" was the decided answer, as Mrs. Snowdon moved away.

"Tavie, dear, do go; we *must* have him; he always obeys you, and you would be such a public benefactor, you know."

Without a word Octavia wrote a line and sent it by a servant. Several minutes passed, and the gentlemen began to lay wagers on the success of her trial. "He will not come for me, you may be sure," said Octavia. As the words passed her lips he appeared.

A general laugh greeted him, but, taking no notice of the jests at his expense, he turned to Octavia, saying quietly, "What can I do for you, Cousin?"

His colorless face and weary eyes reproached her for disturbing him, but it was too late for regret, and she answered hastily, "We are in want of some new and amusing occupation to wile away the evening. Can you suggest something appropriate?"

"Why not sit round the hall fire and tell stories, while we wait to see the old year out, as we used to do long ago?" he asked, after a moment's thought.

"I told you so! There it is, just what we want." And Sir Jasper looked triumphant.

"It's capital—let us begin at once. It is after ten now, so we shall not have long to wait," cried Rose, and, taking Sir Jasper's arm, she led the way to the hall.

A great fire always burned there, and in wintertime thick carpets and curtains covered the stone floor and draped the tall windows. Plants blossomed in the warm atmosphere, and chairs and lounges stood about invitingly. The party was soon seated, and Treherne was desired to begin.

"We must have ghost stories, and in order to be properly thrilling and effective, the lights must be put out," said Rose, who sat next him, and spoke first, as usual.

This was soon done, and only a ruddy circle of firelight was left to oppose the rapt gloom that filled the hall, where shadows now seemed to lurk in every corner.

"Don't be very dreadful, or I shall faint away," pleaded Blanche, drawing nearer to Annon, for she had taken her sister's advice, and laid close siege to that gentleman's heart.

"I think your nerves will bear my little tale," replied Treherne. "When I was in India, four years ago, I had a very dear friend in my regiment—a Scotchman; I'm half Scotch myself, you know, and clannish, of course. Gordon was sent up the country on a scouting expedition, and never returned. His men reported that he left them one evening to take a survey, and his horse came home bloody and riderless. We searched, but could not find a trace of him, and I was desperate to discover and avenge his murder. About a month after his disappearance, as I sat in my tent one fearfully hot day, suddenly the canvas door flap was raised and there stood Gordon. I saw him as plainly as I see you, Jasper, and should have sprung to meet him, but something held me back. He was deathly pale, dripping with water, and in his bonny blue eyes was a wild, woeful look that made my blood run cold. I stared dumbly, for it was awful to see my friend so changed and so unearthly. Stretching his arm to me he took my hand, saying solemnly, 'Come!' The touch was like ice; an ominous thrill ran through me; I started up to obey, and he was gone."

"A horrid dream, of course. Is that all?" asked Rose.

With his eyes on the fire and his left hand half extended, Treherne went on as if he had not heard her.

"I thought it was a fancy, and soon recovered myself, for no one had seen or heard anything of Gordon, and my native servant lay just outside my tent. A strange sensation remained in the hand the phantom touched. It was cold, damp, and white. I found it vain to try to forget this apparition; it took strong hold of me; I told Yermid, my man, and he bade me consider it a sign that I was to seek my friend. That night I dreamed I was riding up the country in hot haste; what led me I know not, but I pressed on and on, longing to reach the end. A half-dried river crossed my path, and, riding down the steep bank to ford it, I saw Gordon's body lying in the shallow water looking exactly as the vision looked. I woke in a strange mood, told the story to my commanding officer, and, as nothing was doing just then, easily got leave of absence for a week. Taking Yermid, I set out on my sad quest. I thought it folly, but I could not resist the impulse that drew me on. For seven days I searched, and the strangest part of the story is that all that time I went on exactly as in the dream, seeing what I saw then, and led by the touch of a cold hand on mine. On the seventh day I reached the river, and found my friend's body."

"How horrible! Is it really true?" cried Mrs. Snowdon.

"As true as I am a living man. Nor is that all: this left hand of mine never has been warm since that time. See and feel for yourselves."

He opened both hands, and all satisfied themselves that the left was smaller, paler, and colder than the right.

"Pray someone tell another story to put this out of my mind; it makes me nervous," said Blanche.

"I'll tell one, and you may laugh to quiet your nerves. I want to have mine done with, so that I can enjoy the rest with a free mind." With these words Rose began her tale in the good old fashion.

"Once upon a time, when we were paying a visit to my blessed grandmamma, I saw a ghost in this wise: The dear old lady was ill with a cold and kept her room, leaving us to mope, for it was very dull in the great lonely house. Blanche and I were both homesick, but didn't like to leave till she was better, so we ransacked the library and solaced ourselves with all manner of queer books. One day I found Grandmamma very low and nervous, and evidently with something on her mind. She would say nothing, but the next day was worse, and I insisted on knowing the cause, for the trouble was evidently mental. Charging me to keep it from Blanche, who was, and is, a sad coward, she told me that a spirit had appeared to her two successive nights. 'If it comes a third time, I shall prepare to die,' said the foolish old lady.

"'No, you won't, for I'll come and stay with you and lay your ghost,' I said. With some difficulty I made her yield, and after Blanche was asleep I slipped away to Grandmamma, with a book and candle for a long watch, as the spirit didn't appear till after midnight. She usually slept with her door unlocked, in case of fire or fright, and her maid was close by. That night I locked the door, telling her that spirits could come through the oak if they chose, and I preferred to have a fair trial. Well, I read and chatted and dozed till dawn and nothing appeared, so I laughed at the whole affair, and the old lady pretended to be convinced that it was all a fancy.

"Next night I slept in my own room, and in the morning was told that not only Grandmamma but Janet had seen the spirit. All in white, with streaming hair, a pale face, and a red streak at the throat. It came and parted the bed-curtains, looking in a moment, and then vanished. Janet had slept with Grandmamma and kept a lamp burning on the chimney, so both saw it.

"I was puzzled, but not frightened; I never am, and I insisted on trying again. The door was left unlocked, as on the previous night, and I lay with Grandmamma, a light burning as before. About two she clutched me as I was dropping off. I looked, and there, peeping in between the dark curtains, was a pale face with long hair all about it, and a red streak at the throat. It was very dim, the light being low, but I saw it, and after one breathless minute sprang up, caught my foot, fell down with a crash, and by the time I was around the bed, not a vestige of the thing appeared. I was angry, and vowed I'd succeed at all hazards, though I'll confess I was just a bit daunted.

"Next time Janet and I sat up in easy chairs, with bright lights burning, and both wide awake with the strongest coffee we could make. As the hour drew near we got nervous, and when the white shape came gliding in Janet hid her face. I didn't, and after one look was on the point of laughing, for the spirit was Blanche walking in her sleep. She wore a coral necklace in those days, and never took it off, and her long hair half hid her face, which had the unnatural, uncanny look somnambulists always wear. I had the sense to keep still and tell Janet what to do, so the poor child went back unwaked, and Grandmamma's spirit never walked again for I took care of that."

"Why did you haunt the old lady?" asked Annon, as the laughter ceased.

"I don't know, unless it was that I wanted to ask leave to go

home, and was afraid to do it awake, so tried when asleep. I shall not
tell any story, as I was the heroine of this, but will give my turn to
you, Mr. Annon," said Blanche, with a soft glance, which was quite
thrown away, for the gentleman's eyes were fixed on Octavia, who sat
on a low ottoman at Mrs. Snowdon's feet in the full glow of the firelight.

"I've had very small experience in ghosts, and can only recall
a little fright I once had when a boy at college. I'd been out to a party,
got home tired, couldn't find my matches, and retired in the dark.
Toward morning I woke, and glancing up to see if the dim light was
dawn or moonshine I was horrified to see a coffin standing at the bed's
foot. I rubbed my eyes to be sure I was awake, and looked with all
my might. There it was, a long black coffin, and I saw the white plate
in the dusk, for the moon was setting and my curtain was not drawn.
'It's some trick of the fellows,' I thought; 'I'll not betray myself, but
keep cool.' Easy to say but hard to do, for it suddenly flashed into my
mind that I might be in the wrong room. I glanced about, but there
were the familiar objects as usual, as far as the indistinct light allowed
me to see, and I made sure by feeling on the wall at the bed's head
for my watchcase. It was there, and mine beyond a doubt, being
peculiar in shape and fabric. Had I been to a college wine party I
could have accounted for the vision, but a quiet evening in a grave
professor's well-conducted family could produce no ill effects. 'It's an
optical illusion, or a prank of my mates; I'll sleep and forget it,' I said,
and for a time endeavored to do so, but curiosity overcame my resolve,
and soon I peeped again. Judge of my horror when I saw the sharp
white outline of a dead face, which seemed to be peeping up from the
coffin. It gave me a terrible shock for I was but a lad and had been ill.
I hid my face and quaked like a nervous girl, still thinking it some
joke and too proud to betray fear lest I should be laughed at. How
long I lay there I don't know, but when I looked again the face was
farther out and the whole figure seemed rising slowly. The moon
was nearly down, I had no lamp, and to be left in the dark with that
awesome thing was more than I could bear. Joke or earnest, I must
end the panic, and bolting out of my room I roused my neighbor. He
told me I was mad or drunk, but lit a lamp and returned with me,
to find my horror only a heap of clothes thrown on the table in such
a way that, as the moon's pale light shot it, it struck upon my black
student's gown, with a white card lying on it, and produced the effect

of a coffin and plate. The face was a crumpled handkerchief, and what seemed hair a brown muffler. As the moon sank, these outlines changed and, incredible as it may seem, grew like a face. My friend not having had the fright enjoyed the joke, and 'Coffins' was my sobriquet for a long while."

"You get worse and worse. Sir Jasper, do vary the horrors by a touch of fun, or I shall run away," said Blanche, glancing over her shoulder nervously.

"I'll do my best, and tell a story my uncle used to relate of his young days. I forget the name of the place, but it was some little country town famous among anglers. My uncle often went to fish, and always regretted that a deserted house near the trout stream was not occupied, for the inn was inconveniently distant. Speaking of this one evening as he lounged in the landlady's parlor, he asked why no one took it and let the rooms to strangers in the fishing season. 'For fear of the ghostissess, your honor,' replied the woman, and proceeded to tell him that three distinct spirits haunted the house. In the garret was heard the hum of a wheel and the tap of high-heeled shoes, as the ghostly spinner went to and fro. In a chamber sounded the sharpening of a knife, followed by groans and the drip of blood. The cellar was made awful by a skeleton sitting on a half-buried box and chuckling fiendishly. It seems a miser lived there once, and was believed to have starved his daughter in the garret, keeping her at work till she died. The second spirit was that of the girl's rejected lover, who cut his throat in the chamber, and the third of the miser who was found dead on the money chest he was too feeble to conceal. My uncle laughed at all this, and offered to lay the ghosts if anyone would take the house.

"This offer got abroad, and a crusty old fellow accepted it, hoping to turn a penny. He had a pretty girl, whose love had been thwarted by the old man, and whose lover was going to sea in despair. My uncle knew this and pitied the young people. He had made acquaintance with a wandering artist, and the two agreed to conquer the prejudices against the house by taking rooms there. They did so, and after satisfying themselves regarding the noises, consulted a wise old woman as to the best means of laying the ghosts. She told them if any young girl would pass a night in each haunted room, praying piously the while, that all would be well. Peggy was asked if she would do it, and being a stouthearted lass she consented, for a round sum, to try it.

The first night was in the garret, and Peggy, in spite of the prophecies of the village gossips, came out alive, though listeners at the door heard the weird humming and tapping all night long. The next night all went well, and from that time no more sharpening, groaning, or dripping was heard. The third time she bade her friends good-bye and, wrapped in her red cloak, with a lamp and prayer book, went down into the cellar. Alas for pretty Peggy! When day came she was gone, and with her the miser's empty box, though his bones remained to prove how well she had done her work.

"The town was in an uproar, and the old man furious. Some said the devil had flown away with her, others that the bones were hers, and all agreed that henceforth another ghost would haunt the house. My uncle and the artist did their best to comfort the father, who sorely reproached himself for thwarting the girl's love, and declared that if Jack would find her he should have her. But Jack had sailed, and the old man 'was left lamenting.' The house was freed from its unearthly visitors, however, for no ghost appeared; and when my uncle left, old Martin found money and letter informing him that Peggy had spent her first two nights preparing for flight, and on the third had gone away to marry and sail with Jack. The noises had been produced by the artist, who was a ventriloquist, the skeleton had been smuggled from the surgeons, and the whole thing was a conspiracy to help Peggy and accommodate the fishermen."

"It is evident that roguery is hereditary," laughed Rose as the narrator paused.

"I strongly suspect that Sir Jasper the second was the true hero of that story," added Mrs. Snowdon.

"Think what you like, I've done my part, and leave the stage for you, madam."

"I will come last. It is your turn, dear."

As Mrs. Snowdon softly uttered the last word, and Octavia leaned upon her knee with an affectionate glance, Treherne leaned forward to catch a glimpse of the two changed faces, and looked as if bewildered when both smiled at him, as they sat hand in hand while the girl told her story.

"Long ago a famous actress suddenly dropped dead at the close of a splendidly played tragedy. She was carried home, and preparations were made to bury her. The play had been gotten up with great care and expense, and a fine actor was the hero. The public demanded a repetition, and an inferior person was engaged to take the dead lady's part. A day's delay had been necessary, but when the night came the house was crowded. They waited both before and behind the curtain for the debut of the new actress, with much curiosity. She stood waiting for her cue, but as it was given, to the amazement of all, the great tragedienne glided upon the stage. Pale as marble, and with a strange fire in her eyes, strange pathos in her voice, strange power in her acting, she went through her part, and at the close vanished as mysteriously as she came. Great was the excitement that night, and intense the astonishment and horror next day when it was whispered abroad that the dead woman never had revived, but had lain in her coffin before the eyes of watchers all the evening, when hundreds fancied they were applauding her at the theater. The mystery never was cleared up, and Paris was divided by two opinions: one that some person marvelously like Madame Z. had personated her for the sake of a sensation; the other that the ghost of the dead actress, unable to free itself from the old duties so full of fascination to an ambitious and successful woman, had played for the last time the part which had made her famous."

"Where did you find that, Tavie? It's very French, and not bad if you invented it," said Sir Jasper.

"I read it in an old book, where it was much better told. Now, Edith, there is just time for your tale."

As the word "Edith" passed her lips, again Treherne started and eyed them both, and again they smiled, as Mrs. Snowdon caressed the smooth cheek leaning on her knee, and looking full at him began the last recital.

"You have been recounting the pranks of imaginary ghosts; let me show you the workings of some real spirits, evil and good, that haunt every heart and home, making its misery or joy. At Christmastime, in a country house, a party of friends met to keep the holidays, and very happily they might have done so had not one person marred the peace of several. Love, jealousy, deceit, and nobleness were the spirits that played their freaks with these people. The person of whom I speak was more haunted than the rest, and much tormented, being willful, proud, and jealous. Heaven help her, she had had no one to exorcise these ghosts for her, and they goaded her to do much harm. Among these friends there were more than one pair of lovers, and much tangling of plots and plans, for hearts are wayward and mysterious things, and cannot love as duty bids or prudence counsels. This woman held the key to all the secrets of the house, and, having a purpose to gain, she used her power selfishly, for a time. To satisfy a doubt, she feigned a fancy for a gentleman who once did her the honor of admiring her, and, to the great scandal of certain sage persons, permitted him to show his regard for her, knowing that it was but a transient amusement on his part as well as upon hers. In the hands of this woman lay a secret which could make or mar the happiness of the best and dearest of the party. The evil spirits which haunted her urged her to mar their peace and gratify a sinful hope. On the other side, honor, justice, and generosity prompted her to make them happy, and while she wavered there came to her a sweet enchantress who, with a word, banished the tormenting ghosts forever, and gave the haunted woman a talisman to keep her free henceforth."

There the earnest voice faltered, and with a sudden impulse Mrs. Snowdon bent her head and kissed the fair forehead which had bent lower and lower as she went on. Each listener understood the truth, lightly veiled in that hasty fable, and each found in it a different meaning. Sir Jasper frowned and bit his lips, Annon glanced anxiously from face to face, Octavia hid hers, and Treherne's flashed with sudden intelligence, while Rose laughed low to herself, enjoying the scene. Blanche, who was getting sleepy, said, with a stifled gape, "That is a very nice, moral little story, but I wish there had been some real ghosts in it."

"There was. Will you come and see them?"

As she put the question, Mrs. Snowdon rose abruptly, wishing to end the séance, and beckoning them to follow glided up the great stairway. All obeyed, wondering what whim possessed her, and quite ready for any jest in store for them.

≈ *chapter VIII* ≈

JASPER

SHE led them to the north gallery and, pausing at the door, said merrily, "The ghost—or ghosts rather, for there were two—which frightened Patty were Sir Jasper and myself, meeting to discuss certain important matters which concerned Mr. Treherne. If you want to see spirits we will play phantom for you, and convince you of our power."

"Good, let us go and have a ghostly dance, as a proper finale of our revel," answered Rose as they flocked into the long hall.

At that moment the great clock struck twelve, and all paused to bid the old year adieu. Sir Jasper was the first to speak, for, angry with Mrs. Snowdon, yet thankful to her for making a jest to others of what had been earnest to him, he desired to hide his chagrin under a gay manner; and taking Rose around the waist was about to waltz away as she proposed, saying cheerily, "'Come one and all, and dance the new year in,'" when a cry from Octavia arrested him, and turning he saw her stand, pale and trembling, pointing to the far end of the hall.

Eight narrow Gothic windows pierced either wall of the north gallery. A full moon sent her silvery light strongly in upon the eastern side, making broad bars of brightness across the floor. No fires burned there now, and wherever the moonlight did not fall deep shadows lay. As Octavia cried out, all looked, and all distinctly saw a tall, dark figure moving noiselessly across the second bar of light far down the hall.

"Is it some jest of yours?" asked Sir Jasper of Mrs. Snowdon, as the form vanished in the shadow.

"No, upon my honor, I know nothing of it! I only meant to relieve Octavia's superstitious fears by showing her our pranks" was the whispered reply as Mrs. Snowdon's cheek paled, and she drew nearer to Jasper.

"Who is there?" called Treherne in a commanding tone.

No answer, but a faint, cold breath of air seemed to sigh along the arched roof and die away as the dark figure crossed the third streak of moonlight. A strange awe fell upon them all, and no one spoke, but stood watching for the appearance of the shape. Nearer and nearer it came, with soundless steps, and as it reached the sixth window its outlines were distinctly visible. A tall, wasted figure, all in black, with a rosary hanging from the girdle, and a dark beard half concealing the face.

"The Abbot's ghost, and very well got up," said Annon, trying to laugh but failing decidedly, for again the cold breath swept over them, causing a general shudder.

"Hush!" whispered Treherne, drawing Octavia to his side with a protecting gesture.

Once more the phantom appeared and disappeared, and as they waited for it to cross the last bar of light that lay between it and them, Mrs. Snowdon stepped forward to the edge of the shadow in which they stood, as if to confront the apparition alone. Out of the darkness it came, and in the full radiance of the light it paused. Mrs. Snowdon, being nearest, saw the face first, and uttering a faint cry dropped down upon the stone floor, covering up her eyes. Nothing human ever wore a look like that of the ghastly, hollow-eyed, pale-lipped countenance below the hood. All saw it and held their breath as it slowly raised a shadowy arm and pointed a shriveled finger at Sir Jasper.

"Speak, whatever you are, or I'll quickly prove whether you are man or spirit!" cried Jasper fiercely, stepping forward as if to grasp the extended arm that seemed to menace him alone.

An icy gust swept through the hall, and the phantom slowly receded into the shadow. Jasper sprang after it, but nothing crossed the second stream of light, and nothing remained in the shade. Like one possessed by a sudden fancy he rushed down the gallery to find all fast and empty, and to return looking very strangely. Blanche had fainted away and Annon was bearing her out of the hall. Rose was clinging to Mrs. Snowdon, and Octavia leaned against her cousin, saying in a fervent whisper, "Thank God it did not point at you!"

"Am I then dearer than your brother?" he whispered back.

There was no audible reply, but one little hand involuntarily pressed his, though the other was outstretched toward Jasper, who came up white and startled but firm and quiet. Affecting to make light of it, he said, forcing a smile as he raised Mrs. Snowdon, "It is some stupid joke of the servants. Let us think no more of it. Come, Edith, this is not like your usual self."

"It was nothing human, Jasper; you know it as well as I. Oh, why did I bring you here to meet the warning phantom that haunts your house!"

"Nay, if my time is near the spirit would have found me out wherever I might be. I have no faith in that absurd superstition—I laugh at and defy it. Come down and drink my health in wine from the Abbot's own cellar."

But no one had heart for further gaiety, and, finding Lady Treherne already alarmed by Annon, they were forced to tell her all, and find their own bewilderment deepened by her unalterable belief in the evil omen.

At her command the house was searched, the servants cross-questioned, and every effort made to discover the identity of the apparition. All in vain; the house was as usual, and not a man or maid but turned pale at the idea of entering the gallery at midnight. At my lady's request, all promised to say no more upon the mystery, and separated at last to such sleep as they could enjoy.

Very grave were the faces gathered about the breakfast table next morning, and very anxious the glances cast on Sir Jasper as he came in, late as usual, looking uncommonly blithe and well. Nothing serious ever made a deep impression on his mercurial nature. Treherne had more the air of a doomed man, being very pale and worn, in spite of an occasional gleam of happiness as he looked at Octavia. He haunted Jasper like a shadow all the morning, much to that young gentleman's annoyance, for both his mother and sister hung about him with faces of ill-dissembled anxiety. By afternoon his patience gave out, and he openly rebelled against the tender guard kept over him. Ringing for his horse he said decidedly, "I'm bored to death with the solemnity which pervades the house today, so I'm off for a brisk gallop, before I lose my temper and spirits altogether."

"Come with me in the pony carriage, Jasper. I've not had a drive with you for a long while, and should enjoy it so much," said my lady, detaining him.

"Mrs. Snowdon looks as if she needed air to revive her roses, and the pony carriage is just the thing for her, so I will cheerfully resign my seat to her," he answered laughing, as he forced himself from his mother's hand.

"Take the girls in the clarence. We all want a breath of air, and you are the best whip we know. Be gallant and say yes, dear."

"No, thank you, Tavie, that won't do. Rose and Blanche are both asleep, and you are dying to go and do likewise, after your vigils last night. As a man and a brother I beg you'll do so, and let me ride as I like."

"Suppose you ask Annon to join you—" began Treherne with well-assumed indifference; but Sir Jasper frowned and turned sharply on him, saying, half-petulantly, half-jocosely:

"Upon my life I should think I was a boy or a baby, by the manner in which you mount guard over me today. If you think I'm going to live in daily fear of some mishap, you are all much mistaken. Ghost or no ghost, I shall make merry while I can; a short life and a jolly one has always been my motto, you know, so fare you well till dinnertime."

They watched him gallop down the avenue, and then went their different ways, still burdened with a nameless foreboding. Octavia strolled into the conservatory, thinking to refresh herself with the balmy silence which pervaded the place, but Annon soon joined her, full of a lover's hopes and fears.

"Miss Treherne, I have ventured to come for my answer. Is my New Year to be a blissful or a sad one?" he asked eagerly.

"Forgive me if I give you an unwelcome reply, but I must be true, and so regretfully refuse the honor you do me," she said sorrowfully.

"May I ask why?"

"Because I do not love you."

"And you do love your cousin," he cried angrily, pausing to watch her half-averted face.

She turned it fully toward him and answered, with her native sincerity, "Yes, I do, with all my heart, and now my mother will not thwart me, for Maurice has saved my life, and I am free to devote it all to him."

"Happy man, I wish I had been a cripple!" sighed Annon. Then with a manful effort to be just and generous, he added heartily, "Say no more, he deserves you; I want no sacrifice to duty; I yield, and go away, praying heaven to bless you now and always."

He kissed her hand and left her to seek my lady and make his adieus, for no persuasion could keep him. Leaving a note for Sir Jasper, he hurried away, to the great relief of Treherne and the deep regret of Blanche, who, however, lived in hopes of another trial later in the season.

"Here comes Jasper, Mamma, safe and well," cried Octavia an hour or two later, as she joined her mother on the terrace, where my lady had been pacing restlessly to and fro nearly ever since her son rode away.

With a smile of intense relief she waved her handkerchief as he came clattering up the drive, and seeing her he answered with hat and hand. He usually dismounted at the great hall door, but a sudden whim made him ride along the wall that lay below the terrace, for he was a fine horseman, and Mrs. Snowdon was looking from her window. As he approached, the peacocks fled screaming, and one flew up just before the horse's eyes as his master was in the act of dismounting. The spirited creature was startled, sprang partway up the low, broad steps of the terrace, and, being sharply checked, slipped, fell, and man and horse rolled down together.

Never did those who heard it forget the cry that left Lady Treherne's lips as she saw the fall. It brought out both guests and servants, to find Octavia recklessly struggling with the frightened horse, and my lady down upon the stones with her son's bleeding head in her arms.

They bore in the senseless, shattered body, and for hours tried everything that skill and science could devise to save the young man's life. But every effort was in vain, and as the sun set Sir Jasper lay dying. Conscious at last, and able to speak, he looked about him with a troubled glance, and seemed struggling with some desire that overmastered pain and held death at bay.

"I want Maurice," he feebly said, at length.

"Dear lad, I'm here," answered his cousin's voice from a seat in the shadow of the half-drawn curtains.

"Always near when I need you. Many a scrape have you helped me out of, but this is beyond your power," and a faint smile passed over Jasper's lips as the past flitted before his mind. But the smile died, and a groan of pain escaped him as he cried suddenly, "Quick! Let me tell it before it is too late! Maurice never will, but bear the shame all his life that my dead name may be untarnished. Bring Edith; she must hear the truth."

She was soon there, and, lying in his mother's arms, one hand in his cousin's, and one on his sister's bent head, Jasper rapidly told the secret which had burdened him for a year.

"I did it; I forged my uncle's name when I had lost so heavily at play that I dared not tell my mother, or squander more of my own fortune. I deceived Maurice, and let him think the check a genuine one; I made him present it and get the money, and when all went well I fancied I was safe. But my uncle discovered it secretly, said nothing, and, believing Maurice the forger, disinherited him. I never knew this till the old man died, and then it was too late. I confessed to Maurice, and he forgave me. He said, 'I am helpless now, shut out from the world, with nothing to lose or gain, and soon to be forgotten by those who once knew me, so let the suspicion of shame, if any such there be, still cling to me, and do you go your way, rich, happy, honorable, and untouched by any shadow on your fame.' Mother, I let him do it, unconscious as he was that many knew the secret sin and fancied him the doer of it."

"Hush, Jasper, let it pass. I can bear it; I promised your dear father to be your staunch friend through life, and I have only kept my word."

"God knows you have, but now my life ends, and I cannot die till you are cleared. Edith, I told you half the truth, and you would have used it against him had not some angel sent this girl to touch your heart. You have done your part to atone for the past, now let me do mine. Mother, Tavie loves him, he has risked life and honor for me. Repay him generously and give him this."

With feeble touch Sir Jasper tried to lay his sister's hand in Treherne's as he spoke; Mrs. Snowdon helped him, and as my lady bowed her head in silent acquiescence, a joyful smile shone on the dying man's face.

"One more confession, and then I am ready," he said, looking up into the face of the woman whom he had loved with all the power of a shallow nature. "It was a jest to you, Edith, but it was bitter earnest to me, for I loved you, sinful as it was. Ask your husband to forgive me, and tell him it was better I should die than live to mar a good man's peace. Kiss me once, and make him happy for my sake."

She touched his cold lips with remorseful tenderness, and in the same breath registered a vow to obey that dying prayer.

"Tavie dear, Maurice, my brother, God bless you both. Good-bye, Mother. He will be a better son than I have been to you." Then, the reckless spirit of the man surviving to the last, Sir Jasper laughed faintly, as he seemed to beckon some invisible shape, and died saying gaily, "Now, Father Abbot, lead on, I'll follow you."

A year later three weddings were celebrated on the same day and in the same church. Maurice Treherne, a well man, led up his cousin. Frank Annon rewarded Blanche's patient siege by an unconditional surrender, and, to the infinite amusement of Mrs. Grundy, Major Royston publicly confessed himself outgeneraled by merry Rose. The triple wedding feast was celebrated at Treherne Abbey, and no uncanny visitor marred its festivities, for never again was the north gallery haunted by the ghostly Abbot.

❧ *Afterword* ❦

Behind a Mask: The Unknown Thrillers of Louisa May Alcott was first published by William Morrow and Company July 1, 1975. The next morning I was interviewed about those unknown thrillers by Barbara Walters on the *Today* show. The hoopla had begun.

The excitement continued, centering upon the stunning disclosure that America's best-loved author of juveniles, the creator of *Little Women*, the revered "Children's Friend," had also operated behind a mask. Louisa May Alcott, it was apparent, had been as familiar with murder and mayhem, drug addiction and the war between the sexes as she had been with loving families and the wholesome delights of apples and ginger cookies.

Radio and television interviews were punctuated by critical appraisals of Alcott's page-turners and the detective work that had led to their recovery: "The discovery is, in itself, a literary thriller. *Behind a Mask* and not *Little Women* shows us what might have been" (*St. Louis Post-Dispatch*). "Miss Alcott towers in style, imagination, plot and veracity of character. . . . [The stories] are wild melodrama and mad passion and just as entertaining as they can possibly be. They don't date. They simply are themselves and irresistible" (*Cleveland Plain Dealer*).

But perhaps the most perceptive review was the one that appeared in *Publishers Weekly:* "A most fascinating find. Never again will you have quite the same image of this particular 'little woman.' " Actually, the fact that Alcott had lived a double literary life had been revealed as early as 1943 when Leona Rostenberg published her discovery of the Alcott pseudonym in a scholarly quarterly. All who read that article would know that the author of *Little Women* had, like her heroine Jo March, taken "a plunge into the frothy sea of sensational literature" and produced thrillers either anonymously or over a pseudonym.

It was not until 1975, however, with Morrow's publication of *Behind a Mask: The Unknown Thrillers of Louisa May Alcott,* that the precise nature of those thrillers was made known to an avid public. Then, at long last, well over a century after they had first emerged from the Alcott attic, four of the author's cliff-hangers were once again made available. Those four stories included Alcott's first success in the genre, "Pauline's Passion and Punishment," a tale of feminist anger and revenge that won a $100 prize from New York publisher Frank Leslie in 1863 and in 1994 provided inspiration for a musical entitled *The Sweet Revenge of Louisa May;* "The Mysterious Key and What It Opened," a suspenseful narrative originally published as a dime novel and posthumously reprinted by the New York publisher of cheap books Frank M. Lupton; "The Abbot's Ghost, or Maurice Treherne's Temptation," a Gothic romance with English background serialized over the pseudonym A. M. Barnard; and the title story.

"Behind a Mask, or A Woman's Power," also serialized over Alcott's pseudonym, remains one of her most powerful feminist tales. Dominated by the manipulating heroine, Jean Muir, who happens to be a highly effective actress, the story convincingly portrays a favorite Alcott theme, woman's power over all male antagonists. "Behind a Mask" was charmingly dramatized by Karen L. Lewis and performed to enthusiastic applause in 1983 at New York's Theater of the Open Eye.

Indeed, with publication of the collection entitled *Behind a Mask,* many eyes were opened and many eyebrows were raised. Only then was it realized that Louisa May Alcott had written with both hands, one producing classic domestic novels, the other shaping narratives of violence and revenge, pride and passion, intrigue and suspense, narratives acclaimed by *The New York Times* as proceeding "from title to thrilling conclusion at a swift pace. Real page-turners."

The general public agreed, and *Behind a Mask* was reprinted, and issued in an English edition and a Bantam paperback. At the same time, the scholarly world set about its revisionist course, reinterpreting "The Children's Friend" in the light of her anonymous and pseudonymous shockers. The darker aspects of Alcott's life and character were spotlighted, and the new criticism was applied not only to the author's persona but to her entire oeuvre. The sexual politics in Alcott's newly uncovered sensation fiction was traced, her "midnight fantasies" examined, her "gender relations" explored. The result of this reexamination was of course a new image of Louisa Alcott, who was now viewed as a far more complex writer than had been supposed. Alcott's tales of power and passion made readers along with scholars aware that their creator was a many-faceted professional as adept at the sensational as at the sentimental. Her forays into the realms of blood and thunder have disclosed hitherto unsuspected dimensions in her work. She was, it turns out, a far more adventurous writer than had been believed. Her complexities have been acknowledged, as her reputation has been extended and her stature increased.

The new image of Alcott, disclosed twenty years earlier, was reacknowledged in 1995 with publication of a full-length sensational novel entitled *A Long Fatal Love Chase* originally rejected by its intended publisher. In addition, in 1994 a highly praised new film version of *Little Women* based upon Alcott's domestic novel conveyed to a large public her skill in depicting a loving family and a gloriously independent heroine. Although *Little Women* has never been out of print since its first publication in 1868–69, a new readership has been reminded of its perennial pertinence. Both those events—publication of a previously unpublished sensation novel and the film of *Little Women*—are reminders if not revealers of Alcott's versatility.

Just so the timely reprinting of *Behind a Mask* recalls the acclamations evoked at its first appearance and anticipates its reception today by yet another generation of readers. Surely they will be captivated by the twofold nature of Louisa May Alcott, who dealt in brightness and in darkness and illuminated both.

—MADELEINE STERN, 1995